Praise for Shannon K. Butcher
and the Sentinel Wars Novels

Finding the Lost

"Exerts much the same appeal as Christine Feehan's Carpathian series, what with tortured heroes, the necessity of finding love or facing a fate worse than death, hot lovemaking, and danger-filled adventure." —*Booklist*

"A terrific grim thriller with the romantic subplot playing a strong supporting role. The cast is powerful as the audience will feel every emotion that Andra feels from fear for her sister to fear for her falling in love. *Finding the Lost* is a dark tale, as Shannon K. Butcher paints a forbidding, gloomy landscape in which an ancient war between humanity's guardians and their nasty adversaries heats up in Nebraska." —Alternative Worlds

"A very entertaining read ... the ending was a great cliff-hanger, and I can't wait to read the next book in this series ... a fast-paced story with great action scenes and lots of hot romance." —The Book Lush

"Butcher's paranormal reality is dark and gritty in this second Sentinel Wars installment. What makes this story so gripping is the seamlessly delivered hard-hitting action and wrenching emotions. Butcher is a major talent in the making." —*Romantic Times*

continued ...

Burning Alive

"Starts off with nonstop action. Readers will race through the pages, only to reread the entire novel to capture every little detail . . . a promising start for a new voice in urban fantasy/paranormal romance. I look forward to the next installment." —*A Romance Review* (5 Roses)

"This first book of the Sentinel Wars whets your appetite for the rest of the books in the series. Ms. Butcher is carving her way onto the bestseller lists with this phenomenal nonstop ride that will have you preordering the second book the minute you put this one down."

—*Affaire de Coeur* (5 stars)

"Absorbing. . . . Butcher skillfully balances erotic, tender interactions with Helen's worries, and intriguing secondary characters further enhance the unusual premise. Fans of Butcher's romantic suspense novels will enjoy her turn toward the paranormal." —*Publishers Weekly*

"Ms. Butcher offers fresh and delightfully creative elements in this paranormal romance, keeping readers engaged as the story unfolds. *Burning Alive* is a well-crafted beginning to this exciting new series, and will have fans of the genre coming back for the next adventure in the Sentinel Wars."

—Darque Reviews

"An exciting romantic urban fantasy. . . . Shannon K. Butcher adds her trademark suspense with plenty of tension and danger to the mix of a terrific paranormal thriller."

—*Midwest Book Review*

"*Burning Alive* is Shannon Butcher's first foray into paranormal romance, and what a doozy it is! Filled with sizzling love scenes, great storytelling, and action galore, fans of paranormal romance will rejoice to have Ms. Butcher finally join the genre!" —ParaNormal Romance

"A different twist on the paranormal genre. . . . Overall, Shannon K. Butcher has done a good job with *Burning Alive*, and I will definitely be reading the next in the series."

—Fallen Angel Reviews

Also by Shannon K. Butcher

NOVELS OF THE SENTINEL WARS

Running Scared
Finding the Lost
Burning Alive
Living Nightmare

LIVING
ON THE
EDGE

AN EDGE NOVEL

SHANNON K. BUTCHER

A SIGNET ECLIPSE BOOK

SIGNET ECLIPSE
Published by New American Library, a division of
Penguin Group (USA) Inc., 375 Hudson Street,
New York, New York 10014, USA
Penguin Group (Canada), 90 Eglinton Avenue East, Suite 700, Toronto,
Ontario M4P 2Y3, Canada (a division of Pearson Penguin Canada Inc.)
Penguin Books Ltd., 80 Strand, London WC2R 0RL, England
Penguin Ireland, 25 St. Stephen's Green, Dublin 2,
Ireland (a division of Penguin Books Ltd.)
Penguin Group (Australia), 250 Camberwell Road, Camberwell, Victoria 3124,
Australia (a division of Pearson Australia Group Pty. Ltd.)
Penguin Books India Pvt. Ltd., 11 Community Centre, Panchsheel Park,
New Delhi - 110 017, India
Penguin Group (NZ), 67 Apollo Drive, Rosedale, North Shore 0632,
New Zealand (a division of Pearson New Zealand Ltd.)
Penguin Books (South Africa) (Pty.) Ltd., 24 Sturdee Avenue,
Rosebank, Johannesburg 2196, South Africa

Penguin Books Ltd., Registered Offices:
80 Strand, London WC2R 0RL, England

First published by Signet Eclipse, an imprint of New American Library,
a division of Penguin Group (USA) Inc.

First Printing, March 2011
10 9 8 7 6 5 4 3 2 1

Chapter 1

Lucas Ramsey's target stood out from the swirling masses of perfumed, sequined gold diggers on the ballroom floor. There was something different about her—a watchful, focused quality that none of the other women at this fancy shindig possessed. Then again, there were three other women flirting with the flabby, older man she was hanging on. Maybe she was worried she'd lose her sugar daddy.

Too bad Lucas wasn't a rich man, 'cause he'd love to sign up for that job, even if for only one night.

The weapon in his shoulder holster felt odd through the thin cotton of his tuxedo shirt, and the shiny leather shoes didn't have the same gripping traction of his combat boots. He was as far out of place here as a man could get, but Sloane Gideon was here, so he was, too.

She was his last chance to repay a man he owed everything to. And the job was simple. All he had to do was keep her from catching her flight on a private jet in ninety-eight minutes.

No sweat. Even a washed-up soldier like him could handle that. In fact, Lucas could think of more than one way to make her miss that flight. The Old Man had said to use any means necessary to keep her in Texas, and as the list of the more interesting possibilities formed in Lucas's head, his body temperature kicked up a couple of degrees.

There were hundreds of people here, all as well dressed as the room itself. Silk draped the walls, and fine linen cloths covered the tables. No polyester there.

A tidy crew of unobtrusive waiters wove among the guests, offering an endless supply of champagne in crystal flutes. Live music swelled from the raised platform where a small orchestra played. Elegant harmonies wove their way through the room, and on the far left, couples danced to a waltz Lucas recognized but could not name.

He was more of a beer and rock-and-roll kind of guy, but that didn't mean he couldn't appreciate the finer things in life.

Like Sloane Gideon. She was definitely fine.

Sloane was lovely in an untouchable sort of way. Perfect hair, perfect makeup, perfect dress flowing over perfect curves. She was walking perfection, and he'd bet his last dollar that she knew it. Decked out in diamonds and a dress that probably cost more than his car, she was way out of his league. Of course, if a man managed to strip her of all that flash and sparkle, the playing field would be a lot more even. And a lot more interesting.

All he had to do was pry her off the arm of Moneybags.

Lucas made his way across the ballroom, through the glittering upper-crust socialites. He ignored the women who glanced his way, and the men who sized him up, staring at him as if trying to calculate his net worth. Not much, he knew, but he'd played enough roles in his life that this one wasn't much of a stretch. At least here no one was shooting at him, which made this a walk in the park by comparison.

He mimicked the rigid posture of the other men here, donned an air of casual indifference to the ridiculous amounts of wealth being displayed, and moved toward his target.

His knee throbbed as he forced it to accept his weight without limping. He wasn't sure how he was going to hit the dance floor with Sloane without giving away his weakness, but he'd think of something. Maybe a nice, long slow dance would come their way.

Even with a busted knee, Lucas could still come up with at least a dozen ways he could make her forget about her flight. Hell, if he wasn't too rusty, he might even be able to make her forget what day of the week it was. That would be a nice change of pace from his recent, unwelcomed, lengthy celibacy.

Any means necessary held a cargo ship load of possibilities.

Lucas had a hotel room upstairs all ready and waiting, stocked with enough wine to knock a man his size unconscious. Come morning when his debt to the Old Man was repaid, he'd leave Sloane satisfied and sleeping while he walked away from his old life with a clean slate and a clean conscience.

His new life held little appeal, but that, thankfully, was a problem for another day.

A movement in his peripheral vision stopped him dead in his tracks. He wasn't yet sure what he'd seen, but his instincts were: trouble. The urge to duck and cover screamed inside him, making his pulse skyrocket.

He turned his head, just enough to see the threat.

On a raised platform behind the orchestra was a thick arrangement of huge potted trees and plants. Sticking out of those plants was the last six inches of a rifle's barrel.

And it was aimed right at Sloane.

The man crossing the ballroom toward Sloane had been born to wear a tux.

She let her gaze slide up and down his body, appreciating the way the fabric hugged his broad shoulders and accentuated his trim waist. The fit was so good it almost hid the bulge of the weapon beneath his jacket. Almost.

She tightened her grip on the arm of her client, signaling to him there was trouble.

"Time to go," she whispered into his ear, smiling as though she'd just said something seductive.

Edward Henning looked at the three cosmetically engineered gold diggers fawning over him and giggling, then back at her like she was crazy. "I don't think so."

Sloane squeezed his arm harder. "Move. Now."

She'd scoped out the place earlier, and her best bet was the eastern stairwell exit. She gave her client a not so gentle tug, but the man refused to budge. Hanging on whatever bimbette number three was saying, he stayed glued to the spot.

Mr. Tuxedo and his concealed weapon were still fifty feet away, but he was making progress through the crowds easily. Men parted from his path, pulling their wives and dates out of his way. Not that she could blame them. Any woman in that man's path was a target—whether for sex or violence, Sloane wasn't sure, but it was definitely one of the two. Maybe both.

The bimbo trio giggled at something her client said, and she felt his chest puff up. At sixty-three, Edward Henning was turning to flab, spending too much time at a boardroom table and not enough in a gym. Then again, if he'd been in better shape, maybe he wouldn't have needed to hire her to watch his back. Out-of-shape flab with deep pockets was her job security. And Sloane loved her job—loved the danger and adrenaline rush. If it hadn't been for her friend Gina, she never would have even considered taking vacation time.

But Gina needed her. Now. Another half hour of guard duty and Sloane was officially off the clock. Her private flight left in ninety minutes, and it couldn't happen soon enough. It had taken all day and she'd called in a lot of favors, but she'd managed to make arrangements for a whole lot of firepower to be waiting for her in Colombia. No matter how deep a mess Gina had gotten herself into this time, one way or another, Sloane was going to get her out of that godforsaken country in one piece.

Mr. Tuxedo stopped for a split second, then fixed his gaze on her and picked up speed with more than a hint of desperation hurrying his pace.

Now it was *really* time to go.

Sloane plastered a vapid smile on her face and stomped over whatever bimbette number two was saying. "It's time to go, Edward. I have twin twentysomethings back in our room waiting for us, and the girls won't wait naked all night."

Edward's eyes rounded with shock, and her absurd distraction worked well enough that when she tugged on his arm this time, he went.

"What is going on?" he asked under his breath as they hurried toward the exit.

"A man with a gun is headed right this way. I thought now would be a really good time to leave."

Edward cast an apologetic look over his shoulder at the girls. "Why didn't you say so?"

"I did," said Sloane, refusing to allow her frustration to enter her tone.

"No, you said it was time to go. You didn't say anything about a gun."

"You hired *me* to protect you, rather than one of the big, beefy men I work with. That tells me that you really didn't want a lot of people knowing you needed a bodyguard. I was trying to be discreet."

"By telling everyone I'm going to have sex with twin girls?"

Sloane shrugged, urging Edward to hurry the hell up. The exit was only twenty feet away. "Would you have preferred guys?"

He sputtered in outrage, but at least she'd gotten his blood moving enough that he had picked up speed.

Just not enough.

Hot, strong fingers closed around her bare arm, jerking her to the side. Her grip on Edward failed, and she stumbled toward Mr. Tuxedo.

"Run," she shouted at Edward.

"Get down," barked Mr. Tuxedo.

He tried to push her to the floor, but Sloane had other plans. She had a perfect track record at the Edge, and she wasn't about to ruin that now by leaving her principal unprotected.

She spun her arm, breaking Mr. Tuxedo's grip. She needed to reach Edward and get him out of harm's way. Running in heels was an art all its own—one she'd spent hours working on—but the laws of physics hadn't changed because of that training, and she found herself slipping on the glossy ballroom floor.

Edward hadn't moved. He stood staring at her in shock, his mouth hanging open, his flabby body trembling with indecision.

"Go!" yelled Sloane. She'd catch up with him on the stairwell once she'd disarmed Mr. Tuxedo.

Behind Edward, only inches from his head, a glass wall sconce exploded into shrapnel. A large gaping hole opened up in the drywall where a bullet had shredded it.

"Gun!" shouted Mr. Tuxedo, an instant before he tackled her to the floor, covering her with his bulk.

Screams filled the ballroom. Confused panic skittered through her system.

Mr. Tuxedo's heavy body crushed the air from her lungs, and black spots formed in her vision. Through them, she saw Edward turn tail and run, pushing open the heavy stairwell door.

Now all she had to do was get out from under Mr. Tuxedo and join Edward. Not that she was going anywhere until she got a little oxygen.

Another shot went off, fracturing a section of the exit door, and people started stampeding.

"We're going to get trampled." Mr. Tuxedo's mouth was right next to her ear, allowing her to hear him over the panicked screams of the partygoers.

His weight disappeared, and in the next instant, she felt weightless as he lifted her to her feet and pulled her toward the exit. She jerked away, dodging him in the crowd. The doorway was already clogged with people, pushing and shoving as if that would help them escape faster.

For one split second, she thought about going back to find the shooter and take out the threat to her principal. She knew better; she knew her job was to keep Edward safe, not hunt down scum, but the urge was still there, and she had to fight it every step of the way. There were at least two gunmen here so far. Who knew how many more there might be flooding out the doors toward her unprotected client?

Someone stepped on her foot, hard, but she didn't dare look down to figure out who it was. Beside her, an old woman gasped and slipped beneath the shoving bodies.

Sloane reached for her but was too late, and the frail woman went down beneath a herd of lethal spiked heels.

Sloane tried to turn around to face the mob, hoping to stop them before they killed the woman. She was swept along in their wake, forced to move with them or fall herself. The crush of shoving limbs was unrelenting, and it took her too long to face the oncoming crowd.

She pulled in a breath to scream for them to stop when she saw Mr. Tuxedo behind her with the frail woman in his arms.

He gave her a grim, determined nod. "Go," he told Sloane. "I've got her."

Seeing him protect the old lady gave Sloane pause. He was supposed to be the bad guy. Wasn't he?

Okay, so clearly he wasn't the shooter—that shot had come from across the room. But if he wasn't here to hurt Edward, why had he been heading their way with a gun under his jacket?

There wasn't a whole lot of time to contemplate that question before Sloane squeezed through the door, and down the steps, and found Edward waiting for her on the ground floor.

She didn't even slow, but grabbed his arm and headed for the rear exit of the hotel, where the armored limo was supposed to be ready and waiting to pick them up.

Mr. Tuxedo still had an elderly woman in his arms to deal with, and Sloane hoped that by the time he did, she and Edward would be long gone. She really would have liked to know what his part in all of this had been, but her job was to get her principal out safely, and that was exactly what she was going to do.

Lucas had lost her. One minute she was right in front of him, and the next, she was gone.

He set the little old lady on a bench and checked to make sure she was going to stay upright. Her white hair had come free of its sparkling combs and was now a mess. The sleeve of her silk gown was torn, but she looked healthy enough.

"Are you okay?" he asked.

She gave him a shaky nod.

"Are you hurt?"

"Just banged around a bit. I'll be fine. Thank you." She sounded breathless, but Lucas figured she had a right to be. That whole mess had probably scared the hell out of her.

She reached up to pull at her mangled sleeve, and her hands were shaking so badly, they looked like they might fly off her wrists. A dark bruise was forming on her forearm, beneath pale, papery skin.

Shit. He couldn't leave her like this. What if she'd hit her head?

"Sit tight. I'm going to find you some help."

Lucas flagged down one of the confused bellboys and hauled his pimply ass over to the woman. "You stay with her," he ordered the kid, jabbing a finger into his skinny chest. "Do not let her out of your sight until a paramedic has checked her out. Understand?"

"Yes, sir," said the kid.

Police and other emergency vehicles were swarming into the parking lot. Lucas flagged down the first paramedic he saw and dragged him bodily to the old woman. The wide-eyed EMT went to work, glancing nervously over his shoulder every few seconds. At least he seemed capable enough to handle the situation.

It was going to have to be good enough. Lucas still had to find Sloane and keep her off that flight to Colombia. His best chance now was to intercept her at the small airport where her plane would depart.

In eighty-eight minutes.

As he headed for his car, he dialed the Old Man.

"Is she with you?" he answered on the first ring.

"No, sir. There was a situation here. Shots fired. She got away."

"Shots? Is she okay?"

"Yes, sir."

"I swear to God, Ramsey, if so much as one hair on her head is harmed, I'll hold you personally responsible."

Lucas slid behind the wheel of his car. "Yes, sir."

"Find her. Stop her. Do not let her step foot on that jet. I don't care what it takes."

He eased out of the parking lot as more emergency vehicles came into view down the street. "I'm on it, sir."

"I chose you for this because you're not a man who knows how to fail. Was I wrong?"

"No, sir. This was just a minor setback."

"Any idea why there were shots fired at some charity ball?"

"None. But I can tell you that the shooter was aiming right for her."

"Dear God," breathed the Old Man, sounding like he'd just aged twenty years in a heartbeat. "Are you sure he wasn't aiming at her principal?"

Lucas merged onto the highway, heading away from Dallas toward the airstrip. "Principal, sir?"

"She's a bodyguard, of all things." He spoke like the mere thought chapped his ass raw. "Are you sure the shooter wasn't aiming for her client?"

A bodyguard? Seriously? Well, that would certainly explain how she knew how to break his hold without so much as batting an eye.

Lucas wondered why this little bit of info hadn't been passed on to him earlier. Must've been need-to-know.

"No, sir. I guess he could have been the target. She was hanging all over him, so it's hard to be sure exactly where the gunman was aiming. I assumed that since she was my target, she was also the shooter's."

"Anything's possible with that woman, but I hope you're wrong."

"Is there anything else about her I should know, sir?"

"Now that you've lost her, you mean?"

Lucas gritted his teeth and gunned the engine, maneuvering around the late-night traffic. "Yes, sir."

"Like what?"

"Like why it's so important that I stop her from getting on that flight. What's so important about some chick bodyguard?"

"That chick bodyguard happens to be my daughter."

Daughter? No way. The Old Man couldn't have a child. He wasn't human. He was frigid logic. He lived and breathed strategy and tactics. He was walking death with any weapon created by man, and had at his disposal some of the most lethal men on the planet. All of whom feared and respected him. He couldn't have a kid. That was just . . . spooky.

"Uh. Sorry, sir. I didn't realize you had a daughter."

"Not many people do. See that you keep it that way."

"Yes, sir."

The Old Man hung up, leaving Lucas reeling. The stakes had just been raised, big-time. If he failed to stop Sloane and she ended up heading toward one of the most dangerous countries on the planet, he wouldn't have to worry about a new line of work. The Old Man would kill him.

Chapter 2

Sloane's flight left in thirty-two minutes, and if she didn't get to Colombia soon, the chances of her ever seeing Gina again were somewhere below zero.

She parked at the small private airstrip, where the pilot was waiting, got out of her car, popped the trunk, and grabbed her luggage. The canvas bags weighed as much as she did, but chances were she was going to need every last advantage she could get, so she'd packed accordingly.

Sloane's phone had rung in the middle of the night last night. It was Gina.

I'm not sure exactly where in Colombia I am, Sloane. All I know is that I'm surrounded by jungle and he won't let me go. His name is Lorenzo Soma. He . . . changed after we got here. I thought he was some rich exec, but I was wrong. There are men with guns here. Lots of guns. They lock me in at night. I'm scared, Sloane. I—

Whatever else Gina had started to say had been cut off abruptly.

Sloane had spent the last twenty hours making arrangements to find and rescue her former boarding school roommate. She only hoped that things weren't as bad as she feared—that Gina was exaggerating again.

The sick, twisty feeling in Sloane's gut told her she was fooling herself.

"Need a hand?" came a deep voice from behind her.

Sloane was on edge, revved up from the adrenaline rush at the hotel. Before she could think through what she was doing, she whirled around, ready to strike at the throat that had made that statement.

It was Mr. Tuxedo, and he was faster than she was. He grabbed her wrist before her strike landed and pulled her forward, using her own momentum against her. She ended up spun around, her back to his chest, her own arms wrapped around her like a straitjacket.

"Whoa. Calm down," he said into her hair. "I'm not going to hurt you."

Maybe not, but she wasn't so sure she could promise him the same. "Let me go."

"Not until I'm sure you're not going to try anything stupid."

"Who are you?"

He paused as if debating his next statement. "A friend."

"You say that like I should know who you are. I don't." She would have remembered a man who looked and moved like him. There was not a single doubt in her head about that.

She could feel the hard heat of his body behind hers, the subtle contours of his pecs against her shoulders. His arms were thick and unyielding beneath the sleeves of his tux jacket, holding her in place. A faint, clean scent hovered around him, and Sloane couldn't help but pull it into her lungs.

A deep, primal part of her mind perked up, sparking a kind of interest in him she hadn't felt in a long, long time. Maybe never.

If it weren't for the fact that he was an armed stalker,

she might have been interested in seeing whether or not that instinct was right.

"That doesn't answer my question. Why are you following me?" she asked.

"I can't let you get on that plane."

Sloane's body stilled inside his hold. If he didn't want her going to Colombia, then his appearance at the charity ball earlier tonight hadn't been about Edward. It had been about stopping Sloane before she could reach Gina. Which meant he had to know something about her abduction.

"Where is she?" Sloane demanded.

"She who?"

"Gina. Where have you taken her?"

He loosened his grip and turned her around to face him. "I don't know what you're talking about. I don't know any Gina. I just came to keep you off that flight."

Sloane studied his face, watching the minuscule movements of his mouth and eyes, searching for a sign he was lying. She found none.

What she found was even more disconcerting than a lie. There was pain hiding in his expression. She saw it in the tightness of his mouth and the redness rimming his eyes. He was hurting, and she had to shove away a fleeting moment of concern.

He was handsome. Not in the way of models—all perfect angles and symmetry—but deeper than that. More alluring. His nose had been broken at least once, and there was a small scar bisecting his upper lip. He'd shaved today, but the shadow of his beard darkened his wide jaw. His hair was a shiny deep black, swept back from his forehead in a sleek style that fit perfectly with the tux.

Sloane hated it that she couldn't stop staring. She had things to do. A friend to save.

"I'm getting on that plane," she told him.

"No, you're not."

If she hadn't been watching him so intently, she wouldn't have seen the smirk playing about his mouth or sparkling in his eyes. But she was watching, and she saw his amusement for what it was.

A challenge.

A tingle of excitement bubbled through her veins. This was going to be fun.

She gave him a sweet smile, one that made him relax his hold on her arms. It was all the room she needed to strike. One well-placed blow to the temples, and he crumpled and was out for the count.

Lucas knew the woman had game, but he had no idea how much until he was staring up at the stars, wondering what had happened.

His head throbbed, both where she'd hit him and where he'd hit the asphalt. Rather than moving it, which seemed a really bad idea, he lifted his arm and checked his watch.

He'd been out for only a few minutes, but long enough that her private jet was gone.

Shit. Now he had to call the Old Man and admit how he'd fucked up such a simple job.

Failure grated along his insides, making his stomach churn. No wonder he'd been kicked out of the U.S. Army Rangers. He couldn't even subdue one unarmed woman.

Lucas pushed himself to his feet, forced his throbbing knee to take the punishment he gave it, and dialed the Old Man.

"She got away, didn't she?" answered the Old Man.

"Yes, sir."

"You underestimated her, didn't you?"

"Apparently, sir."

There was a long, uncomfortable silence on the other end of the line, before he spoke again. "Can I safely assume you won't make that mistake twice?"

That sounded suspiciously like a second chance—something the Old Man rarely gave. The chance for redemption flared bright and hot inside Lucas, and he gripped the phone tighter, hoping he wasn't wrong about the man's intentions. "Absolutely, sir."

"Good. I'll arrange for you to fly out immediately. You'll go to Colombia and drag her ass back. Is that understood?"

"Yes, sir."

"You can't be gentle with her. Believe me, I've tried."

"I don't want to hurt her, sir. She's your daughter."

"I'd rather see her in a hospital bed than a body bag. If that's what it takes, that's what you'll do. Whatever it takes. Are we clear, Ramsey?"

"Crystal, sir."

Sloane Gideon was going to have the world's shortest visit to Colombia. One way or another. Lucas refused to fail the Old Man again.

Bella Bayne waited patiently while Tanner wiped blood from his broken nose and the stream of tears from his eyes. He wasn't crying. Hell, no. Tanner O'Connell was too tough to cry, but even a tough guy leaked a little when his nose broke.

She was more interested in how he'd handle the blow to his pride than whether or not those were tears of pain.

The sparring mat was soft under her bare feet, and the smell of hot sweat filled the air of the training room. Around them, her men and women—her mercenaries—gathered to watch her beat the new guy to a pulp.

"If you can't beat me," she told the interviewee, "why

should I hire you? Because your brother works here? Are you looking for special treatment?"

"I don't want to hurt you," said Tanner, his voice ringing with a swollen nasal twang.

Bella laughed, though she had to force it out. There'd been a time not so long ago when she'd been weak and helpless—a victim just about anyone could have hurt. But not anymore. That life was over. "At the rate you're going, neither one of us has to worry about that, do we?"

Tanner clenched his fists, which he held up, ready to defend himself against another blow. "You never said that part of the interview would involve beating the hell out of a woman."

"There are a whole lot of things I haven't said yet. Quit whining and show me what you've got. Or do I have to grow a dick before you'll man up?"

The onlookers laughed, and Tanner gave a resigned sigh, shaking his head as he closed the distance between them.

She had to give him points for that. Seven out of the last ten men she'd interviewed hadn't gotten past the bloodied nose phase. They'd packed up their muscles and gone home.

Now, the women, on the other hand . . . they had no trouble coming at her, fists, elbows, knees, and heels flying without concern.

"Bella," came Payton Bainbridge's voice echoing across the training room. "A word."

She didn't dare take her eyes off Tanner now that he was showing promise. "I'm busy. Make an appointment."

"You can bludgeon that young man later. This can't wait."

Great. The bills from the Mexico job must have come in.

Bella called a halt and bowed to Tanner. "If you'll

please excuse me. We'll have to pick this up again later."
She turned to her right-hand man. "Riley, could you give
Tanner a ride over to Leigh's office to get his nose set?"

"Yes, ma'am." Riley scrubbed his sweaty, shaved
head with a towel and tossed it into the hamper. "I'll
make sure she makes him all pretty again."

There were at least a dozen people in the training
room, and every one of them had something to say
about how pretty the new guy was. Bella left, and the
door swung shut on a particularly vile comment regard-
ing Tanner's pretty mouth.

She smiled, wishing she could stay and join the fun,
but there were consequences to face, and Payton was
going to make sure she did.

Bella followed Payton down the hall toward her office. Air cooled the sweat on her body, and the shiny
tile floor was cold under her bare feet. The seam down
the back of Payton's perfectly cut suit jacket barely
shifted as he walked. Every one of his gray hairs was
in place.

"Hey, Payton," she said behind him. "Does your hair
ever grow?"

"Of course it does."

"It always looks the same. I've known you for what,
twenty years, and I've never once seen you with shaggy
hair."

"That's because I've never *had* shaggy hair."

"No, I mean, I've never seen you come in looking like
you just got it cut. It's always the same exact length. Do
you have some kind of secret superpower I don't know
about?"

Payton glanced over his shoulder without slowing,
and said, bone dry, "Yes. Clearly that must be it. I'm the
Amazing Never Needs a Haircut Man. Now that you
know my secret, I'll have to kill you."

She kept bugging him, because she knew her turn

was just around the corner. Literally. Once he got her into her office, she was going to have to sit and listen to him gripe about stuff she had no interest in listening to. "I'm just saying you must get it cut every three days or something."

As they rounded the corner, Lila, Bella's secretary, stood and held out a bottle of chilled water.

Lila was dressed in her usual burlap brown attire, which hid every bit of proof she was a woman. Her mousy brown hair was pulled back into a ponytail, held in place by a plain rubber band—not even the kind meant for hair. A gnawed pencil was behind one ear and her nose was bright pink.

Lila had been crying again.

A warm, gushy spot opened up in Bella's heart for the woman. She'd been through hell, and yet here she stood, alive and kicking. Or at least she'd be kicking by the time Bella was done with her. For now Lila was out of her soon-to-be-ex-husband's house and supporting herself, which was a huge step in the right direction.

"Thanks," Bella said as she snagged the water and disappeared into her office with Payton right on her heels.

He shut the door with a carefully controlled click. "That woman needs a makeover."

"No. She needs a good right hook and maybe a concealed-carry permit."

"Bringing in the strays again?" he asked, as he settled himself on the edge of the chair on the other side of Bella's glass desk.

"You know me. Allergic to cats. Gotta have something soft and cuddly around."

"Indeed," he said. "Shall we move on with the business at hand?"

Bella propped her bare feet up on her desk, just because she knew it would drive Payton crazy. She loved him as much as she did her own father. She really did.

But the man was such an easy target, she couldn't help herself sometimes.

He stared at her bright purple toenails for an extended moment before he pulled a tri-folded sheet of paper from his jacket pocket. "Do you have any idea how much money your latest . . . escapades cost us?"

Bella opened the cold water and chugged half the bottle before responding. "More or less than they paid us?"

"More."

"More than last time?"

Payton sighed. "This is not a guessing game, Bella. I'm being serious here."

"Oh. Sorry. I thought we were playing twenty questions. My mistake."

"It usually is," muttered Payton.

"I heard that."

"Good. Then perhaps you'll finally hear this: We're in business to make a profit. When you blow up property, we have to pay for it. That cuts into our profit. Substantially."

"There's more to life than profit."

Payton laughed. "No. There isn't."

"You seriously need to get laid."

He held up a finger. "What is rule number one?" he asked in a paternal tone.

"Don't discuss your sex life," recited Bella, rolling her eyes.

"I believe the term was 'love life,' but I'll take what I can get."

"Apparently not. Otherwise you wouldn't be nearly so grumpy all the time."

Payton waved the paper at her. "You cost us every penny of income from that job and then some. This cannot happen again. What fun is it to be in business if we don't make a profit?"

"You didn't get to see that building explode, or you wouldn't be asking that question."

"Bella," he warned.

"I took pictures. Wanna see?"

"No. I do not."

"I even got pictures of the weird shit inside."

An unnatural stillness settled over Payton. Only his eyes moved, locking with hers. "How weird?"

"Really weird. All kinds of medical equipment I've never seen. Big tanks full of who knew what. A freaking snake's nest of wires, tubes, and cables leading from nowhere to nowhere, like someone had disconnected something big and hauled it out of there before we arrived."

"Where are these photos?"

"On my phone. I'll e-mail them to you later."

"No," he said too quickly. "No need. I'm sure it's nothing."

"What the hell has you spooked?" she asked.

He pulled in a long breath. "The bill, Bella. Paying this bill has me spooked."

She waved a negligent hand. "Oh, come on. You're made of money, and that place needed to be blown up."

"That wasn't the job you were paid to do."

"No. We were paid to make sure that those human traffickers no longer had a place to hide. And that's what we did. By blowing up their hiding place."

"I see you've learned to think outside of the box."

She gave him a wink. "I learned from the best."

Payton sighed, folded up the bill and put it back in his pocket. "Your mother would have been proud."

Bella liked to think so. She'd done well for herself—made a name in a man's world as one of the most dependable mercenary companies around. Sure, Payton had footed the bill at first, but she'd paid his initial investment back threefold. Even including all the collateral damage she'd caused along the way, which wasn't nearly as much as Payton thought, and a hell of a lot less than she'd *wanted* to inflict.

Some of the things she'd seen made her want to raze entire towns. The things people would do to other people for money was beyond her comprehension. If she spent too much time thinking about it, she'd never get to sleep tonight, so she locked the door on those memories and moved on to happier topics.

"I signed a new contract today," she told Payton. "Lots of major buckage."

"The diamond shipments?"

"That's the one. I'll be getting a team together this week. I was hoping Sloane would be on it, since she's worked with them before, but she had some personal emergency to deal with and took vacation."

"You'll pick only the best, I hope."

Bella gave him her widest smile. "That's all I hire."

"Try not to blow up any buildings while you're there?" he asked in a sickly sweet tone.

She walked around the desk and kissed him on the forehead. "I'm not making any promises."

Chapter 3

It took Lucas twelve hours to find her, and during every one of them, he could practically feel the Old Man breathing down his neck.

He had no idea what she was doing this far out into the jungle, in the middle of yet another tiny village. This was the third one so far today, and each time, it had cost Lucas some of his dwindling cash to find out where she'd gone.

All he'd managed to discover was that she was looking for someone who had apparently come this way. No one would tell him who she was searching for.

Fucking wild-goose chase. For all he knew, these people were simply telling her what they thought she wanted to hear, milking her for her pretty American cash. They sure as hell were gouging him.

Losing sleep last night had taken its toll on his knee, making it throb. He had a bottle full of pain pills, but couldn't risk the haze they caused, or the chance they'd slow him down. Unfortunately, that meant he could no longer hide the limp when he walked across the street toward the run-down shack that served as this village's tavern.

Sloane had walked in there seconds ago, and when

she came out, it was going to be willingly, or slung over Lucas's shoulder—whichever it took.

A brief flash of another day, just under a year ago, filled his head. The day he'd carried Jerry's body out of that firefight. Heat had seared Lucas's skin, sucking all the moisture from it. Sand stung his eyes and grated against his teeth. He was too dehydrated to spit it out, too busy fighting his way free to reach for his canteen.

Lucas pushed the memory away with a force of will. If he had to carry Sloane out, he'd use the other fucking shoulder. *Get over it already.*

A boy on a battered bike raced past him, ringing a bell. Lucas jumped out of the way, glad to be snapped back to the here and now. He hadn't realized he had stopped dead in his tracks in the middle of the dirt street. With his luck, Sloane would slip out the back while he took a mental-breakdown moment.

Wouldn't that be fun explaining to the Old Man.

Lucas hurried across the street and in through the open tavern door. There was almost no light in here, and even less air. The place reeked of stale sweat, booze, and smoke. A fuzzy ceiling fan twirled lazily overhead, doing nothing but hauling the odors up to his nose for his enjoyment.

There were six tables, and men at two of them. A bar made from loose planks of wood stacked on two barrels ran along the back wall. Perched there with her lovely butt on a barstool was Sloane. She pushed cash across the stained wood. The bartender pocketed the green and crooked his finger for her to lean close.

The men at the tables eyed Lucas, and though it was way too early in the day for hard drinking, three of them were up to the task. Their bloodshot eyes followed him, their heads turned sluggishly as he crossed the scarred wooden floor.

A young woman with long black hair worn in a thick braid and a colorful flowing skirt came out of the back room carrying a tray full of clean glasses. She was barely out of her teens and pretty in a natural, unfussy way that reminded Lucas of his little sister. One of the men beckoned her over with a sharp word and imperious hand gesture. The woman did a bad job of hiding the cringe that crossed her face before straightening her spine and going to the customer.

The bartender whispered something to Sloane, who hadn't yet noticed Lucas had come in.

He approached her slowly. This time, he wasn't going to be taken in by her beauty or distracted by her curves. As sweet and pretty as she appeared, she had wicked fast hands and knew how to use them.

Too bad she was the Old Man's daughter, or he might consider showing her just how good he was with his hands, too.

Just the idea of touching her bare skin made his body heat and his pulse kick up a notch. And before he'd known who she was, he'd had enough time to form all kinds of interesting scenarios.

But Sloane was the general's daughter, and Lucas liked his balls way too much to risk pissing the man off.

He sat down next to her, interrupting whatever the bartender was whispering to her. Lucas was close enough to grab her if she tried to dart, but not so close he wouldn't see her hands flying toward his face. Again. No more sucker punches for this sucker.

"Hello, Sloane," he said, keeping his voice low so it wouldn't carry across the room.

She stiffened and turned his way. Her eyes narrowed, and he could see now that they were a soft shade of green. Just like the Old Man's, only his weren't nearly so pretty.

The bartender eyed Lucas up and down, sizing him

up, then made the intelligent decision to walk away and leave them alone.

"Why are you following me?" she asked.

"Why are you here?" he countered.

"If you're going to be following me, you can at least tell me your name. You apparently know mine already."

"Lucas Ramsey."

Behind Sloane, the young woman serving drinks made a sudden move, drawing Lucas's attention. One of the sweaty drunks was pawing at her, but he was too slow to catch her. Unfortunately, she moved right into the reach of the next table and one of the men there pulled her onto his lap.

"Did Bella send you to watch my back?" asked Sloane.

"Nope. Don't know anyone named Bella."

The drunk pinned the girl's arms and held her there while he squeezed her breast. She struggled for a moment before going dead still. The look of revulsion on her face screamed that she was not a willing participant.

A swift, hot rage built up inside Lucas. He knew this was none of his business and he had a mission to complete, but there were some things a man simply couldn't ignore.

Sloane couldn't see the situation that was playing out behind her, and she continued to speak while Lucas debated how to best make the pervert suffer. "If Bella didn't send you, then you must know why I'm here. This would go a lot faster if you just took me to Gina."

Lucas had no idea who Gina was, but he knew an opening when he saw one. He'd let her think he was taking her to this Gina woman, so she wouldn't fight him all the way back to the plane.

Lucas kept his expression neutral and let none of his anger seep into his voice as he rose from his stool. He let out a resigned sigh, paused as if thinking it over, then said, "Okay. You win. I'll show you where she is."

"I'm armed," warned Sloane.

"Lady, you're armed even when you're weaponless. Don't think I'll make the same mistake twice."

The young girl whimpered as the man's dirty hand tightened on her breast. His friends leered, laughing.

"That would be smart," said Sloane.

The girl saw him watching, saw him stand and flex his fists. Her wide, dark eyes pleaded with him, though whether she was asking for help or for him to stay out of it, he had no idea. He knew which he was going to do, though.

"Just hang tight for a minute," he told Sloane. "There's this one quick thing I need to do."

Sloane could tell Lucas was lying about taking her to Gina. But that didn't mean he didn't know where she was. Sloane was running out of options. The bartender had taken her money but told her little about how she could find Lorenzo Soma. Once she mentioned his name, people clammed up. At this rate, she was going to run out of cash and still have no leads.

Following Lucas was her only option at this point, so she'd do that until she came up with a better idea.

Too bad Gina had called from a satellite phone, or tracking her down might have been a lot simpler. As it was, all she had was a name and a country. The resident computer guru at the Edge, Mira Sage, had found a small bit of info online that led her to believe Soma operated in this part of the country, but that wasn't much to go on.

Whoever Lucas was, he had to be connected to the mess Gina had gotten herself into. He was just the kind of man Gina went for: tall, muscular, a little rough around the edges. Panty-melting sin wrapped up in smooth, tan skin.

Hell, he was the kind of man most women went for. Including Sloane. At least he would have been under normal circumstances.

Today was far from normal.

Lucas crossed the small tavern toward a table where three men sat. A young woman was struggling against the abusive pawing one of the patrons was giving her.

Sloane stood there, shocked at the open display. By the time outrage had burned away her shock, allowing her to move, Lucas was already dealing with the situation.

"Let her go," he said in a voice low and menacing.

The girl said something in flowing, frightened Spanish.

The man laughed and shot back a string of harsh words.

The girl's eyes began to tear up. In halting, heavily accented English, she said, "Go. I can care of myself."

Lucas's gaze never wavered. "Sorry, honey. I'm just not built that way. Somebody's got to teach this asshole a lesson."

Sloane was more than willing to help.

She stepped forward.

Lucas ignored her. "Let go of the woman," he said, his words more demanding.

The man pushed the girl from his lap and she fell to the floor in a sprawl. He stood, wavering unsteadily on his feet. His eyes were bloodshot and his hands shook as he pointed an accusing finger at Lucas. She caught the words *American* and *pig* but that was enough to get the gist of the insult.

Sloane moved around the men to help the girl to her feet. Tension hummed through the air as the other men rose from their seats. There were five of them and they were all eyeing Lucas like they wanted a piece of him.

This was going to get ugly fast if she didn't do something.

"They'll kill him," whispered the young woman.

"Get out of here. Go somewhere safe." Preferably out of the range of stray bullets.

The girl left, and Sloane stepped up to Lucas's side and drew her pistol, holding it low at her side. She didn't aim it at any of the men, but they all saw she was armed. "We're not doing this," she told Lucas.

"That man molested her. Someone's got to make sure it doesn't happen again."

"That noble streak you've got going there is cute and all, but if we go shooting the locals, we will end up in jail."

Lucas shifted his stance a small fraction, but Sloane read it as the beginning of a withdrawal. "I just want to hit him once."

"I know. So do I, but if you do, it'll just make it worse for the girl next time. Unless you're going to kill him. Are you going to kill him?"

The men were looking at one another, their expressions growing wary. Apparently, they spoke enough English to understand some of what they said. Or perhaps they simply understood Sloane's loaded weapon and Lucas's clenched fists.

Behind them, Sloane heard the unmistakable sound of a pump-action shotgun.

"Get out of my bar," said the bartender. Suddenly, his English was a lot better than it had been when she'd questioned him about Lorenzo Soma's location. She was sure that wasn't a coincidence.

"Time to go," said Sloane. "You can come back later if you still want to beat the hell out of him. I'm not carrying your carcass out of here, understand?"

His face twisted in anger, but he backed up and headed for the door. Sloane covered his back, keeping her weapon at her side. At the doorway, she announced, "I'll shoot anyone who tries to follow us. Don't even step foot out of this door until we're long gone."

The bartender's twin barrels followed her out, but the men stayed put. As they moved away from the building, Sloane kept a careful watch on the doorway.

The young woman was waiting outside, crying silently.

Lucas reached into his pocket and pulled out a wad of cash. "Find a different job," he told her as he pressed the money into her hand. "Don't go back there. They'll hurt you."

She looked at the money in shock, and then flung her arms around Lucas's neck, hugging him. He gently detangled her. "Go now, before they gather up the courage to come out here."

She wiped her eyes and straightened her shoulders, then looked at Sloane. "I heard you ask about Lorenzo Soma. I know where he lives."

Sloane kept her expression neutral, not wanting to get her hopes up. "No one else was willing to tell me."

"He took my brother," she said. "There is a place where small planes come. He takes people there, gives them to a man. Many people have been taken."

That sounded a hell of a lot like human trafficking. No way was Sloane going to let Soma do that to Gina. "Do you mean an airstrip? A runway?"

"Yes. Like that. It's near my childhood home."

"Can you draw a map?" asked Lucas. He dug in a pocket, extracting a small notepad and a stubby pencil.

The woman drew the map while Lucas moved a few feet away and kept watch on the door to the bar. "Be quick."

"If you do not find him here, then he may be at his southern villa. But if you go there, be careful. He has his own army."

"How many men?" asked Lucas.

"Thirty. Maybe more."

Sloane kept her eyes on the map as it emerged at the tip of the short pencil. It was small and not to scale, but there were enough landmarks to indicate that it would at least get her closer to Gina's location.

"His villa is near the secret building," said the woman. "My brother and I went there once when we were children. Our friend was caught by armed guards and never seen again."

"What is this building? What do they do there?" asked Lucas without looking away from the tavern's doorway. His hand was at his side, no doubt on the weapons Sloane knew he had hidden under his loose shirt.

"Bad things. Secret things. Spirits of the dead live there."

Sloane wasn't buying into the whole haunted-building theory, but any landmark they could find was helpful.

"The men are moving around. Time to go."

From inside the bar, Sloane could hear men's voices getting louder. They were either arguing or planning an attack, but she didn't want to stick around to find out which.

"This is where Soma's villa is," the woman said, pointing to a small star on the map.

Sloane nodded and shoved the map in her back pocket as Lucas neared. No way was she going to let him see it. She was going to lose him the first chance she got, and she didn't want him to be able to find her because he knew where she was headed. Unless he already did.

"Thank you," the woman said to Lucas. "I won't forget you." She lifted the hem of her skirt, and darted away.

"I'm leaving. I don't need an escort."

Lucas wrapped his fingers around her arm as they hurried away from the tavern. "I'm out of cash, so there's no getting rid of me now. Don't even try it."

They left the shadow of small huts into the thick, growing heat of the day. As they skirted between rough hovels, they kept out of sight of the tavern, hoping to avoid any encounters with the drunks.

"We're taking my ride," she announced, pretending she accepted his decree that they'd stay together, rather than fighting about it. And if she couldn't give him the slip, she'd still have all of her equipment with her once she got to Gina. There was no way to know what she was going to need to get her friend safely home.

"Fine. Lead the way. Anywhere away from the bar works for me."

Her Land Rover was parked well out of sight of the tavern, at the side of the road leading into this village. She had obscured it as much as possible by the creeping green of the jungle and paid a local farmer to guard it while she was away. The Rover was ugly as sin, fitted with mismatched sheets of rusted metal plates for armor that was hell on her MPG, but as long as the bad guys didn't have large-caliber or armor-piercing rounds, it could take a pile of gunfire and keep going. In this part of the world, she'd take ugly armor over pretty bullets-rip-through-it-like-tissue paint any day of the week.

The man she'd paid to stand guard over her stuff was sitting there, snoozing against one of the wheels. Sloane peeked inside, saw her stuff was untouched and the doors still locked, then nudged him with the toe of her boot. He woke without a word, and held out his hand for the rest of the cash she'd promised him.

She handed it over and waited for him to shamble off before she faced Lucas.

"Give me your gun," she demanded.

Lucas crossed his arms over his chest, making the tight green T-shirt he wore under the looser shirt wrinkle between his pecs. "What makes you think I'm armed?"

"You were packing under a tux in a nice, civilized part of Dallas. The chances of you not carrying here in the middle of the jungle are nonexistent. Now, hand it over."

"I'm not going to shoot you."

"I know you're not. You're not going to have a gun. It's either that, or I'll find my own way."

"You can trust me."

Sloane laughed at him. "Is that what you said to Gina, too, before you abducted her for your boss?"

"No." A slight shift in his expression gave Sloane pause. He was surprised by her words, which meant she'd guessed right, or he knew nothing about Gina. Either way, Sloane was in more trouble than she thought.

"Where is she, Lucas?"

"I'll have to show you."

"Fine. Just tell me the general direction." Sloane had the map the young woman had drawn. Lucas had been so busy watching the tavern, he hadn't paid any attention to it. She knew which way she was headed to find the man who went by the name Gina had given her. Lorenzo Soma. Everyone here knew him, but only a few were actually brave enough risk their lives giving her information. If Lucas hadn't rescued that woman, she might still be groping in the dark.

"North."

Lucas was wrong according to the map, which meant he wasn't who he said he was. Unfortunately, it also meant that Sloane's curiosity was piqued, and she wanted to know who he was even more now. And there was only one way to find out.

"Fine," she said. "Give me your gun and you can get in."

His wide shoulders drooped in defeat, and he reached under the loose shirt hanging open over his T-shirt and pulled out a semiautomatic. He handed it to her butt first.

Sloane released the magazine, opened the slide, and made sure the weapon was safe before she stuck it in her waistband. The magazine went into her pocket. "And your holdout weapon."

He scowled at her for a prolonged second before he propped his foot on the tire and ripped his ankle holster free, weapon and all. A grimace of pain flashed across his face for a brief second, as if the movement had hurt him, but when he handed the weapon to her, any sign of pain was gone.

The pistol had a safety, which was on. She tucked the whole rig alongside the driver's seat, and shut the door.

Showtime.

Sloane gave him her most seductive smile—the one that Bella had taught her years ago as the best way to really disarm a man. Lucas's mouth began to lift in a smile of his own when she lashed out at him.

He was big and heavy, but she had the element of surprise on her side. She shoved him against the truck, pressing the blade of her forearm against his throat. He was tall enough that it was a bit of a reach to apply the appropriate amount of pressure, but not beyond her ability. With her left hand, she grabbed his balls just hard enough to let him know she had a good grip without hurting him.

Lucas froze, and a slow, hot smile warmed his mouth. "If you wanted to handle my goods, all you had to do was ask."

He wasn't afraid. Sloane wasn't sure what to make of that. Maybe she was losing her touch, or maybe he was just playing along, letting her pin him.

"You're going to tell me why you're here, and you're going to do it now, or I'll twist and keep twisting until I hear a pop."

He moved so fast, Sloane wasn't sure what had hap-

pened. One minute, she had him where she wanted him;
the next, she'd somehow traded places. Her back was
against the Rover, and her hands were locked behind
her, pinned at the small of her back in one of his big fists.
His fingers spanned her throat, touching but not hurting
her—letting her know that he could if he wanted.

Her breasts were pressed flat against his hard body,
and heat poured off of him, making her sweat in the
thick jungle air. Even as hot as she was, she felt her nipples bead up, pressing against him.

She told herself it was a response to adrenaline, nothing more. The fact that he was a handsome man with a
hard body that smelled like temptation, and said body
was flattened against hers, had nothing to do with it.

He stared down at her, his nostrils flared with anger
and his navy blue eyes narrow. "Don't think that I'm
some kind of weakling just because you surprised me
in the airport parking lot. Anyone can get in a sucker
punch now and then. Even you."

"It was more than a sucker punch, and you know it."

"No. I don't. But it doesn't matter. What matters is
getting you back to the States in one piece, which is exactly what I'm going to do."

"Who the hell are you? Why do you care where I go?"

"I don't. Your father does."

Her father.

Sloane froze in place, and not even the scalding heat
coming from Lucas could do anything to warm her. She
hadn't spoken to her father since she called to tell him
Mom had died, and it had been even longer since she'd
actually seen him. Five years to be exact.

She shoved away the rage and grief that threatened
to crush her, and forced her voice to come out cold and
steady. "I no longer have a father."

"Bullshit."

"Think what you want. I don't care. Just get your damn hands off of me and let me go."

"Not going to happen. I'm putting your ass on a plane and you're damn well going to stay there if I have to chain you to the seat to make it happen."

Sloane stared up at him, venting years of frustration and anger on a man who didn't rightfully deserve it. Whatever. He was convenient and that was good enough for her. "I will kill you if you try."

Lucas had the audacity to laugh at her, letting out a single humorless bark. "You're outclassed, little girl. You may be tough, but you're not even close to being tough enough to take me out. Better men than you have tried and failed."

"How much is he paying you? I'll double it."

"He's not paying me a dime."

"Then why? Why risk your life coming after me?"

"That's personal."

"Is he blackmailing you? Threatening you?"

Lucas studied her face. She felt his dark gaze slide over her cheeks and mouth before coming back to her eyes. "Do you even know the man? He'd never do something like that."

"Clearly, you're the one who doesn't know him. You're just like all of his other good little soldiers, sucking up to the glorious general like he's some kind of god."

"I've never known a better man."

Sloane had to laugh at that. She'd never known a worse one, unless mass murderers, pedophiles, and serial killers were included in the comparison. "You really need to get out more."

"You're not going to go easily, are you?"

"What? Did the part where I threatened to kill you not sink in?"

Lucas nodded, his mouth flattening with distaste.

"Fine. Have it your way. The Old Man said you wouldn't come quietly."

Oh, no. He had a plan. She could see it in his eyes. He was going to knock her out, or drug her unconscious or tie her up. He was bigger and stronger than she was, and as good as Sloane was, she didn't think she was good enough to overpower a man trained by her father.

Before it was too late and he implemented his vile plan, Sloane said, "Okay. I give up. I'll go with you."

"You're lying."

"No. Once you get me back home, you can tell him you succeeded."

His dark blue eyes narrowed. "And you'll hop the next flight back here, and I'll be chasing you again, right?"

Sloane shrugged as much as her position would allow. "You don't have to tell him that part."

"He'll know. He's got your name flagged. Any passenger manifest listing you leaving the country is going to show up on his desk."

Sloane had no idea her father had kept tabs on her. Why would he bother? He'd given up on her years ago, right after the last time she'd run away from boarding school.

"I'll use a different name, then. Bribe someone to keep me off the manifest."

"And when he finds out you were killed here, poking your nose where it didn't belong? What then?"

"Are you worried he'll dishonorably discharge you?"

His eyelids fell to shadow his eyes. "Not possible. I'm no longer in the U.S. Army."

"And you're still working for him?"

"I owe him," was all he said.

"And he wants me to stay out of Colombia, right?"

"Right."

"He didn't have any trouble when I went to South

Africa, or India, or any one of the dozen other countries
I've been in this year. Why does he care if I'm here?"

"He has his reasons. He always does. You'll be happier if you don't question them."

"You *are* a good little soldier, aren't you?"

"I was," he said with a mixture of pride and regret.
"Now I'm simply an escort, but I'll do that job as well
as I'm able."

Sloane refused to care about the hurt she heard in
his tone. She didn't care if he hurt. He was a messenger
of evil, sent straight from her father. "I'm not leaving
without my friend. She's trapped here, somewhere, being held against her will. There's nothing you can do to
stop me, short of locking me up or killing me. As soon as
your back is turned, I'll be right back here, doing what
I need to do."

Lucas's hand loosened on her throat, sliding down a
scant inch. The feel of his callused fingers on her skin
should not have even rated notice with her. But it did,
and she hated herself for it.

He stared at her for a long time, and she could see the
wheels turning inside that thick skull of his. "How long
will it take to find your friend?"

Hope lit up inside her. He was going to let her go.
She could feel it. "Not long. I should have her back by
tomorrow night." It was a bit of a lie, because she wasn't
sure what kind of fortifications Soma's airstrip might
have. She hoped that Gina would be safe with her by
then, but there were no guarantees.

"And as soon as Gina is with you, you'll go home and
not come back?"

"I promise." At least that wasn't a lie. She hated this
place and its thick, stifling heat.

Lucas nodded slowly. "Okay. We'll go after her. Together."

All that hope shriveled up into a tarry, black pile. "I'm sorry," said Sloane, "but there's no way in hell I'm going to willingly spend as much as ten minutes with one of my father's goons, much less an entire twenty-four hours."

"It's a good thing I'm not giving you a choice, then."

Chapter 4

Lucas wasn't sure if he wanted to strangle Sloane for stubbornly refusing his help, or slide his hand down a little farther and see if the rest of her was as soft as the damp skin under his fingers. Both options were only going to land him in trouble, so he resisted.

"You need my help. I need to not piss off one of the most powerful men in the country. It's a match made in heaven."

She stared straight at him, and her green eyes brightened with anger. "I don't need anything from anyone connected to my father. If I needed help, I would have asked for it from people I trust."

As if she couldn't trust her own flesh and blood? What kind of relationship did they have? Certainly nothing like the comfortable one he had with his folks. "I don't have some nefarious purpose here. I've been straight with you."

"Even if you are telling the truth—which I question— you're just going to get in my way."

"You won't even know I'm there."

She looked him up and down, snorted, and one dark eyebrow shot up. "That's highly unlikely. But if you go back to the hotel by the airport and wait for me there,

I'll pretend like you dragged me back to the United States kicking and screaming. My father will love that. You'll earn all kinds of brownie points."

"I'm not leaving you," he stated, cold and hard.

She stared at him for a long minute, her mouth pressed into a frustrated line. "Fine. Follow behind if you must, but I swear if you draw any unwanted attention my way, I'll shoot out your tires."

"You're a violent thing, aren't you?" he asked.

A slow, devilish smile curved her lips. "You have no idea."

Lucas's gut tightened instinctively, though he couldn't tell if it was the surge of lust her sexy smile caused, or the fact that he needed to be ready to take a punch. Either way, the reaction was both unwanted and unsettling.

The Old Man's daughter was off-limits. Now all he had to do was get his body to recognize that fact. When the general had said *by any means necessary*, he sure as hell hadn't been thinking what Lucas was thinking.

"Where's your ride?" she asked.

"Not far. I'll be back here in two minutes."

He stepped away, giving her room to get in her vehicle, which she did faster than he'd expected. She slammed the door shut, locked it, and started the engine. Through the glass, she said, "Sorry. I'm not waiting."

Lorenzo Soma stared out over his domain. The lush green landscape soothed him, easing away the tension that had been growing behind his eyes since one of his guests had defied him

Gina wasn't going to make that mistake twice.

"There's a woman asking about you in the nearby villages," said Jeremy Block, Lorenzo's right hand, the only man he truly trusted.

"There are always women asking about me. It is the nature of power to draw women."

"She's American."

Lorenzo gripped the iron railing and felt it vibrate with his anger. No more American women. They were too independent and hard to control. The last one had caused him far too much trouble. "What does she want?"

"To find you."

Lorenzo turned around and studied his lieutenant. Block's mud brown gaze never wavered—something that most men could not do when Lorenzo stared them down. "Send men to find her."

"And when they do, should they bring her here?"

"No. Kill her. I can't have any more disruptions. We have to leave to meet Mr. Brink soon, and can't afford to let a distraction make us late."

"Brink needs you. A little tardiness isn't going to turn a man like him away."

"We need each other. My father's empire is crumbling. Moving product over the Mexican border is becoming increasingly difficult. I've lost millions this year alone." A fact that grated his nerves raw. If he couldn't get his drugs onto American soil, his profits were going to decline to the point where he no longer had the power to control the men around him.

Wealth and power were the same thing, and there was never enough of either to go around.

Adam Brink was going to change all of that.

Block inclined his head. "I'll see to the nosy American."

"Send the men to do the job. I want you with us when we leave to meet Mr. Brink. If he reneges on our deal, I'm going to need you to kill him."

Block's eyes narrowed. "I've never once disobeyed one of your orders, and I swear to you I'll do whatever you ask or die trying. But my gut tells me that if you give me that order, trying to kill Brink will be the last thing I do."

"Do you think he can best you?"

Block nodded. "I know he can. Death follows that man wherever he goes."

"Then let us hope for both our sakes that Adam Brink is a man of his word."

Sloane tried not to smile. She really did. Tricking Lucas was one thing, but rubbing it in was not at all kind.

He stood there, shaking his head as if she were some kind of naughty girl. Then again, he'd probably learned that move from the best. Disappointment was something Sloane had seen so often on her father's face it no longer fazed her.

At least that was what she'd always told herself.

Whatever. She didn't need him slowing her down, anyway. Time to move on.

She reached into her back pocket for the paper with the map on it, but found nothing but lint.

"Looking for this?" Lucas asked, pressing the map to the window.

Shock rattled through her. How had he slipped that out of her pocket without her feeling it? Clearly, she'd been too distracted with the way his body felt pressed against hers, or the way his fingers felt slightly rough against her throat. That was how.

"Not nice," she told him.

He smiled. "I'm not here to play nice. Guess you'll have to follow me."

He sauntered off, and Sloane couldn't stop herself from staring. Faded denim hugged his butt and thighs, which were nice, regardless of his connection to her father. Even she was a big enough person to admit that.

As he rounded a corner, she thought she saw the

faintest hint of a limp. Maybe she'd been wrong, or maybe he was perfectly fine and simply playing on her sympathies. But if not, then not only was he a liability; he was an unarmed one. She still had both his sidearm and holdout weapons.

Great. Now, not only did she have to save Gina, and do it with a tagalong; she also had to make sure that her tagalong didn't get himself killed.

Two minutes later, Lucas's Jeep rolled by. Sloane had no choice but to follow him, watch his back, and pray that they all got out of this hot, sticky hellhole alive.

Three hours later, Sloane's shoulders ached from keeping the Rover on the rutted dirt road. This far from a major city, there were sections of road that were nearly gone—washed out by heavy rain—leaving a dizzying drop to the valley below. They climbed steadily, heading up toward the heavy clouds, which would release torrents of rain at any moment.

Ahead, Lucas came to a skidding stop. Sloane had been following at a distance to spread the weight of two vehicles out over the aging road, so she was able to stop before ramming into the back of his Jeep. Barely.

She rolled down her window, stuck her head out, and shouted, "What's up?"

"Something's not right," he shouted back. "Turn around."

Sloane hadn't come this far only to be driven off by some soldier's hair-trigger instincts. Still, she rolled up her window and slid one of her semiautomatics out of the holster clinging to the side of her seat, just in case.

As soon as she got his vehicle behind hers, she'd move on without him, map or no map.

A bullet whipped through the foliage and splintered a chunk from the trunk of a tree a few feet away from Lucas's Jeep.

Okay. Maybe his instincts weren't faulty.

As adrenaline shot through her system, she realized that Lucas had no weapon. She'd taken them.

Great. Now she was responsible for putting him in even deeper danger. Time to find a plan that was going to get both of them out alive.

Sloane slouched in her seat to put more of herself behind the Rover's armor, and scanned the area where she thought the shot had come from. She couldn't see anything through the thick vegetation, but maybe she could buy them some time to turn tail, run, and regroup.

She lowered her window just enough to get the barrel of her weapon out, and fired in the general direction of the shooter, hoping it would make him keep his head down and prevent him from hitting her unarmed, unarmored travel partner.

The Rover was nimble, but she was going to need more road to get it turned around, so she backed up. She drove one-handed, splitting her attention between the road behind her and keeping her shots going in the right direction.

She was driving much too fast for the narrow road, but Lucas was right on her front bumper as he backed up, keeping pace with her, urging her to go faster.

If she was weaponless, she'd be doing the bat-out-of-hell routine, too.

The shooter fired again. Sloane spared a swift glance at Lucas to see if he was okay. He was still upright, but a spiderweb of cracks appeared in his windshield. They were running out of time for her to come up with that plan.

A sharp left turn was coming up fast, and Sloane knew she couldn't make it at this speed. She'd slide off the edge of the road and plummet down into the thick vegetation clinging to the mountain. She had to slow down, but not until the last moment possible. Hopefully,

Lucas would slow with her and not slam into her front bumper and send her flying over the edge.

Sloane looked over her shoulder as her speed increased, in order to gauge the distance to the turn, and saw a battered truck sling around the bend. A man standing behind a mounted machine gun balanced in the back of the truck. He aimed over the roof of the cab.

Panic grabbed Sloane hard, making her hand lock onto the steering wheel. This was not going to end well if she didn't do something fast. Time for plan B.

Sloane slammed to a halt, skidding her vehicle sideways. She had all the firepower she needed to take that truck out in the back of her SUV. The trick was going to be getting to it before they were shot to pieces.

The first barrage of bullets slammed into the side of her Rover, but the ugly armor held, and the rounds pinged off into the jungle. The bulletproof glass was marked, but holding fine. She had time to pull out the big guns.

Lucas's Jeep slid to a halt, lining up parallel with her vehicle. He made the maneuver look easy, though she knew it was anything but. Sloane unlocked the doors, hoping he'd get out of that death trap and into her armored ride, but not wasting the time telling him something he should already know.

She shimmied over the console into the back, heading right for her favorite toy.

Outside, a deep boom blasted through the air. Either the bad guys had gotten way too close, or Lucas had a toy of his own.

Sloane lifted her head from her weapon long enough to peek, and sure enough, Lucas had a shotgun in his hands, firing at the machine gunner.

Good man. He'd bought her enough time to get Constance loaded.

Another boom exploded out of Lucas's shotgun.

Sloane took the opportunity to squeeze herself and Constance out of the back door between the cover of the two vehicles.

Lucas shoved shotgun shells into his weapon and glanced her way. His gaze stalled out on Constance and he lifted his brows. "A grenade launcher?"

"Every girl should have one."

"You're one scary chick. Glad you're on my side."

"Says who?" asked Sloane as she steadied the launcher on her shoulder and took aim over the hood of her vehicle.

The grenade sliced through the air and slammed into the battered truck's cab. A ball of flames exploded, killing the two men in the truck instantly, and sending the gunner flying out of the truck bed. He hit the dirt road and didn't move.

A swift thrill of victory surged through Sloane. Then a second later, a bullet tore across her shoulder, and she knew she'd begun the celebration too soon.

There was still at least one more shooter behind them, maybe more.

Pain radiated out from her arm, but she could still move it, so that was good enough for her. Time to take out the next asshole in line.

Lucas glanced at her arm and a feral snarl tightened his mouth. "How bad?"

"Just a scratch. Can you see where he's hiding?" Sloane asked Lucas.

He peered into the jungle, squinting. "No, but I'm going in. I'll find him."

"I can just blast things in his direction."

"Don't you want to know why they're shooting at us?" he asked.

Sloane shook her head. "I already know why. Gina."

"Maybe, or maybe we've encroached on some drug lord's or weapons dealer's territory."

"I hope so. Otherwise, we're going the wrong way. That's who has Gina."

He stared at her like she was crazy. "Did you think that perhaps it would have been better to sneak in?"

Sloane shrugged and it made her shoulder burn. She felt blood leaking along her skin, but not so much that it worried her. "I'm not good with stealth."

He nodded toward Constance. "Clearly. Good thing I am. Sit tight and try not to shoot me."

"You can't go in there."

"Why not?" he asked.

"This is my problem. I'll deal with it."

"You're hit, a fact that may already mean I'm a dead man once your father finds out. Nothing to lose now." With that, he left his shotgun behind and slipped off into the foliage, disappearing within seconds.

More shots dug into the Jeep's hood. Sloane ducked and covered as best she could, but this was not a good spot. She wanted as much metal between her and the shooter as possible so she could lay down some covering fire for Lucas.

Try not to shoot me.

Easier said than done, but she knew where he'd gone into the jungle. She could aim away from that. So long as she kept the bullets barking in any direction, the shooter might keep his head down and stay in one place long enough for Lucas to find him.

Sloane pulled out her semiautomatic and began making strategic shots, hoping Lucas stayed the hell out of her line of fire.

Lucas found the shooter hiding behind a thick tree trunk. Sloane's shots had him pinned down, making him an easy target.

Lucas had his knife in easy reach. His feet were silent

over the damp, rotting vegetation. His knee throbbed, but the thrill of the hunt blunted the pain and sharpened his senses.

The shooter never saw him coming.

Lucas wrapped his thick arm around the man's neck and squeezed until he blacked out. It took only a few brief seconds of flailing arms before he subsided and Lucas eased him to the ground. He used the plastic flex cuffs that the Old Man has insisted he'd need for Sloane to secure his hands behind him, then waited for the man to wake up.

He had some questions, and with any luck, his Spanish was good enough to get some answers.

Lucas had just settled against a tree to wait for the man to wake when he heard another flurry of gunfire ring out from where he'd left Sloane alone.

There were more gunmen out there, and he was too far away to do a thing to stop them.

Chapter 5

Mira Sage heard the computer room door open over the hum of dozens of fans. She could tell by the heavy, sluggish fall of the footsteps that Clayton Marshall had walked in. "You're late," she said without turning around.

Normally, an intrusion into her electronic sanctuary would have made her nervous. Her network wasn't operating perfectly at the moment, and that made her antsy. But it could wait. Her friend couldn't. Bella probably wouldn't notice the slight network sluggishness, anyway. That kind of subtlety was beyond Mira's boss.

Mira plugged the cables into the updated server and powered it up. "Where've you been?"

Clay settled carefully into a chair as if every move hurt. "Overslept."

Mira knew it was a lie, but she and Clay had been friends since they were kids, and he'd tell her the truth only when he was good and ready. Whatever he was hiding, it was killing him slowly, and had been for the past several months.

The hum of fans and the extra air conditioner used to keep the servers cool filled the computer room. It was a soothing sound, but not soothing enough to keep worry from creeping inside of her.

Her best friend was in trouble. She could feel it.

Mira unsnapped the wire from her wristband and let the protective electrostatic discharge device dangle. She'd have to skip lunch in order to stay on schedule, but that was probably for the best anyway, if the way her slacks were trying to strangle her was any indication.

"Bella was looking for you earlier. She wanted to know why you're late. She's gathering up a team to head to South Africa."

Clay rubbed his temples and let out a weary sigh. He looked thinner—the hollows under his cheekbones more pronounced. "How deep is the shit I'm in?"

"I covered for you," Mira said. "Told her I'd sent you out to pick up some cables for me."

"Thanks, squirt. I owe you."

No. She still owed *him* for saving her life when they were kids, even if he didn't remember doing it. *She* remembered, and she could never do enough to repay him for helping her escape her father.

Mira sat down across from Clay and rummaged in her desk drawer until she found her bottle of aspirin. She poured a small pile out into her hand and offered them to him. "You look like you could use these."

"Thanks." He popped them in his mouth and chewed, making Mira gag. She handed him her now cold coffee, hoping he'd wash down the pills so she could stop cringing. He guzzled it down, seemingly uncaring that it had gone cold.

"You know," she said, trying to sound casual, "you should go see the doctor. I think you might be sick. You've lost more weight."

"Not gonna happen, Mira. Let it drop."

"She's nice. You'd like her."

"I hate doctors. You know that."

"But she's different from a normal doctor—not at all stuffy like the last one. She's beautiful, and a redhead, too," added Mira, hoping that might sway him. He had a weakness for redheads, and it had been too long since she'd seen Clay go out on a date. As his honorary sister, she had made it her duty to play matchmaker.

"I don't care if she's composed entirely of perky, bouncing tits and practices medicine naked. I'm not interested."

Mira lowered her voice. "You have to do something. You're getting worse."

Clay shoved his fingers through his dark hair, messing it up. "I'll be fine. I've just had a bit of insomnia, that's all. It'll pass."

"If it doesn't, I'm going to talk to the doctor for you."

"Don't." He issued the order in a hard, cold voice. "It's none of your business."

"I love you. Of course it's my business."

He shook his head slowly. "Don't think playing the sappy card is going to get you off the hook. I mean it. Stay out of my business. I'm dealing with things in my own way."

"If you were dealing with it, then there wouldn't be a problem."

"Let it go. I'm serious. Don't make me do something I'll regret."

"Holy cats, Clay. You can bluster all you want, but I know you'd never hurt me."

A flash of fear crossed his face, making his amber eyes brighten. "I'd never hurt you on purpose, but lately . . ." Fans hummed, filling the silence he'd left hanging.

"Lately what?"

He waved his hand as if forcing the subject away and plastered a fake smile on his face. "Just give me some time, okay?"

Mira nodded. "Whatever you need."

And she meant it. Even if she had to piss him off, she'd make sure he got whatever care he needed.

Sloane couldn't see exactly where the new shots had come from, but there were at least two more men out there firing at her, maybe three. And judging from the angle of the bullets ripping through the leaves, if she didn't stop them, chances were they were going to hit Lucas.

She didn't want the man anywhere near her, but she didn't want him dead, either. Besides, if he failed, her father would only send two more in his place.

That thought was enough to get Sloane's blood flowing.

She aimed Constance and fired toward the shooters; then, while they were hopefully dodging bits of debris, she grabbed a rifle and moved around to the far side of the Rover. If Lucas hadn't taken out the bad guy up the slope, she was a sitting duck here, but she'd have to take that chance and hope that it *was* her father who'd trained him. And that he'd learned well.

Smoke billowed up from the jungle where her grenade had exploded. It was too wet out here to start a fire, but all that moisture went up in steam, obscuring her line of sight.

A movement sixty feet out caught her eye. Sloane targeted it and fired.

A deep grunt of pain rose up from the jungle, giving her a fierce sense of satisfaction that she'd hit her mark. She'd have made one hell of a sharpshooter. Too bad her father had blocked her every attempt to join the military. He didn't want his little girl putting herself in that kind of danger.

If he could only see her now.

A grin stretched her mouth. She loved this kind of danger, loved living on the edge. Dad had always said this unladylike streak was his genes coming out in an inconvenient display, but she preferred to think of it as her own personal rebellion. Dad deserved a little payback for imprisoning her in boarding school all those years.

The man she'd hit stood up and hobbled toward cover, spraying bullets in her direction. They pinged off the Rover's armor plating. Sloane waited for his assault rifle to empty, popped her head up, caught him in her scope, and fired. He went down, and this time, she didn't see him move again.

Four down.

She peered through her scope, scanning the area, looking for any sign of movement or flash of color that didn't belong among the thick green and brown foliage.

Another volley of gunfire sliced through the trees, bouncing off the Rover's armor. Bark from a tree behind her showered her back, biting into her skin. Sloane flinched, but swiveled her rifle around to where the shot had come from.

There, in the trees, she saw a glimpse of bright blue. She couldn't tell what it was, but Lucas was in green and faded denim, so it wasn't him. She took aim and fired. A sharp howl broke through the jungle and whoever she'd hit let loose with a steady stream of foul curses and automatic gunfire.

Something hot and heavy crashed into her from behind and drove her to the ground, pinning her there. A blistering surge of rage welled up inside her, making her thrash around beneath the weight.

"It's me," shouted Lucas over the noise.

His voice settled into her, calming her nerves enough that she was no longer fighting in blind fury. She pulled in a deep breath, preparing to bellow at him to get the hell off of her when more shots ripped through the trees. Bark splintered from the trees behind them, showering them with sharp, stinging chunks of wood. Lucas covered her head with his arms and curled himself around her.

His scent surrounded her, filling her lungs, making her dizzy. The heat of battle, combined with the artificial scent of soap and a deeper, more natural hint of something she couldn't name wove around her, soaking into her skin. For one long, breathless moment she was wrapped up inside an odd feeling of protection that—for once in her life—didn't chafe her nerves raw.

Then, as quickly as the bizarre feeling had come, it was gone, and she was once again herself—ready to give him hell for finding her lacking and in need of protection, like some kind of child.

Sloane hadn't been that little helpless girl for a long, long time.

"Get off me." She hit him with her elbow hard enough that he grunted. "I've got to take him out."

"Are you nuts? You'll get yourself killed if you poke your head up there."

"One of us has to stop him."

"Then I'll do it. Stay put."

He rolled off of her and moved away before she could grab him. He scooped up her rifle, leveled it over the hood of the Rover, and started shooting. Her rifle. Her target.

Hell no. This was not going to happen. She was not some wilting female in need of a rescue. He could save that shit for a woman who wanted it. Sloane didn't need to be rescued. Not ever. It was a matter of personal pride, and one she was fairly sure she'd protect with her life, if need be.

She crawled under the Rover and came out on the driver's side. The doors were unlocked, making it quick work to grab the .45 from under the seat. Sure, it didn't have the same range as the rifle, and there was no scope, but it had plenty of stopping power and a spare magazine, just in case.

Things had gone eerily silent. No shots pounded at her ears. The nearby wildlife was quiet. No breeze rustled the leaves.

Sloane picked up a rock and slung it over the vehicle. It thrashed through the undergrowth, drawing fire from both Lucas and the man shooting at them.

Within half a second, she'd located the shooter, spotting the bright red bloodstain on his shirt. The .45 barked in her hands three times as she fired. The third shot did the trick and sent the man crumbling to the ground.

Once again, silence settled over them.

"Nice shot," said Lucas.

"That's five. Do you see any more?" she whispered.

"One way to find out."

He shifted, and for a second she thought he was going to do something stupid like stand up to draw enemy fire. Instead, he stripped out of his shirt, draped it over the rifle, and held it up tentatively, like he might be peeking out to check.

No one shot at them, which was a good sign.

"What do you think?" he asked.

Sloane glanced his way and her gaze stalled out at his back. It was wide and smooth and rippling with muscles. Even with all the little cuts and scrapes he'd gotten, she still couldn't remember ever having seen anything quite so perfect. She hadn't meant to notice, but her adrenaline was all revved up, coursing through her system, and apparently, the rest of her hormones had followed its lead.

A wave of heat slid through her, making her mouth go dry. A bead of sweat trickled between her breasts, forcing her to become all too aware of how her nipples had tightened. Lust was not new to her, but she'd never felt it while on the job before. The men she worked with might as well have been eunuchs for the notice she gave them.

But not Lucas. She was noticing him. And then some.

He turned his head, looking over his shoulder at her. His eyes were dark blue, with pale blue shards radiating out like a starburst. Sweat slid over his temple and down the side of his thick neck. His brow was lined with concern. "Sloane? You okay?"

She swallowed, cleared her throat, and nodded. "Yeah."

His frown deepened. "You're flushed. You're not going to pass out on me, are you?"

That question slapped her back to reality. How dared he think she was some kind of weakling? "Hell no."

He nodded once. "Good. Stay sharp, just in case we didn't get them all."

As if he needed to tell her that.

Sloane shook herself, steadied her weapon, and braced it against the vehicle. Her hand had started shaking at some point—something that had never happened to her in a fight before. Put her up in front of a crowded room and ask her to speak, and she'd tremble like an earthquake with Parkinson's, but in a firefight she was always rock steady.

Except this time.

Gina's life was at stake. Maybe that was the difference. It was personal now, and if she failed, someone she cared about was going to suffer. That was the only thing that made any sense.

She saw Lucas disappear into the jungle. One minute he was there, and the next he was gone, leaving no trace of his passage. She had to admire skill like that.

Sloane sat tight, weapon ready, but not overeager. She didn't know exactly where Lucas was anymore.

A few tense minutes later, he yelled he was coming out, and then appeared less than twenty feet from her position. "I counted two bodies in the jungle. The guy I'd intended to question regained consciousness and got away."

In the distance, she heard the hum of a small engine—like a lawn mower or a motorcycle.

"Does that sound like some kind of ATV to you?" asked Lucas.

"It does, which means we'll be having company."

"We should get ready for it."

Sloane checked the road. "The truck will serve as a roadblock on that side, at least for a while."

"We can't keep going. We have to turn around."

"Feel free," said Sloane. "I won't stop you."

"You know I can't leave without you."

A few fat drops of rain began to fall. Sloane gathered up Constance and the rest of her weapons. "Not my problem. And I'm not going to argue with you."

Lucas wrapped his fingers around her arm. Even through her cotton shirt, she could feel the heat coming off his skin. She looked up at him and his eyes were bright with anger. "You're going to get yourself killed. Clearly these men mean business. And they're well equipped."

"Which is all the more reason not to dawdle here with you. Gina's out there. She needs me. Now let go, or you and I are going to have a problem."

His lips flattened and blanched of color. "I'm riding with you, where I can keep an eye on you."

"Watch me all you like—just don't get in my way."

Raindrops fell with increasing speed. Soon the road would be a muddy, impassible mess.

"I'll hide the Jeep in case we need a getaway vehicle," said Lucas.

Sloane nodded. "Don't be long. I won't wait." Once she reloaded her weapons and stitched up her arm, she was out of here, with or without him. On one hand, this might be her best chance to get away from him, but on the other, she knew that he was capable and steady in a fight, and Gina might need a man like that around if things turned ugly.

Which they would. Situations like this always turned ugly.

Gina Delaney wasn't exactly sure what she'd gotten herself into, but it was up to her to get herself right back out.

The mansion where she was being held was a veritable fortress. Sure, it was trimmed in marble floors and crystal chandeliers, but it was still a fortress. Armed guards patrolled the lush grounds outside Lorenzo's home. The suite where she'd been locked away was nicer than any hotel she'd ever stayed in, but the door had been locked from the outside.

Guards watched over the delivery of her meals as the little old bent woman rolled a cart into her room and left without lifting her eyes or saying a word. The food was divine, though that might have been because she'd refused to eat it for the first two days she'd been here.

The sun would soon set on day number three of her captivity, and so far, no one had given her a clue as to why she was here.

Gina pounded on the door until one of the guards opened it.

"I want to see Lorenzo," she told the weathered man holding some kind of machine gun.

He gave her a blank look. Clearly he didn't speak English.

"Lorenzo," she said, stretching the word out as she pointed to her eyes. "See Lorenzo. Now."

The guard cocked his head to the side, and then shut the door in her face, giving her no indication if he was going to comply with her request, or if he even understood her.

Great. Looked like she was going to have to do this the hard way.

Gina peered out of her second-story window. It wasn't barred. It wasn't locked. Sure, the fall to the ground could potentially be leg shattering. The drop was at least fifteen feet down, ending on hard stone cobbles rather than nice soft grass like at the boarding school she'd attended.

She'd snuck out of her room in high school so often she could do it in her sleep, but back then there hadn't been armed guards wandering the grounds. Even if she did manage to get down without hurting herself, how was she going to get away before being shot?

"Hurry up, Sloane," she whispered out the window. "I need you."

Gina knew her friend would come for her. Sloane always bailed her out of sticky situations. She had to believe that the separate paths their lives had taken and the lack of time to get together regularly hadn't changed that.

But what if it had? What if Sloane couldn't come? What if she couldn't figure out how to find her?

Gina needed a plan. She had no idea why Lorenzo was keeping her here, but it couldn't be for anything good. As suave as the man was, as easily as he'd drawn her into his seemingly elegant world, she had gotten a glimpse of the snake inside. Just for one brief moment.

But it had been enough to tell her things were not as they seemed. Lorenzo was not suave and elegant. He was not some gallant corporate executive bent on wining and dining her until she gave in to his seductive desires. He walked the walk and talked the talk, but it was all on the surface. Deep down he was just as bad as all the other low-life scum she'd dated.

Guess that just went to prove how screwed up her taste in men really was. If she got out of this alive, she was swearing off men. Even great sex was not worth the fear she was fighting back now with every breath she took.

No. She wasn't going to think about being afraid. She was brave. She was fine. Sloane was coming, and in the meantime, Gina was going to come up with another plan of escape. Just in case.

Lucas was soaking wet by the time he hauled his gear over to the Land Rover. Rain fell in sheets so thick he had to shield his eyes from the heavy drops in order to keep from being blinded. He tossed his duffel in the back and got in on the passenger's side.

Sloane had stripped down to a tank top and was sewing the wound on her arm closed. There wasn't a sign of pain in her expression, but the beads of sweat along her brow and the pale cast to her skin told a different story.

"Need a hand?" he asked.

"I'm good. Just got grazed." Her voice was barely loud enough to hear over the rain pounding on the roof.

"I don't mind. I'm not squeamish."

She twisted awkwardly, trying to see the back side of her upper arm to finish the suturing. Blood mixed with rainwater leaked down her arm, dripping from her elbow. Every time she shifted, trying to find the right angle to see, more blood seeped out.

Lucas let out a frustrated sigh, which was masked by the thrumming rain. Whether or not she wanted his help, she needed it. He rummaged through the first aid kit sitting open on the dash and found a pair of gloves. They barely stretched over his hands, but they'd work.

"What are you doing?" she asked.

"Helping you so you don't rip out the stitches you've already put in."

"I can do it."

He found an alcohol wipe and cleaned off the gloves as best he could. It was far from sterile, but it would have to do. "You've still got another inch left to go. Unless you're planning on sewing it while looking in a mirror, I'm your best bet. Now give me the damn needle."

She stared at him for a long moment. The rain-blurred foliage of the jungle behind her made her green eyes glow, giving them a feline quality. He knew she had the claws to match; the question was whether or not she was going to use them on him. Again.

Her shoulders slumped as defeat took over her posture. "Fine. Just try not to leave an ugly scar."

"I can do quick or pretty, but not both. I figured you'd want quick."

"Spoken like a man. Especially one who's never had to wear a strapless evening gown."

Lucas remembered just how nice she'd looked in one last night. It'd be a crime to ruin something so pretty. "Right. I'll do what I can."

Thankfully, Lucas's hands were steady as he went to work. Sloane didn't flinch once, or make a single sound of pain. Tough woman. Which not only made his respect for her inch up a few points; it also relieved the hell out of him. He wasn't sure if he'd have been able to do this kind of fine work if she'd been hissing and flinching in pain.

"There," he announced. "All done. I'm no plastic surgeon, but I think it'll heal straight. Now, I'll just bandage you up, and you'll be as good as new."

The rain slowed to a steady pace, but was no longer a deluge of pounding noise. The windows had fogged up, and the air inside the vehicle was thicker, scented with disinfectant and a subtle fragrance he'd come to realize belonged to Sloane. It wasn't flowery, but there was a sweetness to it that called to him.

As close as he was to her now, he could simply breathe

her in—something he found himself doing when he wasn't thinking about it.

"How's your back?" she asked. "I saw you got some cuts."

He hadn't paid any attention to them before, but now that she said something, his back started to sting. "Nothing serious. Just scratches."

Lucas stripped off the gloves and tossed them onto the pile of bloody trash accumulating on the console.

Uncertainty wavered in her voice. "I'll, uh, patch you up, if you want. It's the least I can do."

Not wanting to upset their tenuous peace, Lucas nodded. "Thanks. I'd appreciate it. Let me finish here."

In this humidity, tape wasn't going to stick for long, so he placed the sterile pad over her wound and began wrapping her slender arm in gauze. His fingers were bare now, and every time they grazed her skin, the smooth silk of it shocked him. As tough as she was, as hard as she was to get along with, her exterior was as soft as melting chocolate.

A delicate shiver shook her spine.

"You okay?" he asked.

She was staring at her arm, where his fingers met her skin. Her tongue came out to wet her lips before she spoke. "Yeah."

"Are you cold?"

"No."

She didn't feel fevered. Her skin was warm, but not hot. He looked at her face to see if she was flushed, and her cheeks were a bit pink. "You shivered."

She pulled her arm away from his grasp, grabbed the small roll of tape, and turned her back on him, shifting in the seat. "I'll finish. You've done enough."

Okay. Clearly it was a dismissal—or as much of one as she could give him within the tight confines of the vehicle.

Lucas found a small plastic sack, which he claimed for the trash, and began cleaning up. He wadded up the pile of gloves, disinfectant wipes, and gauze, and something sharp dug into the palm of his hand. He jerked back, dropping the trash. "Shit."

The curved needle stuck out of his skin with a short length of suture dangling from it.

Fantastic. As if he didn't have to dodge enough barbs from Sloane, now this.

She'd turned back toward him and saw what had happened. "Are you okay?"

He plucked the needle out and a small drop of blood welled up from the surface of his skin. "Yeah. I just hope you've had your rabies shots."

It was meant to be a joke, but she frantically grabbed a disinfectant wipe and tore it out of its foil package. "I'm healthy. I swear. I get checked out by the company doctor on a regular basis."

"How regular?"

She scrubbed his wound with the small square, nearly wearing away his skin. It stung like hell, but still, the fact that she was willingly touching him was nice. "Every six months. My last checkup was three months ago and I was completely healthy."

"Any sexual partners since then? Specifically ones who didn't wear condoms?" he asked, more because he wanted to know if she had a steady boyfriend than because he was worried.

"No. You should be safe."

She was still scrubbing at his palm, so Lucas gently covered her hand to stop the frantic motion. "I think it's clean now."

Sloane's hand stilled, but she didn't pull it away from his grasp. Her skin was smooth, and her hand felt small inside his grasp, almost delicate. He knew how fast those hands could move, how hard they could hit, but right now, she seemed content to simply be still and let him touch her.

She looked up at him, her green eyes bright with confusion. "Why are you being so nice to me? I've run from you. I've hit you. I've threatened to kill you. Hell, I even knocked you out."

Lucas cringed. "Don't remind me."

"I'm serious. I haven't given you a single reason to be kind to me, and yet you are."

He shrugged. "We're partners now. I'm always nice to the people I work with. That's just good business."

"We are *not* partners."

"Sure we are. I'm going to help you find Gina and you're going to help me save face with your father. I'd say that's a great reason for a partnership. We both get what we want that way."

"You know I really don't care if you get what you want, right?"

He gave her a small grin. "Sure you do. You like me. Admit it."

"I do not."

Lucas simply stared pointedly down at where her hand rested between his. She followed his gaze, snatched her hand back, and her cheeks flushed a guilty pink. He was sorry for the loss of contact, but he'd made his point, at least.

"I don't trust you," she told him, staring right into his eyes.

"You will. I'm good in a pinch. Besides, we work well together. We took out that whole group of men, despite the fact that we were surrounded and outmanned."

"I didn't need your help. I could have handled that on my own."

"Glory hound."

"Excuse me?"

"You heard me. You're a glory hound. Instead of

thanking me for saving your ass, you pretend like you didn't need me when it's all said and done. That's easy to say now."

"It would have been a lot easier to say if you hadn't stuck your nose into my business."

She was getting defensive again, and Lucas didn't want that. Clearly, her independent streak was wider than most, and stepping on it made her twitchy. Time for a retreat.

"Maybe you're right. Maybe you could have handled all those men on your own."

"I could have," she stated with confidence ringing clearly in her voice. "I had Constance on my side. But if you weren't here, I'd have an ugly scar, so thanks for that."

"You're welcome."

She nodded, but didn't look him in the eye.

"The rain's died down," said Lucas. "We should get moving."

"Your back. You should let me check it out, or whatever."

Lucas figured it was as close to an olive branch as he was going to get, so he stripped off his tee and turned in his seat.

The man standing in front of Lorenzo was drenched, muddy, and shaking. Plastic handcuffs still clung to one wrist, vibrating with the man's fear. Blood leaked from a cut above his eye and another on his leg. Dirty water pooled under his feet, making a mess of Lorenzo's marble floor.

"Well?" said Lorenzo. "Are you going to just stand there bleeding, or tell me what you have to say?"

The man's head ducked in shame. "The woman got away."

Anger leaped inside Lorenzo, howling to get out, but he kept it in careful check. He never yelled at his men. It was beneath him. "How is that possible?" he asked in a quiet tone.

"She wasn't alone. And she was well armed."

Lorenzo's stomach tightened. Even a woman could do much damage with enough weaponry at her disposal. "How well armed?"

"She and the man she was with killed all but me."

Lorenzo glanced over at Jeremy Block, who stood waiting for orders. "How many?"

Block's expression never changed. "Five of the six we sent are dead."

All over one stupid woman. Gina had better be worth his trouble. If Mr. Brink said she wasn't the woman he was looking for, Lorenzo was going to be deeply annoyed.

Already, she'd caused him more problems than all the others he'd hunted down for Mr. Brink combined. If he didn't end this here, it would set a bad example. Villagers might think he'd gone soft—that they could take him out. That simply wasn't acceptable. His father's power was now his, and he was keeping it.

Even the thought of someone daring to take what was his made anger rise in his throat like bile.

Lorenzo turned to Block, switching to English. "Clean him up, feed him, let him say good-bye to his children, then execute him for failing me. Make sure the next group you send out sees it happen before they go. And make sure this muddy mess is cleaned up before it gets tracked everywhere."

Block nodded, his mud brown eyes never blinking. "Yes, sir."

Chapter 6

Sloane was good with men, damn it. She was not awkward and stammering. She did not lose her cool no matter what came her way. And yet here she was, blushing like a kid, stammering like an idiot, and shaking so hard she didn't know how she was going to do much more than splash disinfectant at his back.

He was just a man. Sure, he was a handsome man—one who knew his way around a fight and had a body meant for calendars and daydreams—but still, he was just a man. She should have had him eating out of her hand by now, waiting eagerly for her to show up in some hotel room while she finished her job and left him hanging. Instead, he was right by her side, refusing to leave, putting himself in danger that had nothing to do with him.

Lucas had gotten under her skin. Maybe it was his connection with her father that had her feeling off-balance. General Robert Norwood had a way of making everything worse by his involvement. Even holidays and birthdays were ruined when he was around. Good thing it didn't happen often while she was growing up.

Now that Mom was gone, Sloane just wanted to cut

her ties to him and be done. Move on. But no. He had to send Lucas into her life to torture her.

"How bad is it?" he asked.

Sloane gathered herself enough to focus on the task at hand. "Not bad. Mostly scratches."

Even though she didn't need her fingers to see, the smooth planes of his back called to her, begging her to touch. It wasn't every day that she got a man this well built half naked in front of her. It was her womanly duty to enjoy it while it lasted.

His skin was tan, stretched tight over dense layers of muscle. Every breath he took widened his ribs and showed off just how broad his shoulders were. Sloane slid her fingers along his flank, enjoying the feel of his firm flesh. Small cuts and scrapes marred the perfection, but not her enjoyment of her fingertips gliding over his warm skin.

"Are you counting?" he asked, making her realize that she'd been lingering too long.

Sloane cleared her throat. "There's one cut that's deeper than the rest, but I don't think it needs stitches. We can see if it stops bleeding in a few minutes. The rest just need to be cleaned."

"Or you could kiss it and make it better."

Tempting. "I think I'll stick with disinfectant. I also have some antibiotics you can take if you're worried about infection."

"You do come prepared, don't you?"

"I'm not an amateur, nor is this my first trip into the jungle. Lots of nasty bacteria live out here." Sloane popped open the small bottle of disinfectant, soaked a cotton ball, and went to work. Lucas flinched at the first contact, so she blew over the cut to ease the sting.

"So what's the plan for getting Gina out alive?" he asked. "They're well armed and know we're coming."

"They'll be watching the road. I thought I'd go in through the jungle once we located the airstrip."

"You mean 'we'll' go in. We're partners, remember?"

Sloane wasn't convinced about that, but it was better to keep her mouth shut. "I'll have to be careful about what gear I haul in, since I can't carry it all."

"You don't know anything about this place, do you?"

"No."

"So there's no way to know if you're going to need to cut through a fence, pick a lock, or blow out a wall, right?"

"Right."

"So how are you going to plan what gear to take?"

Sloane shrugged. "I'll have to scout the place out first."

"You said stealth wasn't your thing."

"It's not. I'll just have to wing it."

Lucas turned around enough to give her a disbelieving stare. "I thought your father would have taught you better than that."

Resentment tightened her voice. "My father preferred not to teach me anything useful. I've had to learn it all on my own."

"Well, he taught me a thing or two. Plus, I've still got a couple of favors I can pull in. I bet I could get us some satellite images of the place. Maybe some thermals to tell us how many men are waiting and where we'll find them."

A surge of excitement spiked through Sloane, making her feel like it was Christmas morning. "Really?" she asked, trying not to sound too hopeful. She hated accepting help from anyone connected to her father, but if it meant getting Gina out safely, then she'd do it without hesitation.

"Sure. The problem is I didn't expect to be doing any jungle crawls while I was here. I didn't bring the right communication equipment. Any chance you have a satellite phone?"

"Two, actually. In case one failed."

"I like the way you plan."

"I assumed I'd be on my own, and I really didn't want things to progress to the last resort."

He shifted, turning his big body around until he could look at her. "What, exactly, is the last resort?"

The way he was staring so intently made Sloane squirm. She didn't like it, so she straightened her spine and pulled a flippant cloak about her. With a shrug, she said, "Walking up to Soma unarmed and offering to trade myself for Gina."

Hell no. There were going to be no last resorts while Lucas was on the job. Not a chance. She was not sacrificing herself like that for anyone. Lucas wasn't going to let it happen.

But rather than spouting off at the mouth about how he refused to let her do something so foolish, he simply bit his tongue and choked down all the rules he wanted to demand she follow.

He'd seen for himself how prickly she could be when her independent streak was hampered. The Old Man had even said to make sure Lucas packed restraints. The last thing he needed was for her to start running from him again because he didn't play his cards right.

So he swallowed what he wanted to say, kept his voice carefully neutral, and said, "Over my dead body."

Sloane's green eyes narrowed. "Excuse me?"

"I mean it, Sloane. You do that, and they're going to drug you or kill you or worse. And if you think they'll just hand Gina over, you're a fool. They'll keep her, too. You'll both be trapped."

Her jaw clenched and her nostrils flared. "I can

take care of myself. You've seen it firsthand. From the pavement."

The reminder of how she'd gotten in that sucker punch didn't sit well on Lucas's already precarious control. "You knocked me out cold. Good for you. But that's not going to happen if those men get their hands on you."

"Why? Are they better than you?"

"No. But they're not afraid to hurt you. I am. I'd rather take a hit any day of the week than risk breaking so much as your fingernail."

From the way her face flushed an angry red, that was clearly the wrong thing to say. "You're just like him. You're just like my father, aren't you? You think I'm weak and helpless and need to be saved. Well, I've got news for you. I don't want or need your help."

"I believe you don't want it, but you do *need* it. And the fact that you find shame in that makes you a weaker person."

"I am not weak."

"Physically, no. Your character on the other hand could use some work. You need to learn teamwork."

"I work well on a team, just not on one with men like my father."

"So . . . what?" he shouted. "Because your father sent me, you're willing to get yourself killed to prove a point? Are you also willing to get me killed to stick it to your old man and prove him wrong? How far will you go? Will you sacrifice Gina for your pride, too?"

"Fuck you," she growled.

"The last resort of someone with no valid response."

"Get out."

"No. I'm staying, and unless you want to kill me, there's nothing you can do to change that."

Her whole body quivered, but whether it was from rage or something else, Lucas wasn't completely sure.

There was something vulnerable lurking in her eyes—some old pain that called out to him. Part of him wanted to strangle her, but the other part wanted to pull her into his arms and show her that everything was going to be okay. She didn't need to keep her walls of pride so thick and high. She was safe with him, even if she didn't know it.

"Shut up and turn around," she told him. "I'm going to finish what I started so we can get this over with. I'm done wasting time on you."

Lucas thought he heard a thread of fear running through her tone, but wasn't sure. He gave her a silent nod and turned back around. She wasn't as gentle with the disinfectant this time, nor did her soft breath ease the sting, but she did the job without complaining.

It wasn't until he saw her reflection in the window, and saw the pain on her face, that he realized she wasn't angry. She was sad. Worried.

Lucas felt like he'd kicked a puppy. It was bad enough that her friend was trapped and in danger. He didn't need to make it worse by heaping a fresh pile of guilt on top.

Leave it to him to make a bad situation worse. If it weren't for his loyalty to the general, as well as his need to see both Sloane and her friend home safe and sound on American soil, he would have just walked away. He didn't need this kind of trouble. He had no business out here in the jungle, providing backup when he was busted up, washed up, and used up.

Maybe Sloane was better off without him. Eventually, his knee was going to give out and he'd slow her down if he didn't just get her killed.

Stop feeling sorry for yourself. That was what the Old Man had told him when he'd brought up the fact that he was a liability due to his injury. *You still have your brain if you care to use it. You'll need it with Sloane.*

And once again, the general was right. Lucas had been an excellent strategist. That part of him hadn't been broken.

"What if we take your plan and reverse it?" he asked her without turning around. He didn't want her to know he'd seen her emotions plain on her face. He was convinced that would only make her pricklier, and that was not something he wanted to witness.

When she spoke, her voice was thick with suspicion. "What do you mean?"

"Rather than trading yourself for Gina, why don't we take Soma and trade him for her instead?"

"He's got to be guarded, right?"

"Sure, but not all the time. We'll grab him while he's asleep or in the john."

The humidity inside the vehicle was thick, making them sweat. Sloane lifted the hem of her shirt to wipe her forehead. Of course, she didn't know he could see her, so he got a nice glimpse of her bare belly and the bottom curves of her breasts. It didn't matter that she was wearing a bra or that the show had lasted all of two seconds. The image was burned into Lucas's mind, clear and sharp.

His stomach tightened, and sweat that had nothing to do with the stifling heat of the vehicle rolled down his ribs. That fancy party dress hadn't done her justice. It had clung to her curves, but had not shown off the sexy lines of her stomach or the smooth radiance of her skin.

For one long moment, whatever she was saying faded away, eclipsed by Lucas's wayward imagination. What other secrets had that gown hidden? Had she been wearing stockings? Or perhaps nothing at all under the dress? Were her nipples the same dark pink as her lips?

"What do you think?" she asked.

Lucas had no clue what she'd been saying. He'd been deafened by lust. "About what?"

She let out an exasperated sigh. "Will that be enough equipment to spy on Lorenzo and catch him alone?"

"I'm sure," he said, just because he knew he'd make do with whatever was available. Even if it was just the scope on her rifle.

He turned back in his seat in time to see her square her shoulders the way he'd seen the Old Man do more times than he could count. She nodded once as if making a decision. "We'll drive until we find a place to hide the Rover, then go the rest of the way on foot."

"Sounds like a plan," said Lucas, though his knee cringed at the thought of more abuse. It was already aching like a son of a bitch. "On the way, I'll make a few calls and see if we can get some satellite images, assuming you've got the right equipment to receive an image."

"I do. My laptop can hook into the sat phone."

It took the better part of an hour to get his answer, and when he did, it wasn't good news. "They can't retask a satellite right now. Sorry," he told her. "We're on our own."

She gave him a steady nod. "That's okay. I'm used to doing things on my own."

Payton drove home, went to his basement office, locked the door, and dialed the number he'd hoped he'd never need again.

Senator Gregory Kerrington II answered on the third ring. Not even his secretary was allowed to answer this line. Only Greg would know Payton had called. It was best that way.

"What?" answered the senator.

"Is this line safe?"

"Hold on." The line went silent; then a moment later, the senator came back on. "Make it fast."

"Bella found some things."

Irritation tightened the senator's voice. "What kind of things?"

"Familiar things. I saw the photos on her phone." He'd had to steal a peek at them while she showered in the locker room, but the deception was necessary. "It's happening again."

"Impossible! There's no one left alive who would even know where to start."

"Someone must have found the research, then, because I know what I saw."

"Does Bella?" asked Greg.

"No. She was too young then. All she knows is that what she saw upset her enough to destroy the entire building. She razed it to the ground."

"Good. That saves me some effort." Payton heard the creak of Greg's chair as it leaned back. "It was probably a leftover research facility—a remnant of the past."

He'd thought that, too. At first. "Then why was nothing dusty? Where were the cobwebs?"

"You're just being paranoid."

Greg had always been stubborn, but he'd never before refused to see the truth when it was right in front of him. "Do I need to send you the photos?"

"No," the senator hurried to say. "No need. Whatever it was is taken care of now. I assume you deleted the photos."

"Of course." After he'd sent a copy to himself.

He had to delete all of Bella's contacts and other stored information as well to make it look like her phone had gone haywire, but she'd get over that. Having those photos on her phone could get her killed. He loved her like a daughter. He'd lay down his life to protect her.

Greg's tone became dismissive. "Good. We're done here, then. I have a meeting."

"I hope you're right, but what if you're not? What if

someone did find a copy of the research and has begun the experiments again?"

"Then you'd better pray our names aren't mentioned anywhere in that research, or we're both dead men."

Greg hung up, leaving Payton listening to silence. He'd never been as optimistic as the senator, or as deeply mired in denial. Payton was a pragmatist. A realist. And he was convinced that the sins of their youth were coming back to haunt them.

Judging by those photos, the nightmare wasn't over. It was just getting started.

Chapter 7

Gina had no idea why she was here in Colombia or what Lorenzo planned to do with her. The only bit of conversation she'd overheard indicated that he was taking her somewhere tomorrow.

By then she needed to be long gone.

Gina's plan was fairly simple. She would ease herself down to the ground on a rope made from a sheet, then run like crazy until she found someone with a phone. She'd call for help and keep hidden until that help arrived.

The only thing holding her back was that Sloane might be coming. That, and the guns the men outside had. And the fact that she had no food or water and no idea how long it would be until she found some. And her shoes were meant for a party, not a hike. And she had no idea where she was going and could just as easily get herself deeper *into* trouble as out of it.

Okay, maybe there were a few kinks in her plan that needed some work. Patience had never been among her virtues, but if she was going to make it out of this alive, she needed to find some, quick.

If only she knew why she was here, it would make her decision a lot easier. Three days ago, they'd been at a club in New York. Lorenzo had told her he wanted her to see his home. She'd thought it was a romantic gesture right up to the point where he dumped her here and locked her in.

For the third time today, she pounded on the door and demanded the guard take her to see Lorenzo.

The man who opened the door was younger than the last guard. His hair was shaved until only a quarter inch of stubble remained. His eyes were a deep brown and he had a dimple in his chin. He was short, maybe an inch or two taller than her five-two frame. The way his eyes slid over her body gave her a burst of hope.

Gina turned on the charm and flashed Shorty a sultry smile. "Do you speak English?" she asked.

"English. Little."

She could work with that. "I want to see Lorenzo."

"You stay."

Gina ignored the violent implications of the heavy gun strapped over his shoulder and ran her finger down the side of his face. "Can you ask Lorenzo if he'll come see me? I'm so lonely."

Shorty grinned and inched closer. "He works. You stay. I stay."

"Do you want to come in?" she asked. "Keep me company?" Maybe if she got him inside her room, she could overpower him and take his weapon. She wasn't sure how to use it, but she owned a camera. She could point and shoot with the best of them.

"You are joking me."

She let her finger glide along the curve of his ear and down his neck. "I'd never do that."

He captured her fingers and brought them to his lips, kissing the back of her hand. He said something in Spanish she couldn't follow, but it rolled off his tongue, low and fervent.

He was totally into her, and Gina knew exactly what to do with that.

"Come inside," she urged, mentally cataloging all the heavy objects in the room she could use to bash him over the head.

"Later. After dark. I come."

Great. That was not exactly what she was going for, but maybe that was just her impatience talking. If she got his weapon away from him after dark, she'd still be armed, wouldn't she?

Footsteps sounded from around the corner. Shorty hastily pushed her back into her room and locked the door.

She heard voices outside as he spoke to another man briefly. Once she heard those footsteps fading away, she knocked on the door again.

This time it was opened by the first, older guard. He gave her a sour glare.

"Can I get some food?" she asked, hoping they'd bring her something she could stash in a pillowcase and take with her when she ran.

The guard just stared. She pretended to eat, hoping he'd get the idea. He nodded, then pushed the door closed. The staticky sound of a radio filtered through the solid wood.

He wasn't even leaving to go get her food.

Gina leaned against the door and let out a sigh of frustration. Now not only did she have a guard she couldn't distract; she also had an eager young man coming to her room after dark expecting a little somethin' somethin' she wasn't planning to give.

Knowing her luck, Shorty wouldn't even bring his gun to their late-night rendezvous.

Sloane watched Lucas's back as he moved over the rough jungle terrain. He was nearly silent, each movement fluid and careful. There was a grace about him that was mesmerizing. She stared too long, nearly tripping over an exposed root.

She caught herself before she fell. He spun around, and she felt his strong grip steadying her. His hands were warm against her bare arms, and just a bit rough. Concern lined his lean face and she was struck by the fact that he would care. "You okay?" he whispered.

Sloane nodded, at a loss for words.

His hands slid up her arms, grazing against her flesh. His touch was light, but it still managed to raise goose bumps on her arms. He adjusted the shoulder strap of her pack, sliding it more squarely into place. "Let me take some of your weight."

He was already carrying twice as much gear as she was—twice as much weight—but he hadn't complained. She had the feeling the he never would, either.

As resistant as she'd been to have him tag along, she was glad he was here now. There was no way she would have been able to carry all her weapons and gear without his help. And he was right that the best way to get Gina back was through stealth.

"I'm fine," she said. "I can handle it."

"So can I."

He hadn't moved away. He was still in her space, touching her, cupping her shoulders in his big hands, careful of her injury. His navy blue eyes moved over her face as if searching for signs of weakness.

Sloane wasn't going to let him find any.

Lucas reached up and brushed something from her hair. A small bug flew off, buzzing past her ear. He tucked a loose strand of hair behind her ear, giving her an inadvertent caress as he did.

At least she thought it was inadvertent, but the way his eyes tracked the movement before coming back and resting on her mouth now had her thinking otherwise.

She knew she shouldn't let him touch her like this,

but out here, alone in the jungle with no one to know her weakness, she couldn't find it in her to push him away. It had been way too long since a man had touched her, and even though what he'd done was casual, the way he was looking at her while he did it was anything but.

"We should get moving," she said in a voice breathy and quiet.

"We could take a break if you like."

Sloane wanted to say yes, but she was afraid that if she did, he'd keep touching her. And if he kept touching her, she'd be unable to ask him to stop. It felt too nice for her to fool herself by believing otherwise. As handsome as he was, as much as she admired his body and loved the feel of his fingers on her skin, she knew getting involved with him was a mistake. He was one of her father's men. If she showed any signs of weakness, her father would find out and use it against her. She had to remember that. "I think it's best if we keep moving."

He gave her a regretful nod, then lifted his hands from her body and turned away.

Sloane suffered a sudden surge of loneliness, which was ridiculous. He was still right there in front of her. She could still enjoy the sight of his body moving, and that was as much as she was going to let herself have from him. Time to get over it.

It took her the better part of an hour to start feeling like herself again. She was still staring at him, enjoying the power of his body as he hiked, and it was because she was watching him so closely that she noticed the slight pause in his fluid stride. She wasn't sure what had happened until she saw it again, then again.

For the third time, his left knee gave out and he nearly fell. He recovered quickly and moved on as if nothing had happened, hacking at the thick growth wherever it barred their path.

Sloan was hot, sweaty, and miserable in the stifling thickness of the tropical air. Sunset was not far away, and it was going to get really dark really fast beneath the canopy of trees overhead.

"How far have we come?" she asked Lucas.

"At best a mile, mile and a half."

Sloane cringed. It felt like ten times that far. "We should find a place to stop."

"We've got another good twenty minutes of daylight left. I thought you wanted to keep going."

"I'd rather not have to drag your ass back out of here if your knee gives out."

He stopped, turned, and the snarl on his face was heart-stoppingly scary. "My knee is fine. You won't need to drag my ass anywhere."

"So, you can set up camp in the dark?"

"Yeah, as a matter of fact. I can." Then he turned around and kept hiking, his posture rigid and angry.

Okay. Apparently the knee was a tender subject. "I didn't mean to offend you, but I was trained to know my limitations."

"Well, I was trained not to have any, so just drop it. I'll let you know if and when I need a break."

Fine. Let him suffer. What did she care?

A few minutes later, his knee buckled again. She gasped and reached for him.

"Shit," he muttered.

"That's it. We're stopping here."

He was sweating and his face was pale with pain. "I can keep going. I just need a minute."

"No. I'm in charge of this mission and I say we stop here."

He was kneeling on the ground, looking up at her with mutiny shining in his dark blue eyes. "And what would Gina say?"

"That you're far too hot to let suffer. I'd hate to take

away her chance to get to flirt with you by leaving you behind when your knee gives out entirely."

He sighed and bowed his head in shame. "I thought I was stronger than this. I don't want the life of a woman at stake because of some fucking injury."

"I don't think her life is at stake—at least not immediately. If he meant to kill her, he would have already done it." At least that was what Sloane forced herself to believe. She'd moved as fast as she could to help her friend. She had to believe it would be good enough.

"I guess that's something." He didn't look appeased by the notion.

"It's more important that we do this right than fast. We get ourselves killed and Gina's SOL."

Lucas nodded slowly. "Give me a couple hours of downtime and I'll be as good as new."

"I've only got one pair of night-vision goggles."

"We'll find a way to make it work. I won't let you down."

Sloane was beginning to believe him. She could see the lines of pain around his mouth and eyes, but he clearly wasn't going to let that stop him. "I'm not planning to ditch you yet. You make a good pack mule."

He grinned at her, which made Sloane's stomach do a slow, lazy roll. He was one hell of a fine-looking man. His slicked-back hairdo had come undone and a few short locks had fallen over his forehead. Beard stubble shadowed his wide jaw, accentuating the stark angles of his face. But it was his mouth that had her complete attention. His grin was lopsided, tiling his full mouth in a way that had her thinking about how his lips would feel against hers. Would they be soft, or hard like the rest of him? Would they be as warm as his fingers were when he touched her?

He swiped the back of his hand over his mouth and

he gave her a questioning look. "What? Do I have some-thing on me?"

Sloane swallowed before she could speak, forcing herself to look away. "No." She cleared her throat and forced herself to sound businesslike. "We should get settled. I'll find us a good spot. You stay here."

Before he could argue, Sloane turned and headed into the foliage. She needed a few minutes to regain her balance and get her bearings. She couldn't remember the last time she'd been attracted to a man as strongly as she was to Lucas. It was purely physical. She knew better than to think she could ever fall for a man like her father—which Lucas clearly was. All duty, no heart. Hell, he couldn't even take pity on himself enough to call a stop to a hike that was clearly causing him pain.

She didn't need another cold, unfeeling man in her life. She'd already gotten rid of one, and she considered that a lesson learned. Time to move on. She wasn't fool-ish enough to tempt herself with girlish fantasies of hap-pily ever after. Men were in her life solely to scratch an itch. End of story.

Sloane made quick work of locating an area big enough to put the small, camouflaged tent she'd brought. It would keep the rain off and the bugs out, but there was no way she was getting inside that tiny thing with Lucas. She knew what would happen if she did.

Her hormones would go haywire; she'd start feel-ing that itch and start thinking about his mouth again, rather than focusing on getting Gina home. She was too smart to fall for something so easily avoidable. All she had to do was make sure they took turns in the tent and she'd be fine. So would Gina.

Sloane used a machete to cut away some under-growth and pitched the tent. Ten minutes later, she went back to where Lucas was waiting and pulled the heavy pack from his back. She stumbled under the weight of it, wondering how he'd kept up the pace he had while hauling so much.

"We're set up a few yards this way," she said, leading the way.

Lucas had found a stick somewhere and used it like a cane. "Our trail will be obvious to anyone who passes this way, but my hope is no one will stumble across it. I didn't see any signs of passage."

"Just in case, I'll take first watch. You can have the tent."

He gave her a weary nod. "Wake me in two hours and we'll keep moving."

"Sure," she said, knowing it was a lie. She had no intention of waking him in two hours. Moving in the thick darkness of the jungle with only one pair of NVGs was beyond stupid. She'd let him sleep through the night and hope that would be enough to get him back on his feet.

Sloane ate, hydrated, set out a small arsenal of weapons—just in case—and settled back against one of the heavy packs to keep watch. Her arm was aching, her body was sore, she was cold now that the sun had set, and she wanted nothing more than a hot shower and a hotel room bed. Well, that and Gina safely tucked into the bed next to hers.

They'd spent countless nights gabbing until dawn at boarding school. Mostly about how much they hated the prison their school had become. And boys. They'd talked for hours about boys.

Sloane smiled at the memory, thinking how innocent she'd been then. How small her world had been. Her old self would have been stunned to know she would one day be sitting here in the jungle, surrounded by the sounds of the nocturnal wildlife and a whole lot of firepower. With a man as tempting as Lucas only a few feet away.

The minutes slid by. Sloane let herself doze, waking every few minutes to ensure they were still alone. About three hours into her watch, she started feeling sick and her eyes began to burn. She flipped on a battery-operated lantern, drawing a host of flying bugs, but she needed the light to check her injury. Sure enough, it was red and puffy with some kind of infection.

Great. Just what she needed.

Sloane did the best she could to disinfect it again, re-bandaged it, and swallowed a couple of the antibiotics she'd brought with her. It was as good as she could hope for until Gina was out of harm's way.

Sleep pulled at Sloane, but she tried not to doze too deeply and kept waking every few minutes. Lucas had been trained by her father, which meant that between the two of them, he was the more formidable opponent. She hated admitting that, but owed it to Gina to be a realist. Lucas was the one who needed to be at the top of his game. Not her. Gina's life might depend on it.

Gina held her breath in the darkness of her room as she heard the guards changing shifts outside her door. It was getting late, and so far Shorty had not held up his promise to come see her tonight.

Footsteps faded as someone moved down the hall. The scraping sound of metal on metal grated from the lock. The lever-style doorknob turned. The door slipped open slowly, letting light spill in over the wooden floor. Shorty's diminutive shadow slid inside.

She'd been waiting for him so long her hands had started to cramp up around the metal base of a lamp. The thing was heavy, and it was going to leave a hell of a dent in Shorty's skull.

"Hello, pretty," he whispered as he shut the door behind him.

Gina didn't wait for him to figure out she wasn't lying on the rumpled bed waiting for him. She slammed the lamp down against the back of his head and he crumpled to the ground.

Her heart was racing so fast, she couldn't hear whether or not he'd made much noise on the way down, or whether there was the sound of anyone approaching outside her door. If someone was coming, she didn't want to be here when they arrived.

Gina grabbed the pillowcase she'd stuffed with some fruit and bottled water and slipped out through the unlocked door. She flipped the dead bolt so Shorty couldn't get out and raise the alarm, and moved as quietly as her strappy heels would allow.

The place seemed deserted, but she wasn't going to question her luck. She hurried out through the first door she found and sprinted across the manicured lawn.

Thirty feet out, a bank of blinding lights flipped on. A second later, a siren blared out a whining warning that she was getting away.

Gina picked up speed. Her heels sank into the dirt, slowing her. She just needed to find a place in the nearby jungle where she could hide. It was only a few hundred feet away. She could make it that far before anyone had time to catch up with her.

A gun went off behind her, and for one heart-stopping moment, she was sure she was going to be shot, but she felt nothing. Maybe it had just been a warning shot.

Gina wasn't going to stop and ask.

She made a beeline for the trees. She'd almost reached them when she saw a blur coming at her from her left. Something heavy slammed into her. She fell, crushed under the weight of the man who'd tackled her.

She kicked and clawed at him, but before she could do any real damage, he pinned her hands and flipped her over so she was eating grass. His knee dug into her back and he spat something violent at her in words she didn't understand.

The man held her there so long, she was beginning to wonder if he was planning to keep her here all night. Then she saw a pair of perfectly polished shoes come into her range of vision.

Lorenzo gave a rough order and Gina was hauled up to her feet by the man who'd tackled her.

"Exactly what did you think to accomplish by running?" he asked. His voice was calm, but she could see rage tightening his features. His fists were clenched and his shoulders vibrated with anger.

She glared at him. "I think that would be obvious, even to someone with your limited intelligence."

His nostrils flared. He made a motion with his hand and the man holding her arms behind her inched them up a couple of painful inches.

Gina went up on her tiptoes in an effort to avoid the pain, but it did little good.

"If you'd managed to get away, you would have died out there. Is that what you want?"

Gina choked down the smart-ass remark that was trying to claw its way out. She really didn't want a pair of broken shoulders to add to her troubles.

When Lorenzo saw she wasn't responding, he gave her captor a slight nod. The pressure threatening to tear her arms off eased.

"Have you not been comfortable?" he asked. "Have I not given you everything you need?"

"I need you to let me go."

"And I will. As soon as I'm done with you."

"What do you mean by that? You and I are over."

A condescending smile curved his mouth. "Did you really think you were good enough to keep my attention for more than a few brief moments? I was bored with you the first time I fucked you."

"Not from what I could tell." They'd been at it hot and heavy for a whole week before he'd asked her to come visit his home. She'd been foolish enough to think their relationship might actually go somewhere. He'd been kind, attentive, and completely enamored of her. Or so she'd thought.

He gave her a dismissive wave. "It was all an act, of course—done to lure you here where I needed you."

"Why? Why bring me here if you're not interested in me?"

"Because one of my colleagues is interested in you. Very much. You'll be taken to meet him tomorrow, and it's in my best interest to make sure you're safe and sound until then."

That didn't sound good. "Who? And why does he want to meet me?"

"You'll have to ask him." Lorenzo walked away, and the man holding her forced her to follow in his wake.

Instead of taking her straight back to her room like she expected, they took her to another part of the house. Lorenzo unlocked a door and inside was a room lined with beds. He flipped the lights on and several women startled awake. Fear was in their eyes when they saw who had interrupted their sleep.

The woman in the closest bed clutched a small child who had been sleeping with her. A little girl who was maybe three years old.

Lorenzo went to the child, knelt down, and took her from her mother. He walked over to Gina as the child began to cry.

"This is Julia. Tell her hello."

Gina had no idea what he was up to, but clearly the little girl was scared out of her mind. She tried to make her voice soothing as she addressed Julia. "Hi. I'm Gina."

The little girl reached out for her. The man holding

her let go of her arms, so Gina took Julia from Lorenzo, glad to have her out of that asshole's grasp.

There was a commotion outside the open doorway as someone dragged Shorty into view. He was crying, a stream of words fell from his lips, and even though she didn't understand what he said, it was clear he was begging.

"Jeremy," was all Lorenzo said.

A sturdy, muscular man pulled out a gun and fired it into Shorty's head. The boom of the weapon was deafening. A bloody mess erupted onto the tile floor and the women in the room began to wail and weep. Julia screamed and clung to her with strong, chubby arms.

Lorenzo leaned down close so she could see right into his eyes. "If you try to run again, Julia will be the next mess in the hall."

Chapter 8

It was barely dawn when Lucas woke inside the little tent. The first glow of sunlight brightened the camo fabric. It took him a moment to realize what that meant.

Sloane hadn't woken him.

Panic made his hands jerky as he unzipped the tent

Had she left him behind? Had she gotten hurt during the night? Killed? A thousand gut-wrenching possibilities funneled through his thoughts in the few brief seconds it took him to get out of the tent.

She sat only a few feet away, huddled under a thin survival blanket. Her head was bowed as if sleeping, but the second he let out a relieved sigh, she looked up. Her eyes were glossy and red from lack of sleep, but she appeared alert.

"Are you okay?" he asked.

"I should be asking you the same thing. How's the knee?"

"It's fine. Why didn't you wake me?" he asked.

"You needed the rest."

"And you don't?"

"I'll be fine. I napped."

He said nothing about how unsafe that was, because he didn't want to ruin the gift she'd given him. His knee was a bit stiff, but no longer throbbing as it had been yesterday. He'd be fine hiking all day without embarrassing himself. He had her to thank for that.

"Grab a nap if you want and I'll pack up," he said.

Rather than come back with some stinging comment about how she didn't need his help, she simply curled up on her side, pillowed her head on her arm, and closed her eyes.

Guilt weighed Lucas down. Not only had he forced her to take him along, but now she felt like she had to babysit him. He hated the idea that he was slowing her down, and today he was going to prove to her he wasn't just extra baggage. He was going to find that airstrip and get Gina back.

The general was probably sick with worry, so Lucas took pity on the man and snuck off into the jungle to call him while Sloane was asleep. Thankfully, the general was away from his desk and Lucas didn't have to get his ass chewed out. He left a brief message, telling the general that they were safe and on a rescue mission. As soon as they had Gina Delaney in tow, they'd be on the next flight home, likely by sunset tomorrow.

At least that was what Lucas hoped. Rescue missions often had a way of turning into recovery missions.

He snuck back to where Sloane slept and stowed the phone, powered off and exactly where he'd found it. She didn't even stir when he was practically touching her.

That was when he noticed she was shivering. In this stifling heat. Under the blanket.

Lucas pressed his hand to her forehead and felt the heat from her skin burn his palm.

Sloane startled awake, shoving him away as she scrambled backward. Her eyes were wide and wild.

"Easy," he said, holding his hands up so she could see them.

She let out a long breath, deflating in relief. "You scared me."

He kept his voice low and calm. "You're running a fever."

She rubbed her eyes. "Yeah. I started the antibiotics last night. It'll take a few more hours for them to kick in."

If they worked at all. There was no guarantee that even the broad-spectrum stuff would do the trick. "You need medical attention."

"Which I'll get as soon as we find Gina."

He pressed the back of his hand against her cheek, just to make sure he hadn't imagined how hot she was.

He hadn't.

Lucas pulled out one of his clean socks, wet it, then draped it around the back of her neck. "Maybe we should go back. I know your father would send men in to get her."

"No. I can do this. It's not that bad."

"But it could get worse."

"We're already here. We can have her back before anyone else has the time to get here. Let's just get the job done. If the antibiotics don't work in a few hours, then we'll consider the alternatives."

He was going to hold her to that.

"Why don't you stay here and rest? I'll scout ahead and find the airstrip, then come back and get you."

"All that backtracking will eat up too much time. I'll be fine." She pushed herself to her feet, swaying. Lucas grabbed her arm to steady her. Her bare skin felt smooth, but way too hot under his fingers.

"You don't look fine."

She eyed him with a look that told him to back the hell off. "When I need to stop, I'll let you know. Until then, it'd be best for both of us if you didn't try to baby me."

"I wasn't babying you. I was simply offering another alternative. Besides, you're the one babying me by letting me sleep all night. If you hadn't done that, you might not feel so crappy."

"I said I'm fine. Let's go. The map says we need to head south."

Lucas helped her strap her pack on. While he was at it, he relieved her of some ammunition and stowed it in his own pack. She was so bleary-eyed, she didn't even notice, which proved just how off her game she was.

He kept a careful eye on her as they sliced a path through the jungle, checking over his shoulder every few minutes. She was weaving on her feet, but kept putting one in front of the other like a good little soldier. She was definitely her father's daughter, though he didn't dare say that to her.

They'd been moving for two hours when she'd paled so much he worried she'd fall over. He called a halt. "I need to take five," he told her, saving her pride and any argument she might give him.

Sloane nodded and slumped to the ground, not bothering to take off her heavy backpack. She fell asleep sitting up.

That was it. Lucas was done letting her push herself.

He fished some aspirin out of his pack and took them and a canteen to Sloane. "Take these." He pushed the pills into her mouth and gave her a drink to wash them down.

"Thanks."

Lucas pressed his hand to her forehead. Her eyes fluttered closed and she let out a groan as if his cooler skin felt good against hers

She was still fevered, which worried the hell out of him. What if those antibiotics didn't work? How was he going to get her and Gina out of this place? He truly didn't know if he could carry her that far, though if push came to shove, he'd figure out a way to make it happen—call the Old Man for an airlift, maybe.

He kept touching her, smoothing his fingers over her face, trying to draw away some of the heat from her skin. At least that was what he told himself he was doing. He enjoyed the feel of her under his fingertips as much as anything. The fact that she didn't push him away only encouraged him.

"Let me scout ahead," he said. "I'll move faster without all the gear weighing me down. I'll find the airstrip and come back before you even have time to miss me."

"I don't want you to have to come back for me. It's too far for your knee."

"My knee is fine. You're the one who's going to fall over if you keep pushing. Just sit for a while. If I don't see any signs of our target in an hour, I'll come back." And to make sure she complied, he added, "Unless you're afraid to be out here alone."

"Of course I'm not afraid."

"Good. Then it's settled. I'll see you in two hours or less."

The fact that she didn't argue proved just how close to the end of her strength she really was.

Lucas hid her and the gear in some thick undergrowth, made sure she had a weapon handy, and camouflaged her location with some branches he cut from nearby. He didn't want to be away from her for long, so he hustled his ass south, praying their target wouldn't be far.

He'd gone about two kilometers when he heard voices. He ducked, hiding in the thick foliage. The voices got louder as they came toward him, then began to fade as they passed. He couldn't make out what they were saying, but he thought he caught Soma's name.

Lucas kept a good distance between himself and the two men as he followed them. Maybe they were leading him in the wrong direction, but he had to take that chance. If these were Soma's men, then they were likely on patrol, because there sure as hell wasn't anything else out here but more jungle.

Suddenly, one of the men stopped and held up his hand for silence. Lucas crouched low, hoping he hadn't been spotted. He eased his weapon out of the shoulder holster and felt adrenaline slide through his veins.

He really didn't want to kill these men, but he knew if they came this way, that was exactly what he'd have to do.

Payton cringed as he answered his phone, knowing he wasn't going to like whatever General Norwood had to say. "Hello?"

"How the hell could you have let her go to Colombia?" demanded Norwood.

"Hi, Bob. It's great to hear from you. How have you been?"

"You know damn well how I've been. I trusted you to take care of her."

There was no need to ask for clarification as to who "her" was. Payton knew the general was talking about his daughter—the one only a small handful of people even knew he had. "All I knew was that she requested time off work to help a friend in a jam. She never mentioned Colombia. I didn't even know she was there."

"I sent a man after her when I saw her name on the passenger manifest. He couldn't stop her, so now he's there with her, *helping* her go after her missing friend, Gina Delaney. Does that name ring a bell?"

A loud one. Gina was on the List. If she was missing and in Colombia, chances were she was in deep, deep trouble. "You know it does."

"What about Lorenzo Soma? Recognize that name?"

He was also on the List, though he'd be a grown man now. "Antonio's son."

"Who has taken his father's place in the world. Antonio had a sad mishap with an exploding car a few years back and Lorenzo made a nearly seamless transition into his father's drug business. Only somehow he's got access to the List."

A sick sense of dread welled up inside Payton. "There's no way. It's not possible. We destroyed all the copies."

"If that's true, then how do you explain Gina in connection with Antonio's boy?"

"It has to be a coincidence."

"What about Heath Innis? Sophie Devane? Soma took them from the country, too. Their bodies have not been found."

That dread grew to full panic. "Where would he have found a copy?"

"Adam Brink. He came to see me. He wanted the List and thought I had it."

"Why would Adam want the List? He was just a boy the last time I saw him."

"He's all grown-up now, and he didn't say why he wanted the List. I didn't ask. The less contact I have with him, the better. I figured we'd already fucked up his life. The least I could do was stay out of it now."

"Why didn't you tell me he came to see you?"

"Because you didn't need to know. I handled it."

"Apparently not well enough," said Payton. "He must have found a copy."

"Let's say he did. It still doesn't explain why people on the List are going missing, taken by Antonio's son."

"Maybe Lorenzo remembered them from his days in the Colombian facility. Maybe he's looking for answers."

"Answers to what?" asked Bob.

"Lorenzo could be remembering some of what his father had done to him. Maybe he thinks some of the other kids would know something and help fill in some of the mental blank spots."

"Do you think Adam is looking for answers, too?"

"I don't know," said Payton. "Right now I'm more worried about Lorenzo and what he's doing. He wasn't exactly one of our successes. Who knows what aftereffects he might be suffering."

"Paranoia, delusions, hallucinations," said Bob, shame filling his quiet voice. "I remember."

"It makes me wonder what he's done to Gina."

"I have no idea, but I do know that my little girl is crawling around out in the jungle, looking for her friend, and it's your fault."

Indignation burned off some of Payton's fear. "Like hell it is. She's a grown woman, and if it weren't for all of her abandonment issues, she probably would have settled down to a nice, normal life with a couple of kids and a minivan instead of a couple of dozen guns and a need for violence. That's *your* fault. Don't you dare go blaming me for what *you* chose to do."

Payton could hear Bob's fury coming through in the silence filling the line. It took several seconds before he spoke again, and when he did, his voice was a low growl of warning. "You know it was the only way to protect her, to keep her off the List. I never wanted her involved."

"Well, now she is. You said you've got a man with her. You're just going to have to trust that he'll do his job and keep her safe."

"If he doesn't, I'm coming after you."

"You do that," said Payton, completely unruffled by the general's warning. "We both know how that will turn out."

Again, a long silence stretched on, but Payton let it, refusing to rise to the bait of trying to fill it.

Finally, Bob spoke, sounding tired. "I can't lose Sloane. I know we're not close, but losing Abigail nearly killed me. If anything happens to my little girl . . ."

Payton's heart wasn't completely made of stone. He knew what it was like to worry about someone you loved. He still didn't get a decent night's sleep whenever Bella went out on a mission. Not that he'd stop her. Women like Sloane and Bella could not be controlled. The best he could hope for was to appear harmless so when he offered guidance they would listen.

"I'll do what I can," he promised Bob. "If Sloane gets in trouble, she'll call for backup. It's what I taught her— what Bella taught her."

"I should have been the one to teach her."

"We both know why you couldn't. Let it go. It's over."

Bob sighed. "I only wish that were true."

Payton's muscles tensed and he pressed the phone harder against his ear. "What do you mean?"

"There are too many coincidences to ignore. I've seen things, heard things that remind me of . . . everything we did."

"We can't talk about that now, but maybe we should meet."

"I'm on my way to your neck of the woods to wait for Sloane to come back, anyway. I'll come find you."

"Not at work," said Payton. "I don't know if any of the mercenaries will recognize you."

"I was a lot younger back then. A lot thinner and had a lot more hair."

"Maybe, but I'd rather not take the chance. You know how their minds are—how easy it is to set off one of their memories."

"Fair enough. See you tomorrow."

Payton was not looking forward to the reunion.

Four hours had passed by the time Sloane woke. Her fever had eased, and she felt better, though she still wasn't at one hundred percent.

Lucas wasn't sitting around nearby, but she didn't dare call out his name. She didn't know how close they were to Soma's men or how far her voice might travel.

She pushed herself to her feet and searched the immediate area for signs of him. She saw none.

There was no way she was going to be able to haul all the gear—both his and hers—so she grabbed a few necessities and left the rest behind. At least this way, he'd know she was coming back.

Sloane had gone about half a mile when her head cleared enough to realize she wasn't going to be able to find him out here. He'd left no trace of a trail she could follow—not that she was an expert tracker by any means. She was better off going back to the gear and waiting for him to show.

Which put a nasty thought in her head. What if he didn't come back? What if something had happened to him?

She tried to tell herself that it was his own damn fault for following her here, but she couldn't seem to make herself believe that, no matter how hard she tried. He'd come to help. Sure, he'd been sent by her father, but that didn't make him the devil. He just worked for one.

Sloane hiked to the top of a rise, hoping the elevation would allow her to see over all this damn foliage. She'd nearly cleared the top when she saw a blur of motion and a hard hand closed over her mouth. A heavy weight bore her backward to the ground, pressing down on top of her.

Her arms were pinned to her sides, but she kicked, fighting her captor on instinct.

His head pulled back enough for her eyes to focus on his face. It was Lucas, but he wasn't looking at her. He was watching something in the distance.

Relief made her sag in his hold and she suffered through an involuntary shiver.

He leaned down so his mouth was against her ear. She felt the brush of his breath slide over her skin. "Two men patrolling at one o'clock, ten meters out."

Sloane did some quick calculations and realized that if she'd cleared that rise, they would have seen her. Lucas had saved their lives and possibly Gina's as well.

She nodded, telling him she understood, then stayed still and silent. He moved his hand, and she licked her dry lips, tasting the salt of his skin.

He lifted his head and peered out over her again. His weight still held her down, but she didn't dare ask him to move and risk detection.

His heat sank into her; his scent filled her head. She felt surrounded by him, and surprisingly she found she didn't mind. It had been a long time since she'd felt a man's weight atop her, and she couldn't help but enjoy the sensation, letting it trickle through her and calm her nerves. There was something primal in that feeling—a comfort in knowing she was protected from the world by a man who was more than capable of keeping her safe. Sure, she was independent and strong, but that didn't mean she couldn't enjoy knowing she could relax, if only for a few moments.

Sloane blamed her inappropriate feelings on her fever. It was a lot easier that way than owning up to them.

While Lucas watched the patrol, Sloane watched him. His face was shaded by the wavering shadows of leaves and the growth of beard stubble along his jaw. A smudge of dirt bisected his forehead. At this distance, she could easily see the paler blue starbursts in his eyes. His gaze was focused as it followed the men, his breathing slow and even.

Sloane wanted to reach up and trace her fingers over the lines of his face. She wanted to feel the smooth texture of his mouth and the roughness of his chin. Even the messy drape of his hair over his forehead called to her.

She didn't do any of those things. She suffered through the want, feeling it flow through her body, making her languid and somehow soft.

Lucas looked down at her, and because she was watching him so intently, she noticed the way his pupils flared.

She told herself it was just the change in light, the shift from sun to shadow. But then he kept staring and his gaze roamed over her face, settling on her mouth. He licked his lips in an unconscious gesture.

A crazy, screaming part of her begged her to kiss him. It would have been an easy thing to do. She only had to lift her head a couple of inches, make contact, let her mouth do the rest of the work.

She didn't. Wanting to kiss him was just the fever talking. He was one of her father's men, and like all the men who came in contact with General Robert Norwood, Lucas would spend his life trying to emulate the Old Man. She'd rather die alone than end up with a man like her father.

Wouldn't she?

The fact that she even questioned that idea was enough to break the spell. There was no way she was going to let another man control her and cage her for her own safety. She was not going to be ignored, and she sure as hell wasn't going to ever again let someone make her feel as inadequate as her father had. She was a strong, capable woman. Never again would she connect herself with a man who found her lacking the way the glorious general did.

She kept her voice low, barely a whisper. "Are they gone?"

He nodded, still staring at her mouth.

This was the part where she asked him to move off of her. No words came out.

Lucas reached up and snagged a leaf from her hair. His wide hand settled on her forehead. His skin was rough and warm and felt way too nice against hers. "Your fever's better."

The contact wasn't sexual. It was merely his hand on her head. It didn't even involve any naughty parts, and yet Sloane felt like she'd been stroked from shoulder to thigh and back again. Her body vibrated with a needy kind of tension that was centered low in her belly.

She swallowed, trying to free her voice. It came out as more of a croak. "Yeah."

"That's good." He slid his hand back over her hair, stroking her.

She'd almost thought it was a mistake until he did it again, and again. She closed her eyes, unable to stop herself from enjoying the sensation of being petted by a gorgeous man.

If he didn't stop this soon, she was going to forget why she was supposed to dislike Lucas and let her body have its way with him.

Chapter 9

Lucas knew he should move. He knew that what he was doing was beyond inappropriate. He simply didn't care.

Sloane's supple body fit beneath his as if she'd been made for it—and that was with the bulk of their tactical vests between them. Without them, he could only imagine how good she'd feel. But it was the way she closed her eyes and reveled in his touch that was going to be the death of him.

He hadn't meant to stroke her face and hair. He'd only intended to see if her fever had faded. But once his hand was on her skin, there was no turning back. She was as soft as she looked. Her dark hair was silky smooth despite the bits of debris clinging here and there.

Sloane was a formidable woman capable of more violence than many men he knew, but right now, here, lying under him, she was simply a woman. One Lucas was having a hard time remembering not to touch.

A soft sigh of pleasure lifted from her mouth and Lucas had to grit his teeth to keep from kissing her. He knew better. So far he hadn't done anything irrevocable. He could still pretend his touch was platonic. Sure, it would be a lie, because his thoughts were anything but platonic, but it was a plausible lie.

If he kissed her, that would change. She'd know how he felt—that he was attracted to her. It would make the rest of their mission awkward, and that could make things less safe.

He was hard, and his wayward cock chose this moment to jerk toward her, giving away the erection he'd been trying to hide.

Her eyes popped wide open. The look on her face was a mix of panic and need.

Lucas let out a low curse and rolled aside. He was so busted. "Sorry."

She was silent for a long time before saying, "We can't do this."

"I know."

"We're . . . wrong for each other."

"I know." But he didn't like it. She didn't *feel* wrong.

"We need to think about Gina. Get her home safe."

"And then?" he asked, because he couldn't stop himself.

She pushed herself to a sitting position and looked down at him. "And then it won't matter—this thing between us. We'll be back in our own worlds. Where we belong."

Lucas didn't tell her that he didn't really belong anywhere anymore. All he had waiting for him was his parents' desire for him to take over the family restaurant. He'd worked there growing up and hated every minute of it. They were horrified when he'd been injured, but overjoyed that it meant he was now out of the military for good. They assumed he'd come back and pick up where he left off, allowing them to retire.

As much as he wanted to help his folks, he knew that job would kill him—at least the important part of him, the part that made him who he was.

Don't think about it now. The real world would come crashing down on him soon enough. For now all he had to do was focus on his mission and keep his hands off Sloane.

"Where are the packs?" he asked her.

"Where we were earlier."

"Go back there and wait. I'll follow the patrol and see if I can figure out which way the airstrip is from here."

"I should go with you."

"I thought stealth wasn't your thing. Besides, you need to take it easy. Once we find Soma, you're going to need to be in fighting condition."

Sloane stood and brushed off her clothes. Lucas pulled another leaf from her hair, which was dangerously close to putting the two of them right back where they'd been only a moment ago.

He couldn't seem to keep his hands off of her, which was a mistake.

She knew it too, judging by the way she took a long step back. "I won't wait long. If you get back and my stuff is gone, you'll know I went on without you. South."

"Fair enough. Give me an hour. I should be able to get a feel for their route in that time."

Sloane nodded, turned, and left.

Lucas watched her until she disappeared into the vegetation, then hauled his ass after the two men he was convinced worked for Soma. With any luck at all, he'd find the airstrip and they'd be there before nightfall.

Gina didn't dare to even think about escaping again. She could still feel Julia's sweet little arms hugging her neck, feel the wetness of her tears on her shirt.

She hadn't slept since the murder. Every time she closed her eyes, she saw Shorty's hopeful smile superimposed upon the splatter of gore on the shiny marble floor.

She'd tricked him. It was her fault he was dead. Sure, he worked for a murdering asshole, but that didn't mean he deserved to die. She certainly hadn't intended to get him killed.

No way was she going to let that happen to Julia.

And there was no question in her mind that Lorenzo would follow through on his promise to kill the child.

Gina paced the floor, wondering what she was going to do if Sloane actually did show up. She couldn't go with her and risk the life of that child, which left only one option.

Before Gina got out of here, Lorenzo Soma was going to have to die.

A cell phone plopped onto Mira's desk, making her jump and let out a fearful squeak. "Holy cats!"

"Sorry. Did I scare you?" asked Bella.

She was so worried about Clay, she must not have heard the door to the computer room open. But she sure wasn't going to admit to her worry. If Bella thought something was wrong with him, she'd ground him, and if that happened, Mira wasn't sure what Clay would do. He loved his job, but it was almost more of an obsession than anything normal or healthy.

Mira wished for the hundredth time he'd go see Dr. Vaughn and figure out what was going on.

Bella stood there, her slim hip propped against Mira's desk. "All the data in my phone is gone. Can you fix it?"

Mira pressed a hand to her heart, hoping it would help slow its frantic, frightened rabbit pace. "I can try. Did anything happen to it?"

"Like what?"

"I don't know. Like did you drop it in the toilet, or did it get hit with a hand grenade or something?"

Bella laughed and shook her head. "I really need to get you out on the firing range more often."

"Uh. No, thanks. I'm good."

"You're timid, but you're freaky good at what you do, so you get a pass."

Mira let the timid and freaky parts of that comment slide over her and focused on the compliment. "Thanks. I'll see what I can do. In the meantime, you can take one of the spare phones."

"I need people to be able to contact me at my number. I also need my contact list so I can get in touch with others."

"Sure. Give me a few minutes and I'll get you set up. You backed everything up to your PC, right?"

Bella nodded. "I'll be in my office when you're done. I'll try not to sneak up on you next time."

Bella left and Mira grabbed a fresh phone from the shelf. She switched the number over and remotely accessed Bella's hard drive to upload the data to her new phone. The old one would have to wait until she had time to tinker with it, which wasn't going to be today.

Once the upload was done, Mira tested the phone to check it out, making sure the calendar, contacts, and other data seemed to be all there. She got to the photos and what she saw made her hands shake.

She had to be imagining it. That tiny little screen was distorting things. That was all.

Mira frantically brought the photos up on her biggest monitor.

It was one of the labs. She was sure of it. The concrete, windowless walls. The small, claustrophobic rooms barely big enough for a bed and a couple of people to move around in. Crooked IV stands. Abandoned CRT monitors.

Everything was dated and dingy with age, but not dirty from disuse. Mira remembered when it had gleamed fresh and new. She'd been there. Maybe not in this particular lab, but she'd bet money her dad had been.

Mira picked up the phone and dialed Bella.

"Are you done already? That was fast."

"The pictures on your phone. Where did you take them?"

"Mexico. Weird, huh? Even weirder was that the place was in the middle of nowhere. No roads, no helo pad. Nothing."

Mira's voice was shaking, but she couldn't seem to control it. "Was anyone there?"

"No. The place was abandoned. But it spooked me, so I blew it up."

A wave of relief made Mira sag in her chair. Her head fell to the keyboard, causing the computer to *bing* in irritation at her. "That's good. Thank you."

"What's going on, Mira? Do you know that place?"

"No," she lied hastily. "It just seemed wrong."

"Yeah. That's what I felt, too. At least you're not going to gripe at me about it like Payton did."

Mira needed to get out of here. She needed to feel the sun on her face and the wind in her hair. Normally, her dark computer den soothed her, but not now. "I'm going to step out for a minute, but your phone is ready. I'll leave it on my desk."

"Thanks. You're the best, honey."

She sure didn't feel that way right now. She felt sick. Haunted. She'd tried to leave all of that behind and simply not think about it, but sometimes it was harder than others.

She told Bella, "You should delete those photos. They could be dangerous."

"I don't see how."

"Just do it. Please."

"Sure. Okay. Is there something you want to tell me?"

"No. I'm just feeling a little under the weather. That time of month, you know?" Another lie, but one that was necessary.

The nightmare Mira's father had caused was over and she wanted to keep it that way.

By the time Lucas led Sloane to the place where he'd lost sight of the patrol, it was pouring rain.

Her body ached, and she was so tired she wasn't sure how she was going to keep putting one foot in front of the other much longer. Only the mental image of Gina's smiling face had kept her going this far.

Lucas came to a stop and she ran into his backpack. She lost her balance and grabbed his backpack to keep from toppling over onto the ground.

"We'll stop here," he said.

Sloane was too tired to argue. She wasn't sure exactly when she'd let him take over her mission, but right now she was too wiped out to care.

Her fever was back. She could feel it burning in her eyes and joints.

She slumped to the ground, easing her arms out of her pack. She hadn't realized she'd fallen asleep until she felt Lucas's hand on her face, waking her.

"You're not getting better."

"It hasn't been long enough for the antibiotics to do their job. Just let me have some more aspirin. I'll be fine."

He went away. Sloane fell asleep again, and when she woke, she was cold. Even though she knew it was stifling out here, even though the rain was nearly as warm as bathwater, she was still freezing.

Lucas was leaning over her, his face lined with concern. "I pitched the tent so you can get out of the rain."

If she'd had the energy, she would have kissed him for that. "Thanks."

She managed to drag herself through the flap of the camouflaged fabric. She stripped off the soggy armored vest and finally felt like she could breathe.

Lucas's head and shoulders filled the entrance of the tent. "Here's some aspirin. Drink as much as you can, okay?"

Grateful, she took both the pills and the canteen. "I just need a few minutes for the pills to kick in and I'll be good to go. The airstrip has to be close now."

Water dripped from his hair, sliding down his cheek to drip from his chin. "We have to be realistic about this. Neither one of us is in peak fighting form. Soma has at least four different men on patrol. He could have a whole lot more. We're outnumbered."

"Their four against our two is not outnumbered, especially when you consider our superior firepower."

"Just promise me you'll keep an open mind. If we need help, we ask for it."

"If we need it, I'll ask my own people—those I work with at the Edge. I won't ask for anything from my father."

Lucas's mouth tightened in frustration. "You're just as stubborn as he is. You know that, right?"

Sloane didn't like the comparison, but she had a feeling that was why Lucas made it. "Let me rest. I'll do whatever it takes to get Gina home safe."

"Even if it means calling your father?"

She hated herself for the weakness coursing through her and what that weakness might cost her. "I'll exhaust all other resources first, but yes. If Gina needs him, I'll call."

Lucas gave her a satisfied nod and backed out of the tent, zipping it closed.

Sloane fished the bottle of antibiotics out of her soggy

pocket and downed another dose. She really needed to be over this garbage and back in fighting form, because if she did break down and call her father, her life as she knew it would be over. He'd never again let her out of his control. She'd be back to a sheltered life of boredom and inadequacy. Because he'd know she'd failed.

Worse yet, *she'd* know it, too, and Sloane wasn't sure she could live with that.

She lay down, curling into a ball to get warm. She knew the aspirin would help. She just had to get through the next few minutes of bone-jarring shivers.

The tent flap opened. Lucas's head and shoulders pushed inside. "The whole tent is shaking," he said.

"I'm sorry. It'll pass in a minute."

"Scoot over," he ordered.

"Why?"

"Because you're cold, we're partners, and I'm going to help. Now, scoot over."

Sloane was too wrung out to argue. She moved to one side of the tiny space, putting her back to him. When he took off his vest, she knew what he was going to do. She also knew she wasn't going to turn down the warmth of another human right now. Not even if he were Soma himself.

He curled his big body around hers, sliding one arm under her cheek for a pillow and the other over her waist. Their wet clothes conducted his body heat into her, making her groan. He didn't talk. He didn't tell her how stupid she was for not leaving Gina's rescue to someone else. He stayed silent, with only the steady, even sound of his breathing as it brushed past her ear.

She dozed, and when she woke the shivering had stopped and she was blissfully warm. It was time to release Lucas from his obligations, but she couldn't bring herself to drive him away quite yet. She felt too good cradled inside his embrace like this. She could almost pretend that everything was okay, and she didn't want that to end.

"How long was I asleep?" she asked.

"Only a few minutes. Not long enough."

"I know. I also know that this is a serious case of bad timing."

His voice was low and quiet, laced with concern. "How do you feel?"

"Decent. Not great, but better than last night's round of shivering."

"You should have woken me."

Because she needed to rest, or because he could have held her? She almost asked the question, but couldn't quite get it out. "I promise to take a whole week off once we get home."

She felt him tense behind her and turned inside his embrace so she could look at him. "What?" she asked.

"Nothing. I'm just not exactly looking forward to going home."

"Why not?"

"My folks run a restaurant. I worked there every day growing up and the idea of going back turns my stomach."

"You're not close to them?"

"No. We're close. I just don't want to spend my life doing a job I hate, but I also can't face letting them down, you know?"

"Letting them down? How?"

His mouth flattened and he looked at the wall of the tent as if ashamed. "They need me to take over so they can retire. They deserve their retirement. They've worked hard for it. I can't tell them no. Once this job is done, I have to go back."

"If you don't want the restaurant, why don't they sell it?"

"They can't imagine me not wanting to follow in their footsteps. I don't have the heart to break it to them. It's hard not living up to your parents' expectations."

Sloane let out a flat laugh. "Don't I know it. At least your parents claimed you. I was a dirty little secret kept hidden at boarding school so no one would know the great general had mistakenly sired a girl."

"I'm sure it wasn't like that."

"That's because you're under his spell. Not that I blame you. The man has way too much influence and charm. Everyone around him worships him."

"He's a good man," said Lucas, clearly believing every word.

"No, he's good at *appearing* like he's a good man, but I know better. He didn't even go to his own wife's funeral. That's not something a good man does."

"I'm sure he had a reason."

She shook her head in futility. "It doesn't matter what I say. It never has. You and the other men who've worked for him will always take his side."

"I'm not taking sides. I'm just trying to make sense of what you're saying in the context of what I know about the general."

"That's just it. There's no sense to be made. If I'd been born a male, it would have been different. He probably would have taken me under his wing. But no matter how hard I tried, I couldn't live up to whatever mythical standards would turn me from an embarrassment into a daughter he could be proud of. At some point along the way, I simply stopped trying."

She'd wanted to stop caring, too, but she hadn't managed that feat yet. Maybe one day she'd find a way to look at herself without the shadow of failure hanging over her, but that day had not yet come. She wasn't good enough for her father, but she was one of Bella's best mercenaries, and that was going to have to suffice.

"He worries about you," said Lucas. "That's why he sent me."

"He only worries because he thinks I can't take care of myself—because I'm somehow lacking."

"I think you're wrong. I think he cares enough to worry."

She rolled her eyes. "Yeah, he used to say that when I was in boarding school and kept sneaking out with Gina to meet boys. He'd storm into the school, give me hell, shouting how much he cared and how he couldn't stand the thought of something happening to me. I bought that line when I was younger, but it rang pretty hollow after he forgot a few birthdays."

Lucas frowned as if trying to make sense of her words. "That doesn't sound like the man I know."

"Of course not. You see his public face—the one he wants you to see. Me, I got the real man, and let me tell you, the two are not the same."

"So how long has it been since you saw him?"

"Five years. I thought he'd show up for Mom's funeral three years ago, but he was a no-show. As usual." Sloane could still remember delaying the service for more than an hour, thinking he was just running late. She'd held out hope as long as she could, and as soon as they laid her mother's body in the ground, Sloane knew she was never again going to have anything to do with the man who'd fathered her.

"Did he ever tell you why he wasn't there?"

"Not a single word. Not a note or an e-mail. Nothing. Until you showed up. You were the first contact with him I've had in five years."

"No wonder you don't like me."

"Didn't," she said, correcting him.

"What?"

"Didn't like you. Right now, like this, I don't mind you nearly so much. You're kinda handy."

He smiled. "That's good to know. Very fair of you."

"Yeah, well, you're not supposed to shoot the messenger, right?"

"I wish you'd thought of that before you punched me. I'm still bruised."

She gave him a sheepish grin. "Sorry about that. It wasn't very nice of me."

"You could kiss it and make it better."

And just like that, Sloane wanted to. Here, in his arms, it was easy to forget that he had been sent by her father, that he still didn't believe her about the general. It was easy to forget everything except the warmth of his body and the rain pattering against the tent. She hadn't exactly been nice to him, and yet here he was, caring enough about her to keep her warm. Maybe it wasn't a big deal to him, but to Sloane, it was.

She swallowed, trying to distract herself from wanting to press her lips against his cheek, or mouth, or neck. His neck was closest. She could stretch an inch or two and close the distance, taste his skin. "I don't kiss a man if he's involved. Do you have a girlfriend?"

He gave her a slow, bone-melting smile. "Nope. But if I did, she sure wouldn't like what I'm thinking right now."

She wasn't going to ask. Not even with an invitation like that. But then her mouth opened and she said, "What?"

His fingers splayed against her back and slid up her spine, under her thin cotton shirt. The front of her shirt dragged up, along for the ride, snagging beneath her breasts. The feel of his work-roughened hands on her bare skin was almost too much sensation for her to handle. Her toes curled in her boots and a shiver coursed through her that had nothing to do with fever. His fingers slid up into her hair and he held her still while he leaned forward.

She watched his mouth as he got closer, knowing she shouldn't want this nearly as much as she did. She wasn't a woman easily swayed by a handsome face and a killer body. She didn't want to feel anything for a man who idolized her father, but she couldn't help it. She wanted him.

His lips touched hers, and when she didn't pull away, he increased the pressure, letting her feel him for real. He took his time, keeping things light until she was shaking with a need for more. His tongue fluttered across her bottom lip before disappearing. A groan vibrated his chest.

Sloane's breathing sped until she was dizzy. He wasn't giving her what she needed. Not even close.

She rolled him onto his back, held his face in her hands, and kissed him deep—open mouths, sliding tongues, nipping teeth. She didn't even care if she breathed anymore as long as she got her fill of his mouth.

He eased her shoulders back, breaking contact. She was panting, but she didn't care. His face had darkened along with his eyes, and in the dim confines of the tent, the rest of the world simply fell away.

Sloane wanted him. All of him. Right now. And she was used to getting what she wanted.

She went for his belt, telling him in no uncertain terms what she had in mind. Her hand brushed against his straining erection, making him suck in a breath.

This was wrong and out of control, but she didn't care. Her body was hot and eager, and after all that emotional talk, she needed something to ease the pressure inside of her. She felt raw and exposed and wanted him to be right there with her—completely exposed.

She'd worked the leather free when his hands captured hers, stopping her.

"What?" she asked. "I know you want this. You're way too hard to pretend otherwise."

He closed his eyes, but kept a tight hold on her hands. "I want it more than you know. But now is not the time. It's too dangerous. You're sick. We're out in the open. A patrol could come by at any minute. We can't." He said that last part like it hurt.

Sloane went cold as his words sank in. He was right. One kiss and she'd lost her head. Lucas Ramsey was potent stuff.

She would try not to forget again.

Sloane moved off of him and straightened her clothes. "I'm sorry. I should have been thinking."

"I'm kind of glad you weren't," he said. "It's been a long time since I've made a woman lose her head like that."

Clearly, he hung out with too many brain-dead women, because no woman in her right mind would turn down a treat like Lucas.

He rebuckled his belt, and she couldn't stop herself from watching his strong hands move, or from staring at the mouthwatering bulge in his pants. If they got out of this in one piece, she was going to have to convince him to show her what she was missing.

"Now you're just fishing for compliments."

He lifted her chin, pulling her eyes away from his package. "Hardly. Any more compliments from you and I'll forget my good intentions."

Part of her was wishing he would. She'd probably already have him inside her by now, which was enough of a thrill to keep her warm for a good, long while.

"Thank you," she told him, "for stopping me. I should have known better."

He gave her a playful wink. "I'm glad you didn't. I've been wondering what you would taste like from the moment I saw you in that ballroom."

"And?" she asked before she thought better of it. "How do I taste?"

"Good enough that I don't think I'm going forget about it anytime soon. Good enough that when we get back to civilization, I plan on convincing you to kiss me again. And next time, we won't have to stop."

He slipped out of the tent, leaving Sloane shaken and eager to see if he meant what he said.

She hadn't planned to like him, but her plans were being blown to hell one little bit at a time. Any other man would have either left her to suffer on her own, or, if he had come into the tent, he wouldn't have stopped her advances. The fact that Lucas did stop her advances changed the way she saw him. Sure, he admired her father, but a lot of people did. That didn't mean Lucas was like him.

For the first time, she was willing to give Lucas a chance. She wasn't completely convinced it wouldn't end in a fiery ball of chaos, but if he kissed her like that again, she was convinced it would be worth the cleanup efforts afterward.

Sloane pulled herself together, then left the relative comfort of the tent. Time to suck it up and get moving. The sooner they got Gina, the sooner she could see if Lucas was a man of his word, or if this thing between them would evaporate once they were out of danger.

Danger was one hell of an aphrodisiac. Chances were he wouldn't want to have anything to do with her as soon as he once again had his choice of women. Sloane wasn't exactly the most genteel, ladylike person on the face of the planet. And she sure as hell wasn't biddable. For most men, she was simply too much trouble—which worked for her. She felt the same way about most men.

It was still raining. He had a tarp draped over him as he ate one of the MREs she'd packed. When he saw her emerge, he lifted the tarp to make room for her to sit beside him.

She gladly accepted the offer and sat as close to him

as she dared. Heat seemed to roll off of him, sinking into her aching body and driving away the chill of the rain soaking through her clothes.

He offered her a bite of something she couldn't name. "Hungry?"

Sloane opened her mouth and let him feed her the lukewarm bite. It was something Italian, but beyond that, she couldn't recognize it. Whatever. It was calories and that was all that mattered.

"How much farther do you think we have to go?" she asked.

He fed her another bite. "Hard to say. Not far. I can't imagine he'd have patrols out beyond a reasonable dis tance."

"Are you sure they're patrols?"

"I caught a bit of conversation. My Spanish isn't great, but I think I heard Soma's name a couple of times."

"Anything about Gina?"

Lucas shook his head as he fed her more. "No, but they were talking about women."

"Imagine that. Men talking about women."

He grinned. "Yeah. Not exactly conclusive evidence, but they also mentioned a flight coming in."

"Did they say when?"

"No."

"We need to find that airstrip fast, then." Sloane slugged back some more water, then stood up, feeling the rain soaking through her clothes again. The tactical vest went back on, pressing her clammy clothes against her skin. She hated the wet chafe of fabric, but the sooner she found Gina, the sooner she could be back in nice, dry clothes.

Lucas slid his own vest back on, shoved the remains of his meal back into a pack, and hefted it onto his wide shoulders. "We should go east of here. That's the way the patrol went, and where I found something else."

"What?"

"That building the woman in the village was talking about. You up for a little hike? It's not far."

"On the map, the building was only a little north of Soma's airstrip. We've got to be close."

"I agree. Once we get our bearings, we'll find the airstrip and wait for that flight the men were talking about. Maybe Gina will be on it."

That sounded good. Anything that got Gina back and out of this country worked for Sloane.

They made quick work of packing the gear; then Lucas led them about half a mile to where a run-down building stood. They stayed hidden in the foliage, watching for signs of activity. There was none, and judging by the cobwebs across the single visible doorway, the place hadn't been used in a long time.

The building wasn't huge, but it was much larger than anything out here in the middle of nowhere had a right to be. It was a single story, and maybe ten thousand square feet. Made of concrete, the paint that had once camouflaged the building was peeling away. At least an acre of jungle had been cleared at one time, but after years of neglect was encroaching on the structure. Small, young trees had sprouted up, flourishing without the larger trees shading them from the sun. Even the area that had been paved with bricks near the entrance had begun to give way to the new growth of plants springing up.

"Weird, huh?" said Lucas. "No roads leading here— no way to bring in people or supplies."

"How did they even build it?"

"They had to have brought in construction materials via helicopter or hauled things through the jungle."

"For what purpose?" asked Sloane. "Even a drug lab would need a way to move product in and out easily."

"Only one way to find out. Interested?" he asked, lifting his eyebrows in challenge.

Why not? If the locals were as spooked by this place as they were led to believe, it would be a great place to hide. It was obvious the building had been abandoned. For years. "Sure. Let's go check it out."

Sloane approached the door with caution. From the thickness of the vegetation, no one had been this close in years, but she didn't want to cross any nasty trip wires or other traps meant to keep people away.

Now that she was closer, she could see that the knob was bent and rusted as if someone had bashed it with a heavy object. The door no longer latched closed, leaving a small gap between it and the frame.

She cleared away the cobwebs so they wouldn't hit her in the face, and pressed the door open with her boot. The only thing she could see inside was darkness.

Lucas shone a flashlight over her shoulder. "Let me go in first, just in case."

In case of what, she wasn't sure, but she stepped back and let him proceed with the light.

Weapon in hand, Sloane followed a few paces behind him, letting her eyes adjust to the dark confines of the building.

Water dripped from her clothes onto the concrete floor. How in the world they managed to pour this much concrete here boggled her mind, giving her something to distract herself from the creepy vibes she was trying to fight.

There was something sinister about this place—something not quite right.

Yellowed, moldy papers clumped together in the corners of the large open room. Three metal desks lined one wall, and on the opposite wall were several file cabinets. Two small rooms were partitioned off at one end. Through the dirty glass windows, she could see a gurney and IV stand in each room, along with remainders of other medical equipment.

Out of nowhere, a surge of fear slammed into Sloane. She saw a brief memory flash in her mind, its fragmented bits distorted and brilliant. She was young, small. She was screaming for her mother, fighting against the straps holding her down. People watched her through the windows, terrifying her with their cold stares. The room was too bright and there was a dark-haired woman standing over her with a needle in her hand and a fake smile on her bright red lips. Then the woman was flung aside and her father was there, taking her in his strong arms. She could smell sweat and fear clinging to his skin and hear his low, fervent words of comfort.

The memory faded as fast as it came, leaving Sloane reeling. She had no idea what that was. She'd never been in a hospital as a child. She couldn't remember a single time in her life when something like that had happened or why a dingy place like this would have caused the memory to come back to her.

It couldn't have been real. She would have remembered her father saving her like that.

"It looks like a clinic," said Lucas, "but what the hell is it doing out here in the middle of nowhere?"

Sloane didn't answer him. She couldn't. Her throat clamped down, cutting off words.

Lucas turned to her, and the wash of the flashlight over his familiar, angular features comforted her, easing the pressure in her chest.

"What is it?" he asked. He stood right in front of her, ducking his head so he could look into her eyes.

"I'm not sure, but I think I might have been here before. When I was a kid."

"Here? In this building?"

Sloane shook her head, unsure. "Or someplace like it." As soon as she said the words, the memory seemed to evaporate. As vivid as it had been for that one brief moment, she couldn't recall any of the details now as they faded like the remnants of a bad dream. "At least I think so."

"You look like you've seen a ghost."

"I can't have been here before. I'm sure I would have remembered a trip to another country. We never went anywhere when I was a kid. I went to boarding school when I was five." But she'd been younger than that in the memory, or whatever it was.

Lucas rolled a chair over and brushed the dust from it. "Sit down for a minute. You're so pale you're scaring me."

Sloane sat, thankful for the support. Her legs had gone weak, though she wasn't sure if it was from the fever or that odd flash

He crouched in front of her. "What made you think you've been here before?"

She tried to grasp onto a fragment of that flash of memory or dream or whatever it had been, but it was gone. "I don't know. I thought I remembered something, but I guess I was wrong."

He eyed her nervously and covered her forehead with his wide hand. "Are you sure you're feeling okay?"

"Yeah. I'm fine. Just spooked, I guess."

He didn't look convinced. "Sit tight. I'm going to check the place out, then grab the rest of our gear outside, okay?"

She nodded, her mouth dry. Even though she couldn't really remember any details of what she'd seen, she could still feel the fear that had overcome her. She tried to tell herself it was irrational, but that didn't seem to make her hands stop shaking.

By the time Lucas was back inside and had secured the door with one of the metal desks, all she wanted to do was be near him and have him wrap his arms around her as he had earlier.

Her fear and weakness pissed her off, but she was too tired to fight both them and herself, so she tried to ignore it all and focused on stripping out of her gear. Her wet clothes dragged against her skin, chafing. She was sick of being wet and miserable—hot one minute and freezing the next. She couldn't wait to get back to civilization where she could wear dry clothes and sleep on a real bed.

"What do you suppose they used this place for?" asked Sloane.

"You heard the woman from the tavern. Their friend came here and never went back. Maybe it has something to do with black-market organs."

"If that was the case, then why would they put it all the way out here?" she asked. "A human organ is viable for only a few hours after it's harvested, right?"

Lucas dug in one of the packs. "But there's that airstrip nearby, and it sure is a lot easier to hide a facility out here than it would be in a city. Plus, if they're preying on the locals, I think it would be easier to get away with killing people here. Who are they going to report the crime to? And if they do, who's going to come out here and stop it? If men like Soma are involved, chances are they have paid off the local authorities to look the other way."

The idea that someone could have done something so horrible to defenseless people made Sloane want to find that someone and beat the hell out of him. She had seen a lot of bad things, but surely she and Lucas had to be wrong. There had to be some reasonable explanation for a facility like this. "Maybe it isn't so sinister. It could be some group of doctors coming here to vaccinate the local kids or something. There may be a lot more people around here than we know about. It could be they used to come in on foot, which would explain why there was no road."

Lucas gave her a disbelieving shrug. "You could be right. I hope so."

He opened one of the doors at the end of the room. Sloane stood glued to the floor, fighting off the odd sense of panic clawing at her insides.

That whole memory thing had to be some kind of hallucination brought about by the meds. She couldn't think of any other reasonable explanation why this place would set her off, or why she'd be sweating and shaking now, just trying not to think about it.

"Hey," said Lucas from inside the small room. "There's a map on the wall in here. It's faded, but it shows the airstrip."

Sloane forced her feet to move and walk toward him. She peered into the room, bracing herself for some other odd hallucination, but none came. It was just an office with a desk and an ancient, clunky computer monitor.

Lucas pointed at the map. It was a line drawing—like a blueprint. As faded as it was, it was hard to make out, but she agreed that the area he pointed to looked like the plans for an airstrip.

"How far is it?"

"Half a mile."

Even with the rain, she was anxious to be out of this place. "Let's go, then."

Lucas took the pins out of the map, folded it up, and tucked it in his pack. "Just in case we need it."

"We won't," said Sloane, more to give herself a boost of confidence than anything. "We'll have Gina back and be on our way out of this country tonight."

He must have seen some insecurity or fear lurking inside her, because he turned to her with a look so warm with compassion she could almost feel it on her skin. He reached out and touched her face, stroking his thumb across her bottom lip. "Don't worry, Sloane. Things will all work out. Gina will be just fine."

She wasn't used to anyone showing her that kind of compassion, and it caught her off guard.

"You never asked me about her—why I'd risk my life for her. Why not?"

Lucas gave a casual shrug. "It doesn't matter who she is. She needs help, so we help her. It's pretty simple."

"Not to most people, it wouldn't be."

He winked and grinned, melting Sloane's insides. "Guess I'm not most people."

Chapter 10

Adam Brink stepped out of his private jet onto the tarmac, squinting against the evening sun. Heat from the pavement wafted over him, making his skin prickle with sweat. As he'd ordered, a helicopter was fueled up and waiting for him. He'd fly to Soma's airstrip, verify the woman's identity, and if she was a match, he'd have her in Dr. Stynger's hands by this time tomorrow.

After he'd taken what he needed from her.

The small electronic device in his attaché case had been designed by one of the eggheads at the labs. The scientist had been so excited by the challenge of creating the device, he hadn't bothered to ask Adam why he needed it.

It was just as well. Adam had no desire to kill the man who'd helped him.

His phone vibrated at his belt. He retrieved it and read the text message. "Possible subject located. Male. WV."

Adam stopped dead in his tracks, fighting the urge to turn around and hunt down this new subject.

It might be Eli.

But what if it wasn't? What if this man wasn't even on the List? He'd be wasting his time in the air, when he was only hours away from a target that was right here, waiting for him.

She sure as hell wasn't Eli, but she might be a solid lead. A bird in the hand . . .

Adam texted back a confirmation code, telling his contact he'd received the message and would proceed to Wyoming once his work here was done. By that time, he'd have an encrypted message giving him as much information about the new target as Dr. Stynger's men had.

In the meantime, he'd go meet Gina Delany and see if she was going to be of any use. If not, he could let Soma do with her as he pleased.

Riley Conlan hated asking for favors, but in this case, he'd make an exception.

He knocked on Bella's open door. A normal business owner would have had papers strewn across her modern glass-topped desk, but not Bella. The pieces of her favorite .45 were laid out in a neat array, as she lovingly cleaned them.

The smell of gun oil overpowered the faint, sweet smell of Bella's favorite perfume. She'd been wearing it since they were kids, giving him at least one thing he could get her for her birthday he knew she'd love. Besides another weapon.

She looked up at him, her stormy gray eyes crinkled with a smile of greeting. Her black hair was tucked into a sloppy ponytail that stuck out the back of her baseball cap. Her face was freshly scrubbed, devoid of makeup, and with one long leg tucked under her, she reminded him of the scrawny ten-year-old who'd snuck into his house the first night they'd met. At twelve, he'd been old enough to see the bruise on her face and her split lip and know what it meant. He'd hid her from her stepfather for the first time that night, but not the last.

"What's up?" she asked as she slid a cotton pad through the gun's barrel.

Riley forced himself to say the words. "I think I need a raise."

Bella lifted a dark brow. "You think?"

He rubbed his hand over his head, feeling the brush of his buzz cut tickle his hand. "Yeah."

"Care to elaborate on that?"

He wasn't sure how much he wanted his coworkers to know, but this was Bella. She was like a sister to him, and he had to tell someone.

He shut the door to her office and sat in one of the chairs across from her. "I might be having a baby."

Metal clunked against glass as the weapon slid from her fingers and hit the desk. "You're serious?"

She laughed as if he'd just told a great joke. Riley sat in still silence, waiting for her to realize this was no punch line.

He nodded, not sure if he wanted to laugh or cry. This was all so much so fast. He wasn't even sure what to think about it. "There's this woman, Lucille Rosemond."

"Since when? You never date. You're too damn busy working. Or back at the farm, fixing stuff for your mom."

"It was a lark. I was a little . . . antsy."

"You mean horny."

He shrugged, refusing to be embarrassed. "That, too."

"So who is she?"

He stalled for a moment, realizing how little he knew about Lucille. "She's a model. Tall, leggy, make a deal-with-the-devil gorgeous."

"How long have you been seeing her?"

Riley felt his face heat. "Twice. Once for coffee. Once for . . . you know."

"Sex. I only *wish* I knew right now," she said with a wistful sigh. "It's been way too long since I had non-battery-operated company."

He cringed, holding up his hands to ward off any more. "I do not want to hear even one more word about your company—batteries included or not."

She grinned and shook her head. "So you forgot the condoms and now I have a niece or nephew on the way?"

"Actually it broke. The condom. We both got tested right away to make sure we were safe, and that all came back fine. That was six weeks ago. I thought it was over, but then I got this call."

"What call?"

"She left a message for me while I was in Israel last week. She was crying. Hysterical. I understood only part of it, but I definitely heard the word *pregnant*." That, and how her career was over and how angry she was at him. Not that he could blame her. Neither one of them had planned this.

"And you haven't taken the time to pick up a phone and ask? You've been back two days."

"I've called. Repeatedly. She hasn't returned my calls yet."

"So go to her house. What the hell is wrong with you?"

Riley looked at the wall behind her, unable to meet her gaze. "I don't know where she lives."

"But you're having a baby with her?"

"I know. It's crazy. It's not like I planned this. I just went out to have a little fun. Hell, all the rest of the guys hook up with women they don't know all the time."

"Yeah, but you're not other guys. You're better than that. You're responsible."

"Maybe sometimes I get a little tired of being responsible."

Bella stood and moved around the desk. She sat next to him and took his hand in hers. Her fingers were slim and cool and slippery from the gun oil, but it was nice having someone reach out to him. He felt completely at a loss, floundering for some toehold on reality.

He might be a dad. How the hell could something like that even be possible? He was nothing like his own father had been: steady, rock solid, dependable. Riley was too wild, too impatient.

Dad would never have gotten a woman he hardly knew pregnant.

"You can have a raise," said Bella. "And I'll have a baby to fuss over. It'll work out. You'll see."

"I'm setting a bad example for the girls." His three younger sisters. "I promised Dad I'd take care of them."

"And you do. You're putting them all through college and taking care of your mom to boot. You're out at the farm, keeping the place from falling down around her ears, when it would be a lot cheaper just to move her into town and sell the land."

"It's her home. I can't take that away from her."

Bella squeezed his hand. "And that is why I love you. You're a good man. You're going to be a kick-ass dad. So go out there and find your pregnant, leggy model and figure out how you're going to make it work."

When she said it like that, it seemed pretty clear. "I'm not sure how to find her."

"Boy, wouldn't it be nice if we had someone who was good with data? Someone who could probably hack into any database in the state? Someone who could find your baby mama and give you her address?"

Mira. Duh.

Riley grabbed Bella's head and kissed the top of her ball cap. "Thanks, piglet. You're the best."

He left the office, hearing her growl at him for calling her by her hated nickname from down the hall.

*   *   *

Payton was waiting in the restaurant when General Robert Norwood arrived. The man had aged since they'd last seen each other, but Payton figured the general was thinking the same thing about him.

Payton rose, shook Bob's hand, and they both sat.

"Any word from Sloane?" asked Bob.

"None. You?"

"Lucas left one message. I tried to call back, but no one answers."

"I'm sure she's fine. She's tough, smart, and well trained."

Bob nodded. The waiter took their order and disappeared. Payton had chosen this place because the staff was discreet and the tables were spaced out enough to limit the possibility of eavesdropping. Neither one of them wanted their conversation to be overheard. He wasn't even sure how smart it was for them to be meeting at all.

"I need you to tell me what you know," said Payton. There was no need to elaborate about what. Bob knew.

"I swear I haven't heard a word about the project in years. I thought it was as dead as you did."

"As much as I want to believe otherwise, someone has the List. That much is obvious."

"I told you I destroyed all the copies I knew existed— hunted them down one by one."

"Apparently you missed one. The question is, what are we going to do about it?"

"I don't know," said Bob. "I worry that if we do anything, it will expose us. If one of the others is dabbling again, they're not going to want us to know about it."

"How many of the original group are still alive?"

"Not counting the subjects? Six. You, me, and the senator. The other three are in the private sector now, all apparently legit. I checked before I came."

"Could it be someone on the outside stumbled across a copy of the List?"

"It's possible, but they wouldn't know what it meant if they did."

"Unless they were one of the subjects," said Payton. "One of the children now grown. Like Adam and Lorenzo."

"Hell," spat Bob. "They weren't supposed to remember."

"The doctors were wrong. They were wrong about a lot of things."

"You work with some of those kids at the Edge every day. Have you seen any signs of the memories returning?"

"I see signs of stress. It could be memories, or it could be the job. There's no way to know for sure without asking outright. I don't think that's wise."

"Neither do I. We have to be cautious. Anything we do to stir up memories is just going to make their lives worse. We owe them more than that."

Guilt choked Payton for a moment. He took a sip of water, but it did little to clear away his past mistakes. "That we do."

Bob ran his hand over his balding head. "I remember a few of the names on the List. I'll check up on them, discreetly. I'll also ensure that Lorenzo Soma is stopped. Permanently. He's a threat to my daughter, and that can't be tolerated."

"Agreed. A threat to one of them is a threat to all. I think you need to visit the senator as well. He needs to understand that we can't let this get out of control."

"He'll do what I say," said Bob, completely confident. "I know enough about him to ruin his career if he doesn't."

"Blackmail?"

"An ugly word for an effective tool, but yes, if that's what it takes."

Payton wasn't squeamish when it came to the tools of the trade. He'd do whatever it took to protect Bella and the others. Even if it meant killing the general himself.

"I'll keep my ear to the ground," said Payton. "Maybe do a little careful nosing around. We have a therapist on retainer at the Edge. Some of our employees see him. I'll have a little look at his files. If the memories are returning, we'll know."

"The question is, what will we do if they are?" asked Bob.

Payton shook his head. He had no answers. "We'll just have to make sure no one believes them. For their own good."

Chapter 11

"I see six men down there," Sloane said. "All armed. All bored."

Lucas took the binoculars she offered him.

He'd found them a nice, elevated place to scout from that was shielded by lots of foliage. The airstrip was out of pistol range, but it was as close as they could get without being seen. They lay flat on their bellies, watching the men around the airstrip in the shallow depression below.

Lucas peered through the binoculars, counting men and weapons. The airstrip was only long enough to handle small planes, so there wouldn't be a lot of unexpected company from that direction. The road leading here, however, was another story.

The runway had once been paved, but now cracks and potholes were obvious even from a quarter mile away. Jungle plants had sprouted up along the edge, working hard to retake the ground that had once been theirs.

"There are going to be more men inside the shack," he whispered. "And possibly more doing a perimeter sweep that we can't see."

"I can see through the window if I move to the rise on the west."

"Better not chance moving too much. We'll end up in a firefight, and if Soma sees any signs his men are down, he may not even land."

"So you think it's safer to wait and take them all on at once when Soma lands?" asked Sloane. "We'll be shooting right at Gina."

"At least she'll be where we can find her rather than in a plane on her way to who knows where."

"I'd really like to start picking these guys off—put the odds a little more in our favor."

"One gunshot and everyone will know we're here. They could call Soma and warn him off."

Sloane let out a long, frustrated sigh. "You're right. I don't like it, but I think we have to wait."

"I'm going to sneak closer and see if I can hear when they're expecting a flight."

"Wish I'd brought my parabolic mic," she muttered. "Or some comm gear."

"You weren't exactly expecting help on this mission. Don't worry. I'll be quick." He pointed to his right. "I'll go that way through the trees. If shit goes down, that's where not to shoot."

"Right. Got it."

And because he couldn't stop himself, he cupped his hand around the back of her neck and pulled her to him for a quick kiss for luck. She came to him easily, her mouth responding to the touch of his in a hot, sweet instant. Her lips parted, and Lucas couldn't resist the invitation. He deepened the kiss and shifted so he could get a better angle. He cursed the tactical vests between them for denying him the alluring press of her breasts against his chest.

A soft sigh rose from her, almost inaudible, but that faint noise was enough to get his blood pumping and make his cock swell.

Sloane went to his head fast and hard, making him

forget the rest of the world. While his mouth was on hers and the silky feel of her hair filled his palm, nothing else seemed important. Time slowed, and all that mattered was the taste of her on his tongue, her breath in his lungs and the need for more.

If he didn't stop now, he wouldn't be able to in a few more seconds.

Cursing the need for haste, Lucas pulled away. Sloane followed him up, and he had to grab her ponytail in his fist to keep her from ruining his good intentions.

He was breathless when he said, "I need to go now, while the light is still good."

She nodded. Her mouth was dark pink and shiny from their kiss. Her cheeks were flushed and her pupils had swallowed up all but a thin ring of green in her eyes. "You should go."

He wanted to lean forward and give her just one more short, fast kiss, but he didn't dare. Instead, he pushed himself to his feet, adjusted his pants around his erection, and slipped silently into the trees.

He promised himself that as soon as this was over, he'd kiss her the way he wanted—thoroughly, not missing a single spot of her sweet body. It was that promise that kept him moving toward his target, that promise that made him shove his head into the game and figure out a way to rescue Gina.

He wasn't sure if Sloane would still be willing to have anything to do with a washed-up soldier once they were on their way out of here, but he was going to do his best to make sure she was as primed and ready to give it a shot as he was.

Lucas cleared his mind of clutter as he neared the east side of the shack. He hadn't broken the tree line yet, nor would he unless he had no other choice. The thick concealment of the jungle was his best friend right now, and he wanted to keep it that way.

He peered through the open window and saw three men at a table playing cards. Their words were garbled and hard to understand, but he managed to get close enough to hear snippets of conversation.

He listened for close to an hour, hearing nothing of use—just grumbling about being stuck out here instead of the cushier duties awaiting them at Soma's villa.

He'd just shifted his weight to ease the pain growing in his knee when he heard the rumble of a small aircraft.

Lucas eased back away from the shack, the slow movement taking too damn long, but necessary. Once he was clear, he sprinted through the trees back to Sloane.

He heard the aircraft land and the engine shut off.

By the time he reached Sloane, her fingers were clenched so tight around the binoculars, she was shaking.

"Who is it?" asked Lucas as he assumed a firing position and grabbed up a rifle.

The plane landed, but no one got out. "I don't know. I can't see through the windshield. There's a glare."

Lucas peered through the scope on her rifle.

Armed men surrounded the plane. Finally, the door opened. A stocky man wearing body armor and a shoulder holster hopped down onto the aging pavement.

"Is that Soma?" asked Lucas.

"I don't know. I've never seen him."

"Trade me," said Lucas. "Take the rifle. You're a better shot than I am."

She gave him an odd, almost skeptical look, but took the weapon from his hands. "I'm not shooting until I see Gina."

"That's a good idea. You'll blow through the fuselage like a tin can."

Lucas tried to keep his breathing slow and even as they waited. Nervousness bore down on him. A trickle of sweat slid into his eyes.

The stocky man surveyed the area, spoke to one

of the guards, then turned back and poked his head through the open airplane doorway.

"There's definitely someone else in there," she said.

"Yeah. Did you see the man he spoke to?"

"I did."

"That's likely the head guard—the guy in charge of the others, or at least with the most seniority. When the shooting starts, try to take him out as soon as you can."

"I'd rather take out Soma."

"If you think you've got a bead on him, go ahead, but the head guard will be the one the men look to for guidance. Without him, we'll have more chaos, and today, chaos is on our side."

Another man came out of the plane dragging a young woman along with him. He had a firm grip on her arm.

She was petite, blond, and apparently unharmed. Her hair was a mess, and she had on a short skirt and ridiculous strappy heels, as if she'd been dressed for an evening on the town instead of a trip into the jungle.

"Gina," breathed Sloane, her voice radiating with fear.

Lucas put a staying hand on her back. "Easy," he whispered. "We've found her. Now we just have to get her back in one piece. No sudden movements, okay?"

The man holding her—the man Lucas assumed was Soma by his suit and the way the other men shifted a nervous step away from him—dragged her so she was in front of him.

"I don't have a clear shot," said Sloane. "Between that brick of a man and Gina, he's completely covered."

"Wait. We'll give him a minute to relax and feel safe. He'll let his guard down and then you can take him out."

Her shoulders moved as she pulled in a deep breath and let it out. Lucas moved his hand away, worried he might mess up her shot. She was in control of herself now. He didn't have to worry about her doing anything foolish. Sloane was too solid for that.

Soma moved with Gina and his entourage following him until they were out of sight inside the little shack.

"Shit," spat Sloane.

"It's okay. I have an idea. I'll sneak back around to the side of the shack while you start picking off the guards as fast as you can. I'll go in and get her if you aren't able to take out Soma before I do."

"As soon as I open fire, they'll know we're here. They'll run."

"Take out the plane and they won't go anywhere."

"It's too far for Constance."

"The wings are full of fuel. Even if you don't blow the plane up, they won't get far without fuel."

"Okay. We'll do this your way."

Lucas grinned, barely resisting the urge to kiss her. "Give me seven minutes to get over there, then open fire."

Sloane looked at her watch, then back at him. "Be safe, okay?"

"You do like me. I knew you would."

The faintest smile curved her mouth. "In your dreams. I just don't want to leave any of my weapons behind. I like my weapons."

"You like me more."

"You don't make things explode."

He raised his brows and said, "Just wait and see if I don't," before slipping off into the trees.

Arrogant man.

Too bad he was right. Sloan did like him despite her best sense of reason. Despite his connection to her father.

If it hadn't been for his calming touch a moment ago,

she might have lost it right there. Seeing Gina in the hands of that kidnapping bastard, surrounded by armed goons, was nearly more than she could stand.

But he had touched her and settled her nerves, giving her some much-needed mental space to think clearly.

Lucas was always touching her. She'd never before met a man as touchy-feely as him, but she wasn't about to complain now. Unless she was complaining about having to wait to see if this attraction between them was more than a case of adrenaline poisoning.

Sloane checked her watch. Five more minutes.

Below, the men milled around, making a show of being vigilant. She wasn't fooled. She'd seen them when they thought no one was looking. It wasn't until Soma showed up that they started playing the role.

Sloane's scope moved to the shack in the distance. She couldn't see through the windows from this angle, but she could almost feel Gina in there, so fragile and scared. She was depending on Sloane to get her out of this mess. Alive.

Sloane was gripping her rifle too tight. She forced herself to relax and pretend that the stakes weren't quite so high. She needed to treat this like any other mission. Get in, get the job done, get out. Simple, quick, effective. Just like she always was.

The men below wouldn't be the first scum she'd killed. She wasn't a novice. She knew her way around a fight, and this was just another day on the job.

She checked her watch again. Two minutes left.

Sloane scanned the tree line, searching for signs of Lucas. She saw none—no movement or flashes of color that didn't belong. She knew he was there, though. There wasn't a chance in hell that Lucas would abandon her and leave her out here alone to fight for her friend's life.

He was a better man than that.

Time was ticking down. Sloane gauged the distance

to her first target again. He hadn't moved. The wind hadn't changed and in another sixty seconds, her target was going to be dead.

Sloane counted down in her head, pulled in a breath and let it out as she fired.

The shot was clean—right through his head. He crumpled without raising an alarm. A second later, the report of her rifle was heard below. Sloane was already taking her second shot when all hell broke loose.

Men scampered for cover. She spotted one man hiding on the wrong side of a battered truck, unaware of the direction the shots had come from.

She fired, hitting him squarely in the chest. He wasn't dead, but he would be soon. As it was, he was out of the fight, and that was what mattered.

Sloane heard a commotion coming from the direction of the shack. She looked up to see Soma crouched, shielded by men, and Gina, running for the plane.

Sloane shifted her aim and fired at the near wing of the small plane. The round ripped through the wing and fuel spewed out in an arcing spray. She was about to fire again and try to ignite the fuel, but a quick check through her scope showed her that Gina was too close to the plane to risk it.

The stocky man shouted an order, pointing toward Sloane's general location. Several machine guns spun her way and a hail of gunfire ripped through the leaves.

Sloane pressed her head to the ground, hoping none of the shots got lucky. Not that she'd care if they did. She'd be dead, because the only thing the bullets could hit was her head.

The deep boom of Lucas's .45 echoed from below.

She looked up and saw him duck behind the shack to avoid a volley of bullets.

The plane's engine started. Gina was gone from sight. So was Soma. The only way to stop them now was to keep shooting the plane, but with Gina on it, Sloane couldn't take that chance. If she ignited the fuel, the whole thing could go up in flames.

Besides, men were running toward Lucas. If she didn't stop them, he was a dead man. And she only had three rounds left in her rifle before she had to waste time reloading.

Sloane targeted the man closest to Lucas's position, aimed, and fired. His sprint put her aim off, and she only winged him in the arm. He fell, but wasn't injured enough to stop him from lifting his weapon at Lucas.

She fired again, and this time, he didn't move.

Sloane took her last shot, hit one of the men in the hip, but didn't wait to see if he went down or not. She had to reload.

By the time she had a fresh magazine in place, Lucas was gone. She had no idea where he went, and the sudden spurt of panic that hit her made her hands tremble.

One of the men had figured out her location and was running toward her, using the lull in her shots to get close—close enough that he was a real threat.

Ensconced behind a stack of cement blocks, with only the barrel of his weapon visible, Sloane had no shot.

The plane lifted from the ground, roaring over the trees so low Sloane felt it rattle in her chest.

Gina was gone. Lucas was missing, and if she didn't take this fucker out, she was a dead woman.

Four men sprinted toward their buddy—the one who'd figured out where she was. She couldn't get a clean shot, but she fired her weapon anyway, causing them to hit the ground. It wasn't doing her any good, but it was slowing them down, giving her time to find a clean shot.

Her mind was clogged with fear and worry. Was Gina's plane going to go down because she'd shot it? Was Lucas injured, bleeding out somewhere nearby?

Stop it.

She ordered herself to suck it up, calm down, and move the fuck on. She had things to do.

Sloane found a sliver of calm and focused on that, making herself go through the motions. Acquire her target, aim, breathe, fire, repeat.

Another man fell, but the one behind the cement blocks was still a problem.

Dirt spewed up only a yard away from her face.

Sloane ignored it and found another target. It took two shots to finish him off, and by the time she did, the dirt geyser was only two feet away.

Time for a retreat, but to where? She couldn't leave Lucas alone out here if he was injured.

She grabbed her rifle off the tripod and took cover behind a thick tree. She slung the rifle strap over her shoulder and pulled out her 9mm pistol. At this distance, it was just as lethal and a lot easier to handle.

Bark exploded to the left of her shoulder as the men fired on her location.

Her first shot was blind, hopefully making the men duck and cover while she popped her head around the trunk and took a sighted shot.

Her aim wasn't great, but she got close enough to keep one of the men pinned.

Suddenly, her target flew sideways as another deep boom sliced through the air.

Lucas. He was okay—at least okay enough to pull a trigger.

She let herself rejoice, let it give her courage as she popped out again and found another target. This time, her aim was good and the guard grunted in pain. She hadn't killed him with a shot to the shoulder like that, but it was his right shoulder, so she figured his aim would be for suck from here on out.

He crawled back behind the cement barricade to join his buddy.

"Got a clear shot?" yelled Lucas.

"No. You?"

"Get ready. On three."

Sloane immediately started counting in her head. One. Two. Three.

She peeked around the tree, bracing herself for anything. What she saw was Lucas stand up, visible as daylight, drawing the fire of the man behind the barrier.

Panic seized her hard as she realized he was going to get himself killed.

Without thinking, she charged the barrier, running. Elevation gave her just the scantest view of the top of a man's head. She took aim, firing as fast as the weapon would allow.

The enemy fired. Lucas grunted in pain and fell backward.

Sloane screamed in rage, running toward the gunman. Her third shot plowed into the man's skull, and a pink vapor erupted into the air.

There was still one more man behind the cement blocks, but by the time she got there, his hands were raised in surrender. Tears streamed down his face; blood soaked his shoulder. Fast, desperate words bubbled from his mouth as he begged for his life or prayed to God. Maybe both.

Sloane couldn't pull the trigger. Not now.

She kicked the weapons away from him and pointed at a spot on the ground a few feet away. "Lie down."

He hobbled and sat, his whole body shaking. He must not have understood her words, but it would have to do.

Sloane kept her weapon on him and eyes wide-open, looking for signs of any other survivors.

The need to go to Lucas and check on him screamed

through her body, but she didn't dare turn her back on this man with so many weapons lying about.

She went to the dead man, searched him for handcuffs or something she could use to tie the man up with. She found nothing.

There was nothing else she could do on the spur of the moment. Her plastic handcuffs were back with her gear and Lucas might be bleeding out. She wasn't going to take the time to go back for them.

She approached her prisoner, and with a hard, brutal blow to the back of the head, knocked him unconscious.

Without dwelling on her actions too long, she sprinted over to where she saw Lucas fall. She passed the shack, where she saw three men lying dead—men she hadn't killed. Lucas's handiwork.

She veered around the building until she neared the place she'd seen him last. He was in amongst the fallen leaves and rotting vegetation. She could hear him wheezing. He wasn't dead.

Relief made her body feel heavy as she closed the last few feet.

He was on his side, propping himself up on one elbow. Blood ran down the back of his head.

She moved around to his front, searching for signs of the gunshot wound. Her throat was too tight to speak. Her fingers trembled visibly as they moved over his face and chest and arms.

"Vest," he wheezed out. "I'm okay."

Sloane ripped open the straps on his protective vest. She shoved his shirt up, revealing bare skin. He was whole and healthy, though a bruise was already forming along his ribs.

"The shot knocked the wind out of me," said Lucas. "I hit my head."

Which would explain the blood.

She forced herself to calm down. Breathe. Let her panic fade so she could react. She moved behind him and gently inspected the damage. "There's a small cut on your scalp, but it's bleeding like hell. Stay put. I'll go get the first aid kit."

He pushed to his feet. "I'm going with you. I'm okay to walk."

Sloane wasn't so sure, but she refused to argue with a grown man. Instead, she looped his arm around her and shoved her shoulder under his to support him.

He looked down at her and gave her a forced smile. "If I'd known all I had to do was get shot to have you hold on to me, I would have done it sooner."

She stifled the urge to smack him. "Less talky, more walky."

"Taskmaster."

Sloane looked at the ground and blinked against the tears of relief stinging her eyes. She held him tighter, thanking God he was alive and well. She couldn't even imagine what she'd do if he'd gotten seriously hurt. Or killed.

The thought made her insides freeze over until she started to shiver.

She settled him down next to their gear, sparing a quick glance at the man she'd knocked out. He was still out cold, but she found two sets of cuffs and shoved them in her pocket.

Once she had a clean wad of gauze pressed against Lucas's head, she had him hold it in place. "I'll be right back. Need to secure the hostage."

She made quick work of cuffing the man's hands together behind his back and his ankle to that of one of the dead guards. He wasn't going anywhere for a while, which worked for her.

She ran back to Lucas, who watched her with guilty

eyes. "I'm sorry," he said. "I didn't have a clean shot on Soma, and I wasn't fast enough to get to them before they got on the plane."

"Neither was I," she said. "We'll find another way."

He leaned his head back against a tree and let out a rough sigh. "You know what this means, don't you?"

"What?"

"We need to call for help."

Sloane nodded. "I'll make the call to Bella."

"And your father?"

She shook her head. "I won't call him, but I won't stop you. If he can send men to help us find Gina, then I won't turn them away."

"Fair enough, I guess."

The thought of taking anything from her father turned her stomach, but that was just too bad. If Gina needed her father's help, then that was what she was going to get.

Lucas went stiff and his head jerked up as he looked at the sky. "You hear that?"

Sloane listened, but all she heard was the racket of the jungle behind her. "No."

"There's a helicopter and it's getting closer."

"Our mystery man?" she asked. "The one who was coming for Gina?"

"That would be my guess."

Sloane set up her rifle again and settled in behind it as the helicopter touched down. She watched as a tall, dark-haired man got out from behind the controls. "He's alone," she told Lucas.

He shifted so he was lying beside her, looking through binoculars. "I think I've seen that guy before."

"You have? Where?"

"I don't remember."

Sloane watched as he moved cautiously away from the helicopter, surveying the damage they'd caused. He crouched, pressed his fingers against the ground and brought them to his nose, smelling the spilled fuel. He was wearing protective gear, which meant she was going to need to get a head shot. She moved her finger to the trigger.

"Wait," said Lucas. "You can't kill him."

"Why not? He's the reason Gina's in this mess. He's the one who wants her for some reason. I kill him, Soma has no one to sell her to—or whatever he's doing."

Lucas laid down the binoculars. "Soma may also have no more reason to keep her alive."

Shock rattled Sloane and she hastily moved her finger from the trigger. She hadn't thought about that, though she sure as hell should have.

"What do you suggest? Should I take out a leg?"

The man below moved up the slope toward them, heading straight for the man Sloane had restrained.

"No. Hang on," Lucas whispered.

The man was close now, only a few yards away. She pulled her rifle back so it wouldn't be visible and held her breath, not daring to move any more for fear of being seen. Under the overhang of low branches where they lay, she didn't think he could see them there, but as close as he was getting, she didn't want to leave anything to chance.

He scanned the area again as he knelt down next to the wounded man. He slapped his face, dragging a groan from the guard. After several more rough pats to the face, the newcomer finally gave up and pulled a phone from his belt.

"What happened?" he asked in a clear American accent.

"Do you still have her?" He paused, listening to whoever was on the other end of the line. "Of course I still want her, but I'm not risking a trip to you until you can guarantee it's safe. I will come Tuesday night. Late.

Do you think you can manage to regain control of one woman by then?"

He lifted his gaze, his eyes narrowing as he scanned the trees. "I know how well fortified your villa is. I also know that if you make another mistake, it will be the last time we do business. I expect her to be waiting when I arrive. I don't want a repeat of this time." He disconnected the call and replaced the phone on his belt.

With one last study of the area, he turned, got back in his helicopter, and flew away.

Sloane let out the breath she'd been holding.

"I remember where I saw him now," said Lucas, sounding vaguely sick.

"Where?" she asked.

"Your father's office."

Chapter 12

Adam flew straight back to his jet. The urge to go after Gina now that he was so close was hard to resist, but he wasn't going to risk his life going into an unknown situation. Better to go find the man in Wyoming now, before he disappeared again, and let Soma fight off Gina's rescuers. If Soma failed to beat back Sloane and her mercenary friends—and Adam knew the general's daughter was definitely at the root of this inconvenience—so be it. He'd find Gina's body and take from it what he needed. The data would still be there whether she was dead or alive.

And if Soma succeeded in taking down Sloane, it would serve the general right for not cooperating with him. Next time Adam went to the general, maybe he'd think twice about turning him away empty-handed.

Adam still wasn't convinced that Sloane's name wasn't on the List. She'd been in Dr. Stynger's hands long enough to be useful, despite the general's protestations to the contrary.

All he needed was a few minutes with her and he'd know for sure. In fact, all he really needed was her body. There was no way she'd know anything useful; the general would never have allowed her close contact with any of the major players in the Threshold Project.

He'd let things fall where they may and stay far enough away that none of the backlash would touch him. He couldn't risk his own safety now—not when he was so close to finding Eli.

Once he and his brother were together again, he'd take down Dr. Stynger and her whole operation, but until that day, he needed her too much to piss her off. Until that day, he'd be her good little soldier and bring her back anyone he found on the List.

Riley was waiting on Lucille's doorstep when she came home. The September sun was still hot enough to make him sweat, but even if it hadn't been, facing up to the woman who was probably carrying his child was enough to make any man sweat.

He didn't know her. He didn't even know if he liked her. He had no business having a child with her, but it was a little too late to be worrying about that. *Closing the barn door after all the horses were out,* as his dad would have said.

He was struck again by how pretty she was. How elegant. How far out of his farm-boy league.

Her hair was a wild, artful mess, and her microminiskirt showed off enough leg to make his mouth go dry. Based on the overdone makeup she was probably coming from a job.

She saw him and came to a dead stop. Her voice was cold and clipped. "What are you doing here?"

"I thought we should talk."

She dug in her giant purse and pulled out her keys, unlocking her door. "Fine, but make it quick. I'm having people over tonight."

The fact that she hadn't invited him stung, but he understood it was going to take them some time to get to know each other, to find common ground.

When she let him into her home, he was shocked by how sterile it was. A mix of chrome and glass with matte stone accents. Nothing at all like the worn wood and soft fabrics of his childhood home. Even his own apartment—which he used more as a hotel than anything—had more give than this place. A person could sit down and prop their feet up on his coffee table. Not here. Lucille's was glass, topped with jagged metal modern artwork.

It hit him in that moment that this was no place to raise a kid. He was going to have to buy her new furniture if she planned on staying here. And after being in her home for only a few seconds, he could tell there was no way he'd ever convince her to move into his tiny place.

She was an upscale kind of girl all the way.

"Talk," she ordered, propping her hands on her slim hips.

"How are you feeling?" he asked, since he didn't know where else to start. "Are you sick at all?"

"I'm fine." And that was it. She was done talking, leaving him hanging, scrambling for the next bit of conversation.

Time to cut to the chase. "Did the doctor give you a due date?"

"For . . . ?"

"The baby."

She blinked her wide blue eyes twice before answering. "There is no baby."

Confused, he said, "But I got your message. You said you were pregnant."

"I was. Now I'm not."

Understanding dawned and he couldn't help but reach for her. No wonder she was so cold. She was hurting. She'd lost the baby.

A ripple of grief swept through him, but he couldn't be selfish right now. Later, he promised himself, he'd feel whatever he wanted, but right now he had to be strong for her. Support her. "I'm so sorry."

His hand moved toward her and she stepped back, dodging him.

"Don't be. It was a simple procedure. I'm already back at work."

Procedure?

Shock rocked him back on his heels. "You had an abortion?"

"I told you I'd take care of it on the phone."

Numbness settled into his bones, chilling him. He'd just gotten used to the idea of having a child with a woman he barely knew and now this. "I thought you meant you'd see a doctor and get checked out."

"And then what? I'd get fat and lose my modeling job? All for a broken condom and a kid neither of us wants? It's not like we love each other."

"You could have at least told me what you'd planned to do."

"I did tell you. I left a message on your phone. I called a million times and you didn't answer, so I assumed you didn't want to be involved."

Maybe she was telling the truth about telling him, and he just hadn't understood the part of her message about her getting an abortion. She'd been crying so hard. Probably because she'd thought he'd abandoned her—left her to deal with an unwanted pregnancy on her own, like some kind of asshole.

Riley fought off his urge to comfort her because she'd been clear that she didn't want that from him. "I was out of the country. That's why I didn't answer my phone. Not because I didn't want to help you through this."

Her full lips flattened and she sniffed, blinking fast. "It doesn't matter now."

"I would have been there for you. We got into this mess together."

"And I got us out of it." She held up her lovely hands as if to push him away. "We're done, Riley. Just go. There's nothing more for us to talk about and I'd really prefer never to see you again. I'm moving to LA. I got a contract. It's my big break."

She was right. What was done was done and there wasn't a damn thing he could do to change it.

Riley left, got in his car, and drove. He had no idea where he was going, but he was sure that if he drove far enough fast enough, he could outrun the numbness that chilled him to the bone.

Something was not right here. Things were not adding up for Lucas.

He watched the helicopter fly out of sight.

Sloane was speaking quietly into the phone, the guilt of failure heavy in her voice. "I'm sorry I couldn't handle the rescue on my own. I know you depend on me to be better than that."

Lucas wanted to interrupt and comfort Sloane, but he held back. It wasn't his business. He shouldn't have even been listening.

Sloane let out a relieved sigh. "Thanks, Bella. I knew I could count on you."

She hung up and handed Lucas the phone. He was going to call the Old Man, but not until he had some answers.

"Why is a man who had ties to your father trying to get his hands on Gina?" he asked.

"Your guess is as good as mine. I'd say he wanted to get her out of my life to protect me from her wild lifestyle, but she lives in New York. We're both busy with our jobs. And while we try to keep in touch, we see each other only once in a while."

"Do you have any idea what that man might want with her?"

"None. When I got her call, I figured she'd fallen for the wrong guy. When I researched Soma and found out he was a drug lord, I assumed my guess was right. Apparently there's more to it than that."

"What do you know about her? Do you know of anyone who might want to try to hurt her?"

"No. She's a party girl. Fun loving, carefree, everyone's favorite good time. She has an inheritance from her mother, who was some big exec at a pharmaceutical research company. She died our senior year."

"So it could be about money."

"I suppose, but she has no family. No one else has access to the money but her."

Lucas shook his head. "Maybe they plan to force her to withdraw cash or transfer funds, but something about that doesn't fit."

"I thought the same thing. Soma is rolling in cash. His fortune makes Gina's look like a kid's piggy bank savings."

"What else do you know about her?" he asked.

"Gina went to college in New York, got a degree in hotel management, and has been enjoying life and hitting the clubs ever since."

"Why was she at boarding school with you?"

"Her mom was too busy to deal with her. Gina has always been a bit of a troublemaker. It was easier to hand Gina off to a boarding school than it was to deal with the problems herself. Gina always claimed that she was just some experiment to see if her mother could actually breed. Once she knew she could, she lost interest."

Lucas couldn't even imagine what it had to have been like growing up thinking you weren't wanted. He'd never doubted a day in his life that his folks loved him. Sure, some days he wished they didn't love him quite so much—didn't worry about him quite so much—but he'd never felt like Gina had. Or like Sloane.

"What about Gina's father?" he asked.

"As far as I know, she never had one. She joked that her mom went the frozen pop route and got artificially inseminated. After meeting her mom once, I realized it wasn't a joke."

"Siblings?"

"None."

"Any enemies you know of?" he asked.

Sloane shook her head. Her ponytail was askew from all the chaos with several silky strands falling loose about her face. "There were girls at school that hated her, but it wasn't anything more than high school drama. After college we didn't have the same friends, so I have no idea about her current set. Though it's probably huge, knowing Gina."

"There's just something wrong here. What is it about Gina that makes her a target? And why would I have seen the man who has apparently paid someone to abduct her in your father's office?"

"Maybe she got involved in something dangerous. Maybe she's a witness to something."

It made more sense than anything so far. "I'm going to call the general and see if he can shed some light on this mess."

"Don't tell him about the man."

"Why not?"

"You said you saw them together. My father could be part of all this. For all I know, he's the one who wants Gina."

How could she even think such things about her own father? There was simply no room for Sloane's suspicion inside his view of the general.

Then again, he wasn't Lucas's father. He'd only seen one side of the Old Man.

Lucas stood and checked the gauze on his head. The bleeding had stopped, and now he just had a nice, tender knot to avoid. "If I don't ask him, then he won't be able to give me what could be vital information about this man."

"As if he'd share, even if he did know something about him."

"It's worth a shot."

Sloane reloaded her rifle magazines, shoving rounds in, one by one. "Do what you want. You're never going to believe me about him, so I'm not going to bother wasting my breath."

"You really do hate him, don't you?" he asked her.

Her fingers paused, and he could see them shaking. "I used to envy Gina for her frozen pop. At least that way she didn't expect anything. She never got hurt when her birthday came and went without a card. She never even went shopping for a dress for the father-daughter dance, knowing he was just going to cancel. She had no hopes—nothing to shatter." She looked at him and her green eyes were dry, but sad. "It took me a long time to get what Gina has. I'm not going to let you or anyone else mess it up."

She stalked off into the trees. Lucas's heart ached for her, and the need to comfort her rode him hard, but he let her go, respecting her need for privacy. He'd go after her in a minute if she didn't return. Until then, he had a call to make and it was just as well Sloane wasn't around to hear it.

The general answered on the second ring. "Yes?"

"It's Lucas. I'm on Sloane's sat phone."

"Is she okay?"

"Fine. We're both fine."

"When will she be home?" he asked, sounding desperate.

"I don't have an ETA yet. We don't have Gina."

There was a distinct chill in the general's voice. "Forget the girl and bring my daughter back."

"We have to get Gina back. Sloane won't leave without her." He pulled in a long breath, bracing himself for the fallout. "Neither will I."

"Are you refusing to follow an order?"

"No, sir. I can't do that anymore. Remember?"

"Don't play games with me, son. You won't win. Besides, the girl is probably already dead." Something about the way the Old Man said that made Lucas pause. It sounded almost as if he knew something that had him writing Gina off.

Suddenly, Lucas was beginning to question his view of the general. Maybe he wasn't as bad as Sloane believed, but chances were he wasn't as sterling as Lucas had always thought. "Listen, you can either help us or not, but we just saw Gina and she's alive and well."

"Tell me where you are," he demanded.

"I will, but first I need to ask you something."

"Make it fast."

"Last summer, you ordered me to come to your office. It was right before my last mission. There was a man walking out. Tall—really tall—with dark hair and angular features, mid-twenties. Who was he?"

"A lot of people come to my office. Do you have a name?"

"No, but when I came in, you were pissed. I remember that much." And he'd quickly tucked away a file that had been open on his desk. Lucas just remembered that, too. The Old Man had been hiding something, but because of his station, Lucas hadn't thought anything about it.

"Sorry. Doesn't ring a bell."

"He had pale eyes—light gray or blue, maybe." Lucas had seen that today when the man had stared out as if he could almost feel them watching.

There was a long pause, and when the general spoke,

there was no longer fire in his voice. There was, however, a hint of fear. "Why is this so important?"

"That man was here today. We're guessing he's the one who paid Soma to take Gina out of the States."

"He was there?"

"Not fifty feet away."

"Did he see Sloane?" Panic stripped the power from his voice, making it sound old and hollow.

"No, but that's kind of an odd question to ask for a man who has no idea who I'm talking about."

"I won't say his name. All you need to know is that he's dangerous in ways I can't even begin to explain. Stay away from him. Keep him away from my little girl. Understood?"

"I'll do what I can, but we're in need of support. Gina's being taken back to Soma's villa, which from all accounts is heavily guarded. We need backup. Can you send help?"

"Yes. Right now, as soon as I get off the line I'll find some men. They'll be there in less than twenty-four hours."

"Okay. That will work. We'll meet at the villa and extract Gina tomorrow night."

"No. I'll send you coordinates for a safe place nearby. Wait for us there."

"We're on foot. I don't want to go out of our way."

"You won't be. This place is near Soma's villa. Hidden."

"How do you know about it if it's so well hidden?"

"It's a bunker. We built it."

We, meaning the U.S. government, no doubt.

"What for?" asked Lucas.

"I'm not going to tell you that. In the meantime, I'll send you satellite images and whatever other help you need. Just keep her away from that man, understand?"

Lucas had no idea what was spooking the Old Man,

but it was clear he wasn't going to find out today, over an unsecured line. After they were all home safe and sound he'd try to get some answers. Until then, he'd take what the general was willing to give and be thankful.

"Yes, sir." Lucas hung up and packed away the rest of the gear. The phone beeped, and displayed on the screen were the coordinates the general had promised.

It was only a few miles away—some of which they could probably do via road—but it was going to be a fast hike to get to the Land Rover before dark.

Sloane still hadn't come back. Lucas could no longer afford to give her any more time. They needed to get moving.

He headed off in the direction she'd gone and found her sitting on a fallen log. Her head was in her hands and her shoulders were slumped in defeat.

Lucas sat down next to her, searching for something to say to make her feel better about this fucked-up situation. He came up empty and settled on, "You okay?"

"Fine," she said, a little too quickly and with too much fake brightness in her tone.

"Help is on the way. Your father is sending men to help us. We'll have Gina back in no time."

She was quiet for a while, then turned and looked at him. Her eyes were bright green, almost luminous. Guilt pinched her features. "I failed her. She trusted me and I failed."

"You're wrong. She's still alive. We know where she is and we know she's going to be safe for a while yet. As long as she stays alive we haven't failed."

"That's easy for you to say. She's not your friend. And you're not the one with a father who's going to try to lock you away and make you miserable for the rest of your life."

"He's not going to do that to you. He can't. You're a grown woman."

"It's not legal for him to try, but since when has that ever stopped him?"

Lucas slid his hand over her hair, smoothing the wayward strands back in place. The silky texture made his palms tingle and he couldn't seem to stop himself from doing it again. He wanted to pull her against his shoulder and hold her close, but he sensed she'd balk at that—take it as some kind of statement she wasn't strong enough on her own—so he held back.

"We need his help," said Lucas.

"I know. And I'm glad he's offering it, for Gina's sake. I just hate it that he knows I'm a failure."

"I'm sure he doesn't think of you like that."

She turned her body and gave him a hard stare. "Please stop defending him. I know the man better than you do."

"Sometimes the things you say make me wonder."

She was silent for a moment, her mouth tight, moving like she was trying to hold back words. "Have you ever wondered why my last name is Gideon and not Norwood?"

"The thought had crossed my mind. At first I assumed you'd been married."

"Nope. Gideon was my mother's maiden name."

"So you took that because you hate your father so much?"

"No. I didn't take it at all. It was given to me. By my mother. Even though my parents were married, my father refused to let me have his name when I was born." She swallowed hard, blinking fast as if to ward off tears. "I was a newborn. I hadn't done a thing wrong. I hadn't disappointed him—unless you count being born a girl. I was a bundle of potential, and yet he shunned me even then. What kind of father does that?"

Lucas was stunned speechless. He couldn't imagine not wanting to give his child his name—whether or not he was married to the mother. How could the general not have been proud of his baby girl? How could he not have wanted to crow to the world that he had a daughter?

Sloane composed herself during his silence. "Do you see now? He's not the great man you've come to respect. He's not flawless."

His fingers twined with hers, and the warmth of her skin sliding along his own made his heart kick up a notch. "And yet he still has the power to upset you."

She closed her eyes and let out a weary sigh, leaning against his shoulder. "I wish he didn't, but he does. And if you tell him that, I'll make sure you regret it."

Lucas felt a grin play along his mouth—one he wisely hid. "My lips are sealed. He'd never believe stories of you showing any kind of weakness, anyway."

"I only wish I was as tough as you think I am. It sure would make things a lot easier."

"Easy is overrated," he said. "Complicated is a hell of a lot more fun. That's why I like women."

She tipped her head up to look at him. A hint of a smile warmed her eyes. "That's good to know."

The urge to kiss her struck fast and hard. He stared into her eyes, hoping it would go away if he just held out a moment longer.

Instead, the urge grew. Something in his gaze must have given him away, because he felt the shift in her body—a subtle softness sweep over her in a languid wave. Her muscles unclenched and her lips parted.

"You should move away," he whispered.

"I'm always doing the wrong thing. Why stop now?"

Lucas didn't want to be the wrong thing. The more time he spent with her, the more he liked her—thorns and all. She was strong, but not cold as he'd first suspected. Maybe she didn't let a lot of people see her weakness, but it was there, calling to him. He wanted to be there for her and help her through the rough spots.

He wanted her to need him, just a little—just enough that she was willing to give him a shot.

At what?

His folks needed him so they could retire. He owed them the chance to relax a little after all the work they did—after raising him and his sister and putting them through college, after supporting his decision to go into the military and being by his side after his injury. He owed them a lot, and it was a debt he intended to pay.

The only problem was there was no way Sloane would sign up for a quiet small-town life. He knew a fellow adrenaline junkie when he saw one. She had a fantastic job she loved. He couldn't expect her to leave everything behind and come live with him in the boonies. And he knew better than to think a long-distance relationship would work.

Their lives couldn't mesh, so what was the point in trying to make anything work? And why was he even thinking about that when he'd known her for only a few days?

Lucas had no idea. All he knew was that he wanted her. Now. Later. Whenever he could get her, however he could get her. As unfair as it was to both of them, he couldn't make it stop.

He hadn't moved. He stayed completely still, giving himself time to do the right thing. Stand up. Walk away. That was all he had to do.

And then her fingers settled on his cheek, her touch so soft he wondered if he'd imagined the whole thing. She leaned up, moving toward his mouth. She didn't kiss him, but she was so close he could feel her breath warming his mouth, see the tiny dots of brown in the thin ring of green surrounding her widened pupils.

"I didn't want to like you," she said, her lips nearly brushing his, her sweet breath filling his lungs.

Lucas's fingers tightened, curling against the stiff plates

of her armored tactical vest. He'd never hated body armor more than he did right now. He wanted to feel the supple give of her skin, the firm curves of her muscles.

He slid his fingers down to her hip, seeking a bit of bare skin, but found none, only more fabric and the rough edges of her belt.

"I didn't want to feel like this about you," she continued.

Lucas couldn't resist the bait, even though he knew better. "Like what?"

"Intrigued. Attracted." She paused and a frown line appeared between her brows. "Soft."

"You are soft," he said, feeling her stiffen as if she'd been insulted. "Not weak," he hurried to add. "But everywhere I touch you, you're soft and smooth and I can't seem to keep my hands to myself."

Just saying the words put the picture in his head of her laid out naked for his enjoyment. He didn't know what she'd look like under all her clothing, but he was dying to find out. The hints he'd had from her clinging evening gown and that split-second glimpse of her bare stomach were just enough to tease him, just enough to make his mouth water at the thought of more.

His blood heated, speeding through his limbs until he was shaking with the strain of holding back. For her. She was too vulnerable right now. He owed it to her to back away, though he couldn't seem to find the strength to manage.

"I'm not a failure," she whispered, her tone so insecure it nearly made his heart bleed. "You wouldn't want me if I was a failure, would you?"

Lucas figured he'd want her no matter who she was or what she'd accomplished. The fact that he'd considered wanting to keep her in his life was a completely different matter altogether. "No. Not like this."

She closed the scant distance between them, pressing

her lips to his. The first brush was light, almost timid, and nothing at all like Sloane. He knew she was hurting and insecure right now, and he hoped like hell that she wasn't kissing him just to prove something to herself.

But even if she was, he knew better than to think he'd stop. He wasn't that strong of a man.

He let her take the lead, promising himself he'd stop at the first sign of hesitation from her. He kept his hands where they were—one cupping her hip and the other in a tight fist in his lap—and kissed her back.

With every nibbling kiss she gave him, her caution seemed to fade. She grew bolder, sweeping her tongue out over his bottom lip, trying to coax him to open his mouth to her.

Lucas's heart was slamming around inside his chest. Part of him needed to hold steady and let her work out for herself that this was the wrong thing to do. The rest of him was clamoring for him to surrender and take what she so clearly wanted to give.

It was just a kiss. It shouldn't have rocked his foundation so hard. He'd kissed dozens of women over the years, and although he'd always enjoyed it, this was somehow different. There was a desperation in it, a kind of frenetic need. It consumed his world, drowning out all else until he could no longer even remember what his problem had been in the first place.

Defeated and elated all at the same time, Lucas gave in to her onslaught and opened his mouth, letting the tip of her tongue sweep in for a taste.

She groaned, letting out a low, womanly sound of approval, then shifted until she was straddling his knees. She held his face in her hands and had her way with his mouth.

Lucas was more than happy to oblige.

She slid her hands over his shoulders, her nails scoring his skin as they passed. Lucas grabbed her hips and slid them forward until her legs were spread wide and she was pressed against his hard-on. The heat of her sank through his clothes, scalding his cock.

He had never wanted to be inside a woman more than he did at this very instant.

He sucked in a deep breath in an effort to find a bit of control, but all it did was fill his lungs with her scent, driving him even more insane.

Her fingers squeezed between their bodies until she found his belt. "I'm not letting you stop me this time," she warned him. "Don't even try."

Chapter 13

Sloane's head was spinning. Her breathing was labored and her body was covered in a fine sheen of sweat. Every rapid heartbeat made her more desperate, more needy.

There were too many emotions rolling around inside her right now. She couldn't handle them all, so she focused on the one thing she knew had the power to make her feel good.

Lucas.

She knew she was using him, but she couldn't find the sanity to care. He was right here with her, as hot and needy as she was. His big hands clenched against her hips as he kissed her, stealing the oxygen from her lungs. Not that she minded. He could have whatever he wanted as long as he gave her what she needed in return.

And right now what she needed was to feel him sliding inside her, driving away everything else.

She undid his belt and the button on his pants. The zipper went down easily and she reached inside his shorts and took a firm grip around his cock. It was thick, hard, and smooth and throbbing in her palm. She slid her hand along his length, feeling the slippery wetness leaking from the tip.

He pulled his mouth from hers and hissed between his teeth as his whole body went tense. When he looked at her, his eyes were so dark it was hard to tell they had ever been navy blue. His mouth was wet from hers. His cheeks had darkened and sweat dotted his brow.

There was no question that he wanted her—no reason for her to doubt herself.

Sloane used one hand to unfasten her pants while she stroked him. It was taking too long and the impatient grunts she let out told him so.

He lifted her weight and eased her down to the leaf-covered ground. She was sure the movement had to hurt his knee, but if so, it didn't show on his face. The only thing she saw there was the stain of lust and a man on a mission.

He finished unfastening her pants, grabbed all the fabric covering her and yanked them down her legs. Her boots kept him from going any farther, but he grabbed the knife from her tactical vest and cut though the laces on one boot. It loosened and came off easy. Seconds later, he'd freed her leg of clothing.

Lucas paused over her as if he wanted to look, but Sloane didn't want that. She didn't want anything to slow this down—nothing to give her time to think. This wasn't about thinking. It was about feeling, and she knew what she wanted to feel more than anything: Lucas sliding thick and deep inside her.

She grabbed his shirt and pulled him down on top of her. His pants were open. His erection was easy to find, and she guided him right where she needed him to go.

The blunt tip of his cock slid along her labia. She could feel her wetness mingling with his as she widened her legs to make more room for him.

He opened his mouth like he was about to say something and Sloane covered it with a kiss, stopping whatever he might have said. She didn't want words now. She didn't want him to say anything that might make her stop.

Her body was writhing in need, clamoring against the emptiness that plagued her. All she wanted was for Lucas to fill the void.

Her tongue slid against his and finally, finally, his hips moved forward and he began to fill her.

The initial stretch was intense, intoxicating. Every cell in her body was celebrating, letting her know she was getting it just right.

He rocked inside her, inching carefully forward before retreating once again. Each inch he gained drove her higher. She pulled her mouth away, kissing along his stubbled jaw and down his neck. The salty taste of his skin made her mouth water and her blood sing. He tasted so good. She could hardly wait to go down on him.

But that would come later. Much later. After he'd given her what she needed.

Her pants were trapped under their bodies, but she wrapped her free leg around his thighs, working to pull him closer, faster.

As if she could move him. He was too strong for that, taking his maddening time, moving too carefully.

"Faster," she told him, growling the word out against his neck.

He let out an agonized moan and went completely still.

Sloane wiggled beneath him, rocking her hips, forcing him to comply. He pulled back, then drove forward, burying himself fully inside her.

The sensation was so intense, so perfect, she forgot to breathe. Lights danced in her vision and her head swam as he held still, stretching her and filling her in a way she'd never been filled before.

She stroked his back, burrowing under his shirt so she could feel his bare skin on her fingers. It would have been nice to be naked right now—to feel his chest against her breasts, to see his muscles bunching and flexing as he moved over her—but she'd take what she could get. And right now, she was getting about as much as she could handle.

The scratches on his back were rough under her hands. His muscles were hard, shifting smoothly under his skin as he began to move inside her.

Sloane's head fell back in abandon as he gave her what she wanted. With each driving thrust, she inched a bit higher, coiled a bit tighter. She'd never been fast to orgasm, but this time was clearly different. He was built just right, stroking against her clit as he moved, pressing against her every time he seated himself deep.

She let herself go, let him do his thing and simply reveled in the physical sensations. It didn't take long before she knew it was going to be over too soon. She tried to slow down and calm her rampaging nerve endings, but Lucas didn't give her the chance. He moved in a powerful, steady pace that forced her to go right along with him.

She felt him tense, heard him stifle a groan. He shifted slightly and slid against a whole new batch of nerves that she hadn't even known she had.

Lights slammed into her. Color exploded in her head and her body arched as her climax plowed into her, stealing her breath.

Lucas's voice filled her ear—a low, masculine sound of release. He throbbed inside her, driving her up on the edge of another deafening wave. She felt his semen pulse inside her as she slid back down, limp and boneless and too satisfied to scold herself for not being more careful.

Before their breathing had even slowed, Lucas rolled her over so she was lying on top of him, away from the ground. He tucked her head under his chin and idly stroked her hair with one hand, while cupping her ass with the other.

Sloane began to tense, knowing this was the part where regrets kicked in. This was when he told her how wrong it had been and how they never should have let things get so carried away.

"You okay?" he asked against her hair.

"Fine. We should probably get moving, though."

"We will. I just need a minute for my heart to slow down. I've never made love to a woman wearing body armor before. That was pretty intense."

She pushed herself up, feeling him slide from her body. She was still straddling him and his eyes roamed over her nakedness.

Sloane refused to be shy and hide herself now. Let him look. She was still dressed from the waist up. The fact that her breasts still ached for his hands and mouth was proof of that.

"I didn't use a condom."

Ah. So that was what he was worried about. "I'm protected. And clean. No worries."

He sat up and looped his arms around her. He was close enough to kiss now, and heaven help her, she wanted to feel his mouth on hers again. Already.

That itch was supposed to have been scratched.

"Just like that?" he asked. "You didn't even ask if I was disease free."

"You are."

"How do you know? I never told you."

His mouth was so nice. Full and firm and quick to smile. Just not right now.

Sloane shrugged. "If you weren't, you never would have let it go this far. You've got too much honor."

"Even though I was sent by your father?"

"If we're going to talk about him, I'd rather not do it naked."

He pulled her back down so her body fit atop his. "Then let's talk about something else, because I like you naked way too much. In fact, I'm hoping to get you out of the rest of your clothes and go for round two."

Sloane's stomach jumped at the thought. A slow, wet heat slid through her and that odd softness Lucas seemed to cause was back. "We both know that's not a good idea. Gina's still out there. Dark is coming soon, and there's an unconscious hostage tied up by the airstrip."

Lucas sighed and nodded. "You're right. A quickie is all we get. We need to be good and get moving."

"I have friends coming to help us."

He nodded. "The general is sending men as well. He gave me the coordinates of a meeting place. It's safe."

Sloane had to make a conscious effort to trust her father's word about the location's safety. It would have been a lot easier to rebel and pick her own spot, but doing so would have been spiteful and petty. Besides, she didn't have any better ideas, and she couldn't stand to think that her father would let her step into danger. He wasn't that much of a monster. "I'll forward those to Bella so she'll know where she's headed."

He helped her to her feet and knotted her cut shoelace while she righted her clothing. When they were all put back together, he pulled her into his arms and kissed the tip of her nose.

"You're a good woman, Sloane. If I'm ever lucky enough to have a daughter, I'd be proud as hell if she were just like you. Without the sex in the jungle with a near stranger part. She doesn't get to do that."

And if that wasn't the perfect thing to say, she didn't know what was.

Tears stung her eyes, and she cursed her lack of control. She hadn't cried since Mom died, and she wasn't about to start now. She had no idea what it was about Lucas that brought out the emotional side in her.

It dawned on her that that was the only thing she wasn't going to miss when they parted ways. She'd grown to like him. A lot. He was easy to be around, and even though she knew they had no future, it was nice to let herself pretend, if only for the time it took them to get to Soma's villa and get Gina out.

"I'll go deal with the man I tied up," she said.

"What are you going to do?"

She grabbed up the first aid kit. "Patch him up. Let him go. With that gunshot wound he's not going to be following us."

He nodded, his hands slowly releasing her. "I'll figure out the fastest way to the rendezvous point. The general said he'd have men there in twenty-four hours."

Sloane wasn't looking forward to that, but she was a big girl. She'd do what she had to to save Gina, and after that, she'd never need anything from her father again.

"The diamond shipment is going to have to wait. Make the arrangements," Bella told Payton as she passed by his office. She didn't stop to chat. Her team had a plane to catch.

Payton hurried down the hall, catching up with her. "What do you mean?"

"I mean we have another job."

"What job?"

"Sloane called. She needs backup. We're going in."

"In where?"

"Colombia. Call your connections there. I want transportation and weapons waiting for us when we land."

"Slow down, Bella. You can't flake out on the diamond job."

"I'm not going to flake out. I'm just going to be a day or two late."

Payton grabbed her arm and pulled her to a stop. She

faced off against him, cursing every second he made her wait.

Some asshole was holding a woman prisoner. Bella could not let that stand.

"Tell me exactly what's going on," said Payton.

"Sloane went to Colombia to rescue an old friend of hers from a sticky situation. She got involved with some drug lord or something—Lorenzo Soma. Sloane tried to get her out, but it went bad and now her friend is being held in a villa that's a veritable fortress. The job's too big for her to do alone. We're going to help."

Payton turned white, like he'd been spooked, and it took him a minute before he spoke again. "Who's paying?"

"No one. What's wrong with you?"

Whatever had bothered him must have passed, because he was back to his old stuffy self. "We work for profit."

Bella was not wasting time on the dollars and cents. "No. *You* work for profit. I work because I love it."

"You also have to eat and put a roof over your head. And pay your employees. And let's not forget the insurance premiums we pay."

"Like you'd ever let me forget."

"You can't keep doing jobs pro bono."

"Watch me."

He let out a long sigh as he followed her into the locker room. Gage and Riley were already there, getting dressed. She ignored their fabulously bare bodies and began stripping out of her street clothes.

They were planning this op as they went, since every second counted. There was a chance they were going to have to parachute in, and she wanted to be dressed and ready for the possibility.

"Someone has to fund the mission," said Payton. "The jet fuel alone is going to cost a fortune."

"Bill me," she said as she pulled her shirt off, forcing Payton to flee wearing a burning blush.

"I will," he promised over his shoulder as he left the locker room.

Bella had no doubt he would. She simply didn't care.

By the time she was done dressing, both Riley and Gage were waiting for her. Their bags were on the ground at their booted feet, and they stood in silence.

She looked at Riley. He hadn't said a word since returning from his trip to see the woman who might have been carrying his child. "I'm used to the silent treatment from Gage, but I didn't expect it from you."

"Got nothing to say except when do we leave?"

"As soon as the others are here."

"I thought this was a rush job."

"It is."

Riley shook his head. "Then I suggest we stop waiting. The others are on vacation until tomorrow when we were scheduled to leave for the diamond job."

"I told Mira to call them in."

"That doesn't mean they'll answer their phones."

Bella dialed Mira, who answered immediately. "Were you able to get in contact with the others?"

"Riley and Gage should be there any minute if they're not already there. Razor is on a job, so is Reid. I left messages for the others," Mira said.

"Contact me if you hear from them," said Bella, then hung up. She looked at the two men in front of her. "Well, boys, I would have liked to have more bodies, but I guess we'll have to make do with what we have. Sloane won't wait for us if we take forever, and if she goes in alone she's likely to get herself killed."

Gage said nothing, but gave her a slight nod.

Riley picked up his bag and headed for the door.

With these two silent men, it was going to be a long trip.

*   *   *

Payton dialed General Robert Norwood. He was still shaken from Bella's announcement that she was going near Lorenzo Soma. The Threshold Project hadn't been kind to Lorenzo. If he was anything like he'd been as a child, Sloane, Bella, and the rest of their team were in serious danger.

"I'm busy," answered Bob. There was the sound of a jet engine in the background. "Make it quick."

This wasn't a secure line, so Payton had to be careful how he said things. "Bella and two others are going after Sloane."

"We don't need their help."

"We?"

"I'm on my way now."

"So are they. I can't stop them."

"Great. I thought you had more control over that woman."

"I have as much control over Bella as you do Sloane."

Anger radiated through Bob's voice. "What do you want?"

"I need you to make sure she's safe. You can't let anything happen to her."

Bob sighed. "I've got my hands full. I can't watch out for her, too. I have my own daughter to worry about. And you should know that Lucas saw Adam. He's there. In Colombia."

Payton had to swallow twice before he could clear the surge of panic from his throat. "What if Bella sees him and it triggers a memory?"

"Chances are she wouldn't recognize him even if she did see him. They were so young then."

"I don't want Bella anywhere near the Colombian facility. It looks just like the one—"

Bob stepped over his words, which kept Payton from

saying something he shouldn't on an unsecure line. "That facility was closed years ago. I saw to it personally."

Payton pulled in a deep breath, gathering his wits so he wouldn't misspeak again. "That's not good enough. Too many things could go wrong." Things that could ruin Bella's life. He couldn't let that happen.

"My hands are tied," said Bob. "I'll have my men do what they can to make sure she doesn't take a bullet, but that's as much as I can promise."

It wasn't enough, but it was something. "I don't want her to remember."

Bob's voice dropped so quiet it was hard to hear. "I know. None of us do. The fact that she hasn't yet is a good sign."

"I love her like you do Sloane."

"Maybe you should come along and watch out for her yourself."

"I can't. She doesn't know anything about my old life. If I go into a combat situation she'll see right through me. It's better to let her see me as she does now."

"As a pampered pansy with more money than brains?"

"I'm no threat to her like this. She allows me in her life, and that's enough for me. I'm where I need to be to make up for past mistakes."

"Fine. It's your life. You want to play the role of the tame lapdog? Go ahead."

"You'll watch out for her, then?" asked Payton, needing to get Bob to give his word. The man might be a cold son of a bitch, but he always kept his word.

"Yes. If I can't get her to leave, I'll do what I can to keep her safe."

"Thank you," said Payton on a heavy sigh of relief. "I owe you."

"You watched out for Sloane all these years when I couldn't. I'm the one who owes you."

*   *   *

Gina heard the lock on her door move a second before the door swung open. She jerked out of bed and came to her feet, her heart racing. All she could think to herself was what now?

She knew they'd planned to give her to another man at that little airport today. She also knew that it had been Sloane who'd stopped it from happening. Gina was back where she started, but at least she was still alive. At least things weren't worse. That was something.

Sloane would come for her. All she had to do was hang on until then.

A thick, heavily muscled man stood in the doorway, staring at her with his mud brown eyes—the man Lorenzo had called Jeremy. The man who'd killed Shorty.

His gun sat in a holster under his arm. Gina couldn't seem to look away from it.

Was he here to kill her now, too?

"Time to go," he said. His voice was as rough as the rest of him, grating over her frayed nerves.

"Where?"

"Lorenzo wants to see you."

Gina had no desire to see him, but it wasn't as if she actually had a choice.

She walked around the bed toward Jeremy. He took a firm grip on her upper arm, making it clear there was no way for her to escape—at least not on his watch. He marched her down the hall. Gina counted doors as they moved through a labyrinth of hallways and rooms. She tried to memorize her way around in case she got the chance to run for an exit.

If she got an opportunity to kill Lorenzo, she'd run. She might not get far in these strappy heels, but she'd rather take her chances in the jungle than stay here until they did whatever it was they were going to do with her.

Please let Sloane come before that happens.

She stumbled on the slick tile floor and Jeremy jerked her up so she didn't fall. "Don't even try it," he warned.

"I wasn't trying anything. I tripped. Maybe if you got me some different shoes, that wouldn't happen."

He looked down at her feet, then pulled her to a stop. He bent down and slipped one of the high heels from her foot.

"Hey!" she said, resisting the urge to swat at his head. If it weren't for his gun, she probably would have, but self-preservation instincts were screaming at her to be reasonable.

Jeremy forced her to give up the other shoe and carried them in his hand. "There. Now you have no excuse."

Great. She wasn't going to get very far in the jungle with no shoes.

He'd just started moving again when she heard sounds of a scuffle coming from around the corner. He dragged her through the hall, forcing her to run.

Her bare feet slapped against the tile as she struggled to keep up.

They cleared the corner and saw two men on the floor in the midst of a fistfight.

Jeremy let out a frightening growl, his mouth twisting in frustration. He dragged her to a door, pulled out a key, and hastily unlocked it. He shoved her into the dark room, said, "Stay here," then shut and locked it behind her.

Gina pressed her ear to the door, trying to hear what was going on.

"Hello?" came a woman's voice from the darkness behind her.

Gina's heart kicked hard and she scrambled to turn on the lights. The room was bathed in eye-searing brightness and the woman let out a surprised hiss.

Gina saw her cover her eyes as she sat up in bed. She

wore a nightgown and her strawberry-blond hair fell over one shoulder in a thick braid. Her bare arms were covered in freckles, which stood out against her pale skin.

"Who are you?" asked Gina.

"Sophie Devane. Who are you?" She had a Southern accent. Definitely American.

"Gina. I'm being held here against my will."

The woman lowered her hand, her pale green eyes wide. "Me, too."

"Where are you from?"

"Shreveport, Louisiana. You?"

"New York." The urge to grab this woman and run pounded at Gina, but what was she going to do? There was no way out, and even if she did get out, she had no shoes.

"How long have you been here?" asked Gina.

"Three or four months. I think."

That drove all the air out of Gina's lungs. "Four . . . ?" She couldn't imagine staying here that long. The confinement would kill her and that was if she didn't make another stupid mistake and get them to put a bullet in her head.

Sophie climbed out of bed, moving closer. "Are you okay?"

Gina nodded. "Tell me everything you know about this place. We've got to get out of here."

"I tried at first. I never made it very far. Jeremy—the stocky American—found me and brought me back."

The image of Julia played through Gina's head. She could still feel her chubby arms and smell the baby sweetness of her hair. "What did Lorenzo do?"

"Do? He didn't do anything. Just brought me back here. Why?"

"When I tried to escape, Lorenzo had Jeremy kill the man who made it possible. He told me if I tried it again, he'd kill a child."

Horror drove all traces of color from Sophie's face. "Oh, God. A child?" Her hand fluttered to her stomach in a gesture Gina understood all too well.

Shock held her silent for a moment before she could manage to ask, "You're pregnant, aren't you?"

Sophie nodded, her face crumpling, though she held back the tears that threatened to fall. "It's Lorenzo's baby."

"Maybe that's why he hasn't sold you yet."

"Sold me? What are you talking about?"

Gina didn't know where to start. "There's some guy who was coming to meet Lorenzo today. He was coming for me. He paid Lorenzo to find me, seduce me, bring me to him. Apparently I wasn't the first woman he's done this to."

Sophie covered her mouth with her hand and tears welled up in her eyes.

Gina continued. "We went to this tiny airport today to meet him, but shots were fired and we had to run away." She left out the part that it was her friend who'd fired them. She wasn't sure how much she could trust this woman yet.

"Why? Why would Lorenzo do that?"

Gina shrugged. "For money, I guess. What I can't figure out is who this guy he's selling people to is, and what he wants with me."

"None of this makes any sense. Lorenzo seemed like such a nice guy. He was even happy when he found out I was pregnant, even though we hardly knew each other."

Knowing Lorenzo, that was an act, too. That man was way too good when it came to pretending to be who women wanted him to be.

"Have you seen any other people like us? Prisoners?" asked Gina.

"No. I've heard things. I swore I heard an American

man screaming for them to let him go. That was more than a month ago."

Best not to dwell on that. "We've got to find a way out." When Sloane came, Gina needed to be ready, and now that included finding a way to get Sophie out, too.

"We can't leave. He'll kill us."

"Only if he catches us."

"Which he will. I've seen the guards through the window. There's no way to escape. And even if there was a way, where would we go? We're in the middle of nowhere."

Gina wanted to tell this woman she had help on the way, but she didn't dare. For all she knew this woman was a plant—someone meant to get her to tell who attacked today and what they were planning. Gina wouldn't do that to Sloane. It was best to keep her mouth shut.

"We'll figure something out," she told Sophie.

"I don't want to be here, but I don't think I can run. I'm tired all the time. I sleep fourteen hours a day. I feel so weak, especially lately. If I went with you, I'd just slow you down. If you get the chance to run, take it. Go without me."

Footsteps sounded outside the door, getting louder. Jeremy was coming back.

"I don't want to leave you here."

Sophie wrapped her pale, slim arms around Gina. "You can send someone back for me, okay?"

The lock turned. There was no more time to argue.

Gina hugged her back and felt hot tears slip down her face.

The door opened. Jeremy said, "Let's go. Lorenzo's waiting."

She let go of the other woman and tried to pretend she was brave as she went to the door. Jeremy looked past her, staring at Sophie with too much interest. As soon as Gina was close enough, Jeremy's hand gripped her arm again and he pulled her out, locking the door behind them.

Gina wiped her eyes.

"Don't get too attached," said Jeremy.

"Why?" she asked, even though she dreaded the answer.

He looked down at her, his mud brown eyes devoid of all emotion. "Because as soon as the baby comes Lorenzo will order me to kill her."

Chapter 14

Darkness fell an hour before they would reach the Land Rover. Sloane's every step was slow and careful after that, as they made their way through the dense foliage. Lucas insisted she wear the NVGs while he relied on the dim light from a flashlight covered in gauze to guide him.

By the time they reached the vehicle, they were both exhausted and starving.

Lucas loaded their packs into the backseat while Sloane refilled canteens from her water stores and broke out a couple of MREs. "Meat loaf or enchiladas?"

"I'd eat just about anything right now."

Her movements were slow and heavy as she prepared the food, and it was all Lucas could do to keep from taking the job away from her. By the time she was done, he could see her hands shaking with fatigue.

"I don't think I'm safe to drive," she said. "You?"

"I'm good. It's safer to drive at night wearing the NVGs, using no headlights, than it will be to wait until daybreak."

She nodded. "How long will it take us to get to the rendezvous point the general gave you?"

"It's hard to tell. It depends on how much jungle

we're going to have to cut through and where we find a place to hide the vehicle. We'll have to go slow on the road. It's going to be a long haul, so you should get some sleep if you can."

"I'll eat, then crash so I can spell you in an hour or so."

He didn't argue. He had no intention of waking her before he had to. There had been no sign of her fever all day, but that didn't mean she was recovered. "Don't forget your antibiotics."

"Right. Thanks." She crawled into the passenger seat, taking the food with her.

Lucas cleared away the camouflaging branches that barred the path to the road and got behind the wheel. Sloane handed him a wet wipe so he could clean the grime from his hands.

He made quick work of the meat loaf, ate a handful of dried fruit, and started the engine. "You might want to grab a light so you can see to eat."

Sloane didn't respond. She was asleep with her food in her lap, her plastic fork drooping in her grasp.

Suddenly, Lucas felt like an ass for wearing her out. Sure, the sex had been great, but it was completely self-ish for him to let it happen.

Not that she hadn't wanted it. She had. But he should have been more careful with her. She may not have normally been fragile, but she'd been sick.

On the other hand, if they hadn't allowed themselves that outlet, maybe she'd still be awake, rather than sleeping like she needed.

Lucas moved her food and tucked it in the backseat where it wouldn't spill, then buckled her in. He drove the vehicle onto the road, then went back and obscured the tire tracks with the branches they'd cut for conceal-ment. It wasn't perfect, but it made their hiding location less obvious. Who knew when they might need it again?

He strapped on the NVGs and headed toward the hidden bunker.

It was around noon when they reached the coordinates Sloane's father had given Lucas. They were standing on the edge of a steep drop with not a single man-made structure in sight.

"These are the coordinates he sent," said Lucas, checking her GPS device.

Sloane tried not to let her frustration show. It would be just like her father to send them somewhere out of the way while he had his soldiers come in and save the day without them. "I don't see anything. Do you?"

"No."

"Great. I guess we'll just have to camp out here and wait for whoever he sends. If that's really what he's doing." She set her rifle against a rock and eased the pack from her shoulders.

Lucas ignored her dig. "I'm going to look around a bit, but I'll stay in voice range if you need me."

Sloane had slept most of the night in the Rover. Her neck was stiff, but at least she didn't feel like she was going to fall over any longer. There had been no sign of fever today, though she still suffered more fatigue than normal. At least the antibiotics were allowing her to heal. She was going to have to thank Dr. Vaughn for that when she got back.

Sloane sat down next to her rifle and uncapped her canteen.

Lucas's voice came through the trees. "I found something."

She grabbed her rifle and went to see what it was.

They were on the side of a mountain not too far up. A section of ground leveled out into a kind of natural terrace overlooking the valley below. Lucas had worked his way around the edge of that terrace until it came out on the far side of an outcropping of mossy rock. The flat area here was larger than on the other side, but not easily visible unless you were near the ledge. If rains washed away another three feet of earth, there'd be no way to move between the terraced sections—no way back to the road.

"What did you find?"

Lucas lifted up a few branches, showing her a metal door. It was rusted in spots where the protective camouflage paint had bubbled away, but seemed solid enough.

"Can you open it?"

"Yeah. I checked the knob. It's not locked."

Sloane looked up, scanning the side of the mountain. It went up farther than she could see through the thick blanket of clouds above. "Why the hell would someone build a bunker here in the side of a mountain?"

"From the look of it, it's been here for a long time."

"Like that clinic in the middle of nowhere?" The one that still gave her the willies to think about.

Lucas nodded, frowning at the door as if he didn't want to open it. "Yeah. Just like that, as a matter of fact. Stand back while I go check it out."

"Really? You really think I'm just going to hang back and let you take the risk? This is my mission. My risk. If anyone should be standing back, it's you."

He shot her a disarming smile and a wink. "Maybe, but I'm the one who trusts your father. If I get blown to hell, you'll be able to say you told me so."

"And while I do love to say that, I'd feel better if you didn't get blown up."

"That makes two of us." With that he opened the door and stepped inside.

Sloane held her breath, but stayed back. If anything happened to him, one of them had to get them down off the side of this mountain.

Seconds passed with no *kaboom*. Sloane inched closer to the door, anxious to see that he was okay. "Lucas?"

"I'm here." His voice had a metallic kind of echo to it. "I'm fine. We're clear."

She stepped through the doorway into the gloomy confines of the space, giving her eyes a moment to adjust. A second doorway stood in front of her, the door wide-open. Beyond that was a room. It was an odd mix of cement and natural rock. Thick metal poles supported the ceiling of rock overhead. Water seeped down one of the walls, leaving dark streaks. The air smelled musty and damp, but was much cooler than the stifling heat outside.

Twin metal desks sat against one wall. A calendar on the wall displayed a picture of sailboats and the month of June, 1979. At one end of the room were two closed doors. At the other was what appeared to be a bare-bones kitchen with a sink and a two-burner stove, but no oven. A small section of countertop held an ancient percolator. Through an open doorway she could see a bathroom.

Lucas went to the first closed door and opened it. "Bunks. Two of them," he said, then opened the second door. "Storage. There's a generator in here, vented to the outside."

She peered over his shoulder. "Do you see any gas to run it?"

He stripped out of his pack and propped it against the wall. "No, but we're only going to be here for a few hours."

"I need to let Bella know how to find us. She's probably already landed by now."

She reached for the phone sticking out of his pack and he covered her hands with his.

"Be careful what you say over an open line," he said. "I don't know what this place is, but chances are the general isn't keen on anyone finding out about it."

Sloane nodded. "At least there's no freaky medical equipment here."

His hand settled against her face, his thumb stroking along her cheekbone. "That really creeped you out, didn't it?"

"There was something about that place. It was like I'd been there before when I was a kid even though I know I hadn't."

"Maybe it sparked a memory of when you had to get shots or something. That can be traumatic when you're little."

"Maybe," she hedged, but she wasn't convinced. That image had been too real and unexpected. If it was something so mundane then why hadn't she remembered it before? Why hadn't a doctor's office visit triggered the memory? "Whatever it was, I'm glad we're out of there now."

He tucked some loose strands of hair behind her ear. Sloane had been working very hard not to think about yesterday's romp in the leaves, but the harder she tried not to think about it, the more she thought about it. Especially when he touched her. With his hand on her like this, her whole body perked up, craving more of his touch.

She still wanted to know what it felt like to have his big, calloused hands on her breasts. Or his mouth. She'd take that, too.

"You're blushing," he said with a smile lighting his eyes. "I think I like that."

"Yeah? Well, don't get used to it," she warned. And to give her an excuse to run away, she said, "I'm going out to contact Bella and get my gear. Be back in a few."

"Okay. I'll see if we have water. It would be nice to get cleaned up."

Sloane left, sent Bella the clearest message she could without fear of bringing the wrath of her father down on them, and then fetched her pack. By the time she got back, she heard the sound of water running.

He peeked out of the bathroom. "It's freezing. I think it comes straight in from a stream above us. I wouldn't drink it, but if you don't mind the cold, you could wash up."

As sweaty as she was, cold water would be a blessing. She went into the bathroom with her one change of underclothes and her small bottle of liquid soap, and shut the door. The water was cold enough it took her breath away, but by the time she was done, her hair was clean, her skin was tingling, and she felt better than she had since stepping off the plane.

She washed out her dirty clothes and hung them to dry.

"All yours," she told Lucas.

"I did a quick inventory of the storeroom. Most of the stuff is expired, but it looks like there were a few recent additions. Some water and freeze-dried rations."

The idea of cold, soggy, rehydrated food didn't sit well, but it would conserve their food—which she was sharing and had not planned on needing much of before getting Gina out of here. Their rations were dwindling. Neither one of them would starve, but they were getting low.

She took the insulating cover off her steel canteen and used a pair of kitchen tongs to hold it while she warmed some water with a cigarette lighter she found in a desk drawer. By the time Lucas came out of the bathroom scrubbed clean, she had enough hot water for a couple of bags of chicken and noodles.

"Not bad," said Lucas.

"Spoken like a very hungry man."

"Believe me, I've had worse."

She checked her watch. It was just after one in the afternoon. "What time do you think my father's men will show?"

"A few more hours at the earliest. What about Bella?"

"Same thing. I hope she makes it in by dark." In fact, Sloane wished she was here right now. Spending time alone with Lucas in the dark like this wasn't good for her peace of mind. He made her want things she could never have, dream of things that could never be. But most of all, he kept watching her, his eyes gliding over her in the dim light of the battery-powered lantern, and everywhere his eyes passed, she felt as though she'd been touched.

"Do you want to talk about it?" he asked.

"What?"

"Having sex with me."

The words made heat explode in her belly as she remembered just how good it had been. And they hadn't even taken the time to do it right. It had been fast and hard and dirty. And she'd loved every second of it.

Sloane swallowed. "I'd rather not."

"You can't pretend it didn't happen."

"Sure I can. Watch me."

They were only a couple of feet apart, sharing one of the desks while they ate. If she'd been smart she would have put more distance between them, but she hadn't thought it through, and now he was reaching for her.

His fingers slid over her ear, brushing back her damp hair. He was so warm, so gentle. She had to clench her jaw to keep from leaning toward his touch.

"Are you sure about that? Are you sure you can pretend it never happened?"

She had been until just now. Now she was having serious doubts about how she was ever going to walk away from him. And it wasn't just the mind-blowing sex, either. He'd been there for her this whole time, taking care of her when she needed it and backing off when she didn't. No other man had ever held that precarious balance with her before. They either shoved their way into her life, treating her like blown glass, or assumed she could take care of herself and left her to do so. Even though the latter was preferable, there were times when it would have been nice to be able to lean on someone without him making her feel lacking because of it.

Lucas had done that. She still wasn't sure how he'd managed the miracle.

"I don't know," she told him, offering him the bald truth. "I want to put it behind us and move on."

"I don't. I want to build on it. See where it leads us."

"Nowhere."

"Maybe. Probably. But I don't want to think about that now. I'd much rather enjoy the time we have together. Wouldn't you?"

His fingers slid through her hair until he cupped the back of her neck. The roughness of his calluses dragged over her skin, making her shiver. That needy ache flared to life, begging her to give in.

So what if it went horribly wrong? It was right for now. That was precious enough that she was willing to ignore her internal warnings and forget about what might happen tomorrow. All she had to do was revel in what was happening in this moment.

She offered him a slow smile. "This time I'm not wearing body armor."

Hunger flared in his eyes as he pulled her to her feet. "Whatever you want, honey."

As close as he was now, she could feel the heat of his body. His hands were hot on her shoulders, his thumbs feathered over her collarbone. She'd gotten used to his touch somewhere along the way, and now the idea of going without it seemed bleak.

Maybe if she held on to him, he wouldn't pull away this time.

Her hands slid around his lean waist until she could trace the tightly corded muscles running along his spine.

She could smell the scent of the soap they'd used, and under that, the more elusive scent of his skin. She'd come to recognize it, and was convinced that she'd be able to pick him out of a crowd of men even if she were blindfolded.

She tipped her head back and looked at him, trying to figure out something she could say that would change reality.

They'd part ways tomorrow or the next day. Her father would send transport for all of them back to the States, and after that, her time with Lucas was over. She hadn't wanted to like him, and she sure as hell hadn't wanted to want him, but there was something about him that pulled her in and made her forget why she'd ever bothered to try to hold herself back.

He was still inside her embrace; the slow sweep of his thumbs over her skin made her tingle. His navy blue eyes had darkened, but she told herself it was simply the lack of light. Nothing more.

His gaze moved to her mouth. His hands came up to cradle her head, holding her in place while he bent down and kissed her.

Sloane's body let out a rioting cheer, and she went up on tiptoe, trying to get as close to him as she could. Her hands clutched at his back and she opened her mouth, urging him to kiss her deeper.

Lucas gave her exactly what she wanted and then some. His tongue swept over her bottom lip; then he speared his fingers through her hair and tilted her head to the perfect angle.

She knew this was madness, but there wasn't a single part of her that wasn't along for the ride. Her toes curled. She backed him up until they were in the little bunk room and he hit the edge of the bed. She gave him one solid shove to topple him.

Before he could come to his senses, Sloane straddled

his lap and kissed him again, silencing any protests he might think to make. His breathing sped, along with hers, and she kissed her way over his jaw and down to the side of his neck. Her self-control was swiftly spinning away, but while she still had it, she used it to keep the press of her teeth against his skin gentle enough not to hurt him.

Lucas sucked in a harsh breath and pulled her hips tight against his body. His obvious erection was cradled between her thighs, and although she could feel the heat moving between them, there were too damn many clothes in the way. She needed to get them naked completely naked this time.

She went for his belt and despite her shaking fingers, she had no trouble getting his pants undone. She was only seconds away from getting to see every inch of that glorious body.

A fierce smile pulled at her mouth.

"I don't know what you're thinking wearing that smile," he whispered to her, "but I'm dying to find out."

His hands slid under her shirt and he swept it off over her head in a single deft move. Her hair flew around her head, landing across her shoulders in a wild, damp mess. Her breasts were bare—her bra hanging with the rest of her dirty clothes. Lucas's gaze narrowed as he stared at her.

Sloane moved to take his shirt off, too, but he grabbed her wrists and held them still at her sides. "Let me look at you."

Who was she to argue? Besides, the way his cheeks flushed and his nostrils flared as he stared at her made her feel like a goddess. He wasn't even distracted by the bandage on her arm, or was too much of a gentleman to let on that he was.

"Take off your shirt," she ordered, desperate to see what she'd missed last night.

He reached over his head, grabbed a handful of fabric, and whipped it off, revealing one of the most fabulous male playgrounds Sloane had ever had the pleasure of seeing.

She pulled her hands from his grip and splayed her fingers over his chest, reveling in the feel of him. His skin was hot, stretched tight over dense muscles. A trail of dark hair ran down the center of his torso, leading her to what she wanted most.

She scrambled from his lap to crouch on the floor between his knees. From this angle, she had no trouble getting a solid grip on his pants to pull them down. His erection sprang free, jutting up toward her.

Sloane took him in both hands, sliding her fingers over his smooth skin. He jerked in her grip and hissed out his pleasure.

She shivered in response, feeling an answering wave of slick heat swell inside her. Taking Lucas was going to be well worth the effort.

"You should lie down," he said. "Let me take care of you."

"Later," she told him as she swept her tongue over the end of his erection.

Lucas clenched his jaw and gripped the covers on the bed. His whole body was shaking, anticipating her next move.

This was one of her favorite parts of sex—the part where her man was at her mercy and she was in complete control. The feeling of power it gave her knowing she could offer this kind of pleasure was intoxicating. It went to her head, making it spin as she stretched her lips over him and let him slide deep.

A low groan of satisfaction vibrated the air between them. His fingers slid into her hair and he curled his body around her, holding her tight.

He let her have her way for a while, before he pulled

her mouth free and bent to kiss her. His tongue swept inside, flicking over hers.

Most men wouldn't have had the willpower to stop like that, but, as she was swiftly realizing, Lucas was not most men.

She felt him lift her, and the next thing she knew, she was laid out on the bed. The mattress was bare and dusty, but she didn't care. His kisses were potent, causing her head to spin. She hadn't felt like this since she was a teenager, all breathless and tingling and aching for more.

His hand slid up her ribs, cupping her breast in his palm. Her nipple beaded up against his skin, and it was all she could do not to rub up against him. The slight calluses on his fingers grazed across her nipple and wrung a soft cry of pleasure from her chest.

He didn't grope her or squeeze her hard, just stroked and teased until she was burning up inside, silently begging for more.

Heat built low in Sloane's belly. The empty, aching need to be filled clamored inside of her, demanding attention. She spread her thighs wide, fitting herself against Lucas as his hips settled in place. Her blasted pants were in the way, stopping her from getting what she wanted, but not for long.

She shed her clothes in seconds without breaking contact with his mouth. Finally, they were both naked, skin on skin just the way she'd been dying for since that first reckless kiss.

Sloane opened her body to him, baring herself, needing to feel the hot glide of Lucas's body as he filled her. She was wet enough to take him easily, even as big as he was. The only thing she couldn't do was wait.

Chapter 15

Lucas was nearly blind with lust. Sloane wriggled beneath him, spreading her thighs wide, telling him without words exactly what she wanted.

Since the moment her mouth had closed around his cock, he'd been willing to give her anything. He was lost and he knew it. No sense in fighting the inevitable.

He pulled his mouth away from hers because he had to taste more of her. Her skin was so soft. Everywhere he touched, she was silky smooth. The sleek length of her neck called to him, as did the gentle curve of her shoulders. His mouth traced over skin, and the sudden urge to mark her had him breaking out in a sweat.

There would be other men around soon. He knew it was barbaric, but he wanted every one of them to know on sight that she was taken.

He valiantly fought the urge, letting himself nip and lick, but no more. Until she took a firm hold on his cock and slid it along her slick folds.

She ground her hips toward him, rubbing her clit against the tip of his cock, pleasuring herself. A sweet tremor shook her body and a second later, she guided him to her entrance.

There was nothing Lucas could have done to stop

now. Instinct and need took over, tightening his muscles and thrusting his hips forward. She was so hot, so wet, there was nothing to slow him down. He glided inside until they were as close as two people could get, the fit tight and perfect.

Sloane panted, clutching his ass, holding him deep. Her head was thrown back, displaying her neck in open invitation.

Lucas was a goner, his control evaporated.

He began to move inside her as he bent his head to lick and nibble just below her ear. The first brush of his teeth over her skin had her sighing. The second, harder suckling bite made her whole body quiver, inside and out.

He nearly lost his load right there, but managed to hold back.

Lucas lifted himself away enough to drag his fingers over her breast, pinching the tip until she arched into his touch. The need to feel her nipple tight and hard against his tongue was driving him crazy. He promised himself he'd take the time to do that soon—after he'd made her come the first time.

Her nails raked across his back and down his arms. The stinging scratches tingled down his spine, making his cock swell inside her. She was soft now, her body easily accepting every thrust with the sensuous lift of her hips as she greeted him eagerly.

Her sharp teeth scraped across his shoulder and her hot breath stroked over his skin. Every breath she took was a quiet sound of pleasure that drew him closer and closer to the edge.

He wished he'd taken her with his mouth first and made her come at least once, because he wasn't going to last much longer and he was desperate to hear her cries of release, to feel her flesh tremble against his own—his cock, his tongue, he didn't care as long as he got what he wanted.

She pulled his hips against hers, holding him there while she ground herself against him. The friction must have been just right, judging by the way her eyes dilated before her eyelids fluttered shut. A deep red flush spread out over her chest and she pulled her thighs high against his flanks.

Lucas was at the end of his control, so he slid his hand between them and found the tight knot of her clitoris. He didn't know how she liked to be touched here, but he was going to find out. Fast.

The first brush of his fingertip had her sucking in a breath.

"Good or bad?" he found the strength to ask.

"Good. Definitely good."

Now was not the time to get fancy. He kept doing the thing she seemed to like until he felt her tighten around his cock. She let out a ragged cry, then fell apart in his arms as her orgasm hit.

Lucas covered her mouth with his, drinking down her noises while he quickened his pace. The fluttering contractions inside her drove him past all control and he let himself go as his climax choked the breath from his body. Pleasure seared his skin and burned along his nerves, lighting his brain on fire. Semen shot from his body, wringing a hoarse cry from his lungs with every heated pulse. It went on so long he was dizzy from lack of air, but completely and utterly satisfied.

He leaned his weight to the side, hoping he wasn't crushing her, but unwilling to leave her body until he absolutely had to. Once they left the jungle, the chances of him ever getting to make love to Sloane again were slim, and he was going to enjoy it for all it was worth.

She shifted beneath him, pulling away until she was no longer splayed out for his enjoyment, but still pressed along his side.

He'd take what he could get.

Lucas found the strength to prop himself up on one arm and make sure he hadn't done any lasting damage. There was a hickey on her neck that wasn't going away anytime soon, and another on her shoulder, but other than that, she was rosy and glowing.

Her nipples were still tight, and he couldn't stop himself from finally getting to taste them. They hardened further against his tongue as he lavished his attention equally, drawing a sigh of enjoyment from Sloane.

"You keep that up and I'll take advantage of you. Again."

He smiled against her skin, flicking his tongue across one nipple. "Are you sure I didn't take advantage of you?"

"Pretty sure."

Lucas laughed and flopped back onto the bed, drawing Sloane against his chest. She snuggled there, fitting far too well for his peace of mind. "I think we both won."

Sloane groaned. "If I weren't so tired, I'd force you to let me win again."

"If you weren't so tired, you already would have."

Her fingers toyed with his chest hair. He felt her mood shift, like he could almost hear her thinking. "We're going home soon."

He stroked her hair, loving the feel of the strands sliding under his palm. "That's good, right?"

"Yeah. It'll be good to be back where we belong. Back where things make sense."

He tipped her chin up so she could see he meant what he said. "Being with you makes sense. I don't regret making love to you."

"Sex," she said.

"What?"

"That was sex. We both know there's nothing more between us than that. It's just chemistry. A spur-of-the-moment decision."

"Two decisions, both of which I'm happy to have made."

"Me, too. I just don't want you thinking this is anything more than it is."

"And if that's what I want?"

The look she gave him was flatly serious. "Don't want that, Lucas. Just don't."

She was right. He knew she was. It was better not to dwell on what was going to happen and simply enjoy what was happening now without ruining it. "I won't bring it up again until we're back home. It'll give us both time to think about things and decide what's real and what isn't."

"What's real is the way you make me feel. The touch of your hands on my skin, the taste of your mouth against mine. That's real. That's what I want."

Lucas nodded slowly, pushing aside all the nagging thoughts and doubts that were threatening to ruin what little time they had together.

He leaned over her, settling his body between her thighs, ignoring how right it felt to be with her. "Then that's what I'll give you. As much as you can stand."

Lucas woke to the sound of muted voices coming from outside the bunker. Adrenaline slid into his bloodstream, driving sleep away in an instant.

He jerked his pants on over his naked hips, and grabbed his weapon. "Sloane, we have company."

She bolted upright in bed, beautifully naked and rosy from sleep. Panic tightened her features for a split second, but she kept quiet and dressed with fast, fluid movements.

Lucas was a few seconds ahead of her and pulled the door shut slightly to give her time to prepare for whoever might be outside. Chances were it was the soldiers the Old Man had sent, but Lucas wasn't taking any risks.

A light, hollow rap on the door announced their presence.

Lucas had locked them inside, bolting both heavy doors.

"It's me, Lucas," came the Old Man's voice. "Open up."

Oh, no. Sloane wasn't going to like him being here at all. Lucas needed a few minutes to play peacemaker with her father before she faced him.

"It's the men we were expecting," he told her as he grabbed the doorknob. "Take your time getting dressed. No rush."

He shut the door, praying he'd get enough time with the general to ease his worries and send him on his way. Once Sloane saw him, Lucas was convinced all hell would break loose.

The general's voice was impatient. "Don't make me wait all day."

That was not going to make this confrontation any easier. Time to get it over with.

Lucas unbolted both doors, letting the men in.

The general led the way, followed by two men Lucas had met before, briefly. Habit had him standing at attention, saluting the Old Man.

The general was dressed in patterned greens and browns—a civilian Hawaiian shirt and khakis. Out of uniform he looked like any other older man, like someone Lucas would meet at the pharmacy in line for his heart meds. The effect was disconcerting, almost eerie.

"At ease, son. As long as I'm here, I'm just a concerned father. I expect you to call me Bob."

Lucas almost snorted at the ridiculous notion, but held himself in check. "Bob?"

"That is my name. You call me general in front of the wrong people and there'll be hell to pay. So from here on out, no ranks. Just names."

"Yes, sir."

"None of that either. Just Bob."

The two men behind the general squirmed, sharing uncomfortable looks. Apparently neither one of them liked it, either.

"Where's my daughter?"

"Sleeping," he lied.

The door to the bunk room opened and Sloane stood there, beautifully disheveled. She smoothed her hair with her fingers, but not only did that fail to tame the wayward locks, but she also revealed the dark hickey on her neck.

The general surveyed his daughter, and then turned slowly toward Lucas. "I guess the two of you got along well enough after all, huh?"

Sloane stared at her father, shaking. Years of tension and strained relations pulled her tight as a bowstring. She was already stretched thin. She was worried sick over Gina. Her injured arm hurt. Her body was worn out despite the bit of sleep she'd managed to find after sex with Lucas. She wasn't nearly strong enough to face her father right now.

He had aged since she'd last seen him five years ago. His hair was lighter, thinner. Wrinkles that hadn't been there before lined his face. He wasn't in uniform, and it was odd seeing him without that sign of his office. His khaki pants and button-up shirt looked far too normal for the glorious general.

For the first time in her life he looked . . . mortal.

Sloane didn't let it fool her. She knew better than to underestimate him or show even the slightest sign of weakness. If she did General Robert Norwood would walk all over her.

She straightened her spine and marched into the room with her head held high.

He took a step forward as if he was going to hug her. Sloane held up a hand and stepped back, warding him off. She wasn't used to his hugs, and she sure as hell wasn't going to let him use one to put her off balance. Everything this man did was either a strategy or a tactic. She knew better than to think otherwise.

"I'm glad you're safe," he whispered in a voice so full of concern she almost believed him.

"Of course I am. Why wouldn't I be?"

"Ramsey said you'd been shot."

Sloane shrugged, feeling the twinge where the bullet had grazed her arm. "It was nothing."

"I've arranged transportation for you and me back to the States."

Oh, no. She refused to be trapped on a plane for hours, unable to walk away. Not to mention the fact that Gina was still in danger. "I'm not going anywhere with you."

He shot her a look of pure disappointment. "Don't be stubborn."

She took a long step forward before stopping herself. Anger tightened her mouth and her fists were balled at her sides. "Let's get a couple of things crystal clear, shall we? First, I'm allowed to be stubborn. I learned from the best. Second, I'm not going home without Gina. Period."

"You're being unreasonable."

"No, I'm simply not willing to negotiate with you. I'm going after Gina."

His shoulders squared and gone was any sign that age had changed him. "Over my rotting corpse."

She was a grown woman. Now all she had to do was remember that in the face of his authority. She was so used to being his little girl, it was hard to break the habit.

"I'm not going to discuss this with you. I don't need your permission or your approval."

"Like hell."

"So are you going to abduct me? Knock me out and drag me back against my will? I won't go quietly."

"Girl, you've never done anything quietly a day in your life. I thought age would have cured that rebellious streak."

She gave him a malicious grin. "Guess you were wrong."

"You can't stay here. It's too dangerous."

"That's my decision. Besides, if we don't go in after Gina, who will? You? I looked at the satellite images. There are too many men there, which is the only reason I let Lucas call you."

"I'll take care of it. I have connections here. I can get the local authorities involved."

Sloane rolled her eyes. "This man has enough money to bribe anyone you'd send. Until I see Gina walk free with my own eyes, I'm not leaving."

The general sighed. "You're doing this to punish me, aren't you?"

Sloane hated to think she was that petty, but there was a part of her that wanted to get back at him for all those years she'd spent wondering what she'd done wrong—why her own father couldn't stand her enough to keep her around.

The old pain stung, and she gritted her teeth to hold back the need to ask him why—what she'd done wrong. "I don't need to punish you. The choices you've made have done that well enough."

"You're still mad I wasn't at your mother's funeral."

Anger and grief whirled around like a tornado dropping from the sky out of nowhere. She snarled through her gritted teeth. "You were hardly there when she was alive. You were not missed when she died."

It was a lie—a huge one she knew would eat her alive if she let it. She'd felt so alone standing by her mother's grave. So devastated. She'd needed someone to lean on, someone to hold her, but the general was away on business, too busy to be bothered to attend his own wife's funeral and see how his only daughter was holding up.

Sloane didn't think she'd ever be able to forgive him for that.

"I wanted to be there," he said. "I couldn't."

She held up her hands to stop him. "I'm not interested in your excuses. I didn't buy them when I was a kid, and I'm sure as hell not going to now."

"You don't understand. It's more complicated than that."

"Your wife died. You had a week to clear out your schedule before the funeral. The fact that you couldn't do it means you either didn't want to, or there's no one else in the world capable of filling your shoes. I know which of those two seem the most likely to me."

"Your mother would have understood."

"Yeah, well, I don't. I never have and I never will."

"I want you on that flight out of here," he said with finality.

"And I want a father who gives a shit about me. Guess we're both out of luck."

"You're getting on that flight, Sloane." This time, it was clearly a warning—she'd heard that tone too many times not to get the message loud and clear.

"No, General, I'm not. And if you try to make me, you're going to find out just how capable I've become in your absence."

"It's for your own good."

"You gave up the right to tell me what's for my own good the day of Mom's funeral. Don't push me on this. You won't like what happens next."

Her words were big, but the truth was she didn't think

she could actually hurt her own father no matter how much he deserved it. She was going to have to disappear until he left. If she wasn't around to stuff on that flight, there wouldn't be much he could do about it.

She looked to Lucas, who wasn't even trying to pretend he wasn't listening. "I'm going outside to wait for Bella. Get him out of here. I can't work with him."

With that high-handed edict, she grabbed up her rifle and backpack and headed outside.

Chapter 16

Lucas started to go after Sloane. The need to comfort her was something he wasn't even going to try to resist, but when he took the first step toward the door, the general held up his hand, stopping him. "You stay here," he told Lucas. "You two go watch out for her."

The other two men left without a word.

General Norwood looked Lucas right in the eye and let out a blustery sigh. His shoulders drooped as if he were weary. "I always thought it would be nice to have a child who took after me. That was before I realized what a stubborn bastard I was."

"Sloane is no wilting flower of a woman," said Lucas.

The general let out a bark of humorless laughter. "That's for sure. Makes me wish she'd taken after her mother. Abigail was sweet."

"Is that a euphemism for gullible and easily influenced?"

"Talk about my late wife like that again, son, and we'll have a problem on our hands."

Lucas refused to be cowed. There'd been a time when he'd seen the general as infallible, but that time had ended about fifteen minutes ago. "She couldn't have been that great of a woman if you couldn't even be bothered to attend her funeral."

One second they were talking; the next Lucas was shoved against the wall with the general's hand around his throat and his feet barely touching the floor.

The Old Man's face was twisted with rage, his voice barely above a growling whisper. "You don't know anything about it."

"So enlighten me," he choked out.

The general's mouth tightened in a sneer and he shoved away from the wall. "I can't. Anything I say could be used against Sloane, and I won't let that happen."

Lucas rubbed his neck. "What are you talking about?"

"I'm saying that I've made a lot of enemies over the years. There are people in this world who would love to take away anything precious to me. If I'd gone to that funeral, I would have wanted to hold Sloane. And if I'd done that, she would have become a target. It's better to let people believe we can't stand the sight of each other—better yet that they think we're total strangers rather than provide a lever they can use against me."

"I find it hard to believe someone would come after Sloane to get to you."

"So did I. Until it happened."

That stopped Lucas's anger cold. "When?"

The general swallowed and looked at his shoes, nodding his head slightly. "When she was four. I got her back, but it was a close call."

Shock rattled through Lucas as pieces fell into place. No wonder the Old Man was such a hard-ass. Nearly losing a child was not the kind of thing a man got over. Ever.

"I'm sorry," said Lucas, at a loss for any other words.

"I did my best to keep her safe. I even kept my name off her birth certificate, though it nearly killed me not to announce to the world that I had a perfect baby girl. My efforts weren't enough. She was still taken from us." He closed his eyes and shook his head as if trying to ward off the memories. "After her abduction, we kept her away at a string of highly secure boarding schools. It was hard on Abigail to be without her baby, but she went along with my demands." He swiped an aging hand over his head. "Sloane says I ruined her life, but . . . I love her. I couldn't let her be taken again."

Those simple words made the general appear more human than he ever had before in Lucas's eyes. He could just see the man loving his little girl, tripping over himself to do whatever he could to keep her safe and happy.

"I regret that I've never gotten to know the woman she's become, but not as much as I would have regretted her never becoming a woman."

Sloane's face appeared in Lucas's mind. She was brave, strong, capable, and selfless. Sure, she had her rough edges, but that just made getting close to her more of a challenge. More of a prize.

Lucas knew better than to be thinking about her in those terms, but he couldn't help it. Ever since last night, he'd looked at her in a different light. He didn't want to. He knew doing so was only going to cause problems in the long run, but he couldn't help it.

"She won't let me protect her," said the general. "I've made too many mistakes with her—things I can't take back."

"Why wouldn't she forgive you for saving her when she was a child? I've been around her long enough to know that she's not that cold."

"She doesn't remember. She has no idea what happened to her. I want it to stay that way."

"I think she might remember more than you think. You should tell her," said Lucas. "She has a right to know why you had to send her away."

"I promised her mother I wouldn't. Abigail didn't want the violence in my life to touch her, even peripherally."

"But it already has. It changed the course of her life. I think she has the right to know why."

The general's body sagged, displaying his years in harsh relief. "What's done is done. I can live with Sloane's anger as long as *she* lives."

"She's tougher than you think. She would not be an easy woman to kill."

"She's my baby girl."

"No, she's a grown woman who knows her way around a fight. You're underestimating her."

"*You're* underestimating the violence that is just waiting to crash down on her."

"I'm telling you she can take care of herself. Sure, I want to keep her safe, too, but if we push her away, then neither one of us is going to be there to watch her back."

"You've gotten uppity since you left," said the general. "I'm not sure I like it."

"That's just too bad. I've spent a lot of time with Sloane over the past couple of days. I've seen her in action. She's as far from helpless as I am. Maybe more so. Put a little faith in her and she may surprise you."

"I don't want surprises. I want guarantees."

"You know as well as I do there are none of those. Life throws shit at you and you have to dodge or find a way to deal."

"Are you telling me you're not willing to help watch out for her anymore?"

"Of course not. You'd have to lock me up to keep me from going after Gina with Sloane."

"That's all I needed to hear."

"I'm not convinced of that, sir, but we're on the same side. We both want Sloane back home safe and sound.

If you stay here, you're just going to piss her off and get her back up. You're a distraction she can't afford."

"I threatened her, which was not wise. I *know* that. But with her, I lose control."

That was a sentiment Lucas could easily understand. "That's why you need to go. Before you drive her away and she does something rash. She's going back in to save Gina with some folks from her work, and it's best if she does it in a planned, methodical manner, rather than with the need to prove something to you."

"I realize now that I can't stop her—that I have no right to—but I do have a right to do whatever I can to keep her safe and make sure the job goes well."

"Then you need to back down. Call a truce. Give her a peace offering of your trust. Whatever it takes to make sure she comes back out alive."

"And just what would you suggest I offer?"

"Prove to her you trust her enough to do this job by walking away."

The general's mouth tightened as he mulled it over. "If I trust you on this and she gets killed, I'll be coming after you, son."

"If she gets killed, you won't have to, because they're only getting to her over my dead body."

Sloane sensed her father's men hovering nearby, on the far side of the natural terrace. They were trying to pretend like they weren't watching her, but she knew better.

She ignored them and retrieved Bella's message stating she would arrive within the hour. It was already early afternoon, and they had a lot of planning to do before they could hit Soma's villa.

If it weren't for the satellite images her father had provided, she wasn't sure they would have even been able to find the location before sunset. As it was, they knew exactly where it was and approximately how many men guarded it.

While they were waiting on Bella, they needed to come up with a plan of attack.

She turned to go back into the bunker for Lucas, and instead came face-to-face with her father. Words dried up in her mouth as they always did when he was near. The air of authority around him created this impenetrable bubble that made her feel like a little girl.

She hated it, so she thrust her chin up and gave him a defiant stare.

He reached out and cupped the side of her head. Sloane flinched away, unsure what game he was playing. She looked at his hand, expecting to find a hypodermic needle or something else to knock her out and drag her home, but saw none.

"Sloane, you don't have to do this. You don't have to go."

"Stop right there," she told him. "You're wasting your breath and my time. I have a mission to complete and I'm sure you have all kinds of pressing things demanding your attention."

"And you're one of them. I worry about you."

"Then stop. I don't need your worry. I'm fine without it. Or you, as I always have been."

His eyes drooped shut for a brief moment. "I wish things could have been different between us."

Her throat was beginning to tighten, and she felt the telltale sting of tears burning her eyes—tears she could not show. She willed away the sign of weakness and said, "So do I, but it's too late for that. Carry on, General."

Sloane walked past him before she completely broke down. She hated it that he could do that to her—that he could make her feel things she didn't want to feel and want things she didn't want to want. She was a grown woman. Strong and independent. She didn't need him.

Then why did she so desperately want his approval? It shouldn't matter what he thought. She'd proven herself time and time again. And she knew he'd kept tabs on her over the years. Why couldn't he tell her he was proud of her? Why did he have to insist that she wasn't good enough to go and rescue her friend—not good enough for him?

"I hate it that things are like this between us," he said from behind her.

She stiffened and quickly pulled herself together. "So do I. But they are. Neither one of us is very good at bending. I think it's best if we just stay out of each other's way."

"I'm going. I'm leaving two of my men here, along with some supplies."

That shocked her enough that she spun around. "You're not going to fight me? Force me to leave?"

Sadness seemed to weigh him down, dulling his green eyes. "I'm tired of fighting with you. Lucas says you're capable. I'm taking him at his word."

Lucas had stood up for her? Sloane hid her shock, worried this was all some kind of strategy to get her to give in. "I'm sure he'll let you know when we're back in the States. You won't have to worry that way."

He gave her a sad smile. "There are some things I can't control. Worrying about my baby girl is one of them. But I will feel better knowing you're back safe and sound."

He really wasn't going to fight her on this. Sloane had no idea what to make of it. All she could think was that Lucas must have had the magic words she'd never been able to find to make her father back down.

"Thank you," she managed to say, her tone polite to cover her shock, "for the intel and leaving the men behind. I appreciate your help getting Gina home safely."

"If you need anything else, please call me."

Sloane was reeling, searching for a hold on reality.

This was not the father she knew. He didn't use words like "please." He gave orders and expected obedience.

"O-okay," she stammered.

He put his big hand on her shoulder and gave her a single squeeze before he walked away.

Three men she hadn't seen watching her melted out of the jungle and joined him. At least he had an escort back to wherever it was he was going.

Sloane stood there and watched him until he disappeared. She wasn't sure what to make of this new side of her father. She didn't recognize this man and it left her feeling oddly unsettled.

Was it his age? Had he finally come to grips with the fact that he wasn't immortal? Or was it simply a case of him mellowing?

She had no idea. This whole situation was too surreal. She was left feeling off-balance.

She wanted to see Lucas again. He made her feel steady, and maybe he could shed some light on her father's odd change of heart.

She went back into the bunker, where Lucas was leaning over a satellite image spread out on the desk.

"What did you say to him?" she asked.

Lucas turned around, propping his hips against the edge of the desk. He crossed his thick arms over his chest. "Not much. I told him you knew what you were doing. That he should trust you."

"And it worked?"

"He's not the man you think he is. He's a hard-ass, but he has his reasons. Maybe you should sit down and ask him about them sometime, rather than assuming he's doing something for some sinister purpose."

He made it sound like he knew something she didn't. "What did he tell you?"

Lucas turned his back on her and went back to the map. "Ask him yourself."

"He's gone."

"I guess you'll have to look him up when we're back home, then."

Right. Like that would happen. "If you know something, you should tell me."

He stuffed the images in a folder and turned back to her. "Nope. But I will introduce you to the men your father left to help us."

The change of subject was intentional. She could tell. "You're just trying to get the two of us to make up. It's not going to happen, you know. The gap between us is too wide."

Lucas closed the distance until he was standing right in front of her—close enough she could smell the soap on his skin. He looked down at her, his face completely serious. "Then build a bridge, Sloane. He's your father. He won't always be around. One of these days it'll be too late to have any kind of relationship with him and you'll be sorry."

Sloane knew what he meant, but she couldn't let herself think about it. Not here. Not now. Anger was easier. Losing Mom had nearly destroyed her. As much as she disliked her father, she couldn't imagine a world without him.

She lifted her chin. "I think it's best if we focus on the task at hand. I'll deal with my problems on my own."

His mouth turned down in disappointment. "No, you won't. You'll keep ignoring it once it's not right in your face."

"You don't know that."

"Fine. Prove it, then. Once we get back home you show me you're willing to sit down with your father and have a civil discussion."

Now Sloane was the one who was disappointed. "We both know that once we get home our lives will no longer intersect."

"Is that your way of avoiding him or me?"

"Neither. It's just the truth."

"Truth?" he asked, raising a dark brow. "I'll show you truth."

And then he kissed her. She fell into it headlong, abandoning reality for the swift, fiery heat that blazed between them. Everything else fell away, and all that remained was the hard grip of Lucas's hands on her body and the taste of him against her tongue. The world shifted and spun out from under her, and she gripped his shoulders, seeking some kind of anchor to hold her in place.

Lucas lifted his head, staring down into her eyes. "The truth is that you hated me from the beginning because of who you thought I was. You were wrong about me. Maybe you're wrong about other things, too."

He pulled away and went outside to join the other men, giving Sloane a few moments to gather the fragile pieces of herself.

She had no idea what had passed between Lucas and her father in the few minutes they were together, but whatever it was, it had changed both of them somehow. Her father had lost some of his ruthlessness, but somewhere along the way, Lucas had found it.

Which only convinced her further that they could never have a future together. It was best if she cut ties now, while she still could. Heaven knew she had one powerful distraction.

Saving Gina was going to take all her focus. Once they were back home she'd let herself think about what could have been, what she was missing. But right now was not the time for regrets. She needed to pull herself together and get the job done.

So that was what she'd do.

Sloane wiped the taste of Lucas from her lips and squared her shoulders before she went out to meet the men.

By the time she got outside, Lucas and the two other men were grouped together in a tight clump. She didn't know what orders these men were under, but she wasn't about to trust them enough to leave them alone for long.

Lucas heard her approach and lifted his head. His gaze was cool as he looked at her, and she found herself wishing for some of that heat he'd given her only a few hours ago.

"Sloane, I'd like you to meet Victor Temple."

Victor nodded as he eyed her, sizing her up. He looked refined, almost aristocratic. He was incredibly handsome and clean-cut, with a nice, straight nose that Bella would enjoy breaking given the chance. His hair was cut short but not quite buzzed, and he stood with the rigid posture of a man born into the military. He held out his hand, which Sloane shook, noting the calluses along his palm.

Victor might look all cultured and elegant, but he was clearly not a stranger to physical labor.

"And this is Justin Hoyt," said Lucas.

Justin gave her a nod and a wink. His hair was a bit too long and shaggy, and he needed a shave. He wasn't overly tall, though he had plenty of muscle. His eyes and hair were both an average kind of brown, but his nondescript looks would make it easy for him to blend in just about anywhere. "So you're really the general's daughter?"

Sloane lifted a brow and gave him a cool smile. "The less you mention that, the better you and I will get along."

"Leave the lady be," warned Victor. "We were ordered not to upset her."

"Upset me?" asked Sloane, feeling her face heat with fury. "Do I look like a troubled child or an old lady?"

Victor's rigid posture tightened. "Sorry, ma'am. I didn't intend to insult you."

Sloane stepped up to him. She got right in his face, but his gaze didn't waver. He stared straight ahead at something in the distance, standing at attention as if she somehow wielded her father's authority over him.

"Did the general order you to take me home, too?" she demanded. "Did he give you permission to knock me out or drug me?"

"No, ma'am."

"Sloane," said Lucas in a placating tone, "don't take your anger out on them."

She turned back to Lucas, feeling herself quiver with anger. "I have a right to know if my father told them to do something against my will."

Lucas grabbed her arms and his jaw tightened. He dropped his voice, but the rage straining his tone was unmistakable. "I heard your father give them their orders. You want to know what he told them? He told them to protect you at all costs. He basically told them to die for you if that's what it took to get you home safe."

Die for her?

Sloane's anger evaporated, leaving her feeling selfish, deflated, and shaky. Lucas was right. It wasn't fair for her to take years of frustration out on these men any more than it was fair of him to ask them to put her life above theirs.

She eased her arms from Lucas's grip and went to where Victor was still standing at attention. "I'm sorry," she told him. "Perhaps I should try this again."

She put her hand out for him to shake. "I'm Sloane Gideon and I'm not a complete whack job. Most of the time."

Victor shook her hand, giving her a brief, rigid nod.

Justin asked her, "Are you married?"

She blinked in surprise at the change of subject. "What?"

"Your last name is Gideon. Not Norwood like the

Old Man. I thought that might mean you were married, which means Lucas really needs to stop looking at you like that."

Years-old shame bore down on her, and it was all she could do to keep her head high. "I use my mother's maiden name."

"But your folks were married, right?" asked Justin.

"Drop it, Hoyt," warned Lucas. "Focus on the map, not Sloane."

Thankful for the change in subject, Sloane latched onto it like a lifeline. "We're meeting up with the rest of my team before we go in. I want to be clear who's in charge here."

Both men looked to Lucas, who crossed his arms over his chest. "It's her mission."

Sloane wanted to kiss him on the mouth. His vote of confidence and the ease with which he handed her control was as humbling as it was shocking. Still, she knew what she had to do to ensure her friend got out safely.

She cleared her throat. "Actually, Lucas is in charge. He's got a lot more experience in combat and extractions than I do. Most of my work is as a protective detail."

She felt his wide hand splay across the small of her back, and it brought back a riot of physical memories of them together. Her body clamored for more even as she knew there was no chance for a moment alone until this job was done. At which time, they'd go their separate ways.

"Will your team go along with that?" he asked her quietly.

She nodded. "We're professionals. We've worked with the military before. It's not a problem."

"Right, then. Let's do this."

Chapter 17

Gina sat on the bed, hugging her knees. She stared out through the window, watching shadows lengthen across the perfectly manicured lawn.

She'd been too rattled by Lorenzo's interrogation to realize it before, but the more she thought about it, the more convinced she was that the meeting she'd had with Sophie had not been accidental. There were too many rooms in this house Jeremy could have put her in. Hell, he hadn't needed to put her in any of them. He had to know she'd never risk Julia's life by trying to run again. Didn't he? Wasn't that the whole point of showing her the child?

Then again, maybe a man like Jeremy—one who could kill in cold blood—wouldn't think twice about letting a child die.

But if her instincts were right and Jeremy had wanted her to meet Sophie, what was the point? The man was too cold to worry about something as paltry as Sophie being lonely or homesick. There had to be more to it. Did he want her to see what could have happened to Gina—that things could be worse? She could be knocked up by a man she detested, trapped here for months in isolation.

Jeremy didn't seem the type to care what she thought. There had to be more to it than that.

Maybe he thought she was going to try to escape despite the threat to Julia. Maybe he thought that if she slowed down enough to take Sophie with her, they'd have a chance to stop both of them before they could get out.

Her lock scraped and the door opened enough for her to see just the side of Jeremy's face. His hand reached in and he tossed something onto the rug. "I don't kill kids," he said, then shut the door again without another word.

Gina scrambled from the bed and found a pillowcase knotted at the top. She unknotted it and looked inside.

Shoes. Sturdy, ugly as hell, brown leather shoes.

She slipped them on. They fit.

She sat there on the floor in shock, trying to puzzle out what in the world that man was up to. It was almost as if he wanted her to be able to escape.

For one brief, tantalizing second she wondered if he might be an undercover agent of some kind. He could be here trying to take down Lorenzo's organization from the inside.

If that was the case, then it all made sense. Except for the part where he killed Shorty. Surely if he was a good guy he wouldn't have done that. He would have found some way to avoid putting a bullet through an unarmed man's head.

Unless there had been no other way.

Gina had no idea what to make of all this. The only thing she knew for sure was that these shoes were not leaving her feet. If Jeremy was trying to help her, she was going to be ready to run when that help came.

Jeremy was taking a huge risk with the new American woman. If she blabbed about the shoes or seeing Sophie, Soma would find out and have Jeremy's head.

He hurried down the hall toward Soma's room. The man would be done fucking one of the maids any minute now, and if Jeremy wasn't at his post when she left his bed, there'd be hell to pay.

As he passed by Sophie's room, he couldn't help but pause. He pressed his hand to the door, imagining he could feel the heat of her skin through the solid wood.

Soma didn't deserve to have a woman like her bear his child. She was too good for him. Too sweet.

And as soon as her baby was born, Soma would order Jeremy to kill her. He wouldn't care that Jeremy wanted her. That he cared about her. Once she'd served her purpose, Soma would want her out of the way.

Jeremy couldn't do it. He'd killed countless men, but never a woman. Especially not one like Sophie.

In his dreams, he stole her away from here and they ran off together to live their lives somewhere Soma could never find them.

Jeremy knew better than to think he was the kind of man who got to live out any kind of dream. He owed his life to Soma, and he knew without a doubt that one day he'd repay that debt the hard way. It was just a matter of time.

Sophie's only chance to get out of here was Gina and whoever had come after her at the airstrip, guns blazing. Jeremy couldn't do much—he couldn't act openly—but he could make sure that if those people came for Gina again, she'd tell them about Sophie. It was a long shot, but it was the most hope he'd had in months.

In his line of work, hope was such a rare commodity, he'd take it wherever he found it.

Bella and two of her men, Riley and Gage, arrived right on time. Lucas watched Sloane as she hugged Bella, then each of the men.

Jealousy rose up, snarling inside of him. He'd never thought of himself as a jealous kind of guy, but seeing

Sloane in the arms of other men seemed to bring out the worst in him.

He tamped down that inappropriate surge and focused on the task at hand.

"Come meet my friends," said Sloane, waving him forward. "This is my boss, Bella Bayne."

Bella was simply beautiful. She had classic, perfect features that could have graced the cover of any fashion magazine. Her black hair was pulled back in a sleek, shiny bun low at the nape of her neck. Lucas figured her hairstyle was intended for function—allowing her to keep it out of the way—it also served to give her a classy, sophisticated appearance. Her jungle camo and the arsenal of weapons strapped to her long, lean body were clear warnings that this woman was more than she appeared.

She looked him up and down with knowing gray eyes. A slow, sultry smile tilted the edges of her full mouth. "Nice catch, Sloane."

"It's not like that," Sloane hurried to say a little too fast.

Bella's grin widened. "We'll talk later, I'm sure."

Sloane had turned a lovely shade of pink that reminded Lucas all too well of the way her skin flushed when she came. He shifted his stance as the next man stepped up to meet him.

"This is Riley Conlan, Bella's go-to guy."

"Nice to meet you," said Riley, holding out his hand in greeting.

A scant quarter inch of hair covered the man's head. The buzz cut was as no-nonsense as the rest of the man. He had the same kind of relaxed confidence about him as some of the most deadly men Lucas had ever known. He didn't smile. He didn't even blink. He just stared at Lucas with dark brown eyes, making him feel weighed and measured in a single instant.

Lucas shook his offered hand, feeling the too-tight grip of the other man—clearly a warning signal not to screw Sloane over. If only Riley knew that it was a lot more likely to happen the other way around, he might have eased up on the pressure.

"And this is Gage Dallas," said Sloane.

Gage was leaning against a tree in a negligent pose, his arms crossed over his chest, one shoulder propped against the trunk. He said nothing, just nodded his head in acknowledgment.

"It's nice to meet you all," said Lucas. "I'll introduce you to the others and we'll get down to business. We go in right after dark and we'll be out of here before sunrise."

He made quick work of the remaining introductions, then spread the satellite images and a map down on the ground so everyone could see. "Based on the thermals, I'd say this is where the guards spend their idle time," he said, pointing at a small outbuilding near the sprawling walls of the villa. "Chances are it's also where they store their weapons—or at least enough of them to give us trouble."

"I can take that out," offered Justin. "A little C-4 and it's no longer a problem."

Bella pointed to one of the images. "There's a large clearing around the villa. If this guy is like any of our rich clients, chances are he's got motion detectors hooked up to lights and maybe even an alarm. If that's the case, how will you get close?"

"I'll move real slow," said Justin, giving Bella a seductive grin.

Bella shot him a cold look for a long moment. She didn't say a word, but it was clear from the way Justin's shoulders drooped that he'd been completely shut down.

Good. The last thing this mission needed was more emotional hurdles. Lucas and Sloane were more than enough in that department.

"We don't have much time," said Sloane. "That guy

is coming for Gina tonight. We have to have her out of there before he does."

"How will he come in?" asked Victor. "We can ambush him at the road so he'll never make it."

"No good," said Lucas. "He's got his own chopper. And plenty of space to land. That's how I'd come in if I were him."

Sloane shook her head. "Then why didn't he fly here before? Why go to the airstrip?"

"Not enough fuel, maybe? The villa may be too far for him to come without refueling, or it could be he simply didn't want to meet Soma on his own ground."

"It sounds like we need to plan for either method of transport," said Victor. "The general left us with plenty of firepower. We'll be able to handle whatever comes."

"Okay," said Lucas. "We need at least two people going in after Gina."

"I'm going," said Sloane. "She knows me."

Lucas figured trying to talk her out of it would be a waste of breath, so he didn't bother. He was, however, going to be right by her side, covering her back if necessary. "Fine. I'll go in, too. But I think we need one more."

"I'll do it," said Riley.

"Okay. And Justin's taking out the guardhouse. That leaves us needing two sharpshooters."

"Gage and I can do that," said Bella.

"I can handle communications and cover the road," offered Victor. "At least some of us are going to have to approach on foot, but we won't want to exit that way. I'll be ready to pick up everyone once you've freed the woman."

"Sounds good. We'll meet here," said Lucas, pointing out a spot in the jungle near the road leading onto Soma's property.

"We need to get closer and make sure there are no surprises before we split up."

"Before we go, everyone take one of these." Victor opened up a case and took out several comm sets.

After a quick test, they geared up and headed toward Soma's villa.

Riley was in the front, silently leading the way. Lucas let him, not wanting to ruffle any feathers. If he got out of line, Lucas would deal with it, but until then, he gave the other man leave to do what came naturally.

Gage fell back in the group until he was last in line, picking up the rear. The man was so quiet, he couldn't even hear him though he was only a few feet away.

Sloane was at Lucas's side, close enough that he could touch her. He didn't. He wished there were time to find a quiet place where he could talk to her for a minute and beg her to be careful tonight. He had no idea what was in store for them, but he knew he didn't want things between them to end here. Sure, it was probably wishful thinking to imagine they'd have a chance once they were done with this mission—he knew better—but he couldn't stop himself from racking his brain, looking for ways to make it work.

The fact that he came up with none made it that much clearer that tonight was probably their last night together. And they were going to spend it risking their lives rather than lounging about in bed, drawing as much pleasure from each other as they could stand.

At least he didn't have to worry she'd forget him. He knew without a doubt that if they survived this, she'd always remember the guy who helped her save her friend.

It was cold comfort.

Sloane stopped inside the shadows of the jungle. It was dusk, and already the lights of Soma's villa had begun to turn on.

A few feet beyond where she and Lucas hid, the

vegetation had been cleared and there was no conceal-
ment between here and the giant house. They had about
two hundred yards of open ground to clear, and judging from the placement of security lights and cameras,
no one got across that space without someone knowing
they were coming.

They had their plan, and now it was a matter of waiting until darkness covered their approach.

Justin had already begun to creep across the clearing
toward the guardhouse. The fact that Sloane couldn't
see him was a good sign that he knew how to use shadows and the lay of the land to obscure his presence.

Victor had gone back for the vehicle and Gage and
Bella were also getting into position. There were two
machine gunners on the roof, and taking them out was
job number one.

Riley was nearby. He was going in with them, which
was good. If Gina needed to be carried out of there, Lucas was going to need help. His knee had held up fine
so far, but with as much strain as he'd been putting on it
over the last few days, he didn't want to risk it giving out
at the wrong moment.

Sloane shifted her position, trying to move away from
a stick that was digging into her stomach, making her
queasy. Or maybe it wasn't the stick's fault at all. A lot
was riding on this mission and her nerves were running
hot, anxiety jangling through her system, making her
edgy and impatient.

Lucas's hand settled below the small of her back
where she could feel his touch beneath the armored vest
she wore. His touch calmed her nerves, but made other
feelings rise up inside her.

For all she knew this was the last time he'd ever touch
her. Once they closed in on Soma's villa, things would
move fast. There was no way to know if Gina was safe,
or if they'd have to whisk her away to get medical atten-

tion. This quiet moment before the storm might be the last one she had with him.

Sloane rolled to her side. Greasepaint darkened his face, but it did nothing to disguise the intensity of his gaze.

He shoved the lip mic away from his mouth and covered it with his hand. "We should talk."

She knew what he wanted to talk about. The two of them, what happened next when this job was over. There was no next, and if she let him talk, she'd break down. She was already running on nerves and adrenaline. Between Gina and her father, she was on emotional overload. Throwing more emotions onto the pile would send her up in flames. She needed to stay strong, solid, and focused.

She covered her mic. "Not now. Not here."

"Then when?"

"When we get back."

"Promise me," he demanded. "Promise me we'll talk—that you won't run away once we're home safe."

She shut her eyes for a moment, trying to keep her voice steady so no one knew she was crumbling inside, wishing for things she knew she could never have. She and Lucas could never be more than a fling. He would always strive to be like her father—a man he admired and she detested. She would grow to resent it, and him. He deserved better than that. "I promise."

Lucas nodded. He repositioned his mic and let it drop. At least for now.

More lights flipped on inside the sprawling mansion. Sloane lifted the binoculars to disguise emotions she knew would show on her face. She focused hard on what she saw, trying to figure out which way to go through the house for Gina. Their intel couldn't turn up any blueprints, so they had no feel for the layout of the building. They were hoping to stay together once they were inside, but as big as that place was, Sloane was convinced they might have to split up.

A movement in one of the rooms caught her eye. She focused in on it and saw Soma and his beefy bodyguard talking.

Her fingers itched for her rifle. "Soma's on the first floor, three windows from the west wall. I can take the shot."

"No," said Lucas, his voice echoing in her headset as well as from beside her. "We stick to the plan."

"I see him," said Bella in her ear. "I'll take him out right after those machine gunners. Promise."

Bella was a good shot, but Sloane really wanted the joy of blowing that man to hell herself. She tried to convince herself it didn't matter who killed the asshole, just as long as he died. Any man who abducted women to sell them deserved to be cold and rotting in the ground.

Lucas wrapped his warm fingers around her forearm and stroked the inside of her wrist with his thumb. The touch eased some of the tension pulling at her, giving her the space she needed to suck in a deep breath.

It was dark now and just a matter of time before Justin's explosion let them all know it was time to execute the plan. Sloane couldn't lie here any longer. She needed to get up and be ready to go. She pushed to her feet, made sure all her weapons and ammo were in place, and silently urged Justin to hurry the hell up.

Lucas stood beside her now. He took the binoculars from her hands and scanned the house. "I think I found Gina."

Hope surged so hard inside Sloane it drove the breath from her chest. "Where?"

He handed her the binoculars. "Six windows from the east wall. Second floor. She just turned on her light."

Sloane's hands shook so hard she had trouble focusing, but as soon as she caught a wavering glimpse of the

woman in the room Lucas had indicated, she knew it
was Gina. "That's her."

She was still alive. Relief bore down on Sloane, driving the breath from her lungs.

"Can you see the fastest way to her?" asked Riley.
Now that he spoke, she could tell he wasn't far away—
maybe a few yards, though she hadn't seen him in the
darkness of the jungle.

Sloane looked for stairs, but it seemed like the only
way up was the massive double staircase right inside the
front door. "The hard way," she said.

"There's a stairway at the end of the east wing," came
Gage's quiet voice through the headset.

"We'll go in that way," said Lucas. "Riley, Sloane and
I are heading toward Gage's location now. Justin, we
need another ten minutes to get into position."

"I'll follow," said Riley.

Justin said nothing, but as close as he was supposed
to be to the enemy, Sloane didn't blame him for keeping
his mouth shut.

They hurried through the jungle, staying within the
edge of the tree line, so their movement wouldn't be
easily detected. By the time they reached the point
nearest the end of the east wing, they were sweating and
breathing hard.

Sloane removed her armored helmet long enough to
wipe the sweat from her forehead. Her hand came away
covered in greasepaint, and she sure as hell hoped Gina
would recognize her through the goop. The last thing
they needed was for Gina to scream bloody murder because she thought she was being abducted again.

"We're in place," said Lucas. "Anytime you're ready,
Justin."

As soon as the words left Lucas's mouth, the night
was blasted away by a brilliant explosion on the west
side of the property. Sloane felt a rush of air sweep over

her sweaty face. Her chest vibrated with the rumble. The guardhouse went up in flames. Men screamed. Huge banks of security lights flashed on and a siren screamed out into the night.

Gunfire exploded from two locations. One of the machine gunners fell from the roof. The other disappeared, but Sloane couldn't tell if he'd been hit or had taken cover. There was no time to worry about it now. She had to trust that Bella and Gage would cover them.

Sloane set off at a dead run toward their entrance point, hearing the heavy tread of both men right at her back.

Chapter 18

An explosion rattled the glass in Gina's window. Fear shrieked through her, driving her to the floor. She covered her head with her hands, sure the glass would explode at any second.

Sirens blared and she heard heavy footsteps pounding in the hallway outside her door. A dozen angry shouts split the air. She heard someone yelling in sharp, frantic Spanish near her door, heard another man answer in a single curt word; then their shouted conversation faded as both men ran to join the fight.

A giddy corner of her soul rejoiced, knowing that *kaboom* had to be Sloane's doing. That woman loved her weapons the way Gina loved shoes and chocolate.

Gina raced to her door, pounding on it, yelling for the guard to open up. No answer came from the other side, as usual.

Which meant her guard had left. The only thing standing between her and freedom was that door.

Gina picked up the heavy metal lamp and swung it at the doorknob. It bounced off, stinging her hands, but that was it.

She slammed down on it again. This time she left a deep gouge in the wood, but the metal knob was still intact.

Gina gave up the futile effort and ran to the window. Fire burned on the far side of the property. A small building was consumed by flames, and several men were trying to contain it with garden hoses. She didn't think there was any risk of it setting the rest of the villa on fire, but she couldn't be sure. If the fire did spread, it was a lot closer to Sophie than it was to her.

She needed to get out of here. She needed to get Sophie out of here, too. And to do that, she needed to let Sloane know where she was.

Gina ripped a page from a book on the shelf and used her lipstick to scrawl "Sloanc" across the page. She slid it under the door, praying Sloane would see it when she passed.

If she passed. This place was huge with hallways sprawling everywhere. There was no guarantee Sloane would find her.

Panic reeled in her stomach, making her dizzy. She just had to hold it together for a little longer. Just a few more minutes and she'd be on her way home.

Not knowing what else to do, Gina pounded on the door, screaming, "Sloane!" There was so much noise with the sirens going off and gunfire and people yelling, she had no idea if she'd be heard, but she had to do something— anything to help herself get out of this horrible situation.

And once she did, she was never dating another man for the rest of her life. Her taste in men had landed her here. From this point forward, she was a single woman.

Hopefully, she'd get the chance to make good on that promise.

An explosion outside sent shards of glass flying through Lorenzo's office. Shock glued him in place for a brief moment before his body finally began responding to his commands to run.

Jeremy was faster and had moved between Lorenzo and the now broken windows. A large black pistol was in his hand as he stood ready to defend Lorenzo from whatever came.

"That was the guardhouse," said Jeremy.

Rage pooled in Lorenzo's belly, driving away the temporary weakness of fear. "They're here for the girl."

"It's possible. Or they could be here for you. You should get into the safe room. I'll handle this."

"None of my enemies would dare come for me in my own home."

Jeremy shot Lorenzo a brief glance. "They never would have dared come after your father. You are not your father."

"Are you questioning my authority?"

Jeremy grabbed Lorenzo by the arm and dragged him toward the secret entrance to his safe room. "Do you want to scold me or do you want to live?"

Lorenzo jerked his arm away and entered the code on the hidden keypad. A section of wall slid open and he stepped into the armored room, leaving the battle to Jeremy.

After all of this was over, he'd have a talk with the man about his lack of respect, but until then, Lorenzo would have to satisfy himself with knowing he'd live through the battle.

He powered up the monitors and settled in to watch the show.

There were more guards inside Soma's place than Lucas had thought. Either the thermals were bad or Soma had brought more men in since they'd been taken.

At the top of the stairs, a bullet plowed into the wall by Lucas's head. He jerked back around the corner where Sloane and Riley stood on the stairwell. "There are six of them ahead that I could see. They're blocking our path."

"Four more men coming up on your six," said Gage, his voice quiet and calm in the midst of all this chaos. More shots sounded from outside, equally spaced. "Three now."

"Got it," said Riley as he turned and aimed over the banister.

"I'll go low," said Sloane. "Take out a few kneecaps."

She slid past him and the urge to grab her and haul her back pounded at his brain. The only thing that kept him in check was the fact that if he jostled her, it could cost her her life.

She crouched low, popped around the corner, fired four rounds, and was back before Lucas's heart had time to beat three times.

"Got two of them. Wounded. Not dead."

There was a door directly across from them, and no light spilled out from the crack underneath. "I'm going across the hall so we can plow our way through. Cover me."

She nodded.

Behind them Riley laid down a heavy burst of automatic gunfire.

Lucas moved to give Sloane room at the corner and as soon as she let loose, he lunged for the door, twisted the knob, and slammed through the opening. He did a quick scan to make sure the room was empty before turning his back on it.

Sloane's weapon quieted as she ran out of rounds. Lucas took over for her while she shoved a fresh magazine into her assault rifle. She'd left her favorite sniper rifle behind, but she was as capable with this weapon as she had been with all the firearms he'd seen her use.

He knew in that moment that all the future women in

his life would pale in comparison to her. She was a rare find—one he was going to miss like hell.

Don't go there. Not the time or the place.

Lucas pulled his head back in the game and took out another one of the shooters down the hall. That left only two standing, evening their odds.

"We need to move," shouted Riley. "More men coming up the stairs."

Right. Time to end this.

Lucas leaned out just enough to see his targets and finished one off while Sloane took care of the other.

"Let's go," he said.

Sloane grabbed Riley's arm and hauled him into the hallway. They shut the door and Lucas bent the hell out of the knob with the butt of his rifle.

"I'll make sure they don't get through," said Riley as he reloaded. "You two go ahead. I'll be right behind you."

They ran to the bloody mess on the floor, scooping up weapons so the two unconscious men couldn't do any more damage. Lucas shoved them both inside a room and turned the dead bolt that was conveniently on the outside of the door—likely the way Soma controlled his visitors—or hostages.

Sloane was a few feet ahead of him. "Here!" she shouted, excitement ringing in her voice.

"Sloane?" said a woman on the other side of a door.

"Gina!"

"I'm here. Get me out!"

Lucas was by her side now, and turned the dead bolt. Unfortunately the bottom lock was also engaged, and it needed a key. "Stand back, Gina. We're going to blow the door open."

He'd brought a shotgun with breaching rounds with him, knowing they might run into this kind of problem.

Thankfully, it was a nice wooden door rather than thick metal bars that held her here.

He gave Gina enough time to comply, then fired the weapon. It shredded a hole through the wood, rendering the lock useless. One quick hammer with his foot and the door flew open.

Gina ran into Sloane's arms, hugging her around the neck while tears streamed down her cheeks. "I can't believe you came for me. Thank you. Thank you."

Riley jogged up behind them. "We're going to have company soon. Time to go."

"We can't leave without her," said Gina.

"Without who?"

"Sophie. She's being held here, too. I saw her."

"Where is she?" asked Lucas.

"Around the corner. This way."

Gina grabbed Sloane's vest and tugged. They all followed after her for a few seconds until Sloane gently pushed her to the middle of the group. "I don't want you running into any surprises."

They'd gone around two corners when Gina pointed down the hall. "There. Third door down."

Behind them came the sound of booted feet and angry voices.

"Time's up," said Sloane.

Riley's jaw clenched. "I'll get Sophie. You two get Gina out."

"You've got to kill Soma," said Gina, her face pale with panic.

"We're working on it," said Sloane. "We've got sharpshooters on the job. As soon as they have a shot, they'll kill him."

Before anyone could argue more, Lucas was going to take the opportunity to get both women. He handed the shotgun to Riley. "It's loaded with breaching rounds."

"Thanks," said Riley as he slung the weapon's strap over his head.

"This way," said Lucas. He practically shoved Sloane forward to get her moving, but at least she went.

"I don't like leaving either of them here," she snapped.

"I know, but this is the best way to keep Gina safe. You said Riley was good. Let him do his job." And if he couldn't, Sloane and Gina would still be safe.

They came up to the next corner and saw three men heading their way. Lucas fired before any of them had time to react.

They had to step over the dead bodies, and Gina balked for a second before Sloane took a tight hold on her arm and propelled her forward. "Don't think, just move."

A low, pitiful sob erupted from Gina's mouth, but she kept walking.

Finally, they reached the top of the massive staircase. The only way out was down and the foyer was flooded with at least a dozen armed guards.

Lucas jerked back, but not before he'd been seen. "Shit. The exit's blocked. Time for plan B."

"Plan B?" asked Gina.

"Break out a window, rappel down to the ground."

"Right." Sloane turned and went back to the first door along the back wall of the villa. She shoved her way through and went to the window, with Lucas and Gina right on her heels.

She pushed the window up, checked outside, and pulled her head back in. "Hold on one sec," she said. Then she pointed her rifle through the opening and fired. "Okay. We're good now, but not for long."

"I hear you," said Bella. "We'll cover your exit."

Lucas made quick work of securing the line to the leg of a massive bed, then clipped a harness onto Gina.

Sloane slipped her rifle's strap over her head. "I'll go

down first." And then she stepped out of the window before he had a chance to argue. "Gage, Bella, we're coming out through a window on the south side. Don't shoot us."

"I'll help you down," Lucas told Gina. "All you have to do is trust me, okay?"

Gina's chin wobbled, but she held it together. He clipped her harness to the line and helped her out the window where she dangled fifteen feet over the ground. It wasn't far, but it was far enough for someone who was already scared shitless.

Lucas controlled her descent as he went, easing her harness down the line. Sloane was waiting on the ground, and helped her friend until her feet were where they belonged.

A bullet ripped a chip of concrete from the ground only two feet away. Lucas shoved Gina toward the measly concealment of some nearby bushes and fired back up toward the window.

Riley heard the guards going after the others and pressed himself into a doorway, hoping they wouldn't see him. He counted ten men as they passed, all seriously armed.

Who the hell was this Soma guy and why did he have his own freaking army?

Behind him, he heard a frightened, feminine voice come through the wooden door. "Hello? Can somebody please tell me what's going on?"

Riley pressed his mouth close to the door. "Sophie?"

"Who's there?"

There was little time for introductions right now. He had to get her out of here while he still could. "My name is Riley. I'm here to help you, but I need you to listen very carefully, okay?"

"Y-yes."

"Move away from the door. Cover your head with something—your arms if you have to. I'm going to blast it open."

Her voice sounded small and terrified. "Okay."

Riley gave her a few precious seconds to comply, then blew a hole through the door. The noise was deafening, but with all the sirens and gunfire going on, he doubted anyone could have distinguished it from the rest of the racket.

Sophie was crouched in the far corner of the room, clutching a pillow over her face and body. She was small enough that it covered most of her, which made Riley's protective instincts kick up a notch.

He tried to keep his voice calm, but adrenaline was riding him hard, roughening his edges. "We don't have much time. Let's go."

She moved the pillow as she stood. Her thick hair fell in a braid over her shoulder. He couldn't tell what color it was in the light streaming in through the window, but it wasn't very dark. Her eyes were huge and shimmering with tears that made him want to pull her in for a long, hard hug.

Too bad there wasn't time for that kind of indulgence.

He held out his hand, knowing that the way he looked now—armed and covered in paint—had to be frightening, but there was no help for that.

She moved so slowly it made him want to shout for her to hurry, but he held back. She extended a shaking hand and Riley closed his dirty fingers over hers. Her skin was cold and clammy, but so smooth he found himself running his thumb over the back of her hand.

It was late, and she was wearing a loose, knee-length nightgown. It wasn't cold enough to worry about the lack of clothing, but her bare feet were going to be a problem. "Where are your shoes?"

She pulled her hand away and reached under the bed. Little flimsy sandals dangled from her hand, but they'd have to do.

"Put them on. Hurry."

He needed to get her out of here before it was too late. The question was, which way to go? He'd heard Lucas say the front exit was blocked. The only thing he could think to do was take a chance that there'd be a matching staircase in the opposite, western wing of the mansion. If not, they were out of luck because they'd only planned to rescue one civilian, and Lucas was the one with the rappelling gear.

Into his lip mic, he said, "I'm heading out through the west wing. Need some support."

"On my way," came Gage's calm voice.

"I'll handle the east end," said Bella.

Sophie slipped the sandals on and was back on her feet, looking to him for guidance. The amount of trust shining in her pale eyes was enough to make him squirm. And oddly, at the same time, it puffed him up knowing she willingly put her life in his hands.

Riley took her hand, curled her fingers around a strap on the back of his tactical vest so she could hold on, and said, "Stay close and stay quiet."

Chapter 19

Sloane was faster than Lucas. Her first rounds had already left the shooter dangling out the window, dripping blood onto the concrete below before Lucas even had time to aim.

Another man appeared in the window a second later, and this one wasted no time sighting his targets. Lucas shoved Sloane as he leaped aside, wanting to be anywhere but where he'd been a second ago.

As he flew through the air, he saw the man in the window jerk and a pink spray bloomed out from his neck.

"Got him," said Bella in Lucas's ear.

The bodies shifted—likely being pulled away to make room for the next man in line. Lucas wasn't going to wait for that to happen. They needed to be able to run without fear of getting shot in the back.

He pulled a grenade from his vest and lobbed it through the opening. "Run!" he shouted, scooping up Gina by the arm as he hauled ass toward their rendezvous point.

Sloane ran backward, sending a few more rounds into the window to keep the bad guys' heads down.

Seconds later, the grenade went off.

*   *   *

Sophie did her best to keep up with Riley, but the pace he set was so fast she had trouble. At least the cramps she'd been having all day had eased. Not only had they scared her to death—making her think that something was wrong with her baby—she was sure she wouldn't have been able to run like she was now if they'd continued.

She'd spent the day curled up in bed, begging for someone to bring her a doctor. No one listened, not even the father of the child she carried.

If she hadn't already known Lorenzo was a monster, today would have proven that beyond a doubt. Then again, after the things she'd done, she deserved whatever she got.

Countless doors and alcoves slid by her peripheral vision. Sophie kept her eyes on the ground so she wouldn't trip over anything, and a tight grip on the thick strap on Riley's back. He pulled her along easily, as if he didn't notice the added weight of her sluggish body.

Sophie had so many questions she wanted to ask him, but she clamped her lips shut, staying quiet as he'd asked.

He stopped suddenly and she ran into his broad back. He reached his left hand back to steady her, his grip warm and firm on her arm. Once she was solidly on her own feet, he put a finger to his lips for silence and pressed her back against the wall.

He leaned close and whispered, "Stay here." Then he left her there, shaking in the hall as he slipped around the corner.

Sophie stood completely still except for the uncontrollable tremors vibrating through her limbs. Her breathing was too fast and she was scared to death.

What if he didn't come back? What if Lorenzo found her trying to escape? What would he do to her and the baby?

She refused to think about that. It wasn't going to

happen. Riley was coming back for her any second. All she had to do was stay here like he'd asked so he'd know where to find her.

The seconds dragged by. The sound of sirens and shouting were quieter here in this part of the house—quiet enough she could hear the frantic pounding of her heart in her ears.

What was he doing? What was taking so long? Surely if things had gone well he'd be back by now, wouldn't he?

Sophie had nearly convinced herself to go after him when he came back around the corner. A few drops of blood were splattered across his forehead, a few more on the hilt of a wicked-looking knife strapped to his thigh.

She didn't dare ask what he'd done. She didn't want to know.

Riley held out his hand, crooking his fingers for her to come to him. It took her a minute to get her feet moving again, but she made it across the few feet separating them.

"You okay?" he asked. "You're pale."

She wasn't sure she was ever going to be okay again, but she gave him a shaky nod. "Let's just get out of here."

He turned his back, waiting for her to curl her fingers around the strap again, before moving forward. She wobbled around behind him like a balloon on a string as he moved down a long hall.

A flash of movement ahead caught her eye. Before she could figure out what it was, Riley moved and a deafening hail of gunfire blasted out from his body. Instincts forced Sophie to cover her ears and fall to a crouch.

More explosions shook the walls, reverberating in her bones as hot metal bullet casings tinkled to the floor at her feet.

The world went quiet except for the ringing in her

ears. The smell of gunpowder assaulted her nose, choking the air from her lungs.

She felt hot, hard hands moving over her body as if looking for something, but she didn't dare open her eyes.

Riley's harsh voice cut through the tinny buzz in her ears. "Are you hit?"

Sophie didn't understand the question at first. How could anyone have hit her when he was the only one close enough to do it? And why would he hit her if he was going to all the trouble to save her?

She looked at his face. Beneath the smeared black and green paint his forehead was wrinkled with concern, but he wasn't looking in her eyes, he was scanning her body.

"Are you hurt?" he asked, his tone more demanding.

Sophie shook her head.

His wide shoulders sagged a bit before he wrapped his hands around her forearms and pulled her to her feet. "We have to move. I need you to stay strong for me, okay?"

Words were beyond her. She didn't have enough room around all the fear in her chest to speak, so instead, she grabbed her strap to let him know she was with him.

He gave her a brief, fierce smile. "That's my girl."

Sloane saw about ten armed men pouring out of the villa. If she, Lucas, and Gina kept running, they'd be torn to shreds before they reached the jungle.

A large cement fountain was a few yards to their north and she shouted at Lucas, "Fountain!"

He still had a grip on Gina's arm, so when he went, so did she.

They piled behind the barrier just as the shooters opened up.

"We're not going to make it to the trees," she panted.

"We need another exit strategy," said Lucas.

Sloane peeked over the low ledge. Those men were getting closer. Their shots were going to be way too accurate any second. "We can't wait."

"I see two Jeeps," said Bella. "Take one."

Victor's voice came over the headset. "The gate is closed. I'll secure your exit."

Lucas pointed at a gap in some bushes. "There. I'll hot-wire it."

"I'll cover you," said Bella.

"Me, too," said Justin.

"Ready?" Lucas asked Sloane.

She glanced at Gina, who was wide-eyed, but holding it together. "On three, Gina."

"Right," said Gina. "I can do this."

"All you have to do is run. As fast and hard as you can, okay?"

Gina nodded and pushed herself onto the balls of her feet, crouching behind the fountain.

Sloane snapped a fresh magazine into her weapon. "One. Two. Three!"

The first heavy boom of a sniper rifle split the air. Then another. Sloane pulled Gina to her feet and they all three sprinted for the Jeep.

A second later, Gina jerked away from Sloane's grip, falling hard.

Sloane skidded to a halt and looked behind her. A hole had been ripped through Gina's sleeve, just above her elbow. Blood soaked the fabric, spreading fast.

Gina lay still, unmoving.

Sloane stopped breathing and stared down at her friend, too shocked to do anything. "Gina?" Her voice was quiet, but Lucas must have heard it over the headset.

In an instant, he was back at her side. He gave her a little shake. "I've got her. Run!"

Lucas picked up Gina's limp body and settled her over his shoulder.

"Run, Sloane!" came Bella's sharp order, loud in her ear.

Finally, Sloane snapped out of it and fired a continuous burst into the growing crowd of guards flowing out of the villa. She was not going to let Gina take another bullet.

Lucas made it to the Jeep and dumped Gina in back. Sloane hopped in, keeping up a steady stream of covering fire to augment that coming from Bella and the others.

Lucas ducked under the wheel—hopefully hot-wiring it with some really speedy skill.

She picked off another three of the guards by the time the Jeep rumbled to life and they lurched into a fast start.

"Hold on," said Lucas. "This is going to be a rough ride."

Sloane turned backward in the seat, firing shots over the back to slow down Soma's men. Chances of her hitting anything were next to zero, but if she bought them a couple of extra seconds, that could make all the difference.

A bullet pinged off the back of the Jeep. Ahead loomed an iron gate. It was closed.

"Can we plow through?" she asked, reaching into the back to fasten a seat belt around Gina's body.

She couldn't think about what was wrong with her friend right now. That would have to wait until they'd stopped taking fire.

"Victor, how's the gate coming?" asked Lucas.

"Ten seconds."

"That's cutting it close," said Lucas. "Buckle up."

Right. She helped Lucas snap his buckle closed, then did her own.

The gate was ten feet of metal topped with razor wire. Strong. Solid.

"Now would be good, Victor."

A flash of light lit the sky and surrounding landscape. A hot boom followed and bits of metal shrieked and banged as they blasted out into the night.

Sloane ducked and covered her head with her arms.

Very little of the metal flew their way. Victor must have rigged it to explode in his direction.

Lucas accelerated. The Jeep slammed into the broken remains of the gate. The windshield was ripped off until it hung, dragging the ground on Lucas's side.

But they were through.

Behind them was a line of vehicles headed right for them, each one full of armed men.

Sloane pulled one of the grenades from her belt and tossed it at the oncoming vehicles.

"Go faster," she told Lucas. "I'll stop them."

"I'm going as fast as I can on two shredded tires."

The engine growled as he tried to accelerate.

She had only two grenades left, but that would have to be enough. The one she'd thrown exploded in the distance. They were too far away for her to see if it worked, and they'd rounded a corner, cutting off her line of sight with the bad guys.

"You're handy to have in a fight. Anyone ever told you that before?" asked Lucas.

"Once or twice." She tossed another grenade for good measure, saving the last one just in case things got ugly.

Another boom sounded in the distance.

"Any sign of company?" he asked.

"No. Can't see past the turn."

Sloane glanced down at Gina. She hadn't moved. The bloodstain on her shirt had blossomed until it was now as large as her head. She couldn't see if Gina was breathing. The ride was too rough.

Fear gripped Sloane hard, squeezing the breath from her lungs. A cold chill shuddered through her that had nothing to do with her fever.

Please, God. Don't let her die.

Sloane consciously shoved her thoughts of worst-case scenarios out of her mind and looked for other options to get all of them the hell out of here in one piece.

There was a metal toolbox on the floorboards behind Lucas's seat. She hefted it into her lap, opened it, but all that was there was standard handyman gear.

"Fling it out the back," said Lucas. "Makeshift caltrops."

Good idea.

Sloane pitched the metal tools onto the road, including a handful of nails she found in the base of the toolbox. Once it was empty, she tossed the box, too.

Lucas was tense as he drove. The muscles in his forearms bulged and his knuckles were white. Blood seeped from a cut on his elbow, dripping onto his lap. His gaze flipped between the road ahead and the road behind. "I don't see anything."

"How close are we to the Rover?"

"We'll see it any second."

"Stop here. Torch the Jeep. Turn it into a roadblock."

"I like the way you think." He came to a skidding halt and hopped out.

Sloane reached back and took Gina's hand in hers. She was warm and limp.

"We need to stop her bleeding."

"It's not bad. She's going to make it," said Lucas, sparing her a quick glance as he unfastened Gina's seat belt and picked her up.

"I hope you're right. If she doesn't . . ."

"Don't think like that. It won't do either of you any good. Stay focused. We're not out of this yet. She needs you to be sharp."

He was right. She needed to stay positive. Will Gina to live.

"You go ahead," she told him. "I'll take care of the Jeep."

Lucas moved away with Gina over his shoulder. He was limping, but he didn't let it slow him down.

Sloane waited for Lucas to reach a safe distance. She could hear engines getting closer, but she couldn't risk either of them getting hurt. She waited until she saw the beam of oncoming headlights before she pitched the grenade into the Jeep—right next to the spare tank of gas—and ran.

Chapter 20

Riley was doing his best to rid himself of the sickly panic that gripped him. For a second there, he thought Sophie had been hit. She'd fallen to the ground so fast he was sure a bullet had ripped through her slender body.

He'd never been so thankful for a plain white nightgown on a woman as he was tonight. The fact that he'd seen no spots of blood on her clothes had been the only thing that kept him from losing it.

If a woman had been killed on his watch, he knew he'd never forgive himself.

As they neared the stairwell, Riley slowed. He did not want a repeat of that last ambush. One of those bullets had come so close to his head he was sure it had left a shiny patch on his ear.

As he slowed, Sophie pressed closer to his back. He could feel the hem of her nightgown dragging against the fabric of his pants.

He needed to check the stairwell without her and make sure it was clear, but he hated leaving her alone, even for a second. He pulled her fingers from his vest. They were cold and she'd been holding on so tight, her fingers resisted straightening in his palm.

He pushed her into the shallow recess of a closed doorway. "Stay here."

The security lights through the window caught a shiny ribbon of tears flowing down her cheek. Her chin wobbled and her mouth was pulled tight, but she did as he asked.

Riley hated it that he had to put her through this, but it was the only way to save her. Rather than dwell on what he couldn't change, he went to do his job.

Lucas wasn't sure how much longer his knee was going to hold up to this kind of abuse. Gina didn't weigh much, but he felt every pound of the added weight grinding in the joint, sending pain streaking up his leg.

"Where are you, Victor? We need to get out of here. Now."

Headlights bobbed in the distance. "I see you," said Victor. "I'm almost there."

Lucas moved off to the side of the road just as Sloane caught up with him. A second later, Victor slid to a halt and they piled in the back of the vehicle. Gina flopped onto Sloane's lap, leaving a smear of blood on her sleeve.

"Where is the med kit?" asked Lucas.

Victor tossed it into the backseat, then turned the Land Rover around in a nauseatingly fast three-point turn. "Nice roadblock."

"It won't hold them long," said Sloane, her voice tight with worry. "Let's get the others and get the hell out of here."

Through the headset, Lucas heard Bella's calm voice. "Justin and I are almost to the pickup point."

Riley came on a second later. "We're still in the villa. We're not going to make it out in time. You go on. We'll cut through the jungle and meet at the secondary location." The bunker, where they'd left the second vehicle.

Lucas swallowed a curse. The plan was falling apart fast. Sure, they had contingencies in place, but needing them was not a good thing. "Do you need any more support to get out?" he asked Riley.

"I'll cover Riley," said Gage.

"Thanks, man."

Lucas glanced at Gina. Sloane had torn her shirt-sleeve off to inspect the wound. It was bleeding, but not badly. "How's her head?"

"Head?" asked Sloane as she ripped open a pack of gauze with her teeth.

"She hit it when she fell." Lucas slid his fingers through her hair, gently searching for a lump. Instead, he found a sticky, wet spot. He pulled his fingers away and they were red. Blood.

Sloane closed her eyes for a second. When she opened them again, they were filled with determination. "She's still breathing. We'll get her out of this mess. Get her medical help."

"Of course we will," he told her, hoping it would help to hear the words from someone else.

"Sloane, honey, I'm almost there," panted Bella.

Victor slowed the vehicle at the pickup point. Lucas lifted Gina onto his lap and scooted over to make room. It was going to be a tight squeeze getting everyone in, considering the back was still full of gear.

He pushed the door open and Bella jumped in. Justin rode shotgun, and as soon as the doors slammed shut, Victor took off, the wheels spewing dirt behind them.

Victor glanced in the rearview mirror. "We've got company."

With Gina on his lap, Lucas had a hard time seeing behind them. "How many?"

"Two vehicles closing in fast," said Bella. "Anyone have a grenade handy?"

Lucas shifted Gina, lifting her limp arm to reveal the two grenades he had left. "Here."

Bella rolled down the window, grabbed both, pulled the pins, held them for a few nerve-racking seconds, and then lobbed them out the window.

The explosions were so close together they felt like one. Light and noise blasted the back end of their vehicle, giving them a good shake. Victor kept them on the road, but the muscles in his arms were straining to do the job.

"Well, hell," muttered Bella. "Only got one of them."

She put her weapon out through the window to fire, and then a hail of bullets slammed into them from behind.

Sloane was working hard not to throw up with all the fear running through her system. As hard as she tried to stay detached, it just wasn't working. This was Gina, the one person who had stood by her through every disappointment her childhood had offered.

Not only was Gina wounded; she was also unconscious with a bloody head wound. And now they were being shot at. The armor plating would hold, but if the tires were blown out, there'd be no way to outrun Soma's men.

"Constance is in the back," she told Lucas. Sloane needed her hands free to keep pressure on Gina's wounds. The way they were bouncing around the rutted road, she worried the bleeding could get worse.

If Gina bled out before they could get her help . . .

Lucas's warm hand settled on her knee. "We're going to get her out of this mess."

Sloane nodded, swallowing back tears she refused to let fall.

"I'm going to need the window," he said.

They shifted so Sloane was in the middle crammed next to Gina. Lucas reached into the storage area and pulled out the grenade launcher and several rockets. He loaded the ammunition, then rolled down the side window.

Bullets pinged against the plating. Lucas pushed the weapon through the window, keeping his head inside, and fired.

The rocket missed, slamming into the jungle. The vehicle chasing them slowed and the gunfire stopped for a moment. Sloane wasn't sure if this would scare them off or make them more frantic to finish killing their enemy.

Lucas didn't wait to find out. He reloaded, pushed his upper body through the window, aimed and fired again. This time the RPG slammed into the vehicle and exploded. Shrapnel hit the back of the Rover. Lucas jerked his head inside, but she could see a nasty cut along one cheek where he'd been hit.

He wiped away the blood. Behind them was a lot of smoke, but no one seemed to be driving through it to follow them.

"I think we're clear," he said.

"Riley?" said Bella. "Are you out yet?"

There was no answer over the headset.

Sloane tried, hoping Bella's unit had gone bad. "Riley? Gage? Are you guys out?"

Still no answer.

"Are we out of range?" Bella asked Victor, who'd given them all the comm units.

"No. We're not."

A sick feeling bloomed in the pit of Sloane's stomach as the list of things that could have gone wrong filled her head. Those were her friends out there—men she'd spent more time with than her own family. She loved them like brothers and now it appeared they might have been snatched away from her, too. Just like Mom.

With Gina's blood cooling on her hands, Sloane couldn't help but think the worst.

"Riley!" she shouted into the lip mic, letting her desperation come through. "Gage! Answer us!"

All that greeted them was silence.

Lorenzo picked up the phone line that went from his safe room to the outside world and called Block. The wall of cameras showed him nearly every part of his estate.

Block answered, "I'm here. No one has come for you yet."

"They're not here for me. They took Gina. And Sophie."

"Sophie?" said Block, the sound of loss seeping into his voice.

Lorenzo had suspected that Block had a thing for the little redhead, but until now he hadn't been sure. Of course now that he knew the weakness, he had no trouble using it to his advantage.

"She's with a man on the second floor near the western stairwell. I want you to stop them."

"I can't leave you unguarded," said Block.

"I'll be safe here. Go. Bring her back."

"You're more important."

Lorenzo was beginning to think that Block wanted his little redhead to escape. But that couldn't happen. Lorenzo's control was already slipping. He needed proof that he could hold what was his—proof for himself as well as Adam Brink. "Bring her back and I'll let you have her. She'll be all yours to do with as you choose."

"You won't make me kill her?"

"No."

A strangled, victorious howl was cut short as Block hung up the phone. Lorenzo watched him sprint from the room. The man was armed with only a pistol, but he'd seen Block at the practice range and that was all he needed.

Sophie was his. Lorenzo had given her to Jeremy, which meant he didn't have to kill her now. He didn't have to let her escape so she'd be safe. They could be together. Forever. *He'd* keep her safe.

Finally, Jeremy would have something good in his life—something that was his and his alone. With Sophie, he'd find happiness. He knew he would.

Jeremy's excitement was short-lived.

Another man had her. Jeremy couldn't let that stand.

Sophie was his, and he was going to kill any man who dared to take her from him.

Chapter 21

Riley didn't dare respond to his friends' radio call. There were three armed men not ten feet away, guarding the stairs. They hadn't spotted him, and he really wanted to keep it that way.

Sophie was with him again, ready to run. He could feel her pressed tight against his back, right where he wanted her—right where he knew she was safe. In a second, he was going to have to leave her here while he cleared the stairwell. She didn't have any protective gear, and he sure as hell didn't want her winding up like Gina—shot, unconscious and bleeding.

Riley reached back and pressed his hand against her ribs, silently telling her to stay. The thin fabric did little to disguise her body's heat or her delicate bones. He eased away slowly, making sure she understood what he needed her to do—that she shouldn't follow him yet.

Sophie stayed put, her eyes wide, her body trembling, but she was still hanging tough.

He gripped his rifle, slid around the corner far enough to aim, and fired at one of the men below. Riley's target fell, but two more men fired back.

Riley jerked back to save his head. The solid wood moldings held steady under the small-caliber rounds, but eventually one of them would get a lucky shot. He needed to have Sophie out of here before it happened.

She let out a little warning squeak. "Behind us."

Riley took a quick look, saw one stocky man running toward them. He had a pistol in his beefy hand and moved like he knew his way around a fight.

Between the two men armed with machine guns in the stairwell and the one man armed with a pistol running toward them, Riley knew which was a safer bet.

He fired into the stairwell blindly, then followed his weapon, looking for a target that hadn't kept his head down well enough. He got one good shot in, knocking one of the men down several steps. The man bounced hard and Riley didn't stop to see if he quit moving. He was too busy searching out the other man he knew was there.

"Riley." Sophie's voice quivered with fear, her frantic pitch telling him that the man running down the long hall was nearly on them.

He grabbed her hand and pulled her through the doorway, keeping her at his back so any stray bullets would have to go through him first. "Ready to run?"

"Yes."

The man in the stairwell opened fire. Riley fired back, advancing down the stairs with Sophie holding on to his vest. They'd just cleared the landing when the man with the pistol appeared at the top of the steps. Riley saw him out of the corner of his eye, but there wasn't much he could do about him. The only way out was down, so that was where they were going.

He got another burst of gunfire off toward the man who was now rapidly retreating before his magazine emptied. So much for firepower.

"Sophie!" shouted the man upstairs. "Stop. I don't want to hurt you."

Like hell Riley would let that happen.

He pushed forward, stepping over a body near the bottom step. Sophie's grip pulled at his vest like she lost her balance, but she stayed on her feet.

The man at the bottom of the steps peered around the corner. If he hadn't yet realized Riley was out of ammo, he would any second.

Riley was not going to let him get the chance.

He slammed the butt of his rifle into the man's hand, knocking the weapon aside. Bullets spewed out, but none of them was on target. Another slam to the side of the man's head stunned him enough that he fell.

Riley tossed a grenade into the stairwell, grabbed Sophie's hand, and ran down the hall toward the nearest exit.

"Gage, we're coming out."

"Copy," was all Gage said, but that one word gave Riley hope that they might actually make it out of this alive.

Riley barreled through the door, shoving it open so hard the glass broke. Sophie's hand was sweaty in his grip, or maybe he was the one sweating. Either way, he held on tight so he didn't lose his hold on her, urging her in front of him to protect her from any gunfire.

From behind, the heavy boom of a .45 splashed out over the lawn. Half a second later, it was followed by an answering boom from the jungle to their west. Gage.

Riley glanced over his shoulder, saw the stocky guy stagger backward. He retreated back into the house.

"Did you get him?" asked Riley.

"Body shot. He's armored."

"Do you have another shot?"

"Negative."

"Anyone else on our tail?"

"Negative."

Riley didn't dare slow the pace even though Sophie was having trouble keeping up. That white nightgown of hers was like a glowing beacon. She'd be way too easy to target. They weren't out of danger until they were hidden inside the jungle, or better yet, inside that bunker.

He kept a tight hold on her arm so she wouldn't fall down. "Almost there," he told her.

Suddenly, the sirens stopped, plunging them into relative quiet. He could hear the sound of Sophie's labored breathing as well as his own. His heart was pounding hard, and only partially from the run. His fear for the woman was an all-consuming thing that had grown from nothing to the driving force in his world in less than fifteen minutes.

She was way too vulnerable for him not to feel that bone-deep need to protect her. He didn't like it, but there was no more he could do about it than he could make the sun set in the east.

"I'm fifty yards to your west," said Gage.

Riley didn't have any plans to veer that direction until they were under cover. Just a few more yards and they'd be out of sight.

"Faster," said Gage. "Men on ATVs are headed for you."

Sophie wasn't going to make it. Her lungs burned and her legs felt so heavy she didn't know how she managed to keep them moving. Riley's long stride made it hard to keep up, and weeks of being locked in that room had killed her stamina.

Unless it was the pregnancy that did it.

She held one hand over her stomach, praying that all this jostling wasn't hurting her baby. She wasn't used to this kind of fear or activity level, and she vaguely remembered hearing that a pregnant woman wasn't supposed to do any strenuous physical activity she wasn't used to.

Sophie sure as heck wasn't used to running for her life from armed men.

Riley picked up speed, practically dragging her along for the ride. They charged into the trees so fast, she felt branches snap at her bare legs. He slowed only enough to keep from running into a tree.

That was it. She was at the end of her strength. She pulled her arm away. "I need a sec," she panted out brokenly.

"We don't have a sec. Soma's men are headed this way on ATVs. We need to get deeper into the jungle." While he was talking, he snapped a cartridge of ammunition into his gun.

Sophie understood his words, but her legs weren't responding.

Riley slung the rifle strap over his head, put one thick arm around her waist, and lifted most of her weight off her legs. "Move," he ordered in a no-nonsense tone.

Sophie moved. They weren't going very fast, and they were making a ton of noise, but at least she did as he asked. It seemed the least she could do after his daring rescue.

Another man appeared a few feet away. Fear snaked through her as she let out a terrified squeak.

"He's a friend," said Riley.

The other man looked grim, covered in paint and weapons. A huge, long gun rested in his hands. "I'll fall back. Cover your six."

"Thanks. We'll head straight for the bunker."

"Bunker?" asked Sophie.

"Not now. Save your breath. We have to keep moving. Those men won't stop at the trees."

And not just any man. Jeremy had seen her escape. Sophie hadn't spent a lot of time with him, but she was good at reading people. She'd seen the way he looked at her. She knew he wanted her. And he wasn't a kind man.

She was convinced that running away from him was going to piss him off like nothing else could.

Sloane had heard snippets of voices coming from Riley and Gage, but they were filled with static and weren't clear enough to make out. At least they were alive.

And no one seemed to be following them after Lucas's judicious use of Constance. The road behind them was clear, without any sign of headlights on the foliage.

"Did anyone understand what they said?" asked Victor.

"I heard plenty of gunfire clear enough," said Lucas.

Victor adjusted his earpiece. "Unfortunately, I think we've reached the extent of the comm units' range."

Lucas kept watch behind them. "They'll meet us at the bunker, just like they said."

"It'll take them hours to get there on foot," said Sloane. Gina was pale and limp against the seat and every second she stayed that way scared Sloane more.

Lucas glanced at Gina, then met Sloane's gaze. Sympathy and concern creased the skin between his brows, and she'd never wanted to have a hug from someone as much as she did from him right now. Instead, she held herself in check and kept pressure on Gina's wounds.

"We have two vehicles," said Lucas. "We can take Gina to get medical attention while the others wait at the bunker."

"The general has arranged for transport out of the country for all of us. There's an airstrip a few miles to the northeast. A small plane will meet us there and fly us into Brazil."

Two days ago, Sloane would have told him to take her father's arrangements and shove them up his ass. But today was not two days ago. Everything had changed. Gina needed her to put aside her daddy issues and deal with the problem at hand—namely getting Gina real medical attention as soon as possible.

She didn't trust the medical facilities here. Not to mention the fact that there was still some man out there looking for Gina. Sloane had no way of knowing how far Soma's reach extended. All it would take was one person on his payroll to let him know an American woman was being treated for a gunshot wound. Soma and the mystery man would have no trouble getting to Gina in a hospital. She'd be a sitting duck.

No, it was better to get her into the hands of her father's loyal men and have one of the medics treat her until she could get to a real doctor.

Sloane looked at Lucas. "We'll take her to the airstrip. Victor can contact my father and tell him to have a medic available. The others can catch up with us once Riley and Gage show up."

Lucas nodded. "All right, then. That's what we'll do." He looked at Victor in the rearview mirror. "Can you make that happen?"

"Yes."

"How far are we from the bunker?" asked Sloane.

"Less than a mile."

"Are you sure about this, Sloane?" asked Bella. "You could run into trouble."

"I know, but I can't sit around for hours while Gina bleeds or gets worse. I need to do this."

"I could go with you," offered Bella.

Sloane looked at her friend, hating what she had to say. "I'd rather Lucas come with me. We've been together for a few days now. We're a good team."

Rather than bristling with insult, Bella smiled a slow, knowing smile. "I just bet you are."

"It's not like that."

Bella held up her hand, cutting Sloane off. "It's exactly like that, but that's fine by me. Good for you."

Sloane didn't bother to waste time explaining. The fact that Lucas wasn't jumping in to clear the air was a sure sign that he thought things were a little foggy, too.

Whatever. Now was not the time to worry over that. They still had a long way to go before they were all safe and sound.

Sloane bent over Gina's head, talking close to her ear. "You're going to pull through this. You're too stubborn to let a little thing like a bump on the head slow you down. You need to open your eyes and let me know you're okay."

Gina was breathing, but that was all the life she displayed.

Sloane hugged her friend and started praying.

Chapter 22

Sophie's cramps were back, only this time, they were worse. Much worse. She tried to keep moving, but her legs were giving out on her. The need to pull them up against her body was almost uncontrollable.

She slipped on the wet leaves at her feet and would have fallen if not for Riley's tight grip.

Another wave of pain gripped her abdomen and squeezed the air from her lungs. A slick wetness coated her inner thighs and she knew it wasn't sweat. The dark spots dotting her nightgown proved her right. It was blood.

She couldn't control the low moan of agony that ripped from her, though the pain in her heart was much worse than that burning in her body.

Riley pulled her to a stop, bending his knees so he could see into her face. "What it is? Are you hurt?"

If it hadn't been for the concern she saw reflected by the flashlight's glow, she would have kept her mouth shut. There was nothing he could do. But he *was* concerned. The man had just risked his life to save hers, not knowing how little she deserved his kindness. She felt she owed him honesty, even though she hadn't been able to give herself the same thing until this very moment.

Denial was a powerful thing, and she'd clung to it all day despite what her body was telling her.

"I think I'm having a miscarriage." The words fell from her mouth, leaving her feeling hollow and numb. The words made it real, terrifying, and devastating.

She didn't like Lorenzo. He'd tricked her at first, wearing the mask of a kind, attentive lover, but now that she knew the man he really was, she hated him. She hated herself for not having seen through his disguise. But she loved her baby. She had from the moment she realized she was carrying it. Despite her fear, despite the fact that she was being held prisoner, she'd forced herself to be calm for the sake of the baby. She accepted her confinement, knowing that once she delivered, she'd do whatever it took to get their child to safety.

And now it was too late.

Maybe she should have tried harder. Maybe if she'd found a way to escape in the beginning she could have found medical care and kept this from happening.

She'd never know for sure, but she did know that she'd wonder for the rest of her life what she could have done differently to save her child.

Riley's dark eyes widened with shock. His grip on her arm tightened fractionally. "You're pregnant?"

She nodded, unable to answer him, because she truly wasn't sure if she was or not anymore. Lorenzo had denied her medical care. The closest thing she'd had was an old woman who didn't speak English who had spent all of five minutes with Sophie. Whatever the woman had told Lorenzo had appeased him, but she had no idea what it had been.

Riley pulled off his helmet, ran a hand over his buzz cut, and took a step back. "Holy shit. You should have said something."

"When? When you blasted my door in or when we were running for our lives?"

He was breathing hard, pacing the small space, refusing to look at her. "I yanked you around and forced you to run. I did this, didn't I?"

"No. It started earlier today. Before you came."

His shoulders sagged in relief, and for a second she thought he might actually pass out. He looked a little wobbly on his feet.

He was silent for a long time, and she could see some kind of internal struggle going on behind his features. His mouth moved like he was holding in vile words and he kept shaking his head in denial. His hands clenched in time with his jaw, and finally, he bent over at the waist, gripping the sides of his head.

When he stood up again, his expression was calm. He walked up to her, cupped her cheek, and said, "I'm going to get you through this."

In that moment, Sophie's composure crumbled. She couldn't be strong anymore. She couldn't deny the grief pounding inside of her. She'd felt so alone for so long, she'd almost forgotten how good it felt to have someone to lean on.

Tears streamed down her cheeks, but she didn't care. A man like Riley wasn't scared off by flying bullets. He sure as heck wasn't going to be scared off by a few tears.

He put his arm around her. "Come on. We need to keep moving. Just a little farther."

Holy fucking shit. Riley was in over his head so far he'd never find a way to get out.

Sophie was having a miscarriage. Losing a baby. Right here, right now. And he had to be with her to witness it. Hell, he'd already promised her he'd help her get through it.

How in the world was he going to do that when he wasn't sure he was going to get through it himself?

He still hadn't had time to absorb the fact that he'd thought he was a father only to find out he wasn't. He still hadn't had time to accept the fact that he wasn't sure whether to be pissed or relieved at what Lucille had done. There were too many fucked-up emotions swirling around inside his head right now to deal with this.

But there was no other choice. This was happening, and he had to find a way to pull himself together and man up. Sophie needed him.

She stumbled. Her gasp of pain hit his ears like a hammer. Her body curled in on itself like she couldn't control it. Witnessing her pain made a wave of nausea slam into his gut.

He was so damn helpless. There wasn't a thing he could think to do to help her.

"Stop," she begged him. "I have to stop."

With who knew how many men hot on their tail? Not going to happen. "We can't. I'm sorry."

She let out a quiet moan, clutching her stomach. He could feel her body vibrating with tension as she tried to fight the pain. She gripped his arm hard enough to leave bruises, and bit her bottom lip.

Shit. There was no way she could keep going like this. It looked like it was taking all her effort to keep from screaming.

Gage slid into sight, making Riley jump. He recovered, hoping his buddy didn't see the way he flinched. "We've got a problem," said Riley.

"Yeah. About six of them. Coming this way fast."

"She's having a miscarriage. She can't run."

Gage surveyed Sophie, nodded once, and said, "Keep her quiet. I'll go hunting." Then he was gone.

Riley missed him instantly. It would have been nice to have another man here to deal with this. Hell, it would have been even better to be the one out there hunting the bad guys, rather than listening to Sophie's brave attempts to keep her noises of pain to a minimum.

Her knees gave out and Riley eased her to the ground. He stripped his gear from his body, then unbuttoned the shirt he wore over his black undershirt. He wrapped it around her pale shoulders, hoping to hide the telltale glow of that white fabric.

Everything went back on, in case they needed to run. He really hoped it wouldn't come to that.

The flashlight could give them away, but he needed to be able to see her. Even more important, he guessed that going through this ordeal in the pitch-black was only going to make it scarier for her. So he laid the light on the ground and covered it with a few leaves to mute the glow.

Unfortunately, it was still bright enough to see how much blood was on her nightgown.

Holy fuck.

He'd seen injuries before. He'd seen plenty of blood in his lifetime, including his own, but none of that had prepared him for this. This was different somehow. He wasn't sure if it was because of the loss of an innocent life, or the heartbreak he knew it would cause.

Sophie saw the blood, too. She pressed her hands between her legs as if she could somehow make it stop. A silent sob shook her frame and broke Riley's heart open.

He leaned in close, holding her, because there wasn't another damn thing he could do.

Torment trembled through her, and he could feel her tears hitting his shoulder. If he wasn't mistaken, he felt a couple of his own as well.

A single gunshot boomed in the distance, not far away. Gage.

The answering gunfire was a sharper, higher pitch of smaller-caliber rounds, but there were a hell of a lot of them.

Riley held his breath, praying for the next deep boom

of Gage's weapon. If anything happened to him because Riley hadn't found a way out of that villa faster, he knew he'd never forgive himself.

Gage wasn't an easy man to get to know. He rarely spoke and when he did it was few words, but he was a good man. He'd laid his life on the line more than once for someone else and never said a word to anyone about his heroics.

A second rifle shot blasted out, allowing Riley to pull in another breath. Gage was holding his own, just like he always did.

Sophie rocked back and forth on the ground.

"Is there anything I can do?" he asked.

She didn't answer, and Riley hoped it was because she was focusing on staying silent, rather than because she was hurting too bad to hear him.

Slowly, the tension in her body eased and she let out a weary breath. She was sweating and panting, but it seemed the worst of the pain was over.

"Can you move?" asked Riley.

She gave him a weak nod. He helped her to her feet. She grabbed his arm to steady herself and her fingers were covered in blood.

He looked down at her gown. A spot nearly a foot across was stained dark red.

A sick sense of panic wriggled into him. He had no idea how much blood was normal for something like this, but that seemed like a hell of a lot. And even if she wasn't bleeding out, she sure as hell was going to leave an easy trail for someone to follow.

He cut a strip from the bottom of her nightgown, folded it up, and handed it to her. "We can't leave a trail of blood for them to follow."

She closed her eyes in weariness, then lifted the bottom of her gown. Riley turned away to give her privacy to do what she needed to do.

"My shoes are bloody," she whispered.

"That's okay. I'm going to carry you for a while to see if it will slow the bleeding." He had no idea if it would help, but it sure would make him feel better to do something to keep her from exerting herself.

He arranged his gear so it wasn't in the way, helped her slip her arms into his shirt, and picked her up. She helped him by hanging on to his neck and burying her head against his shoulder. He could barely see a thing, but he stumbled through the best he could with only the faint glow of the flashlight dangling from his belt.

Gage fired again—or at least Riley assumed it was Gage based on the sound. That made three shots and likely three kills.

The bunker was a good hour's hike—more like two at this pace. Riley only hoped Gage managed to hold off the bad guys for that long.

Lucas held on to Gina while Victor came to a skidding stop near the second vehicle. Her head lolled to one side and she let out a groan.

Sloane took Gina's face in her hands. "Gina? Can you open your eyes?"

Her eyes fluttered open, then squeezed shut. Lucas found a flashlight and shone it into her eyes to gauge her pupil reaction. She hissed at the light, but everything seemed normal to him. Granted, he just knew the basics, but that was as good as they were going to get for a while yet.

"What happened?" asked Gina.

Sloane smiled and tears of relief shone in her eyes. "You hit your head. But we're safe now."

Gina struggled to sit up, but when she moved her arm, she groaned in pain.

"Sit still," said Sloane. "You were shot. It's not bad, but you don't want to start bleeding again."

Gina settled back on the seat and opened her eyes hesitantly. "I knew you'd come for me."

"Of course I did."

"Where's Sophie?"

Sloane's eyes slid away from Gina's face. "She's with friends."

"Are you lying to me? Did she die? Don't you dare lie to me." Gina was swiftly getting worked up, ignoring her injuries.

Lucas pressed her back against the seat. "She's fine. We had to split up, and just lost contact with the others, that's all. You've got to stay still."

Victor opened his door. "I'm going to head toward the others on foot and see if I can make radio contact with them."

"Do you need company?" asked Bella.

"No, thank you. Stay here and guard the vehicles. I won't be long. I would appreciate it if you'd man your headset, though, just in case."

Bella nodded, grabbed some spare ammunition from the back, and got out. She took up position between the vehicles and the road, donned a pair of NVGs, and settled in like she planned on staying there as long as it took.

Sloane slowly lifted the gauze from Gina's arm. "The bleeding seems to have stopped."

Lucas shone the flashlight on the wound. He hadn't really had a chance to see how bad the damage was earlier. "It doesn't look too bad. Did the bullet go through?"

Sloane shook her head.

Gina's eyes widened. "You mean I have a bullet inside of me?"

"Think of it as a souvenir," said Sloane.

"You mean a reminder to be careful about who I hook up with."

Sloane swept Gina's hair back from her head. "We'll talk about that later. I promise. For now try to get some rest." She looked at Lucas. "We need a plan. Should we move her now or wait for the rest of the group?"

"She's stable, but that could change. It might be best if we leave, though there's security in numbers."

"I want to wait for Sophie, and . . . Oh, God. Julia." Gina lurched up, reaching for the door with her good arm.

Lucas grabbed her arm and used every trick he knew to hold her still without hurting her. "Stop it. Tell us what's going on."

Gina quieted, but her eyes had flooded with frightened tears. "He's going to kill her. I have to go back."

"Who's Julia?" asked Lucas.

"She's just a baby. I can't let him kill her." She tried to reach for the door again.

"Whoa," said Lucas. "You have to stay still."

"I can't. He'll kill her."

Sloane took Gina's face in her hands, forcing her to focus. "Slow down. Tell us what you're talking about."

Gina looked up at Sloane with tears in her eyes. "I tried to escape once. Soma and his men caught me. He took me to this room where these other women were sleeping—servants, I think. There was a little girl there." She broke off on a sob. "He made me hold her. I felt her warmth, smelled her hair, felt her chubby arms clinging to me. He killed a man while I watched, then told me he'd kill her if I tried to escape again."

Lucas's core temperature dropped twenty degrees in that moment as Gina's words sank in.

Soma was going to kill a child because he and Sloane had freed Gina.

"Stay with her," said Lucas. "Your father has an

armed escort coming for you. I'll go back and kill the bastard before he has a chance to hurt the little girl."

If it wasn't already too late.

"I'm going with you," said Sloane.

"Like hell. You're sick and someone needs to stay with Gina."

"If you go back alone, you'll be killed. They'll be on high alert after what we did. There's no way you're getting in. You need backup."

His jaw clenched as he thought of the scared little girl in the hands of that prick. "All I need is a rifle and a clean shot."

Chapter 23

Sloane gave Gina a don't-give-me-any-shit glare. "Stay here. Don't touch anything or you'll blow yourself up. Got me?"

Gina sniffed. "You're going to stop him, aren't you?"

"Yes," she said, unable to lie to her friend. "If he goes back there, he'll be dead before he gets within sight of Soma. That's not going to do Julia any good."

"You're not just saying that because you have some thing for him, are you?"

Sloane had a hell of a lot more than just a thing for Lucas. The idea that he'd put himself in danger made her break out in a sick sweat. She couldn't lose him. She knew they couldn't be together, but that didn't mean she didn't need to know he was out there in the world, somewhere, happy and healthy and whole. He was a good man. He deserved a good life, and she was going to see to it that he got the chance.

She bent down so Gina could see right into her eyes even in the dark. "If I thought he could save that little girl, I'd let him go. He can't. Not like this. We'll find another way."

"Promise me," said Gina, growling out her demand. "Promise me Julia won't die because of me."

Sloane couldn't, so she got out of the car, hoping Gina stayed there for just a couple of minutes. That was all she needed to talk some sense into Lucas.

He was refilling his spare magazines from the supply in the other vehicle. His head was down and his movements were jerky and erratic. Sloane went to his side and covered his hands with hers. "You know you can't do this."

"I have to. You heard what she said."

"That doesn't make it true."

He looked at her and all she saw was the cold, hard man that lurked inside his kinder exterior. "Do you really think she's the kind of person to lie about something like this?"

"Of course not. I'm sure Soma told her he'd kill the girl, but that doesn't mean he will. Men like Soma use threats to get their way. I know you've seen it before."

"But what if this time it's more than a threat?"

"Then we really need to kill the fucker. Going in now, when there's who knows how many men on alert, is only going to get *you* killed."

Bella had come over to them during their heated conversation. "Are you talking about going back to get Soma?"

"No," said Sloane at the same time Lucas said, "Yes."

"He's got a panic room. I saw him scurry in there through my scope before I could get a clean shot off. He'll bolt at the first sign of trouble, assuming he doesn't stay in there for a few days until he's sure it's safe to come out again."

"Fuck," spat Lucas.

"We could blow the whole villa up to get to him," said Bella, "but if there are innocents there, we'd be killing them, too."

Lucas rubbed the back of his neck. "We'll have to draw him out and hope to God he doesn't kill anyone else in the meantime."

"Do you think he'll come after your friend?" Bella asked Sloane.

"I don't know. We still have no idea why he was holding her to begin with. For all we know the guy he was selling her to will be the one to come for her."

"She'll have to go into protective custody."

"She's not going to like that at all."

"Tough shit," said Lucas.

"I'll do whatever it takes," said Gina. She'd gotten out of the car against orders and was now standing behind them, holding her bloody arm.

"The first thing we need to do is get you medical attention," said Sloane. "Soma is probably still counting on his men bringing you back alive. He's not going to do anything until he's sure that's not happening."

"How can you be sure?"

"Because any man who was cruel enough to kill a child to punish you would want you to see it happen."

Gina shivered. "He already killed a man who inadvertently helped me escape. He made me watch that. Maybe you're right."

Sloane sure as hell hoped so. She was no psychological expert, but she'd seen cruelty firsthand enough times to recognize it.

"I'll stick around," offered Bella. "I'll scout out the villa and see if I can take the fucker out."

Sloane shook her head. "I don't want you staying here alone."

"I'm sure the guys will stay with me. You all can go back with the others and I'll meet you in Dallas in a day or two."

"It's not safe," said Lucas.

Bella grinned like she was thinking of pinching his cheek for being so cute. "Of course it's not safe. Safe is boring, honey, and I do so hate to be bored."

"I can stay with you," offered Sloane.

"Like hell," said Lucas. "Your father would skin me alive if I let you stay here. Besides, if Gina is going to be bait, she's going to need you by her side to make sure nothing bad happens."

Gina's eyes widened with fear—the kind of fear that hadn't been there before her abduction. "Me? Bait?"

"You don't have to do anything you don't want. It's just one option we have if Bella doesn't kill him."

"I'll kill him," said Bella, full of confidence. "And if I don't, Gage will. That man could shoot the stink off a skunk at five hundred yards."

Victor came back in sight, his aristocratic features grim. "I was able to pick up a few segments of conversation from Riley, though it was more static than anything."

"What did you hear?" asked Sloane.

"Sophie's bleeding. She must have been shot."

Gina covered her mouth with her hand as tears pooled in her pale eyes. "Oh, God. Is she okay?"

"She's still alive," said Victor. "I think it will take them a bit longer to reach us than we originally estimated."

"She's pregnant," whispered Gina.

Sloane's head whipped around in shock. "Sophie?"

Gina nodded. "Lorenzo seduced her. Like he did me."

Lucas's eyes traveled down Gina's body. "You're not . . ."

"No," Gina hurried to say. "I'm not. But poor Sophie."

Sloane looked to Victor. "How long do you think it will take for them to get within communications range?"

"It depends on how slowly they move. It could be a few minutes, or it could be a couple of hours."

Lucas put his hand on Sloane's shoulder, and until that moment, she hadn't realized how badly she'd needed the comfort of his touch. "We should take Gina now."

"I'm not leaving without Sophie," said Gina. "She doesn't know any of you. I'm sure she's scared out of her mind."

Sloane hated waiting, but she knew better than to try to force Gina to do something against her will. She'd find a way to do it anyway and end up getting herself hurt. "Fine. But you need to get back in the Rover and stay there. It's armored. You'll be safe in there."

Gina poked her finger at Lucas's chest. "I can see those wheels in your head spinning. Don't bother wasting your time. I'm staying until Sophie's out."

"Heya, Vic?" said Bella.

"Victor."

"Whatever. How about you and me go see if we can lend a hand, or at least get close enough to find out what's going on with the girl."

"Stay in radio contact with us," ordered Lucas.

Victor nodded and motioned for Bella to precede him into the trees. "After you."

Jeremy spotted the bright red blood splatters in the beam of his flashlight. There was a nice, neat trail, like bread crumbs for him to follow.

If anyone had hurt Sophie, he was going to rip them apart as slowly as he knew how.

She was his. And he was going to take his pretty new woman home. Not to Soma's. But his real home in the United States, where she'd be happy.

He was sure that once she got used to the idea of being with him, she'd settle into the relationship as if she'd been born to it.

The kid was still a problem, but he could deal with that. If she wanted to keep it, he'd find a way to get both of them away from Soma. Even if he had to kill the man to do it.

He owed Soma his life, but he'd paid that debt. He'd saved Soma more times than he could count. It was time he had his own life. A real life. With Sophie. After all he'd done, it wasn't too much to ask.

She was so fucking pretty. So sweet. When he looked at her he *felt* something. Something warm and exciting. He just knew she was the perfect woman for him.

Jeremy followed the trail quietly, keeping the beam of his light low so it would be less visible through the trees. His Glock rested comfortably in his hand, ready for use. All he had to do was take out the men with her and he'd be home free.

If he got Gina back, too, that would be a bonus, but Sophie was his priority.

He heard voices ahead. One deep and low, one high and frightened. He recognized Sophie's voice instantly.

The assholes that took her were scaring her. They were so dead.

Sophie knew she was going to get them all killed. She was slowing them down, possibly leaving a trail of blood.

"Put me down," she said.

Riley's face was grim as he glanced down at her. "It's only a little farther."

"You said that almost an hour ago. You've got to be exhausted."

"Nope. Not even close."

"I can walk."

"We move faster this way."

The cramps had eased, but she knew they'd probably be back in a few minutes.

Sadness weighed down on her, but she shoved it away, refusing to think about that now. She was already a liability. If she broke down it would only make things worse.

And she would break down eventually. She was fighting hard against it now, trying desperately not to think of what she'd lost.

She'd grown attached to the idea of having a child. Even Lorenzo's child. It wasn't what she'd planned for her life, but plans could change. Hers certainly had.

It was best not to dwell on it. The last few months of her life had been a roller coaster from hell. She'd been through too much to process. She'd thought she loved Lorenzo. It turned out that he wasn't the man she thought he was at all. She'd lost her freedom when he locked her up. She'd been gone so long she was sure she'd lost her job. The few friends she'd made had probably written her off by now. She'd spent the past few weeks fearing that she'd lose her life once the baby was born, and now she was losing her child, too.

"Hang in there," said Riley. His deep voice was quiet—barely loud enough for her to hear. She felt it in her skin, though, as the rumble of sound sank into her. His voice was soothing, as was his matter-of-factness.

He seemed to deal with things as they came without judging or making her feel bad. He'd never asked her how she could have been stupid enough to get knocked up by a psychopath, or what she'd done to cause the miscarriage. He hadn't scolded her for being unable to walk or for the tears she couldn't seem to keep from falling.

He just did what needed to be done and moved on.

Sophie really needed to learn how he did it if she was going to have any hope of moving on, herself. Right now that seemed like an insurmountable task—one she couldn't even stand to think about.

Suddenly, Riley stopped in his tracks and eased her feet to the ground. He held his finger to his mouth for silence, then reached for his weapon. He pushed her back against a tree and he was at her front, blocking out her view.

He was breathing hard, his wide shoulders moving

with each breath. He acted like he'd heard something, but Sophie hadn't. All she heard was the sounds of the jungle.

There was a sudden rustle of leaves to her left; then Jeremy stepped out, his big black gun aimed right for Riley's head. They were only five feet apart. The chances of Jeremy missing were slim.

Riley froze.

"Move away from my woman," said Jeremy.

My woman? Sophie didn't even know what to do with that comment, so she let it slide by, unexamined. "Don't, Jeremy. Please don't hurt him."

"He stole you."

"No, he helped me escape. You know I didn't want to be there."

Jeremy's face twisted in anger, but he kept his eyes on Riley. "Let go of the weapon and move away."

Riley's voice was strong and solid, ringing out into the night. "I can't do that, man. I can't let you hurt her."

"I'm not going to hurt her," said Jeremy, disgusted. He took a threatening step forward.

Sophie could see this ending badly. Before it could, she slipped out from behind Riley and took a step toward Jeremy, blocking his line of fire.

Immediately, Jeremy shifted the gun up so it was no longer aimed at her. His eyes moved down her body until he saw the blood. "What the fuck did he do to you?" he snarled.

"He didn't do anything. I"—she swallowed hard, praying she could get the words out—"lost the baby."

That news didn't even cause a flicker of grief to cross Jeremy's face. Not even a blink. "That makes things simpler."

She was raw inside, hollowed out and weeping from her soul with every breath and he thought it made things simpler? Sophie hadn't seen it before, but she did now.

Jeremy was a monster. He wasn't just some guy who was too dumb to realize what he was doing. He didn't secretly regret his choices. He simply didn't care. Not about her and not about her lost baby.

Sophie reached behind her, feeling the hard heat of Riley's thigh. She found that wicked-looking knife and slid it from its sheath.

"Sophie, no," said Riley.

"Don't you fucking tell her what to do," warned Jeremy. "She's coming with me and there's not a thing you can do to stop her. She doesn't want you. She wants me."

"I don't want either of you," said Sophie. An unexpected sob ripped from her chest and she leveled the knife, pointing it at Jeremy's throat. "I want my baby."

One second Sophie was standing there, ready to shove that knife in to Jeremy's throat; the next, Riley shoved her aside, and trees were zooming past her vision as she flew out from between the men. A ferocious blast lit the leaves and bashed her eardrums as a gun went off. Then another. From the corner of her eye, she saw Riley stumble back and fall to the ground.

Shock pinned her in place as she struggled to figure out what had happened. She was lying on her side on the ground. Smoke curled through the beam of a discarded flashlight. She smelled fireworks and heard a wet gurgling noise.

Riley. He'd been shot.

Sophie scrambled to her hands and knees, ignoring the painful spasm in her belly the sudden movement caused. She crawled over the ground, her movements hampered by the skirt of her nightgown.

She reached Riley's side, but he was already sitting up. He seemed fine.

Relief fell over her, making her sag. Then she heard the noise again—that wet, sucking noise.

She turned and saw Jeremy lying on the ground. His

face was a bloody mess. Part of his cheek was missing. His mouth had filled with blood and he was struggling to breathe. He weakly spit out blood and bits of broken teeth or bone, but it didn't seem to make that noise go away.

She stared, trying to make sense of what had happened. Before she could, strong hands grabbed her by the arms and hauled her to her feet.

"We have to move. Now. That gunfire is going to bring them down on us."

Riley pulled her by the arm, urging her forward. She went, staring over her shoulder until Jeremy was out of sight.

"Gage. If you can hear me, head toward the shots. We're going to need backup."

Sophie didn't hear if Gage answered or not. She focused on putting one foot in front of the other as fast as she could without falling over.

"You were shot," she said.

"Armored vest. I'm fine."

Fine. But it had been so close. Riley could have easily been the one bleeding on the ground rather than Jeremy. And she'd been stupid enough to think that knife would actually make a difference.

"I lost your knife," she said.

"I'll get another. Don't talk. Just run."

Their speed was nowhere close to a run, but she was swiftly running out of breath anyway. And the cramps were coming back.

Somehow, the sight of Jeremy bleeding to death made her numb enough to push though the pain and keep moving. There was no way she was going to risk Riley's life by stopping again.

Gage heard his friend's call for help and broke into a run, heading toward the sound of gunfire. There were at least another two men out here that he knew of, assuming they hadn't headed back to Soma's villa. The other four wouldn't go anywhere until someone carried their bodies out.

He truly hated killing. It made him feel brittle and angry—like he was being used against his will. Which was stupid. He'd signed up for this job. He'd volunteered to come here. He knew what he'd be facing when dealing with drug lords on their own turf.

That didn't mean he had to like it. It was a damn shame he was so good at it.

Gage found the location where the gunfight had happened. Not that three bullets was much of a fight.

He didn't get close enough to see if the man lying on the ground was alive or not. There was so much blood it was only a matter of time until he died if he hadn't already.

Gage veered to the south, making a straight line for the bunker. A few seconds later, he nearly ran right into the woman's back.

Riley's weapon was pointed right at Gage until he saw who it was. He lowered the barrel and his shoulders sagged with relief. "How many?" he asked.

"Ten."

Sophie was hunched over, holding her middle. Her breathing was too fast and her skin was too pale. "How much farther?" she asked.

"We'll stop here for a minute," said Riley.

"No," panted Sophie. "No more stopping. Let's just get where we're going so I can rest."

"Another half mile," said Gage, answering her earlier question.

"I can do that." She didn't sound like she could do it, but Gage gave her points for positive thinking.

Riley looped his arm around her waist and they started moving. Gage hung back, giving them a few yards' lead. The bad guys would likely be coming up from behind, and those few yards were enough of a buffer to give Riley time to get his hands off the woman and on his weapon where they belonged.

With any luck, Lorenzo's men had grown tired of the chase, or were too busy dealing with their own casualties to bother following them this far.

Then again, Gage wasn't exactly the kind of guy who believed in luck.

Chapter 24

Lorenzo heard the heavy beat of a helicopter's blades even through the reinforced walls of his safe room. He checked the exterior cameras, and sure enough, a helicopter was closing in. The fire in the guardhouse was still raging. There were broken windows on all levels of the house—likely as many shot out by his men as shot in by their attackers. His front gates were in ruins and smoke drifted up from where they'd once stood.

His entire domain had been destroyed, and someone was going to pay for it.

The helicopter stopped, hovering above the tree line several hundred yards to the north. Lorenzo's private phone rang. He answered it, already knowing who it was. Mr. Brink.

"I have everything under control," he assured the American.

"It doesn't look like it from here."

"Cosmetic damage. Nothing more."

"And the woman?"

"My men are retrieving her now. Land and I'll see to your comfort while we wait."

There was a long pause before Mr. Brink spoke again.

"I already gave you a second chance. There will be no third. Our arrangement is at an end."

Panic shot through Lorenzo, squeezing his lungs. It was all he could to keep his voice calm and remember to speak English. "You do not mean that."

"I do. I'll find someone else to fill your shoes. It won't be hard."

Without Brink's connections, Lorenzo stood to lose millions. His inheritance was already shrinking. He didn't have his father's knack for this business, and without Brink, he knew his empire would crumble. His respect would be gone. He'd lose everything.

"I'll get her back," vowed Lorenzo.

"No. You won't. She obviously has powerful friends. Let her go. I have."

"Come inside and we'll talk. I'm sure we can reach some kind of arrangement."

Brink's voice was cold. "Good-bye, Lorenzo."

The video screen in front of Lorenzo showed the helicopter maneuver away, going back the way it came.

Rage poured through his veins until his vision began to go black. He took several deep breaths, trying to control himself enough to think.

He needed a plan—some way to undo what had just happened.

Gina. Maybe if he delivered her to Brink himself the man would forgive him. And if not, he'd still have the woman. He'd vent his frustrations upon her for causing so much trouble.

Either option was better than what he had now, which was a burning home and crumbling power.

Gina Delaney was going to pay, and if he could manage it, so would everyone who dared to help take her from him.

*   *   *

Sloane checked on Gina. She'd fallen asleep in the Rover, but seemed okay. A few minutes ago, Riley and Gage had emerged from the jungle with Sophie in tow.

She didn't look good. She was covered in blood, pale and shaking.

Sloane rummaged in the back of her vehicle for a spare change of clothes and helped Sophie get cleaned up.

"I'm sorry about the mess," she said, her voice wavering.

Sloane waved it off, trying to be as matter-of-fact as she could about the whole thing. "It's not your fault."

Sloane stripped her naked in the shelter of some trees and used a wet cloth to wipe away as much of the blood as she could.

"I don't know what I did wrong. Maybe it was the stress or something I ate. The food here was so different from what I'm used do." Her voice dropped to barely a whisper. "Or maybe it was because of what I did. This is my punishment."

Sloane's heart clenched as she saw the woman's pain lingering in her pale eyes. She'd meant to say that the mess wasn't anything Sophie could have helped and instead Sophie had thought she was talking about the miscarriage.

Sloane took the woman's hand in hers. "None of this was your fault. Lorenzo did this. *All* of this was his doing."

Sophie swallowed, staring off into space as she fell silent.

The woman was in shock—likely both physical and mental. The best thing Sloane could do was get her in dry clothes, give her something to drink, and get her home.

Once Sophie was dressed in a spare set of Sloane's clothes, she guided her back to the group.

She didn't get far. Riley intercepted her, his grimace of anxiety driving the blood from his lips. He handed Sophie a canteen. "Here. I threw a bunch of drink mix in there so it'll taste better."

Sophie looked at it like she wasn't sure what to do. She was weaving on her feet.

"We need to get her sitting down," said Sloane. "Resting."

"I'll do it," said Riley, shoving his big body between them so that Sloane had to step away from Sophie.

She said nothing about his proprietary behavior. The two of them had just been through hell together. If he wanted to care for her, so be it.

Sloane went to Lucas, where he was talking to Bella, Victor, and Gage. "We need to roll."

Lucas gave Bella an expectant look. Bella sighed and said, "Gage and I are staying. We need to make sure this Lorenzo asshole is taken care of."

Sloane didn't like it. "I'll tell you what I told Lucas. They're going to be on high alert. It's too dangerous."

"Gage saw how many men were left. We can take them."

"How many?" she asked.

"Ten," said Gage.

"For now. You know that man's going to have reinforcements coming. He's got drug labs in the area. All he has to do is call those men in."

"He's weak now. Off balance. It will take a while before reinforcements arrive. We can take him out."

"And what about the safe room, Bella? You said yourself he could be in there for days."

"We'll wait," said Gage.

Lucas put his hand on her arm. "Let them go, Sloane."

She looked at him. "You want to go with them, don't you?"

"I do, but right now I think Gina needs to be our primary concern. You and I can keep her safe. She's going to need you to convince her to stay in protective custody once it gets boring, and I really don't want to leave you alone. At least not until we're out of the country. Besides, the fewer of us there are here, the less likelihood there is that Soma's men will spot us."

Sloane looked up at Bella, who was easily six feet tall in her combat boots. Her gray eyes were twinkling with anticipation.

"You know you don't need my permission to do anything," said Sloane.

"I know, honey. I also know that this is your show. If you feel better having us escort your friend home, then we'll go with you."

"But you'll come back," Sloane guessed.

"Hell, yeah. I'm not about to let this drug-dealing, woman-abducting low-life scum roam free on my planet."

Gage lifted a brow at Bella. "*Your* planet?"

"I'm a bit possessive. You know this. Back off."

Gage hid a smirk. "Yes, ma'am."

"So what do you say, Sloane? Are you woman enough to let us have all the fun while you babysit your friend?"

"The last thing I want is to spend one more minute in this jungle. Go ahead. Knock yourself out."

Bella grinned. Gage looked more like he was getting ready to clean a Dumpster with his own toothbrush.

Sloane walked away to let them plan. She needed to leave them the Rover, which meant they were all going to have to pile into the other vehicle. Six people would to be a tight fit, but they'd make it work.

She looked at Lucas, who had remained suspiciously quiet through the whole conversation. "I'm surprised you didn't beg to go, too."

"We're not out of the woods yet. We still have to get to that airstrip up north to catch our flight to Brazil. Soma could have men set to guard our exit."

She wasn't sure how smart she was to put her feelings on the line like this, but she couldn't seem to stop herself. "I'm glad you decided to stay with us. I like having you around."

His fingers slid through hers. There was no privacy here, but his touch still sent wicked shivers through her nerves. She remembered how those fingers had felt moving over her skin, how he knew just where to touch her to make her fly apart.

Her hand tightened in his, and for a brief, crazy moment she wanted to keep him. Forever.

He pulled her to a stop. She laid her cheek against his shoulder, breathing in his scent. She stepped as close as she could get, placing her feet alongside his big, booted ones so their thighs touched. All the gear strapped to their bodies denied her his warmth, but she remembered exactly how it had felt to be naked in his arms.

She would always remember it, even if she tried not to.

His hand slid up her arm until he cupped the back of her neck in his wide palm. She knew her friends were watching—she could feel them stare. She just couldn't bring herself to care. Let them look. Her time with Lucas would be over in just a few hours. She was going to enjoy every second of it to the fullest for as long as she could.

"Sloane," he said. "I think we should talk about—"

She covered his mouth with her finger, cutting him off. "No. Don't spoil it. We both know the score."

He looked down at her, his dark blue eyes catching flickers of light from nearby. "But the things I feel for you . . ."

"Are temporary. Once we're back to our real lives and the adrenaline wears off, so will this thing between us."

He touched her face and it was all she could do not to close her eyes and let the world go.

"What if it doesn't?" he asked.

Sloane knew better. Feelings as powerful as those she had for Lucas didn't last. They couldn't. She'd never survive wanting someone in her life every day as much as she wanted him. It was bound to go away.

At least she hoped so. She didn't want to spend the rest of her life getting over Lucas Ramsey, though part of her wondered if it wasn't already too late.

She knew he had to go to his family. Even though he wasn't looking forward to it, he was too good a man to turn his back on them. It was one of the reasons she loved him.

Love. There it was. Pure and simple, too obvious for her to deny. Somewhere along the way she'd fallen for him. All the way.

And because she loved him, she'd never tell him. She'd never make his decision to leave her harder on him than it already was. He had enough to deal with in his life without her adding any extra baggage.

Sloane went up on her tiptoes and kissed him goodbye. She didn't tell him that was what she was doing, but in her heart, she knew it was time.

She held nothing back. She let her love for him swell inside her for this one brief moment, giving in to the need to surround herself with it, to revel in the joy of loving a man for the first time in her life. Her heart was nearly bursting and she felt tears slide down her cheeks.

And then, when she could hold no more, she pulled away, lingering at his mouth for as long as she dared.

She turned her back on him and went to gather the others. Their time in the jungle was over and she needed to put it all behind her. She had to move on. For the sake of both of their hearts.

Chapter 25

Lucas found out from the guard posted at Gina's hospital room that Sloane was staying in the hotel down the street. He knocked on her hotel room door, anxious to see her again. They'd been apart for only a few hours, but after the last few days of being constantly side by side, that felt like a lifetime.

He'd been so busy getting debriefed by General Norwood that he hadn't had a moment to spare since they'd touched down in Houston early this morning. Now he was a free man, his obligations fulfilled—at least with the general.

Sloane opened the door a couple of inches. The security lock was engaged, making him wonder if she wasn't still a little jumpy from the whole ordeal in Colombia.

"Hi," he said, feeling lame and awkward, like a kid at his first dance.

"Hi." There was no warmth in her tone. It was flat, almost cold.

"Are you going to let me in?" he asked.

She hesitated long enough that he began to worry. Surely she wasn't going to throw him out of her life now that they were back home. He knew they had some things to work out, and he knew she had her reservations, but he was counting on his powers of persuasion to see her through that.

There was more between them than just circumstances. He didn't know how much more, but he sure as hell wanted to find out.

Sloane shut the door long enough to disengage the lock, then reopened it. She was dressed in a white bathrobe. Her dark hair was damp and tousled about her face. She had circles under her eyes and a slight sunburn on her nose. Scrubbed clean like this, she looked younger, more vulnerable than he was used to seeing her.

Or perhaps it was just the fact that for the first time since they'd met, she wasn't armed.

Her voice was as chilly as the room, which she'd apparently decided to air-condition the hell out of. "What do you want, Lucas?"

Her curt question took him aback. "To talk. To be with you."

"I need to get back to the hospital. I'm just here to get cleaned up."

"Gina's sleeping. I just checked on her. And she's got an armed guard at her door."

"She's still my responsibility until my father arranges for her protective custody."

"He's already on that, but it's going to take a few hours." Maybe even a day or two. Lucas was counting on using that time to see where he and Sloane stood, because he knew she wouldn't leave her friend's side until she was safe.

Based on her greeting, he guessed they weren't on the same page.

She sagged onto the bed as if she weighed an extra hundred pounds. "Just say what you need to say and go."

"Why are you doing this? Why are you acting so cold?"

"I'm trying to make this easy on both of us. I really wish you'd respect that and go."

"I don't want to go. I want to give us a shot."

She closed her eyes and swallowed as if trying to compose herself. "There is no us."

"There sure as hell was. I didn't imagine that."

"No," she admitted quietly. "But it's over now. We both have our real lives to lead."

"So I was just a mistake? Or was I simply a convenient fuck to distract you from how shitty things were in Colombia?"

"Neither, Lucas. Please. Just stop. You're making things worse."

"Worse than the two of us walking away from each other? 'Cause that's pretty fucking horrible from where I'm sitting."

Sloane clutched the top of her robe closed, and the protective gesture was not lost on Lucas. She was feeling vulnerable right now. He got that. He was feeling a little raw himself.

"Where do you see us going?" she asked him, her green gaze as direct and demanding as her father's had ever been.

"I don't know, but don't you want to find out?"

"No. I don't have to go through the pain to know how it will end. We'll either try to make a long-distance relationship work, which won't be enough for either of us, or one of us has to give up something big—something too big not to cause resentment. If you don't help your family, you'll regret it. The guilt will eat at you until you figure out I'm the reason and start hating me. Or I give up the job I love and become bitter because it's the only thing I have worth getting up for every day."

The obvious subtext being *he* wasn't enough to fill that void. Not that he blamed her. He'd felt the same way every day between the time he was discharged and the night he met Sloane. Making her feel useless and unnecessary like he had was not something he could do.

He loved her too much to destroy her like that.

And suddenly everything came into perspective. She was right. He couldn't be with her. He couldn't hold her back. She had a fantastic life to lead, and as much as it tore him up to not be with her, letting her go was the right thing to do.

But the only way he could let go of her was if he had one more chance to hold her. He needed something to take with him when he went back home—something to keep him going until he found a nice, quiet hometown girl to settle down with. He was a good man—a little battered and bruised, maybe, but good. There would be another woman out there who he could make happy. She might not be as exciting and sexy as Sloane, but few people in this world were. He would learn to settle.

"I'll go," he told her, taking her hands in his so he could pull her to her feet. "But I want one kiss good-bye. Then I'll leave and I won't bother you again."

She looked uncertain, but she nodded. A damp lock of hair fell over her cheek and he brushed it back behind her ear. Her skin was so silky smooth, still warm from her shower. He tried to memorize the feel, but knew his memories would never compare to the real thing.

He stepped close, feeling the knot in the tie of her robe press against his stomach. He was hard and aching, which he'd come to accept as normal whenever they were alone together. But he didn't want to taint these last few minutes by having her ward off his advances, so he was careful to keep his erection to himself.

He cupped her face and leaned down to kiss her. She was so warm and sweet, and went straight to his head. The feel of her lips and tongue responding to his drove him crazy until he was shaking from the force it took to remember his intent.

This was just a kiss good-bye. Nothing more.

His arms tightened around her. Her fingers dug into his shoulders. She was breathing harder now, or maybe that was him.

Her soft sound of yearning filled his mouth, and he drank down the cry, so he could hold it inside himself forever. She was the woman he wanted. She made him feel whole and strong and needed when she let him hold her like this, when he ignited her desire with a mere kiss.

"I wish I didn't want you," she whispered between biting kisses.

A little part of him shriveled up at her words, but the rest of him reveled in her physical reaction. Even if she didn't want him for the long haul, at least she wanted this much of him.

"Take off your clothes," she ordered.

Lucas was torn between wanting it as much as she did, and wanting to leave her unfulfilled and horny. Maybe if she wanted him enough, she wouldn't push them apart.

But in the end, he couldn't deny her. His own need was raging hot and furious, and the idea of leaving her aching was more than he could stand.

He pushed her hands away from the hem of his shirt and ripped it over his head. He pulled the tie of her robe. The knot slipped free and his fingers found smooth, warm skin. His hands fit perfectly in the curve of her waist.

She shrugged the robe from her shoulders, baring herself to him. The sight of her in the daylight, beautifully naked and unashamed, was almost more than he could stand. The glimpses he'd had before were painted in shadows, mysterious and intriguing. Now, here, in the bright light of day, he could see everything. Her nipples were a dusky pink. She had a sprinkling of freckles across each shoulder. Small nicks and scratches marred her skin, along with the bandage on her arm. Every glowing curve, every shaded hollow called to him. Even the small imperfections excited him, making her seem more real and less unreachable.

"You're making me nervous," she said.

"I can't help but stare. You're so beautiful."

A wicked smile lit her face and she splayed her hands across his chest. "So are you."

Lucas closed his eyes, soaking in the feeling of her hands touching him. He didn't want to think about how this would be the last time they touched—he didn't want that knowledge to taint the time they had now. There was little enough of it as it was.

Her fingers went to his jeans. She was rushing things. Then again, Sloane was always rushing things with him.

He covered her fingers to slow her down, and walked her back until she bumped into the bed. That wicked smile widened and she kind of melted down to sit on the bed in a move so graceful he wasn't sure how she'd managed it. She was on eye level with his stomach and her clever fingers were outmaneuvering his.

"This has potential," she said, lifting her eyes up to look at him.

Lucas nearly lost it right there. She was naked, unzipping his jeans, looking up at him like he was something good to eat, and all rational thought left his head.

This was not what he had planned, but God help him, he couldn't remember what his original plan had been. All he knew was that Sloane wanted him. It was more than enough.

She worked his cock free of his jeans, shoving them down a few inches to get them out of the way. Her fingers curled around him, holding him nice and tight while her mouth slid over the tip.

Lucas sucked in a huge breath and held on to her head to steady himself. His heart hammered inside his ribs and a fine sweat broke out over his body. Her tongue swirled around him while her lips slid down another slow inch.

He was going to lose it right there. He was going to come and lose his chance to do this right.

She deserved better than that.

He gripped her hair in his fists and pulled his hips away to stop her. She opened her rosy lips to say something he was sure would only turn him on even more, so he covered her mouth with his and kissed her as he pushed her down to the bed.

She hummed her approval and stroked his back, splaying her legs wide so he had room to settle between. Lucas kissed his way down her neck, nipping at her collarbones as he passed before moving on down to her breasts. She arched up, offering herself to him, telling him with her noises just what she liked.

He could feel the wet heat of her against his stomach. Her hips were squirming beneath him, rubbing herself against him while she clutched at his head. His fingers slid through the dark curls between her thighs until he felt her slick center. He slid a finger inside her, driving a moan from her that made his head spin with a giddy sense of power. A second finger made her fingernails dig into his scalp, leave stinging marks behind.

He could hardly wait to see how she was going to react when he got his mouth on her.

Sloane knew what she was doing was wrong. She knew she was leading him on, but she couldn't seem to stop. Not with Lucas.

Once he was in her room and the door had shut, she knew she was a goner. He seemed to fill the space, and without him around, her world was a bleaker, duller place.

And now he was here, loving her with his mouth and

hands, driving feelings from her body she'd never known she was capable of before him.

Rather than think about after, she gave herself the moment—let herself rejoice in the feeling of being the sole focus of his attention. The man knew how to touch, how to tease, when to pull back and when to give her more. She hadn't even needed to tell him. He just knew.

Right now, what he knew was how to drive her to the brink of a screaming orgasm only to stop her short and pet her until she quieted.

"You're killing me," she panted.

He looked up at her, wiped his mouth, and crawled up her body. "You'll thank me later."

Sloane was done waiting. She wanted him, and she wanted him now.

She grabbed his erection in a firm grip and wriggled her body until they lined up just right. He looked down at her with a challenge in his dark blue eyes.

"Why are you teasing me?"

"I don't want you to forget me too soon," he said.

As if she could. The man was imprinted on her so deeply she worried she'd never be free of her memories of him. Part of her was relieved by that, but the rest of her feared the consequences of keeping even memories of him inside her. It would only make her want things she couldn't have.

"I won't," she promised, looking right into his eyes.

"I won't forget you, either." Then he surged forward, sliding slow and deep.

He kissed her as he moved, never closing his eyes. His stare should have been unsettling, but instead, it drew her in, made her feel everything—the powerful glide of his body, the soft brush of his chest hair across her breasts. She could hear the steadily speeding rhythm of her heart and smell the growing warmth of his skin. He was inside her, surrounding her, filling her like no other man had ever done before. It was more than just sex. It was tender, almost loving. She could feel the care he took with every move he made, gauging her reactions and changing his tempo to please her most.

And he did. He pleased her in ways she hadn't known were possible. The firestorm inside of her was growing, swelling. He pushed her higher, demanding she take what he had to give.

He eased her leg up so her calf rode along his ribs, and the change of angle was enough to release the tension that he'd built inside her. It exploded in a wash of color and light, bursting behind her eyes and sent rioting shivers racing out from her womb. A noise of pleasure she couldn't control ripped from her chest as her back arched against the force of so much pleasure.

Lucas's body tightened around hers. He held her hard as he climaxed inside her, whispering her name over and over as he filled her.

The last quivering pulses of her orgasm eased, leaving her limp and sated.

Lucas kissed her slack mouth and cheek, eased away from her, and ran his hand down her flank. She closed her eyes and enjoyed the feeling of his hands on her as she drifted off into a much-needed sleep.

When she woke a couple of hours later, Lucas was gone. The only signs of his presence were the languid warmth in her body, the slickness of his semen on her skin, and a hollow, empty feeling in her chest.

Sloane pushed herself from the bed, showered the proof of their union from her body, and checked out of the hotel. She compartmentalized, forcing herself to do what she needed to do without thinking about it. Move, wash, dry, dress—all on autopilot.

As soon as she slid the shoulder strap of her bag on, her composure faltered. She gripped the handle of the hotel room door hard enough to leave marks in her skin.

She turned and looked at the rumpled bed, knowing it would be the last place she ever shared with Lucas.

He'd said he would go, and he was a man of his word. Honorable. Trustworthy.

She wished like hell that she wasn't too fucked up to allow herself to be with him. It would have been nice to have someone around to lean on—someone she knew she could trust. But then what? After they crashed and burned—because they would—then what would she do? It had taken her a long time to find her way in the world. To learn to respect herself. If leaning on Lucas weakened her, she knew that respect would disappear. For both of them. And she'd rather die than lose his respect. Maybe that made her shallow or warped, but she couldn't help the way she felt. She was, after all, her father's daughter.

Sloane shoved back the tears and turned the knob. Gina still needed her. Bella still needed her. She had a great job and didn't need to lean on anyone. It was everything she'd ever wanted. Everything she'd worked for.

The fact that it was no longer enough was just something she was going to have to learn to accept. It was time to move on.

Chapter 26

Riley stood over Sophie's hospital bed, watching her sleep. She'd been through hell, but she was tougher than she looked. Thank God.

The light over her head put the sprinkling of freckles across her cheeks on display. They'd let her shower, and her hair lay in a thick, damp braid over her shoulder. She looked small in the midst of the white sheets. Pale and fragile.

Riley's hands tightened on the bed railing. The urge to touch her skin and make sure she was warm enough was digging at him, making him edgy and irrational.

The doctor had assured them she was fine and would recover, but Riley wasn't going to believe it until he saw her walk out of here. In fact, he'd fully intended to escort her home, wherever that was, and see to it that she was settled.

After all she'd been through, it seemed the least he could do.

Her eyes opened and he was caught by her pale green gaze. Her face was so stoic, and there was a tension about her as if she was expecting the other shoe to drop.

"How are you feeling?" he asked.

"Fine."

He accepted the lie rather than pry. He knew she was suffering, and he hated that he couldn't do anything to fix it.

"You don't have to stay," she said.

"I don't mind. I could call someone for you. Family. Friends."

She shook her head. "No, thanks."

"I don't want you to be alone. Let me take you home."

"I'm not sure where that is yet."

"What do you mean?" he asked.

"I mean I've been gone for a long time. I'm sure they've cleaned out my apartment by now after a couple months of not paying rent. I was doing temp work, which I'm sure is no longer available. I may stick around here for a while—at least until I can get some ID and access to my bank account."

Houston was too far from Dallas for his tastes. If she stayed here, he was going to have a hard time checking up on both her and Mom when he was in town. And he *needed* to check up on her. "I'm flying back to Dallas. You could come with me."

"Why?"

"Why not? It's as good a place as any if you're not tied to a specific spot."

"I lived in Dallas once. The people there are nice. They drive like maniacs."

Riley laughed. "That they do."

"Let me think about it?" she asked. "I'm tired. I don't want to make any bad decisions."

He forced himself to back down. The fastest way to drive her away was going to be to push and seem all desperate and needy. "Fair enough. I'm going to grab something from the cafeteria. I'll be back in a minute. Want anything?"

"No, thanks."

"You can call my cell if you change your mind." He

pulled out his wallet and handed her one of his business cards.

He'd almost made it to the door when she said, "You really don't have to come back."

He turned. "I've gotten you this far. I'm not going to abandon you now. Let me see you settled, okay? It'll ease my mind."

She nodded, but said nothing.

Riley left, giving her some space to think about his offer. If he was lucky, he'd convince her to stay with his mom for a while. They could watch out for each other when he was out of town, so Sophie wouldn't have to think of it as a handout. Mom did fine on her own, but Riley worried. Besides, she might enjoy having another woman around to chat with and do . . . woman stuff.

He got a sandwich and hurried back to her room, excited to see what she thought of his idea.

She was gone. Her hospital gown was lying on the bed. The bag of sweats he'd bought for her to change into was empty, the tags discarded across the bed.

Riley tried not to panic. He went to the guard posted outside her room. He was just a kid—too young for Riley's comfort.

"Where did she go?"

"A nurse came to get her for some test. She didn't want me to go with her."

"And you accepted that?"

"Well, yeah. It's not like she's a prisoner."

He went to the nurses' station and all they would tell him was that she checked out AMA. They wouldn't give him any details. He wasn't family.

Anger and fear were clawing their way up his throat, but there was nothing he could do. She was a grown woman. If she wanted to leave, it was her right. He had no control—no say in where she went or when.

Riley was sick of not having any control. Here he'd

thought Sophie was a sweet girl in need of his help. Obviously, he'd been wrong. She'd taken off without a word as if what they'd gone through hadn't mattered. As if *he* hadn't mattered.

Fine. If that was the way she wanted to play it, that was fine with him. He had better things to do. That diamond job wasn't going to plan itself, and with Bella out of the country, the job fell to him.

He'd throw himself into his work and not spend another second thinking about the vulnerable, sweet Sophie Devane. She clearly didn't need him, and he sure as hell didn't need her.

Gage and Bella hadn't caught a single glimpse of Lorenzo Soma since they'd returned to the villa. Through his scope, he'd watched all day, looking for signs of the man. All he'd seen was a steady stream of trucks coming in with building materials and leaving again with bodies of the dead. The broken windows were mostly boarded over now, making it even harder to see what was going on.

"Still no sighting," said Bella through the headset. "You?"

"Negative."

"It's nearly dark now. I think we should go in and have a look around."

Bella was one hell of an ass-kicking woman, but she was still a woman, which Gage had a hard time overlooking. It's not that he didn't trust her ability; it's just that he knew all the bad shit that could come down on her if she happened to get caught. He wouldn't wish that on anyone, not even that asshole Soma himself.

"I'll go," he told her.

"Gage," she said, making his name a warning. "We've

talked about this. I'm not a weakling you need to protect."

Actually, they'd never talked about it. *She'd* talked. He'd listened. "I know."

"Besides, we're not going inside. I just want to check out the garage and see if we can tell if his car is missing."

"I'll take the garage. You take the hangar." It was farther away from the house, which made it safer. Plus, it was closer to her location, making it seem like a reasonable strategy. One she'd accept.

"We'll sit tight another hour before we go so it'll be completely dark."

Gage saw another group of women and children leaving. There had been two more to leave earlier that day. So far they hadn't come back. He didn't know if they were relocating while the repairs were going on, or if the mothers had finally had enough of the violence surrounding them.

It took a hell of a lot of violence to make a person uproot their family.

He moved as close as he dared and snapped a few photos with his phone. The quality sucked, but he hoped they'd be good enough for Gina to tell if any of the kids were Julia. It seemed the least he could do while he was sitting around, doing nothing to kill the fucker who'd dared threaten a child.

Patience. He needed to be patient a while longer. Sooner or later Soma had to leave, and when he did, Gage was going to treat the man to a nice, graphic display of justice.

Night closed in. He checked his watch. Almost an hour had passed.

"Are you ready?" asked Bella.

"Yes."

"This is just a sneak-and-peek. Don't engage unless

you have to. If Soma knows we're here, he'll only stay in his hidey-hole longer."

"Understood."

Gage slipped over the ground toward the detached garage. It was large enough to hold a dozen cars at least. Maybe more. Five overhead doors ran along two opposite walls. There was a walk-in entrance on the east side, which also housed a window.

He made slow progress over the ground, keeping out of line of sight of the motion detectors on the main villa. It took about twenty minutes to move a few hundred yards, but no lights flipped on and no sirens screamed, so what he and Bella were doing was working. Or maybe the motion sensors had been a casualty of the firefight.

Gage peered into the window. It was black inside. He couldn't see a thing.

He'd just pulled out his flashlight to shine through the glass when he heard Bella's voice. "He's gone, Gage. His plane is gone. He must have left between the time we attacked and when the two of us came back."

"Sloane," whispered Gage. "We have to warn her."

It was nearing midnight by the time Sloane got Gina back to her house and settled in the guest bedroom. Gina had chosen using herself as bait over going into protective custody, and Sloane knew no amount of arguing was going to change that.

With Bella and Gage watching Lorenzo's villa, the chances of him escaping alive were slim, but at least this way, Sloane knew that Gina was safe.

The hospital had given Gina some pain meds to hold her over for a couple of days. The drive and all the moving had been enough to force her to pop a couple once they'd reached the outskirts of Dallas.

They were both exhausted, both physically and mentally wrung out. They'd hardly said a dozen words to each other during the drive, though mostly because Gina had slept it away.

Sloane tucked her groggy friend in, double-checked all the locks on the windows in the room. There had been no word from Bella yet, and until Soma was found and dealt with, Sloane wasn't willing to let up her guard.

She checked her phone messages. There was only one, and whoever had called had left only static before hanging up. She didn't recognize the number.

Sloane went to put on a pot of coffee to keep her awake while she waited for the feds to arrive and back her up in a couple of hours. Gina wasn't going to like having the FBI involved, but that was too bad. Sloane had to sleep sometime.

She flipped on the light in the kitchen and Lorenzo Soma was sitting at her kitchen table, pointing a suppressed 9mm right at her chest.

Chapter 27

Lucas stared at the ceiling of his hotel room. He'd been too tired to drive home tonight, but lying here, wide-awake, thinking about Sloane wasn't doing much in the way of getting him rested for tomorrow morning, either.

He was stalling. He didn't want to go back. Or, rather, he didn't want to leave Sloane. He'd even stopped in Dallas for the night, knowing she was somewhere nearby. It was a stupid, sappy thing to do, and he was paying for it now in sleeplessness. He kept thinking that she couldn't be that far away. He could hop over to her place and they could talk.

And maybe somehow, all that talking would magically change reality and his knee would work right, he'd have no family obligations that kept him from her, and she could realize that not every man was as controlling as her father.

Lucas cursed the Old Man silently for not telling her everything. Maybe if he had, Sloane would understand why he'd done the things he had. Maybe then she could get over her disdain for the men of the world and give him a shot.

But the general had refused Lucas's pleas, telling him it was best to leave old wounds alone.

It had taken every ounce of control Lucas had to not call the man a coward. The general wasn't willing to take a risk that Sloane might not forgive him, and Sloane wasn't willing to take a risk that Lucas might not be a mindless zombie slave to her father.

Anger burned deep in his gut, driving sleep away with its bright glow. He wasn't getting any rest tonight. Might as well hit the road and head home.

At least his folks would be happy to see him. Making his mom smile was worth a serious case of red eye.

Lucas slid his pants on just as his phone rang. "Hello?"

The connection was bad, but he could make out a faint female voice. For a second he thought it was Sloane and his heart leaped. And then he heard, "It's Bella. We're . . . villa. Soma's . . ."

"What? I didn't quite get that."

"Soma's gone."

He got that loud and clear. "Where?"

"He . . . His plane . . . could be anywhere."

He could be, but he wasn't. Gina had called Sloane while in his custody. He could have easily found out where Sloane lived through her phone number.

Gina was staying with Sloane until they could make more permanent arrangements.

Holy fuck. Lucas had to get there. Now.

He hung up and dialed the general. "I need Sloane's address. Soma's missing."

To the general's credit, he didn't waste time asking questions. He rattled off the address, giving Lucas an idea of which highway to take to get there fastest.

"I'll send help. How fast can you be there?"

Lucas was already out of the hotel and sprinting toward his car. "Five minutes." He hoped.

Grief and anger roughened the Old Man's voice. "Don't you let that bastard hurt my baby."

"I won't, sir."

Lucas tossed the phone onto the seat and screeched out of the parking lot.

Shock slammed into Sloane, rocking her back on her heels. She was stunned for a second, but recovered and reached for the weapon she'd had strapped to her for the past few days. Of course, now that she was back in civilization, she was no longer carrying a weapon around with her. Her handgun was in the top of her overnight bag, cleaned and ready to fire.

And completely out of reach.

"I suggest you don't scream," he said, his voice only faintly accented.

"I hadn't even considered it," she said, before thinking better about playing the role of tough chick. It was better if he thought her weak and helpless. All she had to do was get close enough to him to reach him.

He rose from the chair, smiling as he moved toward her. Sloane stood her ground, waiting for him to inch closer.

"Back up," he ordered. "Gina told me all about what a talented fighter you are. She threatened me with you more than once. After what you did to my home, I don't think I'll underestimate you a second time."

"What do you want?" asked Sloane, stalling for time to think.

"Gina, of course."

"Why? What's so important about her?"

"She's on the List."

"List? What list?"

Soma shrugged, his dark eyes glittering as they slid over her body. His gaze made her feel dirty and used, but she kept hoping he'd try to make a move. Even if it meant having his filthy hands on her for a few seconds, she could tolerate that long enough to take him out.

"I don't know much more than that. Adam Brink

hires me to find people, and I find them. You'd have to ask him, not that you'll get the chance."

"Are you going to kill me?" she asked, hoping he said no. She wanted him to spew out nonsense about how she was his and he was going to do horrible, nasty things to her until she learned to like it. Whatever. Just as long as he didn't pull that trigger.

"Yes. Let's go wake Gina, shall we?"

Oh, God. He was going to make Gina watch her die. He was going to punish her for escaping, just like he'd claimed he'd do with the little girl Julia.

Sloane planted her feet, not moving. "If you want to kill me, you're going to have to do it right here, right now. I won't help you torture Gina."

Soma opened his mouth and someone knocked on her door.

Sloane froze, caught between possible help at the door and not knowing what Soma would do to whoever was on the other side.

"Sloane? I know you're in there. Open up." It was Lucas.

Every cell in Sloane's body rejoiced at the sound of his voice. Before Soma could stop her, she called out, "Hold on. I'm coming."

Soma snarled a hissing whisper. "You'd better get him to leave."

"Or else what? You'll kill me? You already showed your hand, shit-for-brains. You can't bluff now."

Lorenzo ducked into Gina's bedroom before Sloane could stop him. She lurched after him, but was too slow. Before she'd even crossed the room, he appeared in the bedroom doorway with Gina in front of him. His weapon was shoved into her mouth, keeping her from screaming.

Gina's eyes were wide, confusion and fear melding together in the form of tears. She looked at Sloane, begging for help or answers, or maybe both. The pain meds

were probably making her too groggy and weak to figure out what was going on, which had to be terrifying.

"Don't hurt her," said Sloane, trying to keep her voice
calm for Gina's sake.

"You get him to leave or I'll kill her."

Sloane couldn't tell if he was bluffing or not, and she
wasn't about to take the chance. "I'm going. Just don't
hurt her." She went to her front door and leaned close.
"I can't talk to you right now, Lucas. Go away."

His deep voice seeped through the two inches of
wood, muffled, but strong and confident. "No. Not until
we talk. Open the door."

From behind her, Sloane heard the muted click of a
hammer being pulled back. Gina whimpered.

Sloane cracked the door open. Her heart was pounding so hard, she could barely hear, but when she saw Lucas's handsome face, her pulse still kicked up a notch.
His dark hair fell over his wide forehead and concern
creased the skin between his eyes. He was only inches
away. If she slid her fingers through the opening, she'd
be able to touch his cheek or maybe his hand.

She didn't.

"Let me in," he demanded.

"I can't. I told you, it's over." Dear God, she wished
she could take those words back now. She didn't want it
to be over. In the face of certain death, none of her con-
cerns seemed valid anymore. Of course that was easy
to say now when she knew her chances of surviving the
night were slipping by the second. So were Gina's if she
didn't get him out of here.

And yet if he did leave, she didn't know how she
was going to handle the situation. This was one of those
times when she really wished Lucas could help her. She
didn't even care if that made her weak. She'd take being
weak over having a dead friend any day.

He stared at her, his dark blue gaze steady. "It's not

over. I know you need me. Don't you." It wasn't a question. He was trying to tell her something with his eyes, but she was too rattled to understand. "You need me in there right now. By your side."

Sloane could feel Soma's growing impatience. "Please, just leave."

"Are you in trouble?" he whispered.

Did he know Soma was here? Could he know? If she admitted she was in trouble, Soma would pull that trigger. All it would take was half a second and Gina would be gone. Irrevocably.

"No," Sloane whispered, hoping it saved her friend's life.

"Are you going to let me in?"

"No. But when you see my father, will you tell him something for me?" she asked.

"Sure," he said, his voice cold and uncertain.

"Will you tell him I love him?"

Lucas blinked twice in silent shock. Sloane closed the door in his face, praying he'd figure out her distress signal and bring help.

What she wouldn't give for one huge, heavily armed Texas SWAT team right now.

She turned to Soma. "He's gone. Let Gina go."

Soma shook his head. "We're all going for a drive now. I don't want to take any chance that your friend will come back."

"He won't. I made it clear he wasn't wanted."

"Lovesick men are often foolish."

Lovesick? Lucas? Hardly. A man like him could never fall for her. Not seriously. The sex was fantastic, but her edges were too sharp for anything more. Men liked women who were easier to live with, women who weren't always looking for the next chance to bust some heads. Or balls. What he had felt for her was passing infatuation. Nothing more.

Not that it mattered. If she didn't figure a way out of this mess, her ball-busting days were over.

"Get your keys," he ordered. "We'll go out the back, and I'll keep my gun handy so you'll remember to be a good little girl."

Sloane's teeth creaked she grated them so hard. She hadn't been a little girl for a long time, and she sure as hell wasn't good. At least not for him. She wanted to scream out how she was going to kill him—how she was going to blow as much lead through his insides as she could. Only the gleam of the 9mm barrel in Gina's mouth allowed Sloane to keep her control.

Her keys were in her jeans pocket. She reached in and pulled them out, dangling them in front of him. "I need my driver's license. It's in my bedroom." Where her weapon was.

She took two steps in that direction before his voice froze her in place. "Stop. Drive without it. If you get stopped, I'll kill the police, too."

Frustration and fear ground her down, making her regret the fact that she hadn't already put this man in the ground where he belonged.

He pulled the gun from Gina's mouth and motioned with it toward the back door. "Out. Now."

Red and blotchy, Gina's face was streaked with tears. There was a sheen of confused lethargy in her eyes as she stumbled toward the kitchen, dragged inside Soma's tight grip.

Sloane looked around for some kind of weapon. Something. Anything. All she had to do was incapacitate his weapon hand enough to ensure he wouldn't shoot Gina. After that, all Sloane needed was to have the bastard in her reach.

A knife caddy full of wicked sharp steel stood in the middle of the small island in her kitchen. If she could distract him enough that he wasn't watching, she could snatch up one of the blades and use that. Knife fighting wasn't her forte, but she'd learned the basics. With any luck, Soma hadn't.

He was in the kitchen now, moving slowly with Gina in tow. He kept his eyes on Sloane, clearly not trusting her.

He might be a bastard, but he wasn't a stupid one.

"You go first," he ordered, his eyes narrow as if he suspected her intentions.

Shit. If she was in front of him, she couldn't tell if he was watching her.

Sloane shot Gina a meaningful look, hoping her friend would catch on that she was planning something. Back in high school, they'd been able to communicate with little more than a glance, but it had been a long time since high school. Gina was drugged up and scared out of her mind. She also had a loaded gun pressed against the base of her skull. She had things to think about besides Sloane's looks.

Gina met her gaze, though Sloane couldn't tell if she understood the signal.

Sloane darted her eyes to the right again, indicating Gina should head for the kitchen table when the commotion started. If Gina could just get a few feet away, Sloane could hurl one of those knives at the guy's head. It probably wouldn't kill him, but it might slow him down long enough for her to disarm him.

"Move," barked Soma.

A flash of recognition lit in Gina's face. At least Sloane hoped that was what it was.

"Now!" she shouted.

Gina dropped like a stone. Sloane reached for the knives. A gunshot went off. The wooden caddy flew across the room and landed on the floor, spilling its contents.

The back door slammed open. It hit the wall so hard the window glass shattered.

"Down!" The demand was made with such authority that Sloane found herself falling to the floor before thinking it through. Lucas. He hadn't left her.

Relief trilled through her, and for half a heart-stopping second, Sloane had to hold herself back to keep from running to him.

Another gunshot went off. Sloane ducked behind the island and peered around it, looking for Gina.

Gina had broken free of Soma's grip and was scurrying on her hands and knees toward the kitchen table. There wasn't much cover to be had, but at least she no longer had a gun pointed at her.

Sloane surrendered to another wave of relief while she took stock of the situation. She could just barely see a peek of Lucas's booted foot immediately outside the doorway leading to her backyard. If he stepped inside, he'd be right in the open, an easy target for Soma.

What Lucas needed was a distraction.

Sloane opened a cabinet door and pulled out a stainless-steel mixing bowl. She hurled it toward the last place she'd seen Soma standing, then grabbed another. One by one, her mixing bowls crashed to the floor. Glass and pottery smashed into a noisy mess. More shots were fired, though Sloane couldn't tell from whom. The men were too close together.

She was out of ammunition, so she scooted to the next cabinet. A flash of motion caught her eye as she saw Soma's reflection in the kitchen window over the sink. He was crouched behind the island, moving toward her, his weapon aimed right for her head.

Chapter 28

Lucas didn't have time for any more cowboy antics. He needed Soma dead. Now. Before Sloane or Gina was hurt.

He'd lost sight of Soma, but he had to be nearby.

There was a wide opening between the kitchen and the living room. Soma could be hiding on either side of that opening, just waiting for Lucas to put his head in sight. Or he could be low, hiding on the other side of the island filling the center of the kitchen.

Only one way to find out.

Lucas stepped inside, his weapon raised, his finger on the trigger. Soma was in black and white. Gina was in red. Sloane was in denim and a green top. All he needed was a small glimpse——some body part to help him ID his target.

His boots crunched on the broken glass, giving him away.

He heard a scurrying sound, a feminine grunt of pain; then Soma stood with Sloane's throat clutched in one hand, his other aiming the gun at her temple.

The man's eyes were wide, dark, and wild with the frantic look of a cornered animal.

Anger filled Lucas, choking him. He tried to channel

it into a steely kind of calm, but it wasn't working. That fucker was hurting Sloane and all he could think about was how good it was going to feel to kill him. "Shoot her and I'll kill you before the echo dies down."

Sloane's face was turning a dark red. A choking sound gurgled from her mouth. She pried at his fingers, but it did no good.

"Put down the gun or I'll kill her now," said Soma.

Lucas debated for a millisecond before he complied. Sloane was running out of air, and with it, the ability to fight her way free. All she needed was an opening and Lucas was determined to make one for her. But first he had to get that gun away from her head. One move now and Soma could easily twitch and pull the trigger.

Lucas set the gun on the ground.

"Kick it away."

He did that, too. It slid easily over the polished floor until it came to rest against the carpet of the living room.

"I'm leaving. With both women."

Sloane slammed her elbow into Soma's ribs. Her leg came down hard in a stomp kick on Soma's fancy leather shoes. Whether she didn't know she had a weapon at her head or if she was too desperate to care, Lucas had no idea, but in that one brief second, his whole world narrowed down to a single pinpoint, and inside it, the only thing that mattered was Sloane.

Soma let out a harsh whoosh of air, lifted the gun, and bashed Sloane in the side of the head. She stumbled forward, catching herself against the sink. Soma shoved his hand between her shoulder blades, making her head crash into the hard porcelain.

Sloane staggered and slumped to the floor, unable to support herself.

Rage soared through Lucas, stretching its black wings to fill every corner of his soul. He launched himself at Soma, gliding over the top of the island to tackle him.

Soma's gun went off. Lucas didn't give a shit if he was hit. He was still moving and that was enough for him.

They slammed into the cabinets behind Soma, but he took the brunt of the landing. Lucas balled up his fist and drove it into the side of Soma's head. The blow snapped his head sideways, but the man kept fighting.

Soma had been lifted by Lucas's tackle so that he was sitting on the counter. Soma's feet lashed out, striking a solid blow to Lucas's good knee. The bad one couldn't handle the sudden shift of weight and he fell, ripping off the sleeve of Soma's shirt as he went down.

Soma jumped down, landing hard on Lucas's leg. Lucas scrambled to move back out of the man's reach before he broke something.

Soma snarled and his foot came soaring right toward Lucas's balls.

No fucking way.

Lucas jerked aside, taking the blow on the inside of his bad knee. Pain lanced up his spine, nearly blinding him for a moment. He couldn't breathe, but there wasn't time to worry about that now.

The flash of a kitchen knife caught his eye. He grabbed it and turned back to Soma.

Soma had retrieved his weapon from where it had landed on the counter and aimed it at Lucas's head

Lucas shot up into a sitting position. Something white flew at Soma and smashed into his head. The gun exploded so close to Lucas he could taste gunpowder. He didn't wait for pain to register. He rammed the knife up into Soma's thigh, slicing through an artery.

Soma screamed. Fine, white powder settled across everything. Lucas yanked the knife free and dodged the heavy pulse of blood that spurted from the wound.

Soma collapsed to the ground, holding his thigh. Another pulse of blood arced up, splattering the cabinets. Then another.

The man deserved to die, but not until he suffered in jail for a while, kept as a prisoner the way he'd kept those women.

Lucas whipped off his belt and tried to slip it under Soma's leg to stop the bleeding, but the man kept fighting him, frantic and panicked.

Sloane appeared at Soma's head, on her hands and knees, slipping in the flour coating the floor. She grabbed his shoulders and pushed him down. "We're trying to help you, you bastard."

Within a few seconds, his struggles weakened, but it was too late by then. Lucas's fingers were slippery with blood and by the time he got the belt tightly in place, Soma was already dead.

Lucas couldn't bring himself to care.

Sloane looked at Lucas across Soma's body. "Are you okay?" she asked.

He nodded. "You?"

"Yeah. Thank you."

Lucas wanted to grab her and hold her tight, but not like this—not covered in another man's blood.

"Gina." She turned and hurried to her friend.

Lucas washed his hands in the sink, watching the pink water swirl into the drain. His bad knee barely held him up. His good one wasn't much better. Both were throbbing like a son of a bitch. Now that the fight was over, he felt every scrape and bruise and cut on his body. Every quivering flicker of fear.

He'd nearly lost Sloane tonight. If it hadn't been for her well-timed flour grenade, he'd probably be dead right now.

Lucas looked across the bright kitchen to where Sloane was huddled over Gina. "How is she?"

Sloane's voice was too bright. Too optimistic. "She's great. Soma's gone now. She doesn't have to worry about a thing."

Except massive quantities of therapy, no doubt.

"I'm going to call the police and your father and fetch a change of clothes. I can't stand having this asshole's blood on me."

Sloane looked up at him, her eyes bright with unshed tears. She'd been through hell tonight and all he wanted to do was hold her.

Hell, who was he kidding? What he really wanted was to hold her forever. She'd made it clear that wasn't an option. After charging in here to save her, telling her in no uncertain terms he thought she wasn't capable of saving herself, he bet she'd just added the final tick mark in the he's-just-like the-general column. And after his display of weakness tonight—letting Soma knock him down like a stack of wooden blocks—he knew her opinion of him wasn't going to improve. He was injured and yet he still acted as though he was more capable of taking care of her than she was of taking care of herself.

That was not going to sit well with Sloane, and the fact that she hadn't even looked at him since it was over was proof of it.

Lucas limped out to the car and made his calls.

He'd wait long enough to give his report, then hit the road. If he had to step into that house again and look at Sloane, he knew he'd grab her in his arms. And if he did that again, he knew, this time he wouldn't be able to let go.

It took half the night for Sloane to deal with the FBI and police and explain what had happened. She split her time between checking on Gina, searching for Lucas in the growing crowd in her home, and asking the officer interviewing her to repeat himself.

Lucas had seemingly disappeared, and as much as she tried to tell herself it was for the best, she didn't believe a word of that lie. She needed to see him. She needed to thank him for saving her and Gina tonight. She needed to run her hands over his body and make sure he was okay.

Based on the way the agent was winding up to start asking her the same questions over again—for the third time—she guessed it was going to be a while before she was able to go search for him.

Gina huddled inside a blanket Sloane's mother had crocheted. A female officer was speaking to her, and so far, Sloane had no reason to believe Gina was in distress. She looked confused and rattled, but Gina was tough. She'd pull through this. Sloane would make sure of it.

Sloane's front door opened and her father walked in, surveying her home with a critical eye. She ignored the cop's question and went to confront him. "What are you doing here?"

Her father looked her over. His weathered hand reached toward her face. She'd hit the sink hard enough to split the skin over her eye and his fingers trembled close to the wound as if he wished he could take it away.

Sloane tightened up every bit of resolve she had, battening down the hatches in preparation for his verbal assault. This was the part where he told her how this proved she was incapable of taking care of herself. How she needed to be protected and coddled and he was just the man to make it happen.

She didn't know how she was going to stand him listing all her inadequacies right now, when she already felt brittle and stretched too thin. There was too much going on. She, Lucas, and Gina had all nearly died tonight. There was the blood of a murdering drug lord all over her kitchen. People she didn't know or trust had invaded her personal space. Lucas was nowhere to be seen, and right when what she needed most was a really tight hug. One good verbal hit from her father, and she worried she'd shatter into so many pieces she'd never be able to find them all to put herself back together.

Her father's hand settled gently on her head, stroking her hair. "Are you okay?" he asked, his voice strained.

Sloane gave a tense nod. "Fine. It's just a little cut."

"I'm sorry I couldn't come sooner. It took a while to secure a helicopter."

"You didn't need to come at all. I'm fine."

He nodded. His throat worked as if he were having trouble swallowing. "That's what Lucas said when he called. But I had to see for myself."

"I'm sorry you had to come all this way. It really wasn't necessary."

"You're my daughter. Of course it was necessary. I love you."

A sob swelled inside her chest, threatening to burst free. She clenched her jaw until the urge passed and squared her shoulders. He'd used love as an excuse to control her before. She couldn't let it happen again. "You should go. Everything is under control now."

He took her arm and led her down the short hall into her bedroom, where they had some relative privacy.

His hand fell to his side in defeat, and suddenly, he looked twenty years older. His frame sagged and his eyes misted over. "Lucas was right. I should have told you everything. I didn't, and now I've lost you forever, haven't I?"

"I have no idea what you're talking about. Tell me what?"

"I'm not sure it will even matter now."

Sloane didn't know if he was using her curiosity against her, but she wouldn't put it past him not to use every weapon at his disposal.

She forced a shrug. "Tell me or not, but do it quick if you're going to. I'm sure the police aren't done with me yet."

"I know you think I'm a tyrant. I know you think I didn't want you around, but you're wrong. There were . . . circumstances that forced me to send you away when you were young."

"Circumstances. You expect me to believe that? What possible circumstances could there have been that would make you hate the sight of your own child?"

"I never hated you. Everything I did was out of love for you."

"You had a funny way of showing it. You never visited. You hardly allowed Mom to visit. You didn't want anyone to even know you had a daughter. What kind of father does that? What kind of father is so fucking selfish he can't even give his own flesh and blood his name?"

"I knew you'd be a target. I was involved with some . . . bad things back then. I only wanted to protect you."

Sloane let out an angry laugh of disbelief. "Bullshit. You're just saying that now that Mom's gone and can't clear up any lies you tell. You might as well admit the truth. Go ahead. It's okay. I already know you were ashamed of me from the moment I was born. You wanted a boy who would grow up strong and brave and be just like you."

"You're wrong. I wanted to shout to the world when you were born, but I couldn't."

"Why? And don't even try to feed me that crap about wanting to protect me. That was just a convenient excuse."

"It wasn't an excuse. It's the truth. And even with everything I did, I still failed to keep you safe. They found you when you were four. They took you. You may not remember, but it happened."

That weird flash from the jungle came back, bright as day. She could still taste the fear in her screams for her daddy. He'd told her he'd keep her safe, but strangers had taken her. They wanted to hurt her. They had all those needles. And the lady doctor with the bright red lips kept telling the others to hold her down.

Then her father slammed into the room and batted them all away as easily as if they'd been stuffed animals. He'd scooped her up into his arms and held on to her like he'd never let go.

"I remember." And the memory left Sloane reeling. Her father wasn't lying. At least not about that.

"I never wanted you to know. I didn't want you to be afraid. I had enough fear for both of us."

"Who did it? And what did they want with me?" she asked, her voice shaking.

"It doesn't matter now. I made sure you were always kept safe after that. You hated me for it, but that worked in your favor, so I let it stand. The less contact you had with me, the better."

"You can't use that to excuse how you treated me. You had me trapped as a prisoner at that school."

"They never mistreated you. I made sure of it."

Sloane had to control the snarl of contempt that threatened to come through her tone. "That's easy to say now. I hated it there."

"It was for your own good."

"Bullshit."

Her father let out a heavy sigh. "Think about it, Sloane. You're a security professional. How would you have handled keeping a child safe from her parent's dangerous, violent enemies?"

Because Sloane had nothing to lose, and couldn't stand arguing with her father, she took his question seriously. "I would advise staying in a secret, secure location until the threat was removed."

"And if that threat could not be eliminated? If more permanent arrangements had to be made?"

A child had to learn and have some kind of a life.

Go to school. Have friends. "Electronic surveillance. Around-the-clock armed guards. Carefully screened visitors. Restricted time in public." As Sloane continued the list in her mind, she began to see a pattern.

All those years, her father had rarely made contact, and when he did, it had usually been through a hand-delivered message from one of his men. All the parties and dances he'd forbidden her to go to were those conducted away from school grounds. Even Gina had gone through a security check before they were allowed to room together.

Looking back with adult eyes, she could see his actions in a different light now. Maybe his efforts were less about controlling her in an effort to punish her for not being good enough and more about keeping her safe.

Sloane's whole world shifted, coming into sharper focus. She understood things that had always confused her before, but even that understanding couldn't excuse one thing.

"Why didn't you go to Mom's funeral?"

His face sagged in grief. "I knew you would be there. I knew you'd cry. I can't see you cry and not want to hold you, honey. I still have enemies, and there was no way to guarantee one of them wouldn't show up there with a sniper rifle."

That declaration shocked the hell out of Sloane. Even after all she'd been through in the past few days, nothing had prepared her for that kind of news.

"You're telling me there are people out there who want to kill you? Still? Now?"

He shrugged. "Only other old men like me. I try not to worry about it too much, but I couldn't risk you—not with such long notice for the funeral. Anyone would have had time to prepare for a hit." He looked at his shoes, but Sloane caught the glint of tears in his green eyes. "I went to her grave. I said my own private goodbyes. She would have understood even if no one else did."

"Mom always understood you. I thought it was because she let you walk all over her, but it was more than that, wasn't it?"

"Our relationship wasn't conventional, but it worked for us. I loved her. Just like I love you."

"I've never been as understanding as Mom. You should have told me this before. If I'd known, maybe things would be different."

Her father nodded, sighed. "I thought it was safer not to tell you, even after you were a grown woman. I didn't want you getting mixed up in my mistakes. And the habit of protecting you is a hard one to break. From what Lucas told me, you don't need me anymore. He says you know how to protect yourself."

Lucas told him that? How could he have lied that way after saving her life tonight? If it hadn't been for him, there was a good chance both she and Gina would be dead. "Does this mean you won't be sending any more of your men to follow me around like you did with Lucas?"

He looked her right in the eyes. "Is that what you want?"

"It is. I have to live my own life. I can't keep worrying that you're going to butt in because you're ashamed of me or think I'm incapable of doing what needs to be done."

"I've never been ashamed of you a day in my life. I've spent years in fear for you, but never once felt a moment of shame. I'm amazed at the formidable woman you've become. I'm proud of you, Sloane."

She'd been waiting her whole life to hear those words. A sliver of her that was still Daddy's little girl began to cry on the inside. Outside, she held it together, not wanting to give away how much his words had moved her.

She still didn't trust him completely. Maybe she never would, but for the first time in years, she was willing to give trust another shot.

Sloane wrapped her arms around her father and hugged him hard. He was stiff for a moment before his arms came around her and held her tight. "I love you, Sloane. It makes me sad that I can't show the world, but I'm going to make sure you never doubt it again."

Sloane couldn't speak. She knew she was supposed to tell him she loved him, too, but words were beyond her. It took everything she had to hold herself together and not break down into the kind of emotional scene she knew he'd hate.

And she did love him even though she had told herself for years she didn't. It was easier to pretend than to deal with the rejection by the man who was supposed to love her most in the world.

He pulled back, smoothing her hair away from her face. "Things are going to be different between us from now on. I promise."

Sloane offered him a tentative smile. "I'd like that."

"You'll have to be careful. I still have enemies and they won't hesitate to use you against me."

"I'll be careful. I promise." And she meant it. She wasn't going to make any mistakes and cut short a life that looked more hopeful than ever.

"I don't want to butt in, but I do want to help. Is there anything I can do?"

"I've got it under control. They've already moved the body. I think the authorities will be wrapping things up here soon. I'd appreciate it if you could find Lucas for me, though. I haven't had a chance, and I want to thank him for what he did here tonight."

Her father frowned. "Lucas left before I came in. He called me. Said he was going home."

"Home?"

"Arkansas. He's got family there. I thought you knew."

She hadn't expected him to leave without so much as a word after what he'd done tonight.

Then again, they'd already had their farewell. No point in him staying, right? She'd made it clear there was nothing keeping him here. She wanted him to go and do what he needed to do. His family had to come first.

Her father tipped her face up to study it. "You love him, don't you?"

She didn't have to answer. Apparently there were some things even estranged fathers could see plain as day. "He has obligations."

"I spent a lifetime letting my obligations get in the way of being around the people I loved. It was a poor choice. If you love the man, don't let him make the same mistake."

It was the bleakness in her father's gaze that swayed Sloane. There was a kind of emptiness inside of him so huge, she swore she could almost hear the echo of his regrets. He'd made his own choices and he had to live with that, but she couldn't stand the thought of Lucas suffering that same kind of emptiness. Even if it meant she had to leave her life here behind.

Sloane nearly laughed at the idea of dropping everything for a man. She'd never once even been willing to make a compromise to let a man into her life. She'd thought it was because she was independent and didn't need anyone. Now she realized that she'd just never cared enough before to make the sacrifice.

"Can you help me find him?" she asked her father. "Maybe get the feds to finish up here so I can hit the road?"

Bob Norwood's smile filled his face, stripping away the years. "I'd love to."

Chapter 29

Lucas sat on the front porch of the house he'd grown up in, letting his mother fuss over him. Pam Ramsey was thrilled her boy was home. Who was he to take that away from her just because he wished he were back in Dallas with Sloane?

Mom beamed, grinning from ear to ear as she handed him a glass of milk and a plate of cookies. It wasn't even noon yet and she was already baking up a storm.

Dad was quieter in his welcome, but he hadn't gone more than ten feet away from Lucas since he'd come through the front door early this morning. They'd even closed the restaurant so they could have the day off with him—something Lucas could remember happening only a handful of times in his entire life.

"So, son," said Dad, "you're back for good, are you?"

"Looks like," said Lucas, trying to sound pleased by the idea.

"I wasn't sure you'd go through with it. I mean, I know you love us, but the restaurant has never been your thing."

Lucas shrugged. "I'll adjust. It's not like I don't know the ropes."

Mom patted his knee. "You'll do a great job. You'll

see." She jumped up and headed for the front door. "Oops. Almost forgot the bread."

Lucas pushed the porch swing, letting the motion of it calm him. The neighborhood looked different now. Smaller. Except for the trees. They were huge, looming high overhead, shading the whole yard.

"What's bothering you?" asked Dad.

"Nothing," he lied. "Just settling in."

"How's the knee?"

It still hurt from the blow Soma had landed, but he'd survive. "It works. I'm grateful for that."

"Where were you the last few days? I kept trying to call."

"I was out of the country. I had a . . . friend who needed some help."

"Ah. I see. A woman."

A car turned the corner, heading down the street. Likely another neighbor who'd heard he was home and came to welcome him back. That was the thing about small towns. Everyone knew his business here. He wasn't sure he'd ever get used to that, even if he lived here for the next fifty years.

Lucas grunted. Dad always seemed to know whenever there was woman trouble. In high school, it had been hellishly embarrassing. "It's over."

"Not for you, from the looks of it. Want to talk about it?"

Not even on a dare. "Nothing to say. She wasn't interested."

The car turned into the driveway, the sun glinting off the windshield. Lucas didn't recognize the car, though he imagined it would be a while before he'd memorized every vehicle in town, like he had when he was a kid.

He took a swig of milk, wishing it was something stronger to help him get through this next round of nosiness disguised as well-wishing neighbors.

"I don't suppose that's her getting out of that car, is it?" asked Dad.

Lucas's gaze shot to the driveway. Sloane stood there with the sun shining off her dark hair. She didn't step forward. Instead, she hovered by the car, looking shy and uncertain.

Lucas had no idea she even knew what those things were.

"What the hell are you waiting on, son? Go out there."

Dad was right. He shook off his surprise at seeing her here and went down the steps to greet her. He did his best to hide the limp he couldn't quite seem to control today. It didn't matter if things were over between them. He still had his pride.

Gina got out of the passenger door. She gave him a wink, then walked right up to his dad and introduced herself. Seconds later, both Gina and Dad went inside with a squeak and a slam of the front screen door.

Lucas shoved his hands in his pockets so he wouldn't reach for Sloane. He had no idea why she was here and he didn't want to jump to any awkward conclusions. For all he knew she was here to bring him back for more police questioning.

"Hi," he said. "I didn't expect to see you."

"I didn't expect to come. My father talked me into it."

"And you listened?" he asked, joking, hoping to lighten the weird mood.

"He told me some things—reasons why he did what he did. He said you were the one who convinced him he should. I wanted to thank you."

"You could have done that over the phone. Why are you here, Sloane?"

She looked at the house, the trees, the sky, everywhere but at him. "I like your family's place. It's nice. Gina said it looks just like a real home should."

She was avoiding his question, but he decided to take pity on her. "How's Gina doing?"

"Good. Better. Gage snapped some photos of kids that were leaving Soma's villa and Julia was there with her mom. It's a huge relief, especially for Gina."

"That's great news. But you still didn't need to come this far to tell me that." He could no longer control his hands. He had to touch her. If she shrugged him off, he'd at least have part of his answer.

He stepped forward and slid his hands down her arms until he'd captured her fingers. They were cold. Shaking. She was nervous.

"Why are you here?" he asked again, gently.

"I think I love you." Her words were sharp and laced with just a hint of violence and so much like Sloane he almost laughed. He knew she'd probably slap him if he did, so he kept his grin in check.

"You *think*?"

She glared at him. "Well, I guess I know I love you. I'm just not sure I want to. That's the part I'm thinking about."

Lucas felt something hot and tight in his chest loosen and expand. He pulled in a breath, shocked at how easy it seemed to be now compared to a minute ago.

She loved him. It was more than he'd thought possible. Even her uncertainty about it didn't ruin the giddy feeling that was growing inside him by the second as the reality of her declaration sank in.

He bent his knees to intercept her line of sight with the front lawn, ignoring the throb it caused. "Would it make a difference if I told you I wanted you to love me? That it would sure as hell make it a lot easier for me to admit I love you, too."

Her gaze jumped to his, her eyes narrowing as if expecting a prank. "What?"

"I said I love you, Sloane. It's why I left. I didn't want

you to tie yourself to me when I know how much you love your job."

Her fingers tightened around his. "Screw the job. It's not nearly as important to me as it was a few days ago. That something-to-prove thing I had going on with my dad disappeared." Her eyes filled with tears and her chin wobbled as she whispered, "He said he was proud of me."

Lucas pulled her against him for a hug. He needed to hold her again, but he also wanted to save her pride. If she was going to cry, better she do it into his shirt than for him to watch. "Of course he's proud of you. What's there not to be proud of? You're a fantastic woman."

"You think?"

"I know. That's why I want you in my life. A little. A lot. Up close. Long distance. However I can get you."

"I won't ask you to leave your parents. I know taking care of them is important to you."

Lucas cringed inwardly. "I don't know how much you're going to like it here, but there's nothing I want more than for you to stay. Want to meet them?"

Sloane sniffed and pulled away to look at him. Her eyes were luminous. She was so beautiful it nearly stopped his heart to think he might have a chance with her. He was going to do everything in his power not to fuck it up. Sloane was the One.

"No one's ever brought me home to meet their parents before," she said. "I'm not sure how to act."

He threaded his fingers through hers and pulled her toward the house. "You'll do great. They're going to love you."

They walked into the kitchen where Mom was feeding Gina. Dad looked at Lucas's and Sloane's joined hands and grinned.

"Mom, Dad, I'd like you to meet Sloane Gideon."

He had to bite back the words *my future wife*, because he hadn't exactly talked that part of the deal out with Sloane yet. It seemed rude to assume.

Sloane was adorably nervous, but by the time Mom had shoved a cookie in her hand and sat her down next to Dad, she seemed to relax.

Lucas wasn't worried. His parents would love her, just like he did.

Gina looked up at him with a wistful expression on her face. "Your mom was telling me about your new job running the restaurant. Got any positions for someone like me? After all the excitement, I'd love to settle down in a quiet place like this for a while."

"I don't know. What do you do?"

"I have a degree in hotel and restaurant management. I was assistant manager of a small but posh hotel in New York. I didn't run the kitchen, but I think I could learn how."

His dad looked at Gina in surprise, then shared a meaningful look with Mom. She nodded slightly, a sad smile on her face. Dad said to Gina, "You're hired. You can stay in our guest room until you find a place of your own."

Lucas frowned at his dad. "Uh. Isn't hiring people supposed to be my job now?"

"Son, the restaurant business isn't for you. We both know it. Go and do what makes you happy."

"But it would be nice if you spent a few days," said Mom. "I'd like to get to know your lady friend."

Lucas looked at Sloane. "What do you think? Can you stay here for a few days?"

"I told Bella I needed some time off to take care of Gina. Make sure she's safe here."

"A small town is the safest place she could be," said Lucas. "Everyone knows everyone here. There's no way a stranger can walk around and not be noticed."

"I'll be fine," said Gina. "My arm hurts, but other than needing help to wash my hair, I'm good."

"I'd be happy to help you with that," said Mom. Her smile was back in place now at the idea of having someone to fuss over.

"She'll make you fat," warned Lucas, teasing his mom. "Watch out for the chocolate-chip muffins. They're lethal."

Mom shot him a maternal look of warning. "She could use a little fattening up, so you just back off, son."

"Yes, ma'am," said Lucas, hiding his grin.

"Are you sure, Gina?" asked Sloane. "I don't mind looking out for you for a while. Or we could help you disappear and get a new identity. The man who paid Lorenzo is still out there."

Gina waved her off. "Let your dad give me a new name if he wants, but you know better than anyone how bad it is not to have a life because of possible danger."

Sloane did. All those years of being cooped up felt like wasted ones. She didn't want to do that to her friend.

"We'll watch out for her," said Lucas's dad. "The whole town will."

Sloane hoped it would be enough. In the meantime, she was going make plans with her father to ensure Gina's safety. Even if that meant hunting down anyone who might be a threat. "Promise me you'll be careful and call at the first sign of danger."

"I'll have you on speed dial, but I don't want you butting in. Go have your wild monkey sex with Lucas and leave me in peace."

Dad cleared his throat. Sloane turned red. Mom said, "There will be none of that going on while I'm in the house. Wait until I'm at work. There are some things a mother doesn't need to hear."

Lucas laughed. He couldn't help it. He had everything he needed right here in this room. His folks were happy and going to get the retirement they deserved. He was no longer committed to a job he knew would suck the life from him. Sloane was at his side. And she loved him. She wanted a future with him enough to give up her career. He loved her enough to make sure she didn't have to.

He didn't care who was watching. He scooted her chair out, pulled her to her feet, and kissed her. She was stiff for a second before she forgot they had an audience and went all soft on him. He loved that about her—how she gave everything she had to give, throwing herself into the moment with abandon.

He felt her love for him flowing through that kiss. Or maybe it was his for her. He couldn't be sure, but it didn't matter. It was real. Solid. He could feel it in his bones. They were meant for this—for each other.

He pulled away and watched her eyes open slowly. Desire darkened them. Her cheeks were flushed and her lips were parted as if she was waiting for the next kiss.

He could hardly wait to oblige.

The man in West Virginia living under the name John Doran wasn't Eli.

Adam Brink bit back his disappointment and lowered the binoculars as the man jogged toward Adam's hiding place along the wooded hike trail. He'd know his brother's face anywhere, even after all these years, and John's was not Eli's. John's forehead was too wide, his eyes too dark, and he wasn't nearly tall enough to have the same genes as Adam.

But that didn't mean that his trip was wasted, or that John wouldn't be useful.

Adam waited until the man jogged close before he

stepped out from the brush and fired the Taser. Instantly, John fell to the asphalt path, twitching and gurgling in pain.

Adam made quick work of injecting him with a heavy sedative, then dragged him off the path into the cover of brush. The sun would be down soon, and there weren't many people around, but Adam was a careful man.

He lifted John's shirt and placed the gadget Dr. Stynger's scientists had made for him against John's abdomen. The device vibrated faster and faster until the hum was nearly undetectable.

Adam copied the readout from the device into his notebook exactly as it appeared. Some of the numbers had degraded with time and were unreadable, but others were there—another piece to the puzzle that might lead him to his brother's location.

He stashed the device and hefted John over his shoulder. Adam's truck, complete with a parks and recreation logo magneted to his door, was parked only a few yards away on an access road. He stuffed John into the passenger's seat and buckled him in. He wasn't sure what Dr. Stynger was going to do with this test subject, but it was Adam's job to make sure John was nice and healthy when he arrived.

Adam's phone vibrated at his hip. The text message read: *Possible subject located. Male. ND.*

He texted back his confirmation code. As soon as he got rid of John, he'd be on his way.

Maybe this time the man he found would be his brother.

Hope tried to rise inside him, but he tamped it down, keeping it in check. He'd been through this enough times to know that crushed hopes only made his job that much harder. And it was already hard enough trying to balance his duty to the doctor with his duty to his brother. If Dr. Stynger knew that Adam was using her resources for his own personal quest, she'd have him killed—something he couldn't let happen while his brother was still out there, possibly suffering.

Adam was going to find Eli, even if it meant he had to hunt down every last test subject on the List one by one.

Read on for an exciting preview of the
next Edge Novel by Shannon K. Butcher,

RAZOR'S EDGE

Coming from Signet Eclipse in November 2011.

"**M**r. Chord is pissed," said Roxanne's boss, Bella Bayne, the next morning.

Bella was the owner of the Edge—the growing private security company in Dallas where Roxanne worked. They handled all kinds of needs from threat assessment to protective details to U.S. troop support to ridding foreign countries of any number of pesky criminals. For the right price.

Roxanne's specialty was stealth security for corporate espionage cases. She made sure the bad guys didn't know who she was until it was too late, and she caught them with their hands in the cookie jar. At least that *had been* her specialty. Based on Bella's scowl, she might have been demoted to cleaning the locker room toilets if she wasn't simply fired.

Roxanne really didn't want to walk away from the job she'd come to love. She had to find a way to make things right.

Bella stood to her full, impressive height. She was easily six feet tall in her combat boots, and every inch of her was sleek, sculpted muscle. Her stormy gray eyes narrowed in fury. "Where shall we start, Razor? With the fact that your client's information was stolen? Or maybe with the part where the guy who stole it got away?"

"The data was fake. I planted it. Whoever has it isn't getting anything of value."

"And now they know that, too. Mr. Chord told me how hard it was to architect that setup. Your chance to catch the thieves is gone, and he still has no idea who Mary works for or with."

Roxanne looked down and toyed with her wide cuff bracelet. "Were the police able to get her to talk?"

"Not a word. Not even to a lawyer. And now whoever is doing this knows we're onto them."

What was worse was the fact that the police were now involved—something Mr. Chord had wanted to avoid from the beginning, which was why he hired the Edge to deal with the problem. If word got out that his designs were being stolen, his company's stock price could plummet. He might lose investors.

Roxanne had no idea about the specifics of the devices that had been stolen from him. She didn't need to know any secret information to do her job. But what she did know was that Chord Industries had contributed to several advances in the field of medicine. His machines helped people. Saved lives.

Because of her, he was losing his ability to do good in the world, and that pissed Roxanne off more than her own failure.

"I'm sorry, Bella. I should have realized Mary could have a partner."

"Yes. You should have. So the question is, why didn't you?"

Roxanne considered giving her boss some lame excuse. She could come up with half a dozen that might help her cover her ass, but she couldn't do that to Bella. They were friends. Bella trusted her, and she wasn't going to screw that up by lying.

Roxanne took a deep breath and admitted what she'd hoped she wouldn't have to. "I've been distracted."

Bella crossed her arms over her chest and lifted a dark eyebrow. "Distracted? Care to elaborate on that?"

"My ex, Kurt, he's been sending guys after me, having them follow me. I thought he'd stopped a few weeks ago, but I guess I was wrong. He's not done with his games. A new man showed up yesterday, and I spent so much time losing him before I went in to do the job, I was rushed. I wasn't completely focused."

Bella's face darkened with rage, and her voice became lethally calm. "What, exactly, are these guys doing to you?"

"Nothing. They just watch me. Kurt was the jealous type, and even though we split three months ago, he apparently still hasn't managed to accept the fact that we're over."

"Give me Kurt's address. I'll go speak to him."

"No, Bella. You'd only make things worse if you confront him. I already did, and he denies everything. I know he's lying, and I told him I'd have him brought in for stalking if it happened again. I thought I'd gotten through, but either way, this is my mess. I'll be the one to clean it up."

Bella glanced at Roxanne's arm where the bruise from last night's combat darkened her skin. "Did he hurt you, Razor?" she asked, her hands clenching to fists at her sides.

"No. It was nothing like that. He's not a bad guy. He just didn't want to let go."

"I could make him."

Roxanne had seen Bella mad. She'd seen the woman take down three armed men by herself. And she'd heard stories about that building Bella destroyed in Mexico a few months ago. But Roxanne had never seen this kind of steely, quiet rage, so intense it vibrated through her entire body. Roxanne had heard rumors that Bella had a dark past—one she never discussed with her employees—but seeing this kind of reaction made Roxanne wonder just what that past had been.

"I've got it covered," said Roxanne. "I'll go see him today and make sure he quits playing these games."

Bella swallowed several times before her hands unclenched and the redness in her face abated. "I won't have anyone hurting my people."

"Kurt isn't hurting me. He's just jerking me around."

"Are you protecting him?"

"No. He's an asshole for screwing with me like this, and I plan to tell him that to his face."

"I don't like the way he's treating you."

"Neither do I."

"He interfered with your work, and I can't let that slide."

"I know." Roxanne let out a long, resigned breath. She loved her job, but she knew the score. A mistake like this was too big a thing to simply ignore. "Are you going to fire me?"

Bella's mouth flattened in frustration. "I should. That would certainly appease Mr. Chord. But no, you're not fired. However, I'm not handing out any more chances, either. You blow it again, you're out. Our work is too dangerous for distractions. You need to get your personal shit straightened out before I can assign you any more jobs."

"What about finding the guy who got away?"

"The cops are involved now. They're looking into it."

"So . . . what? We just leave Mr. Chord hanging?"

"No, I'm going to offer him our services for free to calm him down, but he already said he didn't want you back. I'm sorry."

The rejection stung, but not nearly as much as her

failure did. Mr. Chord was right to be mad. She'd let her personal life get in the way of her professional life, which was a big no-no. She knew better.

"I understand. I'll go see Kurt on his lunch break and make sure he understands that his games are over. I should be back by one."

"No. I don't want you back until you're sure you've fixed the problem for good."

Roxanne took a deep breath to keep herself from shouting at her boss. "How long is long enough to convince you?"

"As long as it takes. No less than a week."

A week? If Mr. Chord's thief had left any trail, it would definitely be cold by then. "That's more time than I'll need."

"This isn't negotiable, Razor," said Bella. "If his buddies stay away for a few days, chances are they won't come back. And there's something else, too."

"What?"

"Assholes have a tendency to escalate things when confronted. I'm not letting anything happen to you, so I'm assigning the new guy to you. Wherever you go, he goes. Got it?"

"You're giving me a babysitter?" Roxanne did shout this time, jumping to her feet in anger.

Bella strode around her glass desk and got right in Roxanne's face. "I'm giving you a badass former special operations babysitter—one I want on our team. Don't fuck that up."

Great. Now she wasn't going to be able to look into possible leads on the thief. Her babysitter would no doubt rat her out. "I don't need him, Bella."

"I think you do. And he needs you, too. While he's babysitting, you're going to explain how things work at the Edge. He's already passed all our tests and breezed through training, but he hasn't taken on any real jobs yet. Think of this as his orientation." Bella pressed a button on her phone. "Lila, please send Tanner in."

"This isn't a good idea. I'm a horrible teacher. You need to get Riley to do the training. He's good at that kind of thing."

"Riley's good at everything, which is why he's too busy for this. You, on the other hand, happen to have some free time on your hands. Deal with it, Razor. This is happening."

Fine. Roxanne had screwed up. If this was her punishment, she'd take it like a woman, get through the next few days and be back to her real job in no time. "Let's get this over with."

"Nice to meet you, too," said Tanner as he came in on the heels of her statement.

Bella made the introductions. "Razor, this is Tanner O'Connell."

Tanner was not what she'd expected. She'd been so upset about being saddled with a babysitter that she hadn't even considered that he might be a hot one. And he was. Smokin'. Taller than Bella, even in her boots, Tanner stood with a posture that screamed complete confidence. His shoulders were wide, his back straight, and his blue eyes stayed fixed on her, unblinking. An amused grin lifted one side of his mouth and formed little crinkles at his eyes. His jeans clung to thick, long legs, and on his feet were the worn cowboy boots of a true Texan.

"Tanner, this is your new partner, Roxanne Haught. We call her Razor."

Tanner's dark brows went up at that. "Razor? Is that because you have a sharp tongue?"

"The sharpest," she replied. "You'd better beg Bella for a new trainer, or I'll skin you alive."

His gaze dropped to her mouth. "Might be worth it."

Bella grabbed each of them by one arm and pushed them toward her office door. "I see you two have a lot to talk about. Outside of my office. I have work to do."

"This is a bad idea," said Roxanne, praying for a last-minute reprieve.

Bella ignored her. "And don't think you can come back here in a few hours, claiming you tried to make it work. There will be no trying today. Just doing. Got it?"

"Yes, ma'am," said Tanner. "We won't let you down."

Bella gave Tanner a stern look. "She's going to try to ditch you. Don't let it happen. Some asshole is giving her trouble, and if she gets hurt, you're fired."

All hints of amusement fled from Tanner's rugged face, making his eyes turn cold. He seemed to grow a couple of inches taller and took a step closer to Roxanne. It reminded her of her best friend, Jake, who had a tendency to be a bit overprotective.

Tanner nodded. "I understand."

"Good. I'm glad that's settled. Now get out." Bella shooed them through the door and shut it behind them.

It was time to let the new kid know how things worked around here. "If I'm going to be your trainer, we have a couple of things to get straight."

"Such as?"

"I'm in charge. You do what I say, when I say."

The slightest creases formed at his eyes, but he didn't refute her order. "That it?"

"No. I don't want or need a babysitter. I'm going to deal with my personal problems on my own, without your interference."

"Anything else?"

Wow. He was taking that remarkably well.

"I think that covers the basics. But I reserve the right to change my mind."

He moved, somehow maneuvering her so that her back was against the wall. He nudged closer, breaking the edge of her personal space. His voice dropped to a quiet rumble that Bella's secretary, Lila, would have had trouble overhearing from her desk a few feet away. "Then it's my turn to talk. I don't work for you. I work for Bella, which means she's the one who gets to hand out the orders, not you. So, while I'm happy to learn whatever it is you have to teach me, I'm sure as hell not going to stand around like a good little boy while you deal with your personal asshole problems when Bella specifically told me not to."

Roxanne wasn't sure what she'd expected from the seemingly good-natured man, but it wasn't that. She pulled in a breath to put him in his place, but an instant later, his thick, hot finger pressed against her lips, quieting her.

She was so shocked by the touch, she forgot all about the fact that she should have been upset by it.

A touch of vertigo spun inside her head, and she realized she'd forgotten to breathe. The roughness of his work-hardened finger grazed across her mouth as her lips parted slightly so she could pull in enough oxygen.

"I'm not done," he told her. "You and I are going to be working together, and I'm not going to let you do anything to screw up my chances of keeping this job. I need the work. So you and I are going to get along real nice-like and make Bella proud. Got it?"

As close as he was, she could see deep blue streaks radiating out from his pupils. The creases around his eyes were paler, as if he'd spent a lot of time in the sun, squinting. His scent reminded her of a summer drive in a convertible—warm and exhilarating with just a hint on an incoming storm.

She felt her skin heat up and attributed it to her sudden flash of irritation at his high-handed ways.

Roxanne pressed her hands against his chest to push him back, but as soon as she felt the hard contours of his muscles beneath her hands, her mind stuttered for a moment before she remembered herself and finished pushing.

Tanner stepped back, his finger shiny from her lip gloss.

Roxanne pressed her lips together to fix the damage he'd done to her makeup and swore she could taste him. Salt and earth and something else that made her wish for another taste just so she could figure it out.

Not that she would do that. Bella generally frowned on her coworkers tasting each other.

Roxanne cleared her throat to cover her discomfort. "I can see already that you and I are going to have problems."

"Nope," he said. "Not a single one. We're both going to do what the boss says."

No way was she letting a stranger into her personal life to help her make an ex-boyfriend back off. But he didn't have to know that. "Fine. You win. We'll meet back here after lunch and get started on your training."

By that time, she'd have dealt with Kurt and no longer have anything to hide. She'd throw herself into training Tanner, and in a few days, everything would be back to normal.

Shannon K. Butcher

BURNING ALIVE
The Sentinel Wars

Three races descended from ancient guardians of mankind, each possessing unique abilities in their battle to protect humanity against their eternal foes—the Synestryn. Now, one warrior must fight his own desire if he is to discover the power that lies within his one true love…

Helen Day is haunted by visions of herself surrounded by flames, as a dark-haired man watches her burn. So when she sees the man of her nightmares staring at her from across a diner, she attempts to flee—but instead ends up in the man's arms. There, she awakens a force more powerful and enticing than she could ever imagine. For the man is actually Theronai warrior Drake, whose own pain is driven away by Helen's presence.

Together, they are more than lovers—they may become a weapon of light that could tip the balance of the war and save Drake's people…

Available wherever books are sold or at
penguin.com

S0046